SHADOWDAYS

POLLY SCHATTEL

ISBN: 978-1-68510-015-5 (sc)
ISBN: 978-1-68510-016-2 (ebook)
Library of Congress Control Number: 2021948573

First printing edition: January 28, 2022
Published by JournalStone Publishing in the United States of America.
Cover Design: Don Noble
Editing by Sean Leonard
Proofreading and Cover/Interior Layout by Scarlett R. Algee

JournalStone Publishing
3205 Sassafras Trail
Carbondale, Illinois 62901

JournalStone books may be ordered through booksellers or by contacting:
JournalStone | www.journalstone.com

For Patricia, for Kaye, and yes, for you too, Brett

I was nearly expiring—'twas close of the day,—
A demon advanced to the bed where I lay,
He gave me the power from whence I was hurled,
To return to revenge, to return to the world
Percy Bysshe Shelley, "Revenge"

SHADOWDAYS

melissa

1

There's a curse in the family,
a linger-long something wrong
that no one talks about.
Strange Southern girls
who drink all day
and drown all night
and grow odder
as they grow older.
Quiet, stoic, their insides
twisting rootlike
as the years tread on.
Once in a while they
talk about it, from tangents
and other rooms and hallways,
but it never lurks too long in the air,
(even as it bides in their brains).
Old birds in old houses,
cracks in the curtains
closed against the heat,
gin and tonics sweating,
preachers prescribing from old screens
in far rooms. The upstairs bright
with pale windows,
attic-hot and sheet-draped,
kept for an occasion that will never come.
There's a worm in their brains

and there's nothing they can do—
MS, 8/10/07

2

She could ignore the phone, of course, but Jack's set it to clatter like an old-fashioned party line, sort of like the one that used to hang on the wall in her grandma's kitchen—rust-red plastic and the circular dial and the crack in the mouthpiece from when her brother threw it at her, and if you ever dialed zero it took forever before the little fingerhole made its way back around. And it's her mom on the phone, that's obvious, but right now it's the car she's worried about, driving alone on the road with her eyes closed, listening for that new noise, that air-hiss of the frame just above the asphalt, at this speed it could wrinkle up and bottom her out, who knows. But the air is nice, and through her eyelids the low sun flickers, the whistle of passing trees, in fact all the charm autumn can muster, lovely this time of year but also a good time to croak from a car wreck if it happens that way.

On the last ring she opens her eyes. The car's drifted only a bit, but if another had been coming it would have been not so great. Good to know her shit luck isn't absolute. She hits the answer button. "Mom?"

"Melissa." It's her mom, yep, Melissa's got a sense about these things. Either that or her mother calls a hell of a lot. "Did you get the picture?"

"I did get it," Melissa says. On the seat next to her phone is a photo in a drugstore frame. It's newly restored from a faded old Polaroid and now the colors practically lunge from the image, details coaxed from a murky fog. The Eiffel Tower under a pissed-off sky, school kids and tourists crowded up against the hedges, and in the front are two young people, shaggy extras from a Eurotrash art film—her mom young and smug in her Farrah Fawcett curls, and Dad with his jowly college neckbeard, their faces full of promise, a bright sense of the road ahead of them. "When was that?"

"That was seventy-five. Your father proposed that night." In the picture, her father stands tall and his color is good, his door-gunner smile fastened on straight. "He was healthy then," her mother says. Behind them the mighty tower, a fringe of trees, the hint of buildings low in the background. Other people on the margins—a lady with a baby carriage, a pressing figure stooped and in a hurry, *chapeau* clapped on his head. A woman in a windbreaker and a ribbon in her hair.

"Did you ever see the view from up top?" Melissa says. "I bet it's incredible, the whole city pieced apart and laid out like that. If I went up there I'd never come down."

"No, we didn't get a chance." There's a new apathy in Sandra's tone, a vagueness which makes Melissa worry. "Hey, listen, I put an ad out, I'm gonna sell the ring your dad gave me." This is not a surprise. Her mother's life in the last year has been a sad series of shutting downs, de-escalations, and slow but inevitable reductions into...what? Infirmity? Dissipation? A lone car appears, and Melissa tightens her grip on the wheel and watches it advance, until finally it's gone in a sigh of air. "Honey?"

"What? Sorry, Mom, you're gonna do it?"

"Well, Noah can't know. He would act up, he would..."

Her words trail off. They both know what Noah would do. Noah is Melissa's younger brother, tall and thick like a bowling pin, she can see the two of them now, Mom in the kitchen, Noah in the other room staring glassily at the TV. It's not hard to picture this existence of theirs because they hardly leave the house. "Kinda sad, though," Melissa says. "I mean, your wedding ring and all."

"Not if I'm gonna keep him at home. We need the cash."

"Maybe you could sell it to Jack." A half-laugh from the other side of the phone. Jack is Melissa's fiancé, they're booked to get married later in the winter, if Melissa doesn't murder him first. "The ring he got me's nowhere near as nice as the one Dad got you," she says, and waits for her mother's reply, but there's a hesitation, and Melissa knows that Noah has come into the room.

We goin' to the drug store? a thick voice says on the other end of the line. *I've got seventeen books.*

In the silence, Melissa can almost hear her mother shake her head no at her son. The little GPS that Jack gave her, a disembodied voice that he dialed somehow to sound like a British butler's, says, *Turn left here.* There's a wooden bridge up ahead, narrow and quaint, and a little road that leads through manicured fields. The car thumps across the bridge and now she's headed right into the sun.

"You having a good day?"

Melissa lowers the sun visor. "Yeah, I'm all right."

"I'm serious."

"Me too." On the side of the road there's an old wooden split-rail fence, like that of a farm from the 1800s, heading over the hill. This is bullshit, of course—the fence isn't from the 1800s, this whole neighborhood was an auto graveyard as recent as two years ago. "But look, hey, I'm almost here, I gotta go," Melissa says. "I'll be by tomorrow night. The photo's great, they did a good job, you'll love it."

Her mother exhales, that slight puncture again, it's something she does so much she's not aware of it anymore. "Hookay," she says, already gone, already back in the house, already grimly alone in the fish tank of her life with Noah again. "Be good."

3

Melissa pulls to the gate. Dr. Larry gave her the code—*9717*—which is funny because it's an anagram—Is that what they're called when they're numbers?—of the year she was born. *Star Wars.* Disco. Son of Sam. It'd be cool if she could remember the 70s, it seems like a better and simpler time, like when people were more worried about Anita Bryant and Fleetwood Mac than they were about suicidal ideations or voices in their heads, but maybe that's just her. She leans out from her window and punches in the number, and the metal gate, a white-painted barricade with whimsical birds, lazily swings open.

The blacktop splits into several lanes, leading this way and that through avenues that look pretty much all the same, and Melissa wonders how anyone without a GPS knows where to go. There aren't any landmarks, this neighborhood is flat and featureless, the houses built weirdly, purposefully similar, as though anonymity was part of their appeal. And they're big—new money. The British butler on the GPS, who Jack playfully calls *Sthevens*, with a *thnooty effeminate lithp*, tells her where to go. "*Turn left onto Starling Street. Turn right onto Warbler Way. Turn right onto Crossbill Circle.*"

But when she comes to the house—it's Dr. Larry's place, her new boss, she starts tomorrow morning—the weird thing is how much it actually looks like him. Two stories, a beige exterior with windows and faux balconies and a porch big enough to make a Lexus U-turn. When she first took the job with the clinic (*Silver Star Treatment Center*, it's called, she has yet to learn what the silver star's referring to) she liked Dr. Larry, but thought he was banal in that way exclusive to middle-aged men— generally harmless, mostly good-intentioned, and buttermilk dull. It happened to men when their age edged up and their testosterone drained away leaving them tepid and large and limp. Simians gone soft. But Dr. Larry was nice, and he liked her enough to hire her, so there's that. Other vehicles crowd in the circular driveway and on the street, and she tucks her Subaru among them and kills the engine.

As she gets out, she's aware someone in the upper window is staring down at her, a pale blur of a face, the hint of a hand on the sill. One of the bedrooms or a home office, no doubt, Dr. Larry's daughter maybe. Or his wife. Melissa resists the temptation to wave or even acknowledge them—spying isn't nice—so she makes a show of arranging her blouse and heads up to the porch, fastens on a smile, and opens the door.

Inside, everything is cream and mocha or whatever this year's colors are. Sand. Sahara. Gobi. Death Valley. Parch. Bone. Tibia. It's as though she stepped into a softer world—cushioned couches and love seats and puffy, oversized ottomans like marshmallow dreams. The cold wave of AC hits her as she takes in the scene, maybe twenty or thirty people clumped here and there, cradling drinks and loading up on carbs, they all look weirdly well-to-do for such a hardscrabble town, very different from the dirt-under-the-fingernails working joes and joyces that make up most of the folks around this wretched patch of the world. Too much bright make-up and nails and floral prints on the women, too much sensible tedium—grey suits, blue suits, red ties, blue ties—on the men. Melissa's feeling out of place and wondering what to do when she sees Jack across the room. He sees her too, and starts weaving his way over. She feels better already.

"I thought I beat you here," she says as he comes up. "I didn't see your car." Jack holds a drink in his hand, some kind of rosé in a bulbous glass, she takes it from him and downs a greedy gulp. It's sweet and thin, a cheap brand, no doubt, from the big box store out on the highway.

"You kidding? You drive like an old lady." Jack greedily reclaims his glass. "How we doing?" He's not the best-looking guy in the room, he's doughy and bald with the face of a third-tier boxer, but time and temper have cobbled it all into a kind of pleasant mask. And there's an ease in his posture that tells everyone around him he's approachable, he's open and confident in who he wants to be, he speaks in the same tender tone of voice to adults and children and old people, there's no pretense in him.

"I hate parties," she says. "That's how we're doing."

Jack's smile struggles to stay aloft. "Then why are we here again?"

"You know how these things are. I'm new, I gotta make an appearance. It's part of the game. And it helps to have my hubby here. Tells them I'm stable and happy."

"Ha, then you'd really be giving them the wrong idea."

Melissa watches as a maid, a black maid, dressed surprisingly in old-fashioned black and white, glides from kitchen to counter to snack table. She carries a bowl of potato salad, sets it down, stirs it so the fresh parts are on top. It's been years since Melissa has seen a domestic maid, she didn't know they were still a thing, it brings back her own childhood, her own maid—Corrie, who her mother hired to clean the house after her father took off and diminished her to a single mom, Corrie, her old friend, long departed from experience and memory, dearly missed nowadays and gone for decades. They were close at one time.

But then a hand slides down her back, a little surprising and maybe lower than she's comfortable with, and she turns to see Dr. Wilston creeping closer. Wilston's face is red and ruddy, which is not surprising at all, he was red and ruddy at Melissa's job interview too. Probably one of those doctors who keeps a flask with them—vodka, no doubt, to hide the drink on his breath. The choice of day drinkers everywhere.

"Our best new nurse," Wilston slurs. "Howya doin'?" His hand is even lower now, in the small of her back and heading south.

"Dr. Wilston. Hi."

Jack leans in, maybe sensing Melissa's unease. "And who's this?"

"Jack, this is Dr. Fred Wilston. He's one of the founders of the clinic." She gives them both a skittish smile. "And this is my fiancé, Jack."

Jack thrusts out his hand. His genius at warming up even the most chilly situations is one of the things Melissa most appreciates about him. If the staff are treated like the help, what could be said about the help's *husband?* Even so, an awkward moment like this is still a piece of cake. "Good to meet you, sir." Wilston shakes his hand and assesses Jack with a sloppy smile.

"What do you think of the party?" Melissa asks the older man, looking for some way to tag team it with Jack and tug the conversation back into safer waters.

Wilston tucks his chin and his loose neck wattles over the collar of his shirt. He looks like he needs to belch. "*Most especially must I tread with care in matters of life and death,*" he slurs in his pompous, loaded-by-two-PM voice. It's like a nature documentary narrated by a lush. "*If it is given me to save a life, all thanks. But it may also be within my power to take a life. This awesome responsibility must be faced with great humbleness and awareness of my own frailty. Above all, I must not play at God.*" He winks puckishly at Melissa.

Ah yes, there is that.

4

Wilston's quote is, of course, the Hippocratic Oath. Melissa knows it well from her nursing school days. Whether his words refer specifically to her or not, it doesn't matter, because either way they'd send a bolt of dry lightning rumbling through her guts. By this time, she'd hoped *That Day*, as she's come to call it, would be a distant memory by now, a forgotten ordeal from her past. But it isn't, and it never will be—three years ago, she made a stupid, idiotic, ruinous, devastating mistake, the only one like it she'll ever make in her nursing career. And just as she knew it would, it's followed her for years.

The conference room that day was oddly small for the size of the table inside it, which looked like it had been beamed there from a bigger room in a bigger building—thick oak, a pane of glass sitting atop it like an oil slick. There was a smell in there too, the funk of plywood and old lunch and quiet distress. They were crowded around it—Drs. Larry and Wilston and their pinch-faced office manager, Angie, at one end, and Melissa at the other, it was a little like an inquisition, which Melissa had already anticipated and prepared for.

"What does your...uh, fiancé do?" Dr. Larry asked, looking through his files and glancing up at her. He had a funny habit of tilting his face back and studying you through the bottoms of his lenses. He was almost bald now, once handsome maybe but not anymore, and his round eyes and round glasses seemed constantly surprised by it.

"Jack," Melissa said. "He's studying to be a teacher. Night classes at the community college in Staley. He drove trucks before that, but he never liked it. He likes kids, he wants to work with kids, so now he's student teaching at the elementary school."

There was a mild, condolent silence as they all considered this, and Melissa felt a slight note of disapproval or judgment, as if for some reason these professional people didn't think much of a working man, a blue-collar Mack with his shirtsleeves rolled up, making a lateral pass from one grimly underpaid position to another.

"Noble of him," Wilston said finally. Melissa shrugged, trying to look appealing in her unconcern, no big deal. But it was a big deal, to her it was anyway, the idea that her intended was a man who lived by a code of his own, a moral rulebook that he consulted with to do what he thought was right. That meant he would also try to do right by her too, which made her feel good and safe in a way she couldn't articulate. After three years of dread and fear and guilt, fold upon terrible fold, it was a small, clean, good feeling.

"He says he wants to change the world one child at a time," she added, trying to put a bit more English on it, but it didn't seem to work, the three of them only stared blankly back at her.

"So...this is a bit awkward," Dr. Larry said, getting to the real matter at hand. "But we can assure you. You can be frank with us."

Here it was. She was ready for it, it had taken her years to get back to this place, this dreaded moment, but she was ready for it.

"Okay," she said, and folded her hands in front of her. It was important to seem relaxed, even breezy, but it was hot in here, she hoped her makeup wasn't sinking into her pores and sweating down the oval of her chin.

"Why don't you tell us exactly what happened back in Birmingham? At Baptist Medical?"

Melissa shifted in her chair. One of the legs was uneven, and it took everything she had to keep herself from rocking back and forth like a fidgety child. "Well," she began, still trying and failing after all these years to find a way to make it all sound less horrible. "It was my previous job—"

"Would you like a coffee?" Dr. Larry broke in. This was hard for them too, they must really need her, it was brutal for everybody.

Melissa shook her head. Best to get it over with. "As you know, I was working at the hospital in Birmingham, in the NICU, and…uh. I was supposed to give a little preemie boy some blood thinner. A standard hep-lock, of course. Instead, I…uh, accidentally gave him a full dose of Heparin." Little Joshua James Newcombe, of Mountain Brook, Alabama, she keeps his name close in her mind, a cute little boy with pink skin like fresh from a bath and a scrunched-up little old man face.

And so she told them—blood thinner, it was, employed to keep a preemie's tiny IV lines open. Heparin, at 10,000 units per milliliter, instead of 10 units per milliliter. A simple misread of the bottle, which had a cobalt blue label instead of the usual sky blue. Some pharmacy tech had stocked it there instead of the right one, maybe the tech with the muttonchops and the sweet brown eyes, and Melissa had overlooked the details. She made a mistake. On top of that it had been a rough morning, headaches and rolling chills and fever, she was coming down with something and had misread the bottle. The *something* turned out to be Lyme disease, from a deer tick she never even saw, picked up most likely from the scrubby woods south or east of Birmingham where she'd run once or twice that summer. Two weeks with little sleep, a headache kicking at the insides of her brain, chills, stiff neckaches like wearing a shoulder harness. The Lyme was tough and scary, but thankfully it was taken care of by a six-week "nucular blast," as the other nurses called it, of little maroon antibiotic pills.

Joshua James Newcombe, of course, wasn't so lucky. He died, and Melissa's reputation as a respectable hard-working nurse died along with him. Babykiller, she was called, mostly by herself. Infanticide. Accidental mortality. It was—and still is—devastating.

"That's a thousand times the dosage." Wilston said what everyone already knew. Across the long table, the three people exchanged wary glances again. Melissa knew it would happen that way, until she made them understand how easy and effortless it was to foul it all up.

"Someone stocked the drug cabinet wrong and I didn't notice," she admitted. "I was sick, I felt terrible, I was dealing with undiagnosed Lyme. The labels were almost the same shade of blue. The kid, um…" All she could do was shrug. It was horrible, beyond thinkable—a life, a human life, a beautiful little boy who weighed only four and a half pounds and had everything ahead of him, had been snuffed out. Not to mention her own life and the legal and emotional shitstorm that followed, and it all came down to a remorseful show of helplessness at the lonely end of a conference table. Melissa, fired from her job and investigated, but found innocent. Medical malpractice, the third leading cause of death in the US. The insurance companies coughed up—Melissa wasn't sure how much—but she went into hiding, mostly from herself, had fled the city and the state, moved in with her mom and her brother up in North Carolina, and three years passed before she was herself enough to start looking for another job, and here she was. But there was no way around it, and rightly so—she'd killed someone entrusted to her care. It would follow her for the rest of her days, a little black bird always hovering, always sailing the currents of the stormy sky above her.

"Didn't your system have safeguards?" Dr. Larry asked.

"Less than you'd think. I mean, this was Alabama."

"Birmingham's a medical town. UAB and all that. Things can get pretty first class there."

"Yes. No, you're right. Safeguards have been put in place, partly because of me. Now a minimum of two nurses have to verify any dose of blood thinner for newborns and the PICUs. And there's another system using bar codes to track everything. That was being developed before the overdose, and is still happening, from what I know." Her words sounded hollow, as if they came from the other end of a drainpipe. "All of it. A foul up. The administrators said my error was…unthinkable, given my level of training and experience. I was let go…and, um…hospitalized for depression."

"Jeepers." Wilston again. He seemed to do a lot of smoothing and sandpapering of rough moments between people with meaningless language.

"To make things worse," she went on, *haha why oh why stop now*, getting to the part she really dreaded, "some of the team seemed to think, at least for a little bit, that I did it intentionally. There was an investigation, but no charges were filed. It was officially recorded as an accident, which of course it was, and three years later I'm ready to get back to work."

Melissa unfolded her hands, which were pressed white from tension. But on the other end of the table, Dr. Larry's face was open, and seemed genuinely sympathetic. Maybe he'd been falsely accused before and knew how it felt. "I don't take medication, though I did for a while," she said, hoping her candor counted for something. "I've got nerves of steel. And I'm back to my normal self and ready to get on with things."

Dr. Larry leaned back, and in the silence, Melissa waited for the chair to creak, but it didn't, the adjustment felt suspended, somehow unfinished.

"Accidents happen," he said. "Our business is more high stakes than people realize. But I wanted Dr. Wilston and Angie to hear in your words what happened. Just so everyone's on the same page. I have full confidence in you."

"Well, I can assure everyone," Melissa said, feeling slightly encouraged, hands clasped again, leaning forward now as she had practiced, "that it will never happen again. All of my credentials are up to date, I'm licensed with the NC Board, I've re-certified with the ANCC, I'm caught up on my CEUs, and I'm ready to go. Today, if need be. Right now, this afternoon." Her face felt dry and phony, a mask of failure. The woman, Angie, hadn't changed her expression, not even once—chilly, removed, stern as a Tiki god. Melissa swiveled her smile at Wilston, scanning him for sympathy.

"*Wowee*," was all Wilston said. "*Jee-zus willikers.*"

5

Someone clinks a wine glass then, and Melissa and Jack look over to see Dr. Larry swiveling on his breakfast-bar stool and peering out over the small crowd. His bald head bobs six inches or so above the gathered people.

"Yes yes," he's saying, "thank you all for coming." He takes a moment while the chatter sifts down. "So. A party. A lovely afternoon. Wonderful friends, a busy practice." Around Melissa, people nod their assent, *yes yes yes*. "Before I go too far, I'd like to acknowledge my partner, Dr. Bill Wilston. Bill?"

Near the fireplace, Dr. Wilston leans on a potted palm and raises an empty glass. His eyes are rheumy and beginning to go vague.

"Bill and I have worked together for, what—I don't know," Dr. Larry says. "Fourteen years? It's been a good run, Bill." Tepid clapping. "And my staff—*our* staff. Angie, Grace, the girls, where are they?"

A few pant-suited, middle-aged ladies and younger women in boxy haircuts nod and grin from their collective siege on the snack table. The maid—the only black person in the room—twines quietly around them, picking up discarded plates and glasses. Melissa considers the women's hair and wonders if her own is as unflattering as theirs. She makes a mental note to check herself in the bathroom at home, the one with the two mirrors at ninety degrees to each other so that you can open them just so to see the back of your own head.

"Thank you, ladies, for your wonderful work," Dr. Larry is saying. "Our clinic wouldn't be the same without you." More lukewarm applause.

"So, the numbers are in. Patients who partner with Silver Star Methadone for at least one month officially have a retention rate of eighty-seven percent. A full forty-four percent of our patients are employed, eleven percent are in school, twenty percent are disabled, and another ten percent are in various 'acceptable' categories. Only fifteen percent are in what we would call an unacceptable state. All in all, much better than average. Terrific results."

People start to clap, relief made manifest, but Dr. Wilston raises his glass and clears his throat. Reluctantly, the room hushes again. Melissa reaches over and steals another sip from Jack's wine. It feels like they've been here forever. Or will be here forever.

"As for me," Dr. Wilston says from the corner of the fireplace. The fronds of the potted palm bob in his face. "As for me, I want to...um."

Everyone has turned toward him, and he seems suddenly to feel the weight of their gaze. There's a quiet pressure in the room, as if they're all deep underwater, as if their motions ripple out to affect everyone else. Times like this make Melissa nervous, public speaking is the worst—all the staring, expectant eyes. Once in college she was humiliated in class when she tried bravely and against her better judgment to speak up in front of everyone, to go aloft with a dazzling point only she could make, but her uncertain stammering and her visible fear had slammed her immediately back to the ground. Faceplant. Worse, a faceplant in public. It was mortifying, a vicious embarrassment, everyone avoided her afterwards and she vowed never to speak up again.

"Yes. It's—a good time," Wilston slurs. "A good time...to celebrate." Melissa glances back at Dr. Larry and sees him waiting patiently for his partner to finish. "I wanna let everybody know...that this...this..." The room hesitates, poised on tiptoe, it isn't just Melissa who now seems to feel the moment growing tense, throats are cleared, sips are taken, munching snacks quietly resumed. "That this..." Wilston clears his throat, his eyes are glassier than ever, he looks drunk as a skunk. He seems to try a grin, but on his boozy face it's more like a leer. "This," he says finally, "is a really good time."

People laugh politely, they turn away, relieved. Melissa reaches out and takes Jack's wine again and finishes it off in a gulp. "Let's get the fuck outta here," she whispers.

6

She follows Jack's car home, noticing his right rear brake light is out—*Gotta tell him about that,* she reminds herself, though of course she forgets about it when they see each other twenty minutes later—but on the way, her thoughts circle around the Hippocratic Oath that Dr. Wilston drunkenly recited at the party. She still wonders if it was meant to be a dig at her own past, or a simple reference that she (too sensitively, *That Day* a hammer, everything a nail) wrongly applies to her own situation. The episode with the little boy (*His name is Joshua, Joshua James,* she scolds herself with a somehow nasal sharpness that reminds her depressingly of her mother) will haunt her for the rest of her life, she knew it instantly when it happened, and she knows it now. Worse, she deserves it. She ended a person's life with carelessness and a—rare for her—sense of neglect. She never makes mistakes like that, even when sick with Lyme disease, and *really really never* when it comes to something as important as someone's life. Except that she did that one time and thereafter she and Joshua were forever entwined. Alcohol doesn't interest her, drugs were never her thing, not even when Muttonchops caught her gaze and nodded as she passed in the hospital hallway. Nothing was cleaner than her, she was straight-edge even back in high school when her few friends were sneaking toothpick joints behind the dumpsters near the cafeteria and telling her about Jesse Calley's party on Friday. That's why the whole thing is so strange, and why the enormous pain she carries around with her now for these years is still so heavy. It's hard to remember what happened that day, she has very little direct memory of it, as if she'd stared too long into the sun and burned that part of her brain dead and blind. And so many grim feelings and regrettable sensations have been piled on top of it now, it's become something else, a barrow of remorse and pain that she can exhume forever and never get at the real thing underneath. She wants to feel terrible, to relive it and wallow in the misery like a rhino in a mud bath, so she can finally get clean and feel better. But evidently her brain has other plans.

Jack's car pulls into her neighborhood and she follows. It's a flat circuit board of boxy rental homes, most of them similar aside from a simple detail here and there—an extended porch, a garage on the opposite side, a slightly different paint job. Melissa rented her place almost ten months ago—despite her twenty-eight years, it's the first time she's ever lived alone, and this solo-living thing is hopefully just a rung on the ladder to her getting back on her own two feet. It's a new period of self-sufficiency, and she wants to dig into the risk of it, the accomplishment of it, before Jack moves in, *Hey, look, everybody, I can do it!*

She and Jack have agreed to a wedding but haven't scheduled it yet. Despite Jack's pathetic and even occasionally hilarious appeals, for now she feels it's better to keep things clean and clear. So they live apart, spending most of their waking time together anyway, curled on her lumpy couch, sporking ice cream from the same pint of Breyers, squinting at Dr. Phil on the 19-inch she pulled out of the storage shed at her mother's place. Jack's good like that—he checks out self-help CDs for her from the school library where he student teaches, he grocery shops for her, he cooks for her (and what a cook he is, he should be a chef, she's told him so on many occasions) and even reads to her in bed, mostly from the fantasy novels he likes so much, the magic barbarian-quest books she finds silly but quaint and maybe even sweet in their adolescent male appetites. Jack's good like that.

They met in those brittle months after *That Day*, and even though they hardly knew each other, he was for some reason instantly supportive of the stricken girl who'd made a devastating misjudgment and then fell ill because of it, and he doted on her and almost single-handedly brought her back to life. He helped her relocate herself, to find the solace in small things—dog snores, pear gorgonzola pizza, burning your depression off with grueling evening jogs at the high school track—and, maybe most importantly, when something pushed at her, he taught her to push back. After three years of her drifting and writing terrible poetry, going ever deeper into debt, her student loans whirling like autumn leaves above a windy sidewalk, he seemed not to worry, never to worry, slipping back when she asked him to, stepping forward when it suited her, to let her always find her own way. Or at least think she did.

"Peckish," Jack says now to nobody, ducking around the counter into the little kitchen. The house is small, a bungalow, the dining room and the living room and the kitchen are really just one big room, with an A-frame raised ceiling. It's a 1960s hardware store special, the Brady Bunch on a budget. "You hungry?"

"I had some nibbles at Dr. Larry's."

"*Dr. Larry*," Jack says in a snide voice. He pulls a box of cereal from the cabinet. "Why does he ask you to call him that? Seems kinda weird."

"What's weird?"

"I've never heard that before. It's always Dr. Williams or Dr. Smith or Dr. Whateverstein. Never Dr. *Larry*."

"Maybe it's so he feels familiar. Like a pal. Not like a boss." Melissa sits on the couch and pulls off her shoes. "I think it's cool."

"If he wanted to be a true friend," Jack says, filling his bowl with Captain Crunch, "he would pay you more. And also drop the Dr. altogether and just go with Larry. It's working at cross-purposes with itself."

"*Cross-purposes.*" Melissa leans back, happy to be home again. The tension of the outside world is leaving her already, like rising steam. "Yep."

Jack smirks. After dropping out of high school and working as a truck driver for a decade, in a fit of self-improvement brought about by cross-country listenings to a borrowed set of Tony Robbins tapes—only Number 6 ("Moving Beyond Procrastination") and Number 9 ("How To Increase Your Energy") were missing—he quit his career and went back to college. He'll come out of it soon with letters after his name, his pick of various low-paying teaching jobs, and a better vocabulary, but now he sometimes gets accused of pretension and arrogance, why use a nickel when a dime was twice as good? It's one of his more irritating habits, which he's promised he would try to fix, but he doesn't seem to put that much energy into it. Melissa thinks that after wearing a blue collar for so long, he likes feeling different and smart and making sure everyone around him knows it. He wants them to *hear* that Bachelor of Science.

"It's not clean or elegant is what I meant," he says, pouring the milk. "The Dr. is formal, the Larry's not. It's not that big a deal. Just feels like he needs to shit or get off the pot."

"Oh my God, can we not have people's names be what they want them to be? Let the poor man call himself what he wants." Melissa sits back and looks up to the raised ceiling. Those dusty wooden beams draw her gaze a lot lately, the altitude seems to give her some sort of relief, sometimes she imagines a wild colorful bird hopping around up there from rafter to rafter. "If you wanted to get weirded out by one of them, Wilston is definitely the weirder of the two."

"Holy shit, did you see how drunk he was? He was wasted!"

"I get the feeling he's like that a lot. I can see it in his eyes, on his skin. Total lush."

"Broken veins in the nostrils and cheeks."

"Saggy eye bags."

"Bloodshot pupils."

"Brewer's droop." Melissa laughs. It might be for the first time that day. "You gonna stay tonight?"

Jack shakes his head, chewing. "Tomorrow's your first day. Gotta get your rest."

Melissa gets up and comes over to the counter, leans next to Jack and puts her head on his shoulder as he slumps over his food. The feel of his body, his muscles and his sturdy frame and his funk of sweat and man-musk. She clings to it. "Okay," she says.

7

Melissa goes to bed after Jack leaves, but the nervy feeling in her stomach—what she thinks of as *The New Job Jitters*, or maybe *The First Day at the First Job in Three Years Jitters*, or maybe it should be *The First Day at the First Job in Three Years After Accidentally Killing a Child Jitters*—sticks around. It keeps her up for most of the night, and she's blinking back exhaustion when she pulls into the parking space (RESERVED FOR MELISSA SWEET, RN it says already in yellow stencil, damn that was fast) and she has to take a moment in the car to center herself before going inside. *You'll be all right,* she tells the woman in the rearview mirror, smoothing an eyebrow with a salivated middle finger, *yes yes all right, you'll be all right, honey, you'll be fine.* How bad can it be? The worst happened three years ago.

The clinic's lobby is nice—weirdly nice actually, overdone with thick carpeting and rough-hewn, log-beamed ceilings overhead, and pools of light that spill tastefully in circles on the floor. It's maybe a bit too much, given the fact that many of their patients can hardly afford to be here or have more than a month's rent at any given time, but maybe that's the point: *Come with us,* the office says, *we have the answer, trust us, here, sign this paper.* Angie and another woman—Grace, Melissa thinks her name is, or maybe Gracie, they shook hands briefly at Dr. Larry's party, her wrist as thin and frail as chicken bones—sit behind the desk and watch her approach. They must have been involved in some kind of unpleasant task, because when she smiles and passes by, they both give her the same sour expression.

"Good morning," Melissa says brightly, without expecting an answer. They both seem to have a natural distaste for things, which tells Melissa to stay the hell away.

The morning goes okay. Mostly everyone's pleasant, including Dr. Wilston—who doesn't seem drunk at all, in fact, he's charming and articulate and unexpectedly funny—and Melissa's workstation at the end of a tight L-shaped hallway is well-lit by a window. There's even a cute little plant—she doesn't know the name of it, but it looks like a stubby palm tree that's been sawed off and replanted—and a bright, silver-metallic balloon bounces above it telling everyone to WELCOME MISSY! in all-caps. The misspelling doesn't bother her, clearly it's the thought that counts.

Her first patient is a middle-aged black fellow named Carl Geary. Carl's sweet and agreeable, in a stuttery, rail-thin, bouncy-in-the-knees kind of way, but since Melissa isn't yet an expert on methadone or impairment assessment—

which is one of the ways nurses can tell if their patients are lying to them to secure more of those precious little ruby pebbles—the appointment is led by one of the other nurses, a blotchy, short-haired woman named Karine. Melissa watches as Karine takes Carl's blood and blood pressure, his urine sample, and administers his daily dose. The whole thing takes less than half an hour. *Easy peasy*, what was she so afraid of? The shadow, Melissa reminds herself later while adjusting the height of the stool at her desk and scanning over the new employee manual, is always bigger than the thing itself.

Her first solo assessment is a young white guy named Seth Rainey. Seth's folder mentions he's a Lothario of sorts, or at least considers himself one. Melissa's not worried—in her past life she enjoyed the back and forth with the patients, flirting with the old men, laughing with the salty old ladies, and keeping the young huggers at arm's length. She learned this jiu jitsu in high school and college as a pretty young blonde—how to let the scouting hands scout, but not onto her. But Karine's warning is firm and well-heeded, Seth can be very cute and very sweet and *very* disarming, he has an adorable young daughter, and he's a proud and genuinely loving father. It's a deadly trifecta.

Melissa gives a quick rap on the door and goes into the exam room to find him already sitting on the table. He's slight, not much bigger than she is, wearing a faded Molly Hatchet concert t-shirt, the kind with one of those D&D paintings on them—warriors and bloody axes and skulls. Jack would love a shirt like that. Melissa never really understood what Southern rock bands had to do with fantasy, but hey, maybe that's just her. A decade or so ago she had a boyfriend who would listen to that stuff—Matty, his name was, Matty Truitt. Matty was the one who got her started writing poetry, he was a devotee of Jim Morrison and Charles Bukowski and he had a gorgeous bouquet of red hair that held a curl more than any girl's, Melissa would beg him to let her put it in curlers, to let her put a little makeup on him and doll his pretty face up, but he always refused. Instead, he blasted Molly Hatchet and ZZ Top and 38 Special and Marshall Tucker in his Plymouth GXT or whatever it was, and from what she heard there was certainly no *Lord of the Rings* crap in there, that's for sure. That fantasy stuff was more the Led Zeps and the BÖCs and the Sabbaths, but what the hell did she know? Maybe there was some connection she was missing, she should ask Jack.

"Seth?" she says now, flashing her most practiced, most comforting but still *hands-off* professional smile. How easy it comes back, how good it feels to use it again. "Hi. I'm not sure how to pronounce your last name."

Seth stares back, he probably isn't used to having a young nurse working here, Melissa's the youngest by far, by decades maybe. And he really is a cute guy—baby-faced, round-headed, with swept hair and a scraggly fringe of beard that almost but not quite disguises a pleasant grin. His eyes are narrow and deep-set, giving him a scampish cast, which will only become darker and deeper-set with the years. By middle age, if he ever gets that far, he'll look positively devilish. "You're new," he muses, still looking her over.

"Melissa Sweet. Nurse Melissa to you. Good to meet you."

"Melissa Sweet?" His crooked smile widens. "*Sweet Melissa...*" he warbles clumsily.

It's not a new joke. "How do you pronounce your last name?"

"Rainey. Sounds like, you know. Rainy."

"Rainey, okay." She underlines the first syllable of his last name, as if that will help in any way. "How we doin'?"

Seth purses his lips and studies the floor, suddenly shy. "Ah, well... Things ain't that good, really. I feel all, you know."

"What?"

"Uhhhh...you know, caged up."

She scans his chart. History of Oxycontin and Vicodin, lately a few worrying years of moderate-to-heavy heroin use. If he's not careful, his daughter won't have a daddy soon. "Things have changed, that's for sure," she says, trying to sound like she knows what she's talking about. "The new junk's not like the old junk. Any issues?"

"Not really. But can we do something about that?"

She closes the folder. "Something about what?"

"You don't know what it's like, man. Dolly don't get it."

"*Dolly*?" That term hasn't popped up in the bundles of material she's studied for this job, but there are so many others—*tootsie roll, red rock, spider blue, mud, beast, diesel.* "Is there really a new name for this stuff every fifteen minutes?"

He lets out a raspy laugh. "Aw, man. Got me a baby girl now, you know that. She's really somethin'."

Here it comes, the *coup de grace*. Melissa's guarded, but still allows herself to be led down the path toward the interminably cute little daughter. "What's her name?"

"Sammy." Now his deep-set eyes seem lit up from within, and Melissa can see he's telling the truth, plainly he adores the girl. "Well, Samantha. But...you know." She imagines his daughter, a younger, purer version of him—brown-haired, dark deep-set eyes, olive skin.

"All righty. So." She checks the folder again. "Eighty milligrams. That's what we've got today."

"Okay. Yeah, yeah. But when are we goin' out? It's kinda the rule around here, you know. Mandatory date with Seth Rainey and all that." So, he really is a Lothario. Melissa resists glancing up from her notes, she's more genuinely entertained by this than she expected. "Matter of fact, what are you doin' tonight?"

"I thought you had a kid? Where's your wife?"

"Wife? Ha. Just 'cause I got a kid don't mean I can't date. Everybody knows that."

Melissa retreats back to his folder, back to the shallow end of the pool, *Damn, this guy really is a pro.* "You wouldn't like me, Seth," she says. "I'm not, uh—how do you say it? 'Good with people.'"

His grin is wider now, his cuteness filling the room. "You seem pretty all right to me."

She feels herself flush—*stupid girl.* She's engaged, getting married soon to a very nice man, they warned her about this fellow and she's *still* falling under his spell. Amateur. "Yeah, no," she says. "I'll be back to give you your dolly. If that's what we're still calling it by then." She leaves and shuts the door behind her.

8

"What's the occasion?" Jack's saying. His voice is tinny and high-pitched over the cellphone. After work, Melissa's driving and their connection is weak—she's in the part of town called Saragossa, a neighborhood really, if there are any neighbors, it's a hollow, long and thin like a banana boat or a banana-split bowl, the main road a valley cut into red clay with carpets of kudzu raging up along both sides. The kudzu would fully take over the road were it not for the car and truck wheels that speed past and crush the tendrils until they heal up enough to try it again.

"Mom put her wedding ring on Craigslist."

"Ah, really? Shit. That's too bad."

"I won't be long. What time are you gonna be home?" There's a muted fumbling and she knows that Jack has changed shoulders holding the phone, it's one of his most irritating habits, talking with it against his shoulder while doing other things, and sometimes his voice gets so muffled she has no idea what he's saying.

"Oh, I'm here now," he says. "Finishing my economics paper. 'Black and White and Red All Over: The Production, Consumption, and Transfer of Wealth in the New South.' Discuss."

In the rearview mirror, a car like a shadow has slipped behind Melissa. One of those nondescript vehicles police use, the kind which are so anonymous they practically stand out. She's been seeing it behind her, she realizes with a shock, for the last five minutes. In the mirror, the driver's just a black vagueness in among all the murk.

"Sounds cool," she says, thinking it doesn't sound cool at all. "Well, let me say hi to the fogies and then I'll be by."

"Hey, is everything okay?"

"What do you mean?"

"You sound bothered," Jack says. "Hag-ridden."

"Hag-ridden?" Behind her, the headlights glower, they cast her own shadow onto the dash, the long straight hollow has no turnoffs, how can you turn without any turnoffs? Does she know this person, perhaps a friend who saw her somewhere and wants to flag her down? But she's been a practicing hermit now for the last three years, and during that time she's seen or heard from no one in her past life, all of whom are in another state anyway.

"One of my students used it today," Jack is saying with a kind of self-mocking tone. "I liked it. Told myself to say it more often. Makes me sound smart."

"Mhmm." Melissa reminds herself to quit being paranoid, to stop seeing signs and wonders in every little thing, it's just a car behind her, that's all. Finally, the hollow's walls slip away and side roads appear, and she only half-hears Jack's reply as she takes the first random turn. The car behind her turns too. Melissa takes a quick right, down onto a bumpy gravel road that leads between tight rows of apartments and a railroad track. The other car sails on, the black shadow behind the wheel staring ahead. Melissa pulls the car to a stop.

"Okay-dokey there, perfesser," she says. "Anyway, I'm almost there. I gotta go." She isn't almost there, in fact there's a good quarter hour of open road to go, but Jack gets so sensitive sometimes that it's not worth the trouble to talk to him about anything.

"Right, gotcha," he says, and then the phone goes dead.

Fifteen minutes later, Melissa pulls into her mother's neighborhood, on the southern edge of town, an older collection of neglected ranchers set under sparse platoons of high pines. Melissa knows this neighborhood well, she convalesced here for the three years after *That Day*. Or maybe "hid out" is a better way to think of it, she claimed the empty room next to her brother's in back, it was like being twelve again—long humid afternoons watching the light climb the wall, counting the hairs on the back of her hand, studying the eyelashes in the tight reflections of her glasses, and surviving oblivion. She wrote terrible poetry and listened to the neighbor's beagle, May-May, bark and then grow hoarse and eventually go silent altogether. Since she moved out, that period's already taken on a dreamlike quality, it's like looking at herself preserved in amber or through several panes of rippling, antique glass. For the thousandth time she says a prayer of thanks that things have gotten better and the ground underneath her is solid again. Jack's part of that, for sure, good old Jack. But mostly it's her own stubborn refusal to let herself surrender to the internal tsunami of *That Day*. She's determined to rebuild herself, and so she will.

She pulls in the driveway and grabs the Eiffel Tower photo and goes into the house through the open garage. In the darkness her hand finds the garage door button more from memory than by sight, and she hits it—as ever, she's a little OCD about it—with her middle finger. It takes forever to close. She goes inside through the utility room, past the washer and dryer and into the kitchen, to find her mother standing at the stove.

"Hey there," her mother says. Sandra Sweet is a still handsome woman who was also a nurse, a good one, who retired only after a long and estimable career. No dead babies for her. She's pushing several thick-crusted sandwiches around a skillet with an oil-shiny spatula, her salt and pepper hair bunned-up but tendrils fall around her face and messily, pleasingly, frame it just so. Somehow she looks good without seeming to try, but there was always an air of sadness about her.

Sandra leans over and kisses Melissa on the cheek, which causes a tiny, helpless *frisson* of pleasure, in her weaker moments, Melissa thinks that everything she's done is only a pale imitation of what her mother did earlier and better. Sandra says, "Everything good?"

"Yeah."

"How's the job?"

"It's okay. Good first day. Everybody's super supportive and chill. I was thinking it would be tougher than it really is."

"'Chill'? What a strange term for what that means. In my day we had *groovy*, we had *snazzy*, we had *copacetic*. But chill? It's a reading of thermal energy." For a woman of superior intelligence, her mother spends a terrible amount of time alone, or with Noah, who's not exactly the most scintillating conversationalist.

"Ha. It's mainly a couple of women at the front desk who're marking their territory. Pissing contest and all that. But overall, yeah, it's great."

"Noah!" Sandra yells to the ceiling. "Melissa's here!"

They have a moment to look at each other, to awkwardly smile as they wait, no sense in continuing the conversation now, and then Noah's there, shuffling up and standing in the doorway. He's enormous, a carnival strongman gone to seed. As usual, his eyes are dark and haunted, his hair mussed, the one cowlick he twists over and over, like a weathervane atop his head. He looks like he's just woken up, but that's how he always looks.

"Hi, baby bro," Melissa says, too loudly for some reason, and takes her place at the table.

"We going to the drug store?" Noah says. His voice is slurred, but it's always slurred. Like his father, he's oversized and under-mature, a big baby, and he's got his own special sadness—a feeling of amputation, a promising life that could have grandly gone a thousand different ways, but didn't. It's a low-frequency catastrophe the family live with every day.

Sandra dries her hands on a towel. "Sit down and eat, Noah. Let's eat."

"I want to go to the drug store," he says. His finger twirls round and round the cowlick. Even when a barber cuts it, another exact duplicate springs up in its place.

"First we're gonna have dinner though," Melissa says. "We're gonna sit right here."

"Can we run for something? I've got—I don't know. Seventeen books!"

"Yeah, but right now we're gonna eat some…?" Melissa looks inquisitively at her mother.

"Tuna melts," Sandra says, plating the sandwiches.

"Tuna melts! Yum! How does that sound? I love tuna! Come sit next to me. I want to hear how you're doing."

That's when the doorbell rings. Noah opens his mouth to say something, then snaps it shut. *Oh jeez,* Sandra says with a look Melissa's way. It might be Jeff Dulisch from down the street, he's always raising money for some charity thing or other, he works real hard for it even though he never donates any himself. Or it could be the Johnson kid from the next street over, he sells cookies and chocolate bars for his school, the kind with the edges white from age, which tells you the candy's been stored in some warehouse for longer than anyone lets on. But he always comes selling them at the exact wrong time—someone, some shitty salesman no doubt, told him that dinnertime's when you get people to answer the door.

"Is that the *CI-Ay*?" Noah says, and rushes into the front room to answer it. Sandra puts down the plate of tuna melts and goes after him.

But Melissa's hungry, dammit, she leans over and forks a bite of cheesy tuna that has edged out from one of the sandwiches. She puts it in her mouth—it's warm and good, but too salty—and she reaches for the bottle of salad dressing there on the table, to read the label and suggest Sandra cut them both back no matter how much they're actually using. And that's when the noise—the sudden resounding *BANG!*—comes from the next room.

It makes her blink in surprise with her mouth full. This is no door-to-door fundraiser, no kid from the next street over.

"Mom?" she calls thickly, her mouth full. No answer. She reaches over and lifts another forkful of tuna, looking at the open doorway as she chews, there are dust bunnies on the floor and a pillar of empty cardboard boxes in the corner. The whole place needs a thorough cleaning. *Things just aren't the same around here since I moved out*, she thinks. But then again, after tonight, nothing will ever be the same again.

noah

1

In the cemetery a small crowd huddles among the headstones, which jut like summer-teeth from the smooth mandible of the lawn. No one, not one person, showed up for Noah, and while Sandra Sweet was a terrific mother and loved by many, she was old, and there aren't that many of her friends still around anymore. That's probably for the best, because any friends of hers would have been disturbed—horrified, actually, down to their frail, decalcifying bones—by the manner in which she and her son died.

"Like his father, Thomas Noah Sweet gave his country the best years of his life," the chaplain is saying. He's a bald man with age spots like bad places on a banana, who looks to be a year or two out from retirement. Melissa's never met him before this, though he mentioned earlier that he briefly knew her father. She's packed into cotton and nylon and itchy lace, and Jack stands with her, solemn with one arm around her making her uncomfortably hot. "And Sandra Grayson Sweet, on the other hand, Thomas' dear mother, stayed home and raised two children during the best of hers."

Behind Melissa is Aunt Mina, not really an aunt or even related to them, just an older family friend who everyone called Aunt and who's gone shapeless and puffy with the years. She steps up and puts a hand on Melissa's shoulder, she's older, maybe steadying herself, *too much prednisone*, Melissa heard someone say earlier. The voice comes from a gloomy memory—a warm dim living room, curtains glowing at the edges, old people everywhere plopped onto every sitting surface, doilies and calendars and yesterday's furniture. Melissa, just a kid, leaning in the hallway in the shadows, not wanting to be there but not allowed yet to leave, *Mina's had too much prednisone,* the voice echoes, the owner of it now lost to time, *it makes her swell up like a balloon.*

"Melissa Sweet and her dear departed brother Noah were the beneficiaries of Sandra's loving kindness," the chaplain continues. Melissa watches without seeing him, her body numb, her physical awareness quashed down to a whisper, a mumble, a sliver, maybe not even there at all, aside from the heat. "Together, Noah and Sandra have flown hand in hand, upward to Glory. We ask that you give courage and faith to those who are bereaved, that they may have strength to meet the days ahead in the comfort of a reasonable and holy hope, in the joyful expectation of eternal life with those they love. Amen."

And that's that. Red dirt on the coffins. Hugs and handshakes. Lipstick kisses on the cheek. Cards and phone numbers and business cards and hasty bits of folded paper tucked away and forgotten. Melissa hardly remembers Jack getting her home, there are moments, flashes of staring out the window at the little town as it smears by, but her gaze is turned inward, back to the card catalogs of memory, the stored files of her mother—young and pretty and smoking a cigarette at the playground as little Melly arcs back and forth on a squeaky swing set. Cooking dinner for four as she watches over her kids, born within eighteen months of each other, her father only a vaguely reassuring presence in the next room. A middle-aged single mom as she helps the kids with their homework. Sleepy late-night phone calls, propped on one elbow in bed and lighting a cigarette as she listens to what kind of trouble Noah's gotten into now. And then, her own casket winching itself down into a rust-red hole. A limitless universe of memory and hope and work and yearning and sex, snuffed out like a wick. Planted in the dirt. As Melissa gazes out the car window, a series of emotions pass in front of her, embedded into the passing landscape like nativity displays, crawling across the surface of her brain until they recede into numb, silent obscurity, and are gone.

2

Melissa rented her home with the last smidge of her severance from her previous job. "This'll do just fine for the beginnings of a new family," the landlord told her in his mildew voice. She didn't explain that he had the wrong idea, no new family here, just the ghost of little Joshua James toddling down the hallway. The landlord was older—everyone's older in a town like this—with sallow hair and an undertaker face, he could easily have been the one who tossed the clumps of clay on Sandra's grave. "But once your kids start gettin' big," he said, "you'll wanna look for a new place, a bigger place. More bedrooms. I've got other places if you want." Melissa didn't say aloud what she was thinking—if and when she might ever be ready for kids of her own, that old vulture would most likely be dead.

Jack comes around the car to get her now, they're home already, and as he opens the door and helps her out, there's music, some kind of nasal thrumming jackhammer beat. Heavy metal. But it's not the comforting melodic metal of her teens, not the Priest nor the Poison nor the Crüe, this is metal that cracks your ears and claws at your brain—death metal, doom metal, all abattoir drums and plane-wreck guitars. It's her neighbor, the skinny kid with the sheet of hair who got on her nerves the moment she moved in, he's working on his muscle car now with the hood up and moaning tunelessly along. Jack ignores him and leads Melissa into the house.

He gets her naked and into the shower and leaves her there to clean off, but for most of it she sits on the side of the tub, letting the water spray the wall above her. The world has reduced itself to a blissful, steamy cocoon—her mind almost completely, mercilessly blank, as if her nerves are seared so much there isn't any pain. She's below the pain, sub-pain, hypo-pain, infra-pain, and part of her knows that soon she'll rise like a bubble to the surface and pop back into the world of misery, it will come. She's hoping to feel her way through it, to get ahead of it, but its shape is too large yet to see its circumference, there's only the loss, abstract and vacant and raw. Her mother, her beautiful mother, her soulforce, her link to the universe, *Mater*, the umbilical cord stretching all the way up to the vortex of the whirling cosmos. And then there's Noah—sad, sick, squandered Noah. Taken down by the very thing that seemed to take down their father, bad genes, bad thoughts, broken neural pathways. Not his fault, Noah lost himself and couldn't find his way home. He was always problematic, always complicated, and now he's dead. In a way, it's a relief. Melissa wasn't looking forward to the years after Sandra had passed, when it was just she and him, two siblings who were never really good friends, never close, and him big and difficult and sometimes violent and always troubled, with no one to care for him but her. Maybe murder wasn't all bad?

A careful knocking at the door interrupts her thoughts. "You okay?" Jack's timid voice outside. *Not really*, she thinks, *I'm not okay at all.* The entire shower is soaked, but she's completely dry.

"I'm good," she yells back. "Be out in a second."

Mother. *Mater*. Sandra. What can she do now, with her mother gone? Who will she look up to, who will she imitate, how will she find the path? She pushes herself up from the side of the tub, mindful of slipping on the porcelain, to let the water hit her finally and wash away the old bad memories, and maybe make way for the new bad ones to come.

3

They let her take a few days off at the clinic, it's the least they can do. She sits at her kitchen table, surrounded by molehills of food donated by friends and relatives and even people she doesn't know. She hasn't bothered to peek inside all the Tupperware, nor is she the least bit hungry, on a good day she eats hardly anything, let alone when she's wracked with anguish and wandering through a bitter mist of guilt and grief. Tonight's been hard, she can't seem to find her way out of it, or maybe it can't find its way out of her, and she wants to be touched not at all, she's turned away several times from Jack, his caress seems harsh and grating, as if her skin's gotten sensitive or his hands have grown coarse and rough, back to what they were when he was a trucker, his callouses no longer teacher-delicate and chalkboard-soft. Grief isn't rare, she knows, she's far from the first person dealing with loss, it's happened before and it'll happen again, a billion times over. Small comfort—a shroud of grief hanging over the planet, clouds heavy with tears.

Jack stands at the counter and pries back the lids and sniffs each of the dishes and says something she registers but doesn't hear. When she doesn't answer, he says, "Hello? We gonna go through this again?" His voice a bit more insistent now. Melissa looks up, her dread-reverie pierced for a moment. "Asparagus or broccoli? There's cheese sauce and bacon on everything, so I don't think it makes much difference which one."

The quiet feels good, she only shakes her head. Jack comes over and sits down. Rubs his face with tired hands. She tries a smile for him, he's always so attentive, so considerate, almost irritatingly so, he's the kind of steadily unsurprising beau who was overlooked in school, not the most handsome nor the most exciting, but the one who'll make a half-decent dad. He never attracted much attention from the girls, he's got that face of a clay golem, but he's so sweet, so thoughtful, so boringly, doggedly, goddamn unsurprisingly nice.

"You eat like a bird, Mel," he's saying. Above his words she can hear the hiss of the air outside, the pavement whispering to itself, conspiracies and schemes and machinations, and Melissa tries not to meet his eyes and also not to dwell on how everyone at the funeral looked at her, sad and delicate and quick to turn away, like brushing aside a junkie or beggar.

"Can I ask you something?" Jack carefully arranges his knife and fork, something she's never seen him do before, usually he's got the manners of a domesticated ape. "I can't imagine what's going through your head, with everything that's happened. But weren't we supposed to get married in a couple of months?"

He's right. They'd kinda sorta unofficially set the date for sometime in the fall—Melissa always loved that season, with its frugal days and its chilly nights, its death-festive feel and its orange and gold sifting down onto brown and grey. And Halloween is Jack's favorite holiday—he always loved the candy and the costumes—so they both agreed it was a good time for them to celebrate themselves. But now it's mid-September and no plans have been made, not even the words to research the plans have been made. Right now, with Melissa's brain raw and working at half-mast, any concerns of marriage seem tucked away in an indeterminate faraway blur of days.

"I mean, if you want to wait, I'm cool with it. I get it. I've never had something crazy like this happen, so we're kinda making this up as we go along." He picks up his fork, takes a half-hearted bite of asparagus. "I worked with a lady once," he says, "she was a dispatcher, she'd been through something traumatic—it was a motorcycle accident or something, husband almost killed, ended up paralyzed—and it took her the better part of a year to get back to herself. I mean, it takes time. So, if you're thinking you want to delay it, or call it off altogether, I want you to know I get it. Whatever you need."

Certainly a wedding appeals to her, certainly she can't imagine life without Jack, certainly he's been a part of her life now for years, he's been the one to pull her back from the brink after *That Day* several years ago and is presently pulling her back again from this one. No, the wedding needs to happen, it should happen and will happen, it's just a matter of time. Maybe it'll be a salve, she thinks through all the static in her head, a healing thing, a curative, the thing that will allow her to close the door on these awful episodes and say, *Wow, that sucked, can you believe it? But gimme a kiss.*

She opens her mouth to tell him this when there's a blast of noise from outside. Melissa starts, and drops her fork, and the food—a blandly colorless broccoli casserole—plops into her lap. Some kind of music, scathing and rhythmic and all *basso profundo* growls and grimaces, blares from the front yard.

"Goddammit," Jack says, and gets up and goes to the window. "What the fuck?" He parts the curtains, watching whatever's going on outside. "It's that kid. In his driveway."

"What?" Melissa asks distantly.

"What the fuck!" Jack blurts again, and he slings open the front door and marches out onto the little porch. "*Dude! Dude!*" Jack yells over the music outside.

Melissa stands up and follows him out onto the porch, to see the kid in the twilight, it's her neighbor from next door, the one with the hair. He's washing his muscle car, a GTO it says right on the front grill, and he turns around now that Jack is yelling at him.

"What?" he shouts over the blare of the stereo. The kid's maybe 16 or 17, he's pale and gaunt and seems to own an endless ensemble of long-sleeved black t-shirts. Or maybe it's just the one, but he has that remarkable hair, that long silky brown hair which hangs in a slick and shiny curtain, very unusual for a boy—some girls, Melissa thought the first time she saw him, would kill for that hair. They've never said more than three words to each other the whole time she's lived here, he looks like a hard case, the kind that find themselves in trouble no matter what they do or where they go.

"*The radio, man!*" Jack is yelling. "*Do you mind? We got people in here!*"

The kid stares at him for a moment, as if he's assessing the level of a threat. "Dude, quiet time starts at 10 PM!" he yells back, and then leans in the car and turns down the radio so he can talk. "It's not ten o'clock yet."

"Quiet time?" Jack draws back, like he's trying to keep the words from physically touching him. "It's way loud, man!"

The kid holds up a battered hammer. "Not as loud as it's gonna be. Got some dash work going on."

Jack's face scrunches in disbelief. "You have a fucking *hammer*?" Jack's no fighter, but he does have a temper. Usually it's reserved on behalf of others, that was when Jack's rage truly showed, when it was on someone else's account. Jack thought of himself as a boy scout, a knight, a doer of good deeds, it was his element, but it could get frustrating, all the lengths he would go to on stormy or snowy evenings, helping push vehicles from ditches while Melissa huddled cold and tired in the car and ready to get home.

"How many times I gotta tell you?" the kid says. "Noise ordinance says 6 AM to 10 PM are quiet hours. I looked it up. It's legit."

Jack wipes his face. Obviously, this isn't working. "What's your name?"

"I ain't gotta tell you my name, man."

"I just want to know who I'm talking to," Jack says. "It's called courtesy."

The boy looks up and down the empty street. The neighborhood is flat and the houses are close, and they recede away in depressingly perfect symmetry. Evening is falling and the windows of most of the houses are glowing yellow or blue now as families sit down for dinner or turn on CNN or Fox News, but the yards and driveways and the street are all empty, all uninhabited, it could be a neighborhood from some apocalyptic end-of-the-world TV show. "Gordie," the kid says finally. "My name's Gordie."

"Well, Gordie. I'm Jack. I'm not talking about quiet hours here. But you're playing your stereo at full blast."

The kid grins. "Dude, it's not at full blast. It's only on seven. It just seems so loud 'cause of my preamps. Best fuckin' preamps in the neighborhood."

Jack closes his mouth with an audible snap. He stands there, struck dumb for a moment, helpless against this line of thinking, he seems to be casting back to his own teenage years, trying to find some common ground with this infantile turd, and failing.

"And it's—" The kid says something, something Jack doesn't catch.

"What?"

"I said, it's *Skuggämän*. Sick as shit."

Relying no doubt on his teacher's training, some classroom technique for reaching in and pulling out a petulant kid's better nature, Jack says, "What is that?"

But the kid doesn't answer, he leans into the interior of the car, and with the hammer he starts pounding on something under the dash, a loud whacking in time with the music. The clatter echoes up the street.

Jack turns helplessly to Melissa, where she lingers in the doorway, one hand on the doorjamb, and his face goes white. He looks now like he's seeing a ghost. "Jesus."

"What?" she says.

"You look terrible." He comes to her, puts his arms around her, and leads her back in and closes the door against the banging.

4

Thursday night is when the noises start. Jack's still here, they had a restful couple of days, and Melissa insisted that she's good and just needs the space to process, but he tells her in no way will she spend the night before she goes back to work alone. So after setting up her bed, neatly as a hotel maid, and making sure there's water and a barroom mix of honey-roasted almonds nearby in a little crystal bowl (which he in his clueless dudedom failed to recognize as an unused ashtray), he lays down on his side of the bed, rolls over and, with depressing ease, sinks into unconsciousness.

The *WHOOOOOM!* from the other side of the house comes several hours later. In the dark of her bedroom, Melissa sits up, trying suddenly to listen. It's a little after midnight maybe, Jack's just a tree stump in the bed now—a broad shoulder, an ear, a soft glottal snore. The noise in the other room was like a cross between a slamming door and a plane passing close overhead. Melissa, her instincts telling her not to move, risks a glance at the clock radio. It's long after midnight, 2:39 to be exact, the red numbers glowing in the dark, little slits into some far infernal world beyond.

"Hello?" Her voice rings in the quiet room. Jack doesn't stir. From time to time, she's been worried about break-ins. This neighborhood is supposed to be safe, mostly low on crime—just a bunch of grandmas and grandpas really—but Melissa knows there's always a first time. After what happened last week, she'll never feel safe again. From the bed she watches the doorway, waiting for someone or something to emerge from the darkness, some dim sheeted-shape from a horror movie, or maybe it'll poke its head around in a jack-in-the-box jolt, the doorway a frame of expectation, a perfect ingress to violence, as if someone or something should come through, quick, running or crouching, someone weirdly small like a child, face hidden by the brim of a black hat and holding a sharp edge ready to carve.

But nobody's there.

She can hear Jack's breathing, scraping in and out, certain that whatever or whoever is out there can hear it too. Melissa gathers her courage and slips quietly out of bed. The cool of the air, the whisper of her nightgown sliding down around her calves. Still nothing.

"Jack?" He doesn't wake, he's practically enchanted. Or she is.

She tiptoes to the door and peeps around the corner, down the dark hallway and into the living room. Calm has settled over the night house, not a sound now, not even the wheeze of a car passing outside. The streetlights throw abstract, yellow-tinged shadows through the curtained windows. She steps out into the hall, scans the place. No movement, not even dust motes in the air. But for some unknown reason, she stops. *There.*

On the other side of the kitchen table, in the opening to the foyer, she sees something. A figure, someone crouched. Staring back at her.

The figure hunches over, part of the night itself, obscurity taken visceral form. A long face, a bent nose, the glint of an eye under a wide-brimmed hat. She knew there would be a hat.

Her heart hammers now, she won't let herself think this is a person, *No, it can't be,* just as those men at her mother's house couldn't have been, until they were. The thing's face is in shadow, but with a pulse of dread she realizes he's looking at her—both eyes staring right at her across the room.

Earlier she had put her jacket on the coat tree in the foyer—nobody there then, that was for sure—but it had fallen. Jack picked it up, returned it, but Melissa scolded him, *Stop, you're not my maid.* He shrugged and let it fall again, but now the jacket's back on the coat tree, above the figure hunched on the floor, weirdly small, like a gremlin or a goblin. One knee bunched up underneath.

Looking at her, ready to spring. Crowded, knotty features, a heavy brow and a sharp nose, a beak of a nose, one hand fisted up under his chin like he's posing or thinking. But there's something in his other hand—long, thin, lost in shadow. It's a weapon of some kind, she knows it is.

"Hello?" No answer. She takes a step. Her palms itch. The thing, or the person, doesn't move.

She waits, willing it to shift, to adjust, to move. It doesn't, but remains stock still, ready to leap at her with its dark eyes and the knife in its hand.

Melissa reaches for the light switch and presses it on. In the sudden bright, the thing in the doorway turns into…a cart. A *cart*? A cart of some kind. And a blanket thrown over it. On the side of the cart is written, in a steady, permanent-marker scrawl, *Property of Selleford Elementary Theater Dept.*

It's Jack's. She turns the light off again, on again. The way the streetlights sketch the shadows, it looks like a face, an eye, the bill of a nose. The knife in its hand is only the bottom edge of Jack's work satchel, hung on the coat hook behind it, half in and half out of the light. It amuses her now to see it, a blanket, one of those padded things movers use, piled onto itself over a cart in the foyer.

Night nonsense—night terrors, whatever they call it. Stress. PTSD. But tell that to her body, her heart kicking in her chest, her throat dry and tight. She steps out into the living room, the overhead light doesn't fully dissipate the dread, something's still wrong, but she can't tell what it is. Everyone in the neighborhood is asleep, but maybe someone's been in here, slipped in and out before she got up. What was that noise, the thing that woke her up? The front door slamming? Footsteps across the floor, a presence in the doorway, watching she and Jack sleep?

"Nah," she says aloud, but the word seems to wither in the air before her.

In the foyer it's the same—the front door closed and locked, just as it should be. No handprints, no footsteps, no half-turned handle, there's nothing. She rattles the knob. The deadbolt's firm, fastened from the inside.

Maybe it's the bedroom. Or the bed, maybe that's what's giving her the creeps. If the bed is the problem, she can curl up on the couch and get a good night's rest, it's a terrific couch for naps—a wide mesa of a cushion that allows for decent stretching out. Get comfy and let the clock tick and the night breathe, she'll sleep and nothing will happen. Nothing at all will happen.

Probably nothing will happen.

There was a noise, she's sure of it, it woke her, but she's not gonna check every closet, every possible nook, at some point you have to get your steadiness back, your calm, your faith, your trust, you have to *believe* you won't fall. The thought of what happened at her mother's house—the men's voices muffled and dark, the blood and the brains—returns again to her, not that they'll ever really leave. But she does her best to clamp the lid down, keeps them out, *We're not doing that, not here, good God not tonight.* Besides, lightning doesn't strike twice, does it?

Most likely she dreamed it, the noise, of course she did, or maybe a car backfiring outside as it passed. Do cars backfire anymore? Or a plane passing low overhead. Or a helicopter. It's stupid to think any other way, *There's nothing here, blondie, no one here at all.*

Blood pulses in her neck. She retreats to the bedroom and closes and locks the bedroom door. Jack's breath is innocent, helpless. The clinic needs her fresh. Time to rest.

She uncurls herself onto the mattress, scoots over to Jack and pulls the covers up, trying to let go. But there's a noise now, a slight small grinding, like a vibration, coming from the base of her skull. When she moves her head there's a creak, but the creak is coming from inside her head. Aneurysm? Stroke? Maybe it's mold in the walls, creeping and sprouting in the dark. Black mold. Back in Birmingham she had patients who got sick from it and never came fully back—fibromyalgia, respiratory diseases, headaches, nausea, chills. Auto-immune shit, scary shit that follows people for the rest of their lives, their sad haunted eyes, figures shuffling up hospital halls in their shapeless hospital gowns, so slow and painful it makes your teeth clench.

Melissa can feel her thoughts, skipping and stuttering now, threatening to slide into full-blown panic, and so she lifts this notion out of her mind, quickly, like scooping a cat off a table. She's working herself up, that's all, *sleep*, she needs sleep. Jack's breathing is low and regular. She turns over on her side, an ache in her shoulder now, a dull pang, and lays again on her back. There she is, Melissa Sweet, staring at the dark ceiling, doing her best to think of nothing.

5

In the morning, she floats across the parking lot and hides her exhaustion with a stiff smile. Beyond the glass doors, Angie and Grace see her coming and start to whisper about her again, then the doors open and she's swimming through the cold air and the antiseptic smell towards the counter. She fully expected the strangeness of the other day to return, that weird plausibly deniable intentional miscommunication, but as she gets closer a smile of Angie's own rises on her face, an official smile, a public smile, and she gets up and comes around the counter in her floral scrubs and wraps Melissa in a tight body hug. Melissa lets herself be embraced, but she doesn't squeeze Angie back, it's better that way.

"Melissa, we are so sorry for your loss, for what happened," Angie says. "We're so, so sorry. We want you to know that we're here for you."

"Do I have any messages?" Melissa says flatly. She's not interested in Angie's phony sympathy, or in any of her other emotions really.

Angie releases her and indicates a small pile of envelopes on the far end of the counter. Presumably they're for Melissa. "You've got these here and we all—"

"Besides the cards, I mean."

"Oh." Surprise, and another emotion—rejection maybe, or bafflement that her manipulations, so easily recognized, didn't work. "Well, I don't know. I just got here."

Melissa retreats beyond Angie's reach. "When you get a chance to go through it all," she says, "will you let me know?"

"Don't you want to take a look at the cards?" Angie adjusts the glasses on her nose, and Grace watches them dully from her low seat behind the counter, like a severed head kept alive by mad scientists. "You got quite a few here."

"I'll look at them later." Melissa steps around her and moves off down the hall. As she goes, she can feel the cool exchange of Angie and Grace's surprise behind her back. It doesn't matter, she's already thinking of ways she could've made it worse, made it even more perplexing for that cow and her silent sycophant.

"Melissa?" Angie's voice, distant now. Melissa stops and turns.

The older woman looks deflated, which gives Melissa a small satisfaction, Angie standing backlit from the plate glass doors and the sunlit parking lot beyond that, all the bright bumpers and the shiny windshields, it hurts Melissa's eyes to look. She wonders how Angie and Grace can stand it, being in the front all day with that bright sun, that brilliant chrome gleaming in at you for hours. It seems like punishment.

"Just...we thought you'd be out for the rest of the week, you know, with everything that happened," Angie says. "A long weekend's not really—"

But Melissa's not listening. She's already turned and gone down the hall, around the corner to the nurse's station. She puts down her purse and swivels on the little stool. Thinks about turning the radio on, low and in the background, it might help her exhaustion, might help her to focus, but doesn't, it'll be another drone in the background that only adds more to the wall between her brain and her body. Insomnia, her old pal—that hell of wakefulness, that dreaded disconnection from everything, and it follows you around all day. At its worst, it's an unbearable blear of time, she'll find herself slipping outside of things—where "last night" has no meaning, because it's still today, and your face ravaged with the hollow eyes of too much knowing. To withhold sleep, that tiny dump valve, that comforting little death, is the cruelest thing she can imagine. She opens the desk drawer, looking for something, not sure what, and then closes it again. Swivels on her seat and rests her head in her hands. Maybe Angie's right, maybe coming here so soon was a bad idea after all. Her nerves are coming back, healing slowly, creeping like a light-starved plant budding just enough now to bring the pain.

6

The doorbell rang, and Noah lurched into the next room, and Sandra dashed after him, to intercede in case he started making trouble for whoever was at the door. It wouldn't be the first time. Once two years ago Noah pitched a fit at a UPS delivery guy, had assaulted the man after there'd been some missed or broken communication of some sort (no doubt also Noah's doing), and a lawsuit was threatened but never enacted, and Sandra and Melissa learned not to trust *that* process anymore.

But then Melissa took a bite and her mouth was full of tuna salad and she had a moment to think, *This is way too salty I need to cut them both back.* She reached across the table to pick up the jar of salad dressing—on it was a picture of a chubby-cheeked little boy, antique and blushing and with a cowlick not unlike Noah's own, he was slurping a spoonful of the dressing, with the words *THE MORE YOU HAVE THE MORE YOU WANT!* above him.

That's when the noise—the sudden resounding *BANG!*—came from the next room.

Melissa blinked in surprise. This was no door-to-door fundraiser. "Mom?" she called thickly, her mouth full. No answer. She reached over and got another forkful of tuna, looking at the open doorway.

Then voices—men's voices, angry voices, voices crowded and sloppy with rage and stress. And her mother saying, very clearly from the next room: *"What?"*

A man's voice bellowing, "*Fuck offa me!*"

There was the sound of a scuffle, like two boys wrestling, all slips and steps and grunts and croaks, coming closer, and then—before Melissa could react—a group of men, three or four of them but it was a jumble at first, a kinetic blur of form, burst into the living room pushing Sandra and Noah ahead of them like swimmers tossed in a rough tide.

A low percussive shock rippled across Melissa before she knew why. It took her a white-hot moment, a skip of nullity like a computer glitch, before she understood that each of the men, in their dark intentions to come inside the house no matter what, was wearing a cheap Halloween mask.

No fuckin' way, her brain told her. A leering clown, a grinning dog, what must have been intended to be an alien—it was green with big eyes anyway—and a cartoonishly freakish red-nose, red-cheeked, half-mask which covered only the lower part of the man's bearded face. Oddly, frighteningly, it looked like the grotesque blush-cheeked puppets on *Mr. Rogers' Neighborhood*, when she was younger those faces were so horrible to watch, and she remembered having nightmares where they spoke to her in that spooky sniveling mewl Fred Rogers gave them.

But she was at the table in the kitchen, and the men were in the living room, and it was as though the air and the sound had been sucked from the room into the vacuum of space. Abstractly, Melissa thought *Is this real, am I having a dream?* before she understood indeed it was real. Two of the men held Noah by the wrists and they struggled, yelling and wrenching and pummeling him in the living room. Melissa dumbly at the table, fork poised not twenty feet away, if any of them turned to look they could see her sitting there, but they were busy with Noah, who verged on becoming violently agitated, and Noah was a very big boy.

Melissa understood their concern. Noah had bruised and beat her time and again when they were kids, from as early as three years old he'd become an ever-combustible terror, *Watch out for Noah* was the constant refrain in Melissa's mind when she was a girl, he was a grey, boy-shaped cloud always on the periphery of things, and it only got worse as he got older. The real violence started in his teens—temper tantrums, slamming doors, punching walls, spitefully turning on all the water faucets in the house. Once he went through the rooms, putting all the end tables upside down. It wasn't all terrible, every so often Noah's size and temperament came in handy for her, it was a good useful thing like when schoolyard bullies learned not to mess with her. And it did improve for a year or two when he enlisted in the Army, but then his temper seemed only to get worse when he was kicked out of the military on an *Other Than Honorable Conditions* discharge due to his growing record of camp skirmishes, black eyes, door destructions, and shattered windows. Weirdly, alcohol was never involved.

Noah had been stationed at Fort Hood, in east Texas, and the Army had no idea what they had on their hands. He resisted easy definitions. At first, he was labelled *Oppositional Defiance*, but that soon morphed into *Disturbance of the Order* and *Low Impulse Control.* Finally, one night Noah put several drunken privates in the hospital, and when the Army kicked him out, they said it was

Antisocial Tendencies. But it wasn't any of that, Melissa knew, and her mother knew it too. It was the same *linger-long something wrong* that claimed their father. *Nervous. Anxious. Mental. Marbles. Disturbed. Demented. Psycho. Schizo.* It doesn't matter whatever shitty term the Army or anyone else threw at him, because when Noah got mad, definitions were the least of your problems.

In the midst of all the yelling, Melissa saw her mother throw a glance her way, her eyes—white marbles and terrified in a way Melissa had never seen before—wordlessly telling the younger woman that she needed to get herself out. Without thinking, Melissa slowly put down the jar of salad dressing—*the more you have the more you want!*—and dipped underneath the table. On her hands and knees she backed away, against the refrigerator, then laterally and back again into the darkened utility room. Quietly, gently, with her shoulder she nudged the Dutch door closed until both parts, the top half and the bottom, were open just a crack. None of the men looked over.

Maybe, she thought lucidly, her brain sharpened now to a shiny point, her notions coming with weird cold clarity as if everything was happening in slow motion, *maybe their masks limit a bit of their vision*. The door to the garage, to the outside and the windy night and away from this sudden madness, was right behind her, she could flee now at any time. But something stopped her, the worry that a breeze would gust through, rattle the Dutch door, make a racket somehow. It would surely alert the men, which would only doom her mother. No, she slipped back into the shadows, and in her terror concealed herself there as best she could.

That was when the man—the one with the wild hair and the freaknose mask, he was as big as her brother, Melissa saw, he was really fucking big—punched Noah right in the mouth. The sound was a flat slap, not at all like those deliciously tactile Hollywood punches, but more like the flat carnal slapping of bodies during sex.

Noah fell back against the wall. Unexpectedly, that seemed to shut him up and calm him down. Maybe he finally seemed to grasp the gravity of the situation, it certainly had taken his sister a moment. Or maybe he'd gotten a better look at their guns—their pistols and their large scary rifle-looking things, the kind that Melissa had seen in the news here and there, jowly men walking down the middle of a road carrying them like deadly black baseball bats, and even from the utility room, the black holes of their muzzles seemed to stare down into infinity. Whatever it was, Noah backed up against the wall near the corner, his mouth seeping blood, while Sandra stood with the men, one of them with a calm, coercing hand on her shoulder.

Everyone, it seemed then, took a breath. The sense of violence floated in the air like a mist of blood, but for that moment, at least, things were calmer.

After a quick discussion, the men split up. Clownmask and Dogface moved into the back of the house, toward the bedrooms, while the other two—Freaknose and Alienface, Melissa would call them later, numbly describing this scene to the Selleford police—stood with Sandra and Noah in the front room, their guns pointed lazily at them.

"Where is it?" she heard Freaknose ask. Or maybe it was *Where is she*? Melissa couldn't tell. His voice was odd and startling—definitely not Mister Rogers' effeminate mewl, but a deep southern drawl so dense it was almost a parody of one: *Whar is shay?*

"What?" Sandra managed to stammer. "*What?*"

"The girl! Where is it?" In the utility room, a freezing gust of cold air passed through Melissa. *The girl.* Were they talking about her?

"I— What? We don't—"

"*I don't want the letters!*" Noah called. He was in the corner, growing agitated again. "*Drug store secrets!*" he yelled, his voice sharp and thin now.

Sandra was wilting under the stress—sweat already glossing the corners of her temples and under her arms—but she seemed to steady her voice for Noah's sake. "Noah, please calm down, please."

"I'm gonna ask you again," the man in the freaknose mask was saying calmly. That deep voice held an edge of unexpected tenderness, like he was raised to be polite to seniors. Southern propriety, or maybe just a bit of Falstaffian brio. He noticed a picture on the wall, nicely framed, of the whole family—an early 80s Nolan Mills special, Mom, Dad, little Noah, Melissa in braces and pigtails, gawky and mortified. "This is her, right?"

Sandra seemed encased in some invisible iron maiden, unable to move or respond.

"So where's the girl?"

"I don't— *What—*?"

"*Drug store secrets!*" Noah barked. In the darkness of the utility room, Melissa closed her eyes, feeling the panic beginning to boil up. *Please please please*, she heard herself whisper under her breath. If these men had any idea what Noah could do.

But Freaknose only leaned in and tightened his grip on his rifle. "*Shuddup!*" he shouted.

"*Noah*," Sandra said in a pleasant, shaky voice that didn't fool anybody, "we—these people are real. They're here. You need to quiet down."

But Noah, looking like a performer in a stage musical—feet planted, fists balled at his sides, working to be heard by the back rows—bellowed, "*DRUG*

STORE SECRETS!" to the ceiling. When he was under stress, anything could happen. Melissa and Sandra always tried to keep him calm and gentle—never yell, never curse, never exclaim anything more than a slow and quiet *Oh shoot* or *Oh darn*. Mostly it worked. For several years, Noah had seemed to mellow out of his anger and grew fat and slow in his adult years. But this was bringing it all back up.

Freaknose turned sharply to Sandra, like someone needing an explanation. Melissa watched as Sandra's hands did what they always did when they were nervous—they fluttered to the tiny crucifix around her neck.

"He's got—he's sick," she said, "he doesn't understand." Melissa's heart stung with the thought of Noah in trouble—with the cops, with the Army, with his family. It was a tangle, a riddle, an unsolvable problem.

Alienface shifted his rifle, re-aimed it at Noah. "Let's get this fucking thing, all right?"

"How's it comin' back there?" Freaknose called.

Through the crack in the door Melissa could see most of the kitchen and into the living room. The hallway was visible too—it was a near straight shot—and down the length of it someone poked their head out of Sandra's bedroom. It might have been Dogface. "We're lookin'!" he said.

Freaknose turned to Sandra. "All right, where the *fuck* is it?" The older woman gestured to her purse, and the big man went to it and dumped it all out on the floor on the far side of the counter, beyond Melissa's line of sight. He seemed to sift through it with his foot. "There's nothin' worth shit in here!"

The other guy, Alienface, came into the kitchen and started going through the drawers. Knives and spoons clattered on the linoleum. Melissa retreated further into the shadows and with one eye watched through the crack in the door. Cold sweat had gathered on her brow like dew, slipping down her temples and neck and into her shirt.

"*Can't we go to the drug store?*" Noah shrieked.

"*Shuddup!*" Freaknose shouted, and he stepped over and cracked Noah in the temple with the hard black butt of his rifle. Noah fell against the wall, a dribble of blood seeping now from his ear.

Oh no oh no oh no, Melissa heard a voice whisper, as if in a bad dream.

"Fuckin' *relax*, man!" Alienface called over his shoulder from the kitchen.

"*Why won't he shut up?*"

"*Cigarettes and medicine!*" Noah yelled to the ceiling. His nose was bleeding now too, both from the nostrils and from the cut on the bridge of it and running down the side of his mouth. "*MEDICIIIIIINE!*"

Sandra's voice, polite but more strained than Melissa had ever heard it, said,

"Noah—please let the men get what they want." She tried to stay calm, but it wasn't working, not even close. "Noah, *stop it.*"

"*TIME IS MONEY! TIME IS MONEY!*" Noah yelled.

A new sense of unreality paralyzed Melissa, froze her mind, a distant abstracted feeling as though she were watching it all unfold on some TV, her brain moving as slow and sluggish as it did when she were still on the meds she took in the months after *That Day*, the ones which made her fuzzy and forgetful and sleep all the time.

But then—like an idiot, she was an idiot—her cell phone was with her, she'd had it this whole time stuffed down in the front pocket of her pants, she ordered scrubs with pockets because purses and nurses don't necessarily go together and her phone was right here. She also had bear spray, a long-ago gift from Jack that she'd never used, but that was in her purse in the kitchen and spray wouldn't help against these people anyway. In the dark she knelt and pulled the phone out of her pocket and flipped it open.

"*WHERE THE FUCK IS IT!*" Freaknose roared.

"*Where's what?*" Sandra sobbed.

A voice called from the back of the house: "Dudes, chill! We're checking!"

Noah stood against the hallway door, frantically twirling the corkscrew lock of his hair on top of his head. He was trying to fight it, but that vicious careening out-of-control feeling about him was coming back. "*DRUG STORE! DRUG STORE SECRETS!*"

"*Shut him up! SHUT UP!*"

Sandra looked at Noah and commanded in a quavery voice, "Noah—*be quiet!*"

"*MEDICINE! MEDICIIIIIINE!*"

In the utility room, Melissa's fingers, weirdly clumsy and stupid-thick, hit the nine button and the one and the one. With a shaking hand she held it to her ear, the air felt corrosive now, her lungs were empty and she couldn't breathe and a buzzing droning sensation was moving into her vision from the sides, like clouds of tiny gnats or swarming flies. The other end of the connection rang distantly, and Melissa could hardly keep from shouting with fear, *Pick up pick up pick up!* She kept one frantic eye staring through the crack in the door and watched as Noah swatted the Freaknose man with a huge paw, a mitt, a bear claw of a hand, and the man's mask came off and clattered to his feet.

The room stopped. Everything was silence. Melissa's heart turned to cold dirt. In the kitchen, Alienface halted. They all looked over at the unmasked man.

And there he was—Freaknose revealed. Solid, unshaven, his hair wild, shoulders hunched surely from a lifetime of being too big, too tall, too broad.

His nose leaning, maybe from being broken several times. His eyes bloodshot, weighed by heavy bags underneath, and below his sparse beard his cheeks red and blushing, like a schoolboy, or rosacea. Melissa could almost feel his big-boy shame, which he had no doubt turned into a dirty, deprecating humor, making fun of his own size, swallowing his anger, she could see it burning in his wild gaze. Staring at Noah for a long, long time. Nobody moved. It was as if someone had taken a photograph or made a painting, Freaknose and Noah, the two big boys, two embarrassingly big boys, painfully big, facing off against each other, sympathetic in size and in kind and in another life maybe friends, good pals, good buds. Just not right now.

"*DRUG STORE DRUG STORE DRUG—*"

With a smoothness and speed that defied his large size, the hairy stranger lifted the semi-automatic away from his body—it was connected by a strap—and slipped the barrel under Noah's chin and pulled the trigger. There was a sharp *BRRRLLLAAAPPPP* and a muzzle-flash in the room and before anyone could react Noah's blood-red brains hit the ceiling.

7

The journey from adorable little Noah—four years old and impossibly squeezable for six-year-old Melissa—to the overweight, oversized, over-medicated clot in their lives was long and eventful. But only in hindsight did the slide from volatile loner to head-case become obvious and inevitable. Once as a teen, while she had a friend over, Noah took off all his clothes and laid, babbling nonsense, on the living room floor. Other times he talked about being Anthony Kiedis in secret, or Perry Farrell in hiding. Later, there were appointments with doctors, who used terms that Melissa had never heard before—*vulnerability hypothesis* and *double-bind*, *schizophregenic* and *hebephrenic*. He got worse. Once he was missing for two weeks and was found to be sleeping in someone's dirt basement. Another time he broke every dish in the house, because he said the CIA were using them to listen to their conversations. *I'm doing you a favor!* he'd yelled as Sandra sat at the table and sobbed.

The conversations with the doctors changed then, and began to include words like *sodium amytal* and *Thorazine* and *Clozapine*. His behavior didn't change, but Melissa's reaction to it certainly did. When no one but she and Noah were home, she took to locking herself in her room, or started staying overnight at classmates' houses when she could, and made light of her brother's peculiarities and lack of friends, brushing off the weird looks and the snide comments.

Noah's biggest goal was to become a Marine—he buzzed his hair in a high-and-tight while still a young teen, and made sure to do sit-ups and push-ups and pull-ups everyday. It was his way of staving off his disease, Sandra had said, of maintaining at least a little control. But when the Army discharged him—he never made it to the Marines—it seemed to break him once and for all, he came home medicated and bloated, his face flushed and fat. His eyes were different too—they wouldn't meet your own, they stayed mostly on the floor as he shuffled back and forth from his room to the kitchen. Sometimes he would talk to someone in the garbage disposal, or he would go for walks around the block only to be brought home by cars with red and blue carnival lights on top. The local police got to know him, and the paramedics too.

When her own problems forced her to leave Birmingham and move in with her mom seven hours away in North Carolina, Melissa hoped they could find at least a little sense of the old family, the good old days after their father was gone and it was just the three of them. But that Noah was gone too, he could hardly hold a conversation, let alone make order out of anything more complicated than waffles and syrup. His terrible problem seemed even to dwarf Melissa's own. As bad as the Joshua James Newcombe accident had been, watching her brother slowly lose his mind was somehow worse—he was overmedicated and underserved, he was violent, he was bullied, he was instigator and victim, he was their can of worms, their Pandora's box, their own Gordian knot. Until now.

8

Melissa doesn't remember the burst of gunfire that killed her brother. She was instantly drowning in an airless silence, clawing at it from the inside, the flesh of her face had gone numb, and also the skin of her hands and arms, or maybe she felt so much all at once that it was all noise, all cacophony. Everything in slow motion. A single crazy thought came to her—*Mom and I are gonna have the dickens getting that stain off the ceiling.* The men in the room were frozen, and Sandra too as they watched Noah's knees buckle and then collapse, almost too carefully, as if he was only kidding. It reminded Melissa of those building demolitions she'd seen on YouTube—first the base, then the middle, then the top as it all came crumbling perfectly down on top of itself. Noah knelt lifeless at the base of the hallway door, his legs folded underneath him in a way Melissa had never seen him sit before, his fat knees jutting out of his cargo shorts like blood-spatted stumps. No one breathed.

In the silence a car passed by outside, weirdly loud, playing some kind of music, a rhythmic thumping, funky music, and a voice growled up—*a black boy a white girl just another cruel world*—and then it was gone.

"What the *fuck*, man!" It was one of the voices from the back. Shaky and confused. Less a question than a cry of frustration.

A soft exhale came, and Melissa knew it was her own. She closed her eyes and steadied herself. And realized the phone wasn't in her hand anymore. It was on the floor, near the washing machine. She'd dropped it.

Alienface was looking her way. He'd heard it drop.

9

In that moment Melissa's standing in the hospital corridor, good old Baptist Medical, shiny floors, dark subterranean dead-end. About to go into the little boy's room, that poor little preemie, poor little Joshua James Newcombe. Sees herself push open the door—veiny flesh on wood, her nails dull and ridged and needing to be filed and manicured but they won't let her keep them nice as a nurse, it's against regulations. Inside the room it's cooler, and the smell is different, dryer, more medicinal. The hospital room like a photo—infant in the incubator, alone for now, no other babies, he's all swaddled in clean white linen folded carefully and tucked perfectly over his legs so it won't bunch up near his face. A cabinet on the far side, linen drawers closed and empty, grey sink on the far side, a single box of wet wipes near the edge. The IV stands closer, like a hanger from a strip mall laundromat. A fleeting thought comes— coat hangers we need more coat hangers*—but there's a single clear IV bag, hanging with a port halfway down the tube to gain access. And the blue vial in her hand, tiny and clear itself, the top sterile and the liquid spotless, innocuous and water-benign, as if to say* Hey it's fine it's fine you could drink me all of me every bit of me and it would be juuuuust—

10

She came back when she saw her mother rush over to where Noah was crumpled. A pressure was building, a booming in her ears, and Melissa realized her lip was bloody because she had bitten through it. "*Oh my God!*" Sandra wailed. "*Oh my God!*"

Someone from the back of the house spoke up again: "Everybody all right?

Everybody cool?"

Melissa watched frozen as Alienface stepped closer to the utility room where she was hiding. His hollow eyes stared—some cheap mask-maker, some underpaid graphic designer drew it with Photoshop, she knew an art student in college and he used to make grim jokes about designing shit like this, placemats and fast food menus and crappy disposable Halloween masks—and she withdrew from the crack of light, and made herself as tiny as possible and slipped in beside the washing machine, the narrow crevice there, and in a weird moment of clarity she leaned a leg out and pressed her toe against the bottom half of the Dutch door, keeping it steady.

"No! Everybody ain't cool!" the big man yelled. "Find the fucking key and let's go!"

Sandra was sobbing, lost in oblivion. "*Noah! Oh my God*!"

"*SHUDDUP!*" the big man screamed.

Closer to Melissa, Alienface put the barrel of his rifle against the upper half of the Dutch door and pushed. It swung free and drifted to a stop. She was down low now, crouching off to the side, motionless in the shadows with her toe keeping the bottom from opening. People talking in low voices. "*Jeez, what the fuck, yeah?*" someone said.

"We got it or not?" the big man barked. Or was it *We got her or not?* His cow-belch of a voice was oddly unmuffled by a mask, she'd gotten used to him sounding muted and indistinct and now it was worse.

But Alienface, the tilted eyes of the mask dark and empty—Melissa was right, *visibility is definitely limited in those things*, she thought again with that strange clarity—the eyes stayed focused on the utility room door. He was right there. With the barrel of his gun, the fat hole of it looking down into a void, into another universe of nothingness, the Dutch door fully open now, unopposed. Melissa crouched in the crack of the washing machine, just inside the shadow's edge, and she felt herself wanting to break, wanting to run, to scuttle away like a crab, outside to the carport and then away into the night. But the men would see her, they would chase her, and besides, her mother doesn't deserve that, how could she turn away and try to save only herself, she would never have been able to live like that. And *Noah oh shit oh shit oh Noah*.

But now Alienface was sticking the barrel of the gun inside the utility room, it hovered in the air above her, and a wild thought came—she could grab it, snatch it, take it from him, pull it from his grasp and then turn it on him and on the others. *BRRRLLLAAAPPPP!* indeed. A vision of herself like Rambo, like the Terminator or maybe the lady from the Terminator—cigarette and mirrored aviators, her body jigging as she strafed the kitchen and then the living room, ridding the house of the bad guys as they flew back, arms out in slo-mo blood-splatting Grand Guignol. All of them except her mother.

But then another thought—*Don't you try it you'll never get away with it, they'll shoot you like they shot Noah.* And so, resisting her impulses, she stayed low and in the shadows, hoping against hope the darkness and the crappy mask-vision worked in her favor. The barrel with its evil hole wavered above her as Alienface looked in, examining the tiny room.

Then someone said, "Hey, c'mere." Maybe it was the big guy. Whoever it was, the gun barrel wavered for a moment and then retracted, and Melissa sensed an absence, a vacated space, she could tell that Alienface had turned away from the door and the kitchen and returned to the living room. She caught her breath and dropped to her knees for steadiness and peeked above the Dutch door, to see them all in the living room standing over poor crumpled, unrecognizable Noah. His face was all red and the top of his head was weirdly flat, as though he'd gotten a particularly drastic haircut. Maybe that cowlick wasn't so permanent after all.

One of the other men, Dogface, came in from the back, and stood with them. There was a blurry tattoo on his forearm, she'd seen it somewhere before, the shape of it familiar even from across the room. Then it hit her—King Kong roaring, fist raised, from the Empire State Building. From that old black and white movie, jerky and stupid but somehow still perfectly hypnotic, you couldn't take your eyes away. She would watch it every Thanksgiving, the big ape and the girl and the planes like wasps around his head.

"Fuck," she heard Clownface say. "What about her?"

Her. It took Melissa a moment. *Her. What about Sandra. What about Mom.*

The big man without a mask turned to Sandra. He still had that foggy sense about him of someone who had just woken up from a long nap. Sandra stood against the wall near her fallen son, breathing hard, face ruddy with tears and stress. There was a spot of blood on her cheek. She blinked, pushed her hair defiantly back from one ear.

Melissa watched as the room settled, got quiet again. *Pleasepleaseplease,* she thought.

"She seen you, man," Dogface pointed out. "She knows your face."

The big man exhaled showily. There was humor in it, he was funny. Maybe even charming. In a bar he would be the one telling the jokes. Buying everybody a round. The one to give you a ride home when you had two too many. He could handle his drink, Melissa somehow knew, and he could also handle moments like this.

"I won't," Sandra said in a small voice. A calmness had descended upon her now, it wasn't a fake calm, it was very real, maybe more calm than she'd ever been in her life. "I promise you, I'll let it go." She swallowed thickly. "People came in, ransacked the place. And then left right away. I was asleep. Never saw anyone, never saw a thing. That's what I'll tell them."

"Yeah, no, that's good," the big man said thoughtfully, rubbing his chin. "Heavy sleeper."

"It'll work," Sandra said in her best placid-mom voice. The same tone she used when talking to Noah, that false calm, that faux optimism. "I'm a great liar. I promise you, it'll work. It will."

The big man considered the dead body. "And then of course he attacked us. Nothin' we could do. Self-defense."

Sandra's eyes grew wide as she nodded, right, yes yes, exactly, they were co-conspirators, this will work.

The big man gestured around the room. "But look at your plants! They're dry as Death Valley!" And indeed, from what Melissa could see, the plants were wilted and parched. She hadn't noticed. Before tonight, Noah sucked all the air from the room, he took up all your attention, everything else was dimmed and peripheral when Noah was around. But the big man was right, the plants were not doing well, dried ferns and sad spider plants and Chinese evergreens, their big fan-like leaves wilted and sagged from the windowsills and bookshelves and tabletops. "And if these ain't doing so hot, how can I know you to do what you say?"

Sandra said nothing, only stared, sweating, not sure where the big man was going.

"These plants rely on you, girl, they need you. They let you take them home with the promise being they would take care of you and you would take care of them."

"But I have," Sandra said weakly. She was beginning to cry. "I do my best." Her eyes darted to the half-open Dutch door of the utility room where Melissa was hiding. Surely there was no way she could know her daughter was still back there. Melissa watched her mother swallow dryly. "I can, I promise. You're right, I'm not good with plants, but I'll do my best, I promise."

The big man smiled, he wasn't a bad looking fellow beneath all that girth and hair. If he lost a bit of weight maybe, if he quit smoking and drinking and helped his bad skin clear up. His eyes were bright, and his laugh lines were full and deep, he *was* kind of a Falstaffian fellow. From where Melissa could see, his teeth were full and even, and Melissa knew that he had either been very very lucky or that his parents took care of them. She thought, *Money*. He came from money. He came from privilege.

"Well, hello there," the man said then with his grim, perfect smile, stepping up to Sandra. He tilted his big head, put the barrel of the gun underneath her chin. "You doin' all right?"

11

Melissa blinks and looks up. Back at the nurse's station. Elbows on the counter, fingers laced together like a child in prayer. Someone's in the doorway. Dr. Larry.

"What?" Melissa asks, resurfacing back into the here and now.

"I said, Hello, you doing all right?"

For a moment Melissa looks blankly at him, needing to ask herself this before she can answer. "Good," she says warily.

"Can we talk?" He fills her doorway, colorless and pasty. Like a human cubicle. The more she sees of him, the less she wants. "In my office?"

As if still in a dream, she stands and follows him down the hall and into his office, a corner suite that's oddly dark and very quiet. Dr. Larry waits for her to enter, then closes the door behind her. The blinds and curtains are pulled, and the walls are painted cocoa or mocha or beaver or whatever the hell they're calling light brown these days, so the entire place feels like an organic nest or cave or mole-hole, a retreat away from the rest of the clinic. She can see why he likes it.

"First," he says as he sits in the big leather armchair behind his desk, the cushions exhaling with a tired *whoosh*, and motions for her to find a place in one of the more modest seats on the opposite side, "let me say how horrible I feel. What you've been through. It must have been just…goddamn awful."

Melissa sits up straight. "No, no, thank you so much. I appreciate that. But I'm good."

"We're all grateful to you, you know. For coming in so quickly. It shows your dedication to this practice in an admirable way. But, seriously, I mean, if you need more time…"

Melissa shakes her head but remains silent. Not wanting to get into it, there's a dull tug, like sleep or hunger or gravity, to go back into the misery again, always back into her life of grief. But if she does, it might take her awhile to get back out. Better to be here, with Dr. Larry.

"Well. It's a bit awkward to ask so bluntly, but I get the feeling you wouldn't have it any other way. Which is in itself quite admirable. Work ethic and all that." Dr. Larry seems to pause for dramatic effect. "But, seriously…is there anything we need to talk about?"

"Talk about?" The painting on the wall, behind Dr. Larry, is a floral, playfully colored gouache of toucans all lined up on a branch. Almost feminine, full of folk art whimsy. "Like what?"

"Like, for instance, how you're doing?"

"Me? I'm fine. I mean..." She trails off, not sure what to say. There's nothing to say. Or maybe too much to say, really it's a problem of scale—a wall of white noise, it's hard to isolate any one thing, to make sense of it enough to measure it down into one or two brief pithy phrases that will fit the expectations of this man she barely knows. Wiser to say nothing.

His brow furrows. "What?"

"Nothing. I'm sorry." She wants to pick her nose. "I'm good."

Dr. Larry frowns at her, concerned. "Melissa, are you sure you don't need a little more time off? A little, you know, a break? You've stumbled once, I'd hate for this to become something you regret, or some issue between—"

"Honestly, it helps to get my mind off things. If I can keep busy, I mean."

Dr. Larry's chin juts up as he looks at her through the bottoms of his glasses. He sits forward, his hands folded on top of each other. Sensible. Melissa finds herself wondering if he's secretly gay, his movements are stately and precise, just so.

"Of course," he says. "We need you, Melissa. That's why you're here. You are clearly the best one for the job, and we desperately need you. We lost two nurses in June and the others have been complaining about the load all summer, and Angie's having to schedule and resched—"

"Then let me do my job. Please. That's what you can do for me." She tries to project an air of competence, of readiness and steadfast clarity. "I mean, just let me do my job."

For a long time Dr. Larry stares at her, seeming to consider the ins and outs of her coming back so quickly. There's insurance to consider, surety bonds and liability coverage, things like that. Another accident of the type she's already had would be devastating, not only for her but also for the entire practice. But they need her.

He shifts in his chair, purses his lips and glances down at his mail. There's a lot of it. "Okay," he says with an air of surrender. "Okay."

seth

1

The police station's on the low side of town, down by the wide, shallow river which gives the little town its name. Two plain-clothes policemen, Bogdan and Leverton, meet Jack and Melissa at the dirty glass doors in front, which display the dim smears of handprints and boot-scuffs of red mud on the windows, slightly alarming reminders of earlier ordeals. The inside of the station is all chipped tiling, fluorescent lights and cluttered desks butted up against the walls, it really is like something from an old TV movie.

The two investigators were the ones who showed up at the house that night, and now Melissa watches them lean against their desks and fiddle with their pocket change and adjust their ties, *tsk*ing sympathetically at every detail Jack relates, using their small-town psychology to make her feel better, to make themselves feel better, to manipulate her into getting what they want, she remembers disliking them right away, though one of them seems actually to be sympathetic—the small, serious one, she forgets which one is which. Leverton, maybe, but with her grief and shock and the way she's been dipping in and out of a light catatonia, a mostly pleasant place where the lights are off and nobody's home, she's not entirely sure. When Jack talks, Leverton seems to listen, his eyes flit here and there, concerned and worried, but Melissa knows this is straight out of the police handbook. The other one, a jaded air of detachment hovers around him, he's acting, pretending, not shy in his faux gravitas, there's a good cop and a not-so good cop, and she and Jack are meant to pinball between them until they're worn out.

The night of the murders, after the police and the ambulances had arrived at the house, the place looking more like a frat party than anything else—not a single person wearing paper shoes, just a bunch of corn-fed white boys in body armor and CEDs sitting on the arms of the couch or leaning uselessly in the doorway. One of the EMTs went over and asked, "Is this something?" and showed them an old Bic pen he'd found on the floor with hair stuck to it that was being kicked here and there. Bogdan, the sandy-haired one, took it, smelled it, smudged his fingerprints all over it, before dropping it back down and kicking it once and for all under the couch. *Not my problem.* Now, as she and Jack sit across from them, she can see already in the rigid set of their features they have no news. Or maybe it's only bad news.

"The thing is, we have very little to work with," Leverton admits. His thinning thatch of black hair and his fidgety smile that bows in the middle suggests he may have some Mediterranean heritage in his family. The bottom half of his face is blue with stubble.

"If they're pros—and these guys were pros—they know how to keep it together." This is Bogdan—younger and sharp-faced, with his careful eyes in a mask of arrogance. He gets up and goes around to sit at his desk, a threadbare utilitarian chair, cheap metal office furniture, smooth and shiny where the elbows rest. Leverton remains on the desk itself, his feet up on his own chair, a routine arrangement, no doubt.

Despite the news, Jack is still hopeful. "So…?"

"So we keep going," Bogdan says. "Obviously."

"But we're not optimistic," Leverton says.

"Are there people like that? Armed people? In Selleford? Goddamn *gangs*?"

Bogdan glances at his partner, seeming to confirm something before he explains, *hoo boy.* "There are armed gangs everywhere. Up in Avery, which is nobody's idea of a drug hub, there was a major shootout last year, deal gone bad, that big hotel there by the highway. Blood and bodies and bricks of drugs in the fourth-floor hallway. Media kept it hush hush so the bubbas wouldn't get too freaked out, but yes, they're here. Youth gangs, drug gangs, Latino gangs, black gangs, white gangs. Body-packing drugs, stuffed into car manifolds, dashboards, fentanyl in boat cargo and private planes, motorcycles, you name it."

"*Boat cargo?*" Jack says.

"What works in the city don't work in the country," Leverton explains.

Bogdan digs at the corner of his eye, pries out a crumb of sleep and drops it on the floor. Melissa marvels at his wild eyebrows. "There's more, lots more. Organized crime. Snitching livestock, farm equipment, even grain and tobacco where they can. Everybody wants to know *why, why, why*, so we tell 'em it's mostly jobs and drugs—not enough of one, too much of the other. Which Ms. Sweet here might know something about, her job and all."

Melissa feels the cautious glance Jack tosses her way. When she's in public she hides it well, but she's still in terrible shape—benumbed by recent events, the world listing to starboard, her ship running aground. A part of her disappeared that night and might never come back. The catatonia, which Jack has taken to call *Bye-Byeville,* seems to come and go in waves—sometimes she's here and sometimes she's not. They both understand it's a part of her healing, or at least they hope it is, but the only way out of it is through it, to go into the dark tunnel and out the other side.

"So, right," Bogdan says. "We're workin' it. No leads right now, but that doesn't mean something won't pop up."

"Things change all the time, and really quick too," Leverton says. "Don't be too worried. It'll crack sooner or later. You learn that when things look their worst they could break in a moment, or when things look great it's a false hope, so you don't put your faith in nothin'."

"Of course," Bogdan says, "we want you to be realistic. There are always obstacles. State cutbacks, you know. 'Defund the police.' We're struggling to keep up. We're goddamn *librarians* now."

"How so?" Jack says, still looking at Melissa. She smiles weakly back at him.

Bogdan indicates the rest of the station, as if things were self-evident. "Take a look. We're swamped."

"*Deluged,*" Leverton echoes.

Both Jack and Melissa look, but at first glance the place doesn't seem very swamped. Disordered, yes, cramped, sure, grubby, definitely. But swamped? Across the room, through a half-open door, a movement catches Melissa's attention—a man. He's sitting on the corner of his own desk, much like Bogdan, eating a sandwich and staring right at her. Balding, a subdued mustache, a fat, brick-red tie and 1970s black electrical engineer glasses. When she glances at him she expects him to look away, as anyone with an ounce of modesty would, but he doesn't—he keeps munching his food and watching her. Or looking through her. She'd thought she was invisible, beneath notice, but apparently she was wrong.

"No, we're short on men," Bogdan is saying. "We just got hit with 191."

"*191,*" Leverton emphasizes, *pow,* fist into palm.

Jack frowns. "191?"

"Prop 191. We are now required to check any suspected illegal immigrant for documentation."

"*Obligato,*" Bogdan says.

"Any and every traffic stop takes twice as long, possibly three times. Other scenarios apply."

"*Any* stop," Bogdan repeats. "Every stop."

Leverton sniffs. The stubble on his face comes right up to the very edge of his mouth. Melissa pictures him at a steamy bathroom mirror, leaning across the sink, razor in hand, making precise, tiny, delicate trims. She likes him, she thinks he's honestly trying to do a good job. The other one, maybe not so much. "And if our guys are out there working immigration," he says, "that means less aggravated, less dope, less homicide."

"Comes from above," Bogdan says.

Behind them, in the other room, the man is still eating, still staring at Melissa. She's puzzled by his rudeness, his lack of politesse, but right now with everything—the cops and the cramped room and the soft tidal roar of her thoughts—she has other things to worry about. "Not even homicide?" Jack is asking when she tunes back in. "Shouldn't this be a federal crime or something? Shouldn't you call other cops in? State or FBI or somebody?"

"Sorry to say," Leverton says, "but I want to be straight with you folks. This isn't an elected official. Not a bank robbery. No rape or child molestation. No drugs that we know of, no killin' for hire that we know of. No bombs or unusual nothing. This is a garden variety B and E gone wrong. One step above domestic."

"B and E?" In the fluorescents, Jack's face is almost alarmingly white.

"Breaking and entering." Bogdan looks up, gives Melissa a wink. "No disrespect, of course. Everybody's important. But that means it's just us two, and we're trying to get these guys, I promise you. And we're gonna find 'em. But the reality is we're overtaxed."

Leverton says, "Your case is one of the highest priorities right now—"

"Top of the stack—"

"—and our phones are always open. It's just gonna take a bit more time than we'd like."

Jack sits back, looking deflated. He glances over at Melissa, checking in with her, but she's staring at her lap, sorry that she came, it was a wasted trip and a wasted morning, a wasted week and the shittiest month of her life, Joshua James maybe even included. Her life feels inverted now, submerged and upside down, and in her mind's eye the man is still watching her, still eating and still at his desk and still with his terrible tie and his mustache and his glasses.

"We'll make progress," Leverton assures them. The two detectives glance dryly at each other. "But look. We're trying. But there are no miracles in this business. I used to think so, but not anymore."

2

For the next three days they cuddle at her place on the lumpy couch and watch the little TV. In the afternoons it's cartoons and soap operas and game shows, in the evenings it's *Survivor* and *The Bachelor* and *CSI*. It's a long weekend, some holiday or other that neither Melissa nor Jack has any real personal attachment to, but it gives them an excuse to be off from work and out of the classroom. Occasionally Jack spoons out chunks from the remaining casseroles, almost unrecognizable now with their Saltine crusts turned to pale goo and their textures uncongealed and recongealed from the refrigerator to the microwave and back to the fridge. But Melissa's still strangely silent, still emerging slowly from her private subterranean lair of grief, still squinting and blinking in the sunshine of real life. Jack makes dumb jokes, but they don't really cheer her up.

Much time is spent in her bedroom alone, thinking maybe writing poetry will cheer her up. Her poems are admittedly terrible, flatfooted sonnets and DOA haikus, little self-conscious confessional kinda things that seem oddly bland, that go nowhere or explain too much, that give away the game, so she never lets anyone see them, not even Jack. But there's no other way she knows to ease the tension bubbling inside of her, drugs don't work—the only times she'd been stoned led to nights of epic stupidity and worse paranoia—and alcohol makes her cry. So in times like this, it's the poetry.

Her poems don't rhyme, they never rhymed, not even before she learned it was okay. They're mostly trite little untitled verses scribbled on pieces of paper that she tries to keep track of but ends up forgetting here and there. Most of them get tossed away.

We keep ourselves
in the backseat,
all buckled in, never
saying or doing anything
worth doing or saying.
As if our world held
so few options,
so few ways to be,
and not the broad
endless infinite reach
of the cosmos.

Or

Pain is a blessing,
misery a godsend
meant to wake us up
to the world
and its torment
and its beauty.
So many ways
we could communicate,
tears, screams, sighs, whispers,
but yet we use the terms
which are the worst
translators of all.
So I'll take my pain,
my joys, my sorrows,
and I'll let them stand
for every uttered word.

Or

The wind yanks at my hair.
The world does too.
And I am reminded
that the slippery slobbery
thing we call life
is really just a
little boy sitting behind
me in fourth grade.

It's better than rage or despair or oblivion. Or the corrosive sense of helplessness that came upon her when her brother stormed into one of his domestic fits, tearing up the house, throwing glasses, putting holes in the walls, sometimes even head-butting his mother and slapping his sister and making the world outside of him mirror the turmoil he felt on the inside. Even then Melissa didn't really blame him. She was doing something similar with her poetry, it was more gentle in kind, less blood and fewer bruises, but it was the same essential search for inner and outer balance.

Melissa's pretty sure they both got it from their father, he was odd too. A big man, Noah, Sr. his name was, his face scratchy with stubble, short hair slicked back, round-headed and pot-bellied but still handsome. Ex-Army, though he didn't talk about it much. A career in middle management—hotels, marketing, sales, life-coaching—but for some reason he always seemed to be on the verge of getting laid off or let go or quitting anyway, no one ever got the full story. Only when young Noah started to have issues did Melissa realize Big Noah, as everyone called him, was practically the same—short-tempered, easy to overwhelm, lashing out at those around him when things got even the least bit complicated. And only when Noah the younger was diagnosed in the Army did Big Noah get fitted retroactively with the very same labels.

Which was odd actually, because when Melissa was younger, she and Big Noah had formed a bond, a kind of genuine friendship that she later learned was rare between fathers and daughters. He could be a really nice guy. He arranged birthday parties when Sandra couldn't, took her and her brother to slalom car races, he wore a silly dress and a tiara once to take her trick or treating. The year she turned twelve, he took her to several concerts in a summer—Cyndi Lauper, the New Kids on the Block, and some other loud kiddie band she immediately forgot the name of. Unlike the other dads, who paced in the lobby or sat outside the coliseum in their cars, smoking or reading newspapers by the metal halide glow in the parking lot, her dad was with her in the crowd, bouncing and sweating and seeming to enjoy the music almost as much as the kids. On the way home Melissa watched him, the glare of the passing suburbs pulsing across his face like the rhythmic throb of the lights at the show, with something like wonder or pride.

Big Noah was good with Little Noah too, maybe not quite as tender, but there was a visible warmth between them. They would hug and squeeze and tickle on the carpet in front of the TV. But Big Noah also seemed to think that to understand his burgeoning manhood, the boy needed to be pushed and prodded and tackled and punched, learning to take it was part of being a dude. Melissa remembers times when they'd both go outside and playfully spar in the yard, but somehow little Noah would always come in upset, red-faced and humiliated, and—fighting back tears—head straight to his room.

The signs that all was not right in her father's head made themselves apparent mostly in hindsight. If at one time he was disciplined and bedsheet-tight, now there were bouts of drinking and cursing at the TV—the boxing matches, the football games, the news and awards shows. In her memory Melissa can see him sitting on the edge of his seat or Indian-style on the carpet, staring at the little box and yelling at the players as if they'd insulted him personally.

The family all went to church, not regularly but regularly enough, and sometimes Big Noah would entertain members of his men's worship group in the house, she remembers their looks of surprise when he would burst into a profane tirade at having missed the end of a basketball game or a thrilling horse race on the TV. Soon the men stopped coming over and they gave up on asking him to take on more responsibility in the group, and the family drifted away from the church altogether.

Then came the war—Desert Shield, then Desert Storm, and Big Noah's enlistment was reactivated. He came home one day with a buzzcut, which Melissa thought made his jaw and chin look weirdly large, bulbing out of the bottom of his face like a goiter, and then he was gone, to Iraq or Kuwait or one of those far khaki places she couldn't find on a map. She was twelve years old when he left, and he was gone for the better part of two years.

When he came back, everything had changed. Sandra was stressed from her work, Melissa was tangled up in books and records and her phone calls to friends, and his son, his beautiful boy Noah, had grown quiet and darkly introspective. It was as though a spell of doom had been cast over the house. But Big Noah was different now too, for whatever reason he was more remote, more brooding, and with a sense of latent violence wherever he went. Melissa eavesdropped on late-night, half-heard conversations between he and Sandra down the hall from her bedroom—first there would be tentative words and Sandra's soft assurances, then more drinks and soon he'd be crying, and then the clink of the glasses and the pouring of more drinks and the click of cigarette lighters, and the conversation would dwindle to an awkward, teary end.

And he would get suddenly prickly about little things—the muffled crunching whenever someone ate a bit of ice from a fountain drink, the messy tumble of shoes under the coat-tree, the scattered fuzz of dog hair on the couch. The paying work Sandra asked him about never seemed to materialize, and he would leave for long drives and come home silent and upset, once he came home bloody from fighting.

That was when he started to hit young Noah, harder and harder each time—a *whap!* across the chin, a black eye, a bruised cheek the color of a coming storm. The teenager took to hiding a steak knife under his pillow. Big Noah seemed on the verge of striking the girls too, but thankfully things never got that far. One time Melissa spied him through the crack of the bedroom door, crying and rocking silently on the edge of his bed, and he looked up at her with haunted eyes that seemed to belong to a different person. The pallor over the house had claimed them all. But things took care of themselves—one day Big Noah got in his pickup, the silver Toyota that Melissa had helped pick out but wondered whether they could afford, went for a drive, and never came back. She never saw him or heard from him again.

3

During the long weekend, Melissa stays up late to brush her teeth for long periods as she stares at herself in the mirror, *brushy brushy brush.* She doesn't look any different, but she's sure beginning to feel so, as if she's been quietly swapped with a doppelgänger, or a fairy tale changeling. She feels replaced with herself, like the actors who played Darren in that old TV series, *Bewitched,* at first it's the one guy who's more funny than handsome, then suddenly it's the other guy, completely different, more handsome than funny. When looking back over her own recent days and weeks, it's almost as if it happened to someone else, as if she herself has been quietly re-cast.

Her mind keeps returning to *That Night,* of course it does, she had *That Day,* and now she has *That Night,* in the evening of her house it keeps replaying over and over, a syndicated rerun just for her, the whole evening imprinted on her retinas, her mother's face tormented by fear, Noah's howls of confusion and rage, and the man—the one with the stubble and the messy shock of hair and the teeth and the glint in his eye—grinning and fingering the gun's big trigger. For some reason now in her memories the house is distorted, the ceiling too low, the furniture crowded and tight, as if Memory Melissa was large and outsized, Alice after having her special cake in Wonderland. It's a dream house, a place of contorted memory and warped proportion, it reminds her of a painting of Van Gogh's—his bedroom, a crooked chair, a lopsided bed, that table with its carpentry all askew, a boudoir seen through a tab of LSD.

But if the nights are bad, sleep is worse. In a matter of days the circles under her eyes get darker, and even Jack, who's sweet but as unobservant as a blind, hairless mole, remarks on it.

"You doing all right, honey?" he says in the grocery store that evening. The long weekend is coming to a close and the store's harsh overheads, their color closer to mint green than anything else, makes even healthy people look like zombie invaders.

"Why?" she asks, though the answer is already pretty obvious—despite her relatively good looks and her relatively young age, she's in the worst shape of her life.

"Oh, I dunno," he says vaguely, but his expression tells her he does know. Her body's thin and getting thinner, the bones jutting out in her face of need. All she can do is try to seem unconcerned and look away, *Hey, bananas are on sale.*

The next day is Tuesday, first day back at work, and in a weird way she's looking forward to it, maybe it'll offer a bit of respite from the evil ViewMaster in her brain—the horrific images going *clickclickclick* as they rotate past. It's a rainy, ashen, waterlogged morning, and at her nurse's station she goes over the day's schedule and is happily surprised to see that her third patient is that kid Seth Rainey—he's actually kinda cute and playful in that self-appointed bad-boy kinda way. Maybe he can cheer her up.

When it's time, she comes into the exam room to see him there on the table, sitting with his legs swinging underneath him, white t-shirt, old jeans, tousled hair, looking for all the world like a young hot Brando in that one movie you always hear about but never actually watch.

"Seth," she says, and shuts the door. "How we doing?"

Seth makes a casual movement with his shoulders, halfway between a shrug and a stretch. "Ah, you know."

Melissa pauses. All at once something is pushing at her, insistent and sudden, trying to let itself in, but she can't put her finger on it. *Clickclick*—another viewfinder flash of that terrible night, the living room weird and shimmery, the spatial arrangements distorted and all wrong. She hears herself say, "What?"

Seth smiles sweetly. "Good. I said Good."

"Have you been good?" she says. She can feel him considering the odd tone in her voice.

"Yeah," he says. "Kinda."

She can't stop staring at him, or through him. Something elusive is eating at her, chewing her up from the inside. "Any issues we should know about?" her voice says, echoing from down inside her solitary cave. Her breath coming quicker now, her heartbeat beginning to hammer.

Seth doesn't seem to notice, he only smiles, his charm firing back to life. "Other than hoping you and me can get up sometime?" he says. "Not necessarily."

"I mean—I meant dose reduction. You feeling good and stable?"

"Yeah. I get cravings, you know, at night. They can be pretty bad. But it's nothin' new."

Melissa blows out a breath. The room's too small, the air too thick, rain washes the roof above them, creating a low, rolling patter of white noise that sounds like it's coming from inside her brain. Her throat's scratchy, she wishes she'd taken a sip of water at the fountain down the hall, the one all the patients use and thus all the staff avoid, before coming in here. She resists an urge to bolt from the room, she tells herself to *Calm down, calm down, Mel, it's a panic attack, you gotta get this under control.* If she gives in to it, she'll spend the rest of her life hiding from these feelings that assail her like a gang of thugs, better to take them head on now and let them know who's really in charge.

So as Seth watches her, she allows herself to indulge them for a moment, just slightly give in and let them learn for themselves—*Here, you wanna try it? Try it!*—that there's no bogeyman in her foyer, no scary monster under the bed, the monsters have all left the building.

"Seth, you did time in jail, right?" Melissa works to keep her voice even and steady. A cold, uncertain surge comes on, and she consults his chart to hide it. "For what?"

Seth frowns, hesitant. "What?"

"What did you...?"

Now he cricks his neck. "Aw, man."

"Answer the question, please." The need to prove the bogeyman isn't real has become insistent now, a mission, she will follow it all the way, turn on the overheads, clean out the closets, strip the beds. "It's...it's part of your treatment. We have to know."

Seth purses his lips, then whispers: "*Hamburgle.*"

Melissa doesn't know what that means. She only has a vague sense of the word, taken, she thinks, from an old McDonald's commercial. She shakes her head at him, *I don't get it.*

"Smash an' grab, whatever." Frustrated, but a little louder, "Two years in the pen, if that's what you're asking."

Now Melissa can only stare, seasick with emotion and upsetting memory, her body knows something her brain hasn't caught onto yet. She says, not quite a whisper, "Did you really do it? The thing that put you in there?"

Seth leans away and breaks their confidential space. Confession time over. "Jeez," he protests, adjusting himself on the table. "Sweet Melissa," he appeals to her, restlessly, with his best awkward little boy smile.

Melissa backs off. He's right, there's nothing to be gained by following this particular line of thinking, and it's making both of them feel like shit. She tries to get her focus. "All right. Sleeve, please."

"What's going on?"

"Labs," she says, trying not to look at him.

But when he folds up his sleeve, it is as if someone has kicked her in the gut. Her chest hitches and her throat closes, and suddenly she can't take a breath. On his right forearm is a blurry green tattoo, King Kong, one fist in the air, roaring from atop the Empire State Building.

A rush of blood to her face. The room closes in. *The more you have the more you want* rings in her head like some mindless daytime TV jingle, *the more you have the more you want the more—*

"I'll be right back," Melissa wheezes, and slips out the door.

4

Luckily, the vomit makes it into the toilet. Thank God no one's in the bathroom and Melissa's alone, because it's a bad one—a neck straining, vein popping, stomach-wrenching puke that seems to never end. Drool stringing from her mouth, a little amoeba of brown sputum in the bowl, she only had half a bagel that morning, Jack had been after her to eat more starch, more carbs, and now she's glad she took his advice.

When she's done, she forces herself to look in the mirror. Paler and skinnier than ever, she inspects herself, her winter-branch wrists, her neck already like a 50-year-old's, as she tries to think of something, anything, to tell herself to make it better. Veins cast shadows on her forehead, her eyes are rimmed in red, she turns on the faucet and splashes water on herself, drinks some even though this is the patients' bathroom and disgusting because of that, and the cool slipping down her throat makes her feel a little better. *I can get through this,* she tells herself, *I'm stronger than this. The more I have the more I want.*

But that tattoo. She'd love to convince herself it isn't the same one, but she knows it is.

Her eyes meet in the mirror. Seth was there. No way around it—everything in her body, every sense that she has and maybe a few more she has yet to understand, are telling her the same thing—Seth was there. Seth was part of it.

Before another discussion with herself can come, a babble of terrible thoughts arise—*hurt him fuck him suck him strangle him*—and she pushes it back down. Seth was in jail for drugs and hamburgling and smash and grab and whatever else it's called these days, and she's only a knobby-kneed chick in her 20s who lost her entire family, who's seeing things in the dark, and who can hardly watch a horror movie, let alone live one. She hasn't felt strong in years. What would Jack say about this? Jack would call the cops.

She should call the cops herself, get hold of Cagney and Lacey or whatever their names were. What would they do? Arrest him? Arrest him for what? Of course Seth would talk his way out of it, Seth would run rings around those assholes, he would lie and charm and be buddies with them. Fingerprints? The cops never mentioned them, not even once, haven't talked about them at all. Who knows even if they were taken?

Or maybe hire somebody, get some bruiser to take him down, some moon-dim parking lot behind a bar somewhere, crowbars and brass knuckles, jump him from behind and make him pay. Would that help her? Not really. He'd be free to do it again or she would get busted, one or the other. And anyway, how does she know? How does she really *know*? She doesn't, it's better, she tells her red-eyed reflection, to have certainty. When she knows for sure, then she can decide what to do. The pounding rain on the roof applauds this line of thinking.

When she's collected herself, she goes to the supply station closet, the cubicle where all the inventory is kept under lock and key. She types her name into the computer keyboard, follows the software protocols, fills in the forms, signs her digital signature, and listens as the door unlocks itself. The irregular boxes and bottles stand in rows like a motley platoon—pills, liquids, syringes, vials, droppers. She takes Seth's dosage, a little dispenser of cherry red Kool-Aid in a paper cup—*Better double-check that, sweetie, haha*—shuts the door, then goes back into the exam room where he waits.

Seth's eyes grow wide when he sees her. "Holy shit," he says. "You okay?"

Melissa knows how terrible she looks, but that's all right. "Ready for dolly?" she says, trying to calm her voice, trying not to meet his eye, not to glance at King Kong, but now the tattoo seems to pulse, to glow neon green, drawing her awareness whether she wants it or not. "You say you wanted to meet?" Her voice hollow, from down in the cave. "Outside work?"

In her peripheral vision she sees Seth smile. That charm again. "Yeah?"

"Yeah." He holds out his arm so she can wrap a rubber hose around it. His veins are big and blue—perfect veins. Dreamy veins.

"What if, um—we're, uh…" She shakes the hair out of her face. "You know, we're starting a new study. A new method, a new…reduction method."

"Hm."

"Like—a new…a new thing."

"Yeah?"

"Yeah." She looks at up Seth, maybe a little too long, a strange glint now in her eye making him uncomfortable. Good.

But then he grins, that charm, it's brutal, man. "What is it?" he says. "Do I get paid?"

"Eh, I dunno about all that." She taps his vein, so it straightens out.

"Well, when is it?"

"When would you like to start?" she asks, and plunges the syringe into his vein with a crack of thunder—*BOOM!*

5

She bolts up in bed. The noise was terrifyingly loud. It wasn't thunder.

Someone's in the house, that's perfectly clear now. The doorway's empty, but the noise came from inside the kitchen. Her brain is weirdly calm, she's in bed and there was a noise just like the other night, a slamming, a booming, a roaring kind of noise, like a jet passing too low which woke her from a dead sleep. Well, not exactly a dead sleep—there were nightmares of tight alleys and backseat arguments full of dreadful unremembered things, the meshwork clutter and junkyard debris of uneasy slumber. But she had been asleep.

Jack's not here. He's at his place, he wants to give her space after practically living here since *That Night*, so quietly she gets out of bed, bolder this time, and tiptoes to the door. Takes a moment to muster her courage, then peeks out.

No one there.

It's not as if someone was there and slipped out the back door. The kitchen's empty, truly empty, it feels abandoned, the last person in it had been her, she herself, making a bedtime cup of Egyptian licorice tea. Who knows what the noise was, but it probably wasn't a night intruder. Probably not.

She creeps into the kitchen darkness. Out the window, the sky is padded with clouds and the moon hides, and the only light in the place is from the streetlamp washing in like muddy water. Melissa stands waiting, a denizen of the night herself now, seeing what might develop. The walls and everything leaning, herself a small, bent frame among a larger arrangement of sheetrock and air and metal and dust and wood. Her breath rises and falls—*inhale, exhale*. Through the kitchen window the backyard is a photograph, a lonesome prison backlot of chainlink fences and withered trees.

The inside isn't any better. Despite all the darkness, the house is visibly filthy. A sink of dishes, clothes in the hamper. Stained, used couch, filthy before they brought it home. The clutter's worse in the murk of night than during the day, depression and grief have paralyzed her, she's not been diligent, and Jack's no help, he's cool but he doesn't clean much or very well. Instead of bringing all the food after a funeral, people should come clean your house. She needs help, she needs Corrie.

Corrie. Her family once had help, they had a maid, they'd never lived in such a clean place as when Corrie was around. Melissa still to this day misses that woman, she hadn't thought of her for years before she saw that maid at Dr. Larry's. One day Corrie was there and the next she was gone, practically a member of the family then let go suddenly to fend for herself in the unfriendly wastelands of Birmingham, Alabama. Corrie was Melissa's friend, a mentor in their hours together, she would tell Melissa of her days as a maid in a Chicago hotel, a dishwasher in the vast industrial kitchens, sometimes even helping to make the hotel's signature secret sauce—a one-to-one mixture of ketchup, mayo, and Worcestershire sauce.

For some unknown reason, Corrie moved from Illinois to Alabama, maybe it was family, and she began working as a domestic. Back then, everyone had a maid, maids were too cheap *not* to have one, and her mom would pick Melissa up from school and navigate her big Chevy down the wooded suburban roads to their home and little Melissa would see the black ladies waiting by the bus stop, all of them stooped and laden with purses and paper bags and waiting to be carried back to the city. Melissa was gone to school most of the days Corrie would clean their house, but in the summers she was home and remembers the old woman would let herself in, put her purse down, and go directly to the utility drawer and pull out the biggest clawhammer the Sweet family owned. Apparently, she'd been attacked years earlier, jumped by someone who'd hidden in a closet or a shower, so she went through the house systematically, room by room, every day, hammer cocked and ready to brain anyone who tried to pull anything. Once, little Noah playfully scared her and she put a hole the size of a quarter in the bathroom door.

Corrie and little Melissa would talk at lunch, she would tell of various exploits in her world of poor black life in the Windy City, the shotgun shacks and the utility-pole lives, a different, more uncertain existence up there near the tracks. She married and divorced and yet worked all the time, and finally fled the big city for the South. When her ex-husband died, there was no one to take the body, so they freighted it on a train down to her in Birmingham.

But one day Corrie wasn't there anymore, and every morning thereafter the house was a little emptier, no Corrie coming by today, no one to tease and laugh with and tell of the wild ruthless politics of Chicago hotel kitchens. The house fell silent, the kitchen which was once Corrie's main station empty and deserted, and Melissa's young world of loneliness returned.

In her own kitchen now, Melissa knows what to do. More by muscle memory than anything else, in the dark she goes to the cutlery drawer and pulls out the big chef's knife Jack brought over for the Christmas cooking a year ago. He forgot about it or left it here on purpose, either way it's huge, practically a foot long, the blade at least two inches wide at the hilt. It's a mighty thing, worthy of Chicago hotel kitchens, sleek and solid, and it catches the light from the street and turns it into a willful shimmer.

She slips back to her bedroom and shuts the door and locks it. Then a moment's pause against the door, listening, just to make sure. Nothing moves. She hides the knife under the mattress and sits up in her bed, and in the dark dresser mirror the shadow of herself stares back. Despite everything, she still can't get that King Kong tattoo out of her head. It glares at her from her memories, refracting like a jewel seen at the bottom of a creek, and she can hear it too—the roaring ape, the din of the city, the little biplanes whizzing around like summer wasps. At times it's almost funny, the planes, the big swatting hands, the bared gorilla teeth, those dark terrified eyes squinting out at her, those eyes won't let her go, they seem to want to communicate with her, tell her something.

It's obvious what it is, she's sure of it. The only question now is what she she's going to do about it.

Her brain circles back to the cops, the cops, the cops, of course. Cagney and Lacey. Modern society's perpetual first and last line of defense—just call the cops. Some cops might know what to do with this guy—they're heroes. But these guys? Flatfooted in their Wallabees, taking down her side of the story in their pathetic little notebooks, and then the reactions her story will cause in them—the wry, raised eyebrows, their disparaging silences and their pitying airs, she doesn't trust those two nor does she think they're up to the job. By their own admission they're already bungling *That Night*, and if they're in charge of it, nothing will get done, at best it'll be a tainted investigation, a corrupted accretion of unrelated facts, a split jury, a slightly older and thicker Seth slumped in a courtroom with his new haircut and that shit-eating simper on his face, and no doubt his adorable daughter on the bench behind him and lounging on her father every chance she gets. And they'll never be able to connect Seth to her mother's house. Not like Melissa can, because she was there.

6

The restaurant is *Taqueria Nido*, a cantina on the scattered side of town, the dark and dingy kind of place where you can drink all day and not be pestered. And it's private—the booths sport high wooden beams and fake thatch roofs which give a sense of seclusion and definitely cut down on overheard chatter, making it perfect for intimate, even possibly illegal, conversations. Melissa finds a seat in the back, away from the windows, preferring to look at the aisle leading back to a gloomy dead end, not even a kitchen door or a bathroom, just a peeling chiaroscuro on the wall of fierce mustached *banditos*, their bandoliers slashing black *X*s across their chests. The waitress brings a bowl of watery salsa and a basket of chips—Melissa smelled the rancid oil from the kitchen the moment she walked in—and a glass of water. When she pauses to take Melissa's order, Melissa asks the woman to wait until her boyfriend has come. Please, if she doesn't mind.

Her boyfriend. How fucking depressing.

Across the aisle and a little way back, a young couple sit in a booth shoulder to shoulder. Apple-cheeked and innocent, it's maybe their second date or maybe the third, they're facing the bright, front windows and whisper and giggle confidentially—most likely about her, Melissa decides—and when they both catch her staring at them, they stop laughing. In the last booth behind them, a businessman sits alone, messy fork poised, reading from a worn paperback. Lurid shapes on the cover—a sexy *femme* in an owl mask, a car, a blood-red title that shouts *Pure Homicide!* Below that the blurb says, *My arms! My arms! Where are my arms?*

Then a shadow falls and Seth is coming around, sauntering in that loose-hipped way he has. He sits heavily across from her—the displaced air whooshes past—and he runs his hands through his messy curls.

"*Sweet Melissa,*" he croons tunelessly. "Jeezus sleaze-us, I'm tired." He's wearing a plaid work shirt with the breast pocket half-ripped away.

Despite the jump in her heart rate at his presence—*Dogface, this is Dogface,* her brain keeps repeating—Melissa gives him a cool, professional nod. "What's wrong?" she says. "More smash and grab?"

"What?" Seth looks at her with a kind of innocent, little-boy alarm—something hurt, something sensitive has come into his face. The waitress appears, and Seth blinks up at her. "A beer, please?" he says. "Something dark?" He turns back to Melissa. "I'm allowed to drink, right? Won't mess it up?"

"What do you mean?"

"Your test. Drinking a beer won't mess your test up?"

"Oh. No, yeah. You can have whatever you want."

He grins at the young waitress. "Dos Equis. And a shot, please—tequila. And bring her a beer too."

When the waitress leaves, he smiles at Melissa with his practiced look of harmlessness. He really is a Valentino-type—no doubt there are girls all over town who've had their hearts broken, and maybe their bellies pollinated, by this sweet, fuzzy-chinned little bee. "Crazy," he says. "Here I am having a drink with Melissa Sweet."

"The famous Melissa Sweet."

"You're famous?"

"Maybe one day." At Seth's puzzled look, Melissa only grins, backtracking, sorry she said it in the first place, she needs to be careful here, not utter a word out of place, say the wrong thing and the whole edifice crumbles apart right in her fingers.

"What's it called?" Seth asks.

"What's what called?"

"The treatment. The new medicine. Whatever it is."

She shrugs one shoulder, perhaps in imitation of Seth himself, trying to downplay it all, on the phone she'd told him that the new study is definitely up and running and he should definitely want to be a part of it, but it's unconventional, she insisted, something that isn't quite public yet. "They're still working on that," she says. "Some really long, unpronounceable name."

"Heh." Seth reaches across the table and takes a sip of her untouched water. "Well, I'll be a guinea pig, no prob, won't be the first time. But I ain't gonna regret this, am I?"

Melissa gives him her best fake chuckle. "No, I promise you won't regret anything at all." She laughs for maybe a fraction of a moment too long, she's worryingly new at this. "Not a goddamn thing."

The waitress comes back with two beers and a shot of tequila. She tries to take their orders again, but Melissa tells her she thinks they're just gonna drink, and anyway, there are the chips and salsa. She munches one encouragingly. When the waitress leaves, Seth raises the shot glass in a toast, the liquor a glint of pure gold in the overhead lamp.

"*Sweet Melissa,*" he croons again. "How's that song go? That's all I got. I hear it in the car, but I never really listen to it."

As he downs the shot, Melissa takes out a little pocket recorder she bought on the way over. "To clear you for the study," she says, trying to bring the conversation back around to where she wants it, "I'm supposed to do an interview, an informal interview." She holds up the recorder so he can see it.

Seth smacks his lips and drums his fingers on the table. "Wow, okay. Let's chat!" Such a little boy. Melissa wonders what kind of dad he is, no doubt his little girl adores him, no doubt they roll cutely around on the carpet together.

She hits the red button on the recorder and checks to see the little timecode is counting, then sets it down on the table, on its long edge, teeter-tottering next to the chips. "Okay. So, I need you to be very honest with me. Very…uh, frank. The more you have, the more I want."

"Yes. Okay. Got it."

But something's been tugging at the peripheries of Melissa's attention, and all at once she knows what it is—in the very back of the restaurant, beyond the young couple, the reading man has put down his paperback and is staring openly at her, in fact, he has been for the last three or four minutes. He's balding, with a horseshoe rim of dark hair and a hideous tie that looks several decades out of fashion. He reminds Melissa of the computer engineers in the hospital her mother used to work at—impossibly square and vaguely sinister, men with bad haircuts and worse fashion, malevolent middle-aged dweebs who leered a little too long at the coltish daughter with the thin, nyloned legs. But when Melissa glances over at him now, he doesn't look away, he takes a long pull of his beer, some brown bottle with a label she can't read, but his eyes remain with her the whole time. In the restaurant's dim light, his gaze is dark and almost predatory.

"Um, okay." Melissa turns back to Seth and tries to clear her mind. *Dogface, dogface.* "So. What would you say is your occupation?"

Seth giggles. "Junkie!"

"No. I mean. How did you make your living? Before…this."

He reaches over and dips a chip into the salsa and munches it. "Why do they always make these in triangles? You can't eat a fuckin' triangle. If I owned a restaurant like this the chips would all be ovals. Like, oblong. Mouth-shaped. Perfect salsa delivery devices."

"Seth, please. What kind of work do you do?"

"Oh, jeez, odd jobs? Oil change. Construction. Cable install. You want all of 'em?"

"No. But any, um…" Her heartbeat picks up again, just a little—*Easy, girl, easy.* "Any illegal activities?"

Seth leans back and crunches his food. The vibe seems to shift a bit. His big bravado act is maybe thinner than she thought. "Mmm…well."

"Be frank."

"Shit." A long pause. He leans up and puts the recorder on its fat side, so it won't wobble. "Illegal stuff? Really?"

"Yeah." In her shoes her toes are curling until they start to ache, but her face remains pleasant and open. "It's for the trial medication. Part of their, you know, research."

Seth blows out a breath. He seems unsure, runs another hand through his hair. "Um, damn. Okay. All right. It's cool, it's cool, I'll talk about it. Uh…" He grins now, clearly uncomfortable. "Carjacking. *Mmm.* Smash and grab, like I said. Purse snatching. Petty theft. Stole my neighbor's cable last month."

"Would you say you're completely done with that?"

"The cable?"

"No, the other stuff."

Seth bobs up and down, maybe parsing out still what he's willing to share with her, sorting the mental piles into *Yes* and *No.* "Oh yeah. Treatment. Treatment helps a lot. And my little girl. She's giving me hope."

Hope. Melissa has to keep herself from laughing, what does that word even mean anymore, it's one of those hollow worthless words like *faith* and *trust* and *belief* that time and enough living make irrelevant. "So, you're all done with that?"

"Yes." Seth reaches, another chip, another tentative bite. "Hunnert percent."

"Haven't done it recently, not at all?" Seth nods, *yes,* then shakes his head, *no.* Melissa tries to display to him her disappointment, not too much, she takes a noisy discontented breath through her nostrils and looks concerned. "Well…that's too bad," she says. She reaches over and stops the recorder and looks dejectedly up to the ceiling. Lets out a great sigh, maybe this pretend stuff's not so hard after all.

Seth seems to notice. "Wait. What?"

"This, uh, this study seems to be biased toward…active, uh, offenders."

"What do you mean?"

Melissa shrugs and makes a show of putting the recorder away, back in her purse. *Oh well, we tried,* she wills her actions to say. She takes a sip of beer, her first. It's cold and good. The balding man is still back there, still munching, still staring.

"What's the problem? I mean, I still do things," Seth protests. "Here and there. You know."

Melissa digs in her purse, making sure not to look up at Seth, she's still in obvious closing it down mode, *too bad, so sad, moving on now.* "Do things?"

Seth's reluctant, but he seems desperately to want in on the study. Or wants in on *her,* at any rate. "Okay, okay," he says with a wave. "No. Sometimes people get me and a bunch of guys together…and…"

Her face stony and distant, distracted, fake-digging in her purse, fumbling and bumbling with all of her crap in there. "You and a bunch of…who? Guys?"

"And we…um. Sometimes. Sometimes we go get something they're after." Seth takes a gulp of beer. Melissa feels kinda icky for manipulating him, he's a sweet kid…if you don't count *That Night,* that is. Or any number of other probable *Nights.*

"Okay, now look," Melissa says, bringing the little recorder back out again. "This is in complete confidence." Her voice wavers, a bit stressed from the ill-suited actuality of what she's doing here and the larger uncertainty of her own goals, but she manages to keep it under control. "I need it for the study. It's part of the…the whole thing. They need a certain type of person. Now. Again. You and a bunch of…who?"

"Why? That's so weird."

"These studies are, you know, *specific*. Very specific. Now, you were saying?"

"Me and who?"

"Activities. We have to know your...uh, activities." She gives him her best *I'm being patient here* face. "And people. It's part of the study, Seth. You don't have to if you don't want to, but it's...you know, it's part of the study."

Seth stares at her, reading her agitation, clearly worried now and maybe a little suspicious too, but Melissa knows she can work around that. "Okay," he says, "um. Usually there's a few folks involved. Nobody wants to go into a place alone."

Melissa curls her toes again. "Why not?"

"I mean. Could be a dude with a fuckin' Walther PPK semi-automatic in there, you know what I'm saying?"

"Ah." Her throat's dry, she swigs her beer, but part of her wants to shriek, to scream and launch herself across the table at Seth and claw out his eyes. But she doesn't, she's surprised to find a certain knack for this subterfuge, she's a decent actor, must've been those theater classes in high school, *Got yourself a new talent, girl.* "So, you have help," she says coolly. Like a lab professor. "Friends."

"Well. I *am* the help."

"What does that mean?"

Seth shifts in his seat. "Do we really gotta...?"

"I can't sign you with the study, Seth, unless you're completely transparent here. I've...sworn the Hippocratic Oath, you know."

"The hypo...critical what?"

"*Don't hurt anybody,*" she paraphrases. "You've heard it before. It's on the wall of every doctor you've ever visited. So, who hires you?"

Seth only takes a swig of beer and looks unhappily at the salsa bowl. He tilts it and a bit of watery red sauce spills out onto the tablecloth, and he pushes it around with the uneaten edge of a chip. "I—I'm not gonna tell you that."

"Who is it?" she says again, a little harsher this time. *I don't need you, Seth,* she's hoping to say with her tone, *but you need me. And trust me—the more you have, the more you'll definitely want.*

"I mean, look. It's nothing too bad. Just housebreakin'. Once in a while."

"Housebreaking? Is that what's it called?" Surely it was called *That Night*, by everyone whose house they broke in on. "Who are the other guys, Seth?"

Seth shifts in his seat. Reluctance oozes from his pores, this is breaking the code, she understands, the informal agreement between crooks, for whatever that's worth, you can't do that. "Come on, Sweet Melissa."

"I'm not asking you to turn anybody *in*, for God's sake. I'm not an officer of the law. This is confidential. This is for the study. *Science*, remember, empirical evidence and all that. This is where you get to help out and give back."

Seth only waggles his jaw from side to side, looking curdled, caught between pleasing her and disappointing them, whoever *they* are. But he's just a kid, a fresh-faced kid, low man on the totem pole, and giving away names is the thing you never do. "Who knows," she says vaguely, "your daughter may even be helped by this study. What's her name?"

"My girl? Uh, Sam."

"Who knows, you know? It may actually help out Sam one day. Tell me about her."

"Sam. She's small for her age. My ex would put Pepsi or Mountain Dew in her baby bottle and all that shit. It's why she's with me most of the time now."

"I bet she looks just like you." Sips from her beer, back to trying to look official. "I bet she's gorgeous."

"But look—I can't see how me talkin' about my buddies helps you with your thingy. I just—" He shakes his head.

Up the aisle, beyond the couple who are now eating quietly, the chewing man is gone. The booth empty, the table clean. She didn't notice him leaving. The bandoliered bandits stare back from the shadows, refusing to comment one way or another.

She takes another swig of beer. It's a little warmer now but still good. She swallows another, longer drink, alcohol was never her favorite thing and, lo and behold, she may now be feeling the very beginnings of a buzz, but maybe not, maybe it's the adrenaline she's trying to hide. "You know what?" she says, setting down the bottle with a hard thump. "You're right. Enough of this. Let's go. Let's fuckin' go to your place."

7

Seth's trailer is down a rutted frontage road near the interstate, in a corner of town she never knew existed, in her three years in this little cracker-town she's never once been back this way. The *whoosh* and *hiss* of the highway is loud as her car bounces along, bottoming out here and there as they curve through the trees, the lights of the highway nearby like disembodied fireflies behind the pines and the power lines.

"You live here?" she says when they pull up and get out, and immediately regrets it, of course he does, it's a single trailer in a clearing cut from the pines—cinderblock supports, rusted skirts, the occasional sinister dark hole underneath where an animal might go to die or a diseased, veiny arm might reach out and snatch at your ankle.

Seth turns to consider his home. "You don't like it?" he says, his hurt voice like a little boy's.

Melissa chides herself, *Gotta be smarter than that, girl.* "No. It's perfect. Just perfect."

Seth looks at her strangely, clouds crossing his face. "For what?"

"For you, Seth. It's perfect for you."

Inside, it's exactly what the exterior promises—paneled walls, ripped carpet, fast food bags, a fecund and fertile garbage can like its own little wildlife habitat. The tiny TV no bigger than Melissa's own, opposite a flabby couch under *Charlie's Angels* and St. Pauli's Girl posters.

"You want a beer?" he says. There's a clatter that makes her jump, and she sees Seth's wallet and keys have made their way to the kitchen counter.

Her hands aren't sure where to go, she's telling herself to relax, to not freeze up. "Uh. Yes."

Seth goes to the fridge and opens it, there's a glimpse of egg cartons, old condiments, onions growing tentacles, and a sad quarter-wedge of lettuce turning brown in the back. In Melissa's buzzing nerves a vision comes—a flash of when she was a teen, 12 or 13 years old maybe, and her next-door neighbor, a middle-aged housewife named Bonnie Poulson, hired her to go and help clean an apartment her college-age daughter had abandoned. *Fuckin' kids fuckin' morons* is what Mrs. Poulson said again and again in the car on the way over, flicking her cigarette out the crack in the window. Melissa was never certain on how long it had been since her daughter left, but it had evidently been a good amount of time, because though the apartment was dark and completely empty, like some malodorous cave you could sense something was drastically wrong, and the refrigerator itself turned out to be a charnel house of horrors.

The apartment's power had been cut off for maybe a month or more, and when the daughter—Daisy was her name, Melissa remembers now—when Daisy left, the various food items in the dark fridge in the hot and humid summer grew and mutated. When she opened the door to the fridge, the smell was like nothing she'd ever encountered—sweet and musty, rancid and rotten, with a sharp, sour umami that somehow rose up behind the other smells and capped them all off. The horrible things that grew in there—fibrous, slimy, veiny, curling up and around inside the trapped cell of the fridge—reminded her of that movie about the men fighting that crazy alien creature down in the south pole or wherever, it was difficult to look at, let alone swab out with gloves and a sponge and a wet dishrag. Mrs. Paulson stood back and smoked and supervised as young

Melissa crouched on the floor, retching and sweeping the various moldy horrors into a—

"*Hello*, Sweet Melissa," Seth's voice says now from the kitchen, and she realizes she's been staring at a photo on the counter, a picture of a young girl, four or so years old, impossibly darling, her brown hair stringing in her eyes and laughing while a goat nibbles at her belt buckle. A pet farm, it looks like. Seth comes around the counter and passes her a cold can of beer, already opened, and for a moment they stand stiff and silent together in the center of the dim room.

He gestures to the old couch, and with her purse still in her lap, Melissa sits uneasily on the edge. Her nerves are jangling now, her behavior erratic, jumpy, she's afraid to let her things get too far out of her grasp but she knows there's not much she can do about it anyway. And the incessant ambient hiss of the highway outside, the refrigerator kicks on and fills the room with an electric hum, and Seth grinning at her. Melissa tries to loosen up. She has to admit that, even in this half-light—maybe especially in this half-light—he's pretty hot. A curl of hair has fallen over his ear and he desperately needs a haircut, but it's charming in a summer-romance-with-the-greaser-lifeguard kind of way.

"*So,*" he says, mock-pretentiously.

"So?"

"We...gonna get started?"

"Oh. Yes." Melissa moves her purse to the coffee table and digs inside it. First, she takes out her rubber gloves and snaps them on. Then she removes the vial of clear liquid—*Careful with this stuff, girlie-girl*—and the syringe. Seth watches wide-eyed as she unwraps it, tosses the wrapper aside, upends it, and meticulously fills the needle to the four-milliliter mark.

"*Cotdamn,*" he says. He takes a nervous swallow from his beer. "That's a lot."

"Oh, it's nothing," she says. "Weak. That's why it's still experimental."

"What is it?"

"Ah, you know. An analgesic. A, uh, hydromorphone derivative. Meperidine, kinda. But non-addictive. It's new."

Seth sits back with the beer between his knees with that rakish half-smile on his face, full of darkness and light and terrible things all at once. "What the hell you doin' here, Melissa? This ain't about the study, is it?"

"You kidding me, it's all about the study." Okay, she's a terrible liar, her tone doesn't even convince herself, she'll be glad when this little moment of dire adventure is over, she'll never lie again. She thumps the barrel of the syringe and the little bubbles all rise to the top.

"I ain't filled out no forms," Seth says, thumbing off the label of his bottle.

"And I ain't done nothin' official. I was part of some kinda study once before, and the paperwork was nuts. Took me an hour or so, and that's with the lady helping me out and telling me everywhere to sign. Got a hundred fifty bucks for it though. But with you—nothin'."

"Right. Yes. I was thinking we'd do the paperwork later."

"There any money in it?"

"Uh, yeah, but not for this one." Melissa shoots a tiny bit of clear liquid out of the needle, and it arcs out over the coffee table and into the matted carpet. "But I think you'll be happy all the same."

There's movement beside her, when she turns she's surprised to find Seth's face close to her own. Before she can react, he tilts in to kiss her—and to her surprise she takes it. She hasn't kissed anyone but Jack in years, Seth's lips are soft, softer than Jack's, but rimmed with a stubble both prickly and somehow sensual. Seth kisses differently too, and shockingly, she finds that she likes it.

They break and lean back. The stillness of the air in the trailer is almost loud, the wheeze of the highway outside is like another person in the room. She wonders if it drives Seth crazy or if it helps him sleep. Maybe both.

"I ain't never kissed no nurse before." He wipes his mouth with the back of his hand.

"I ain't never kissed no junkie before."

Seth pulls away, looking hurt, the sad-eyed little boy in him always right on the surface. "Aw, come on. I'm a good guy. A good dad."

Melissa, sorry but not wanting to apologize, glances over at the little girl in the photo. "Are you? Really?" she asks, more from real curiosity than disbelief. The girl's long face, a slippery nose that may turn knockout beautiful or not, hard to say now, but they do look alike, father and daughter.

"You bet I am. Child support—dadimony's what I call it—every month and on time too."

"But you said she lived with you."

"Well. Sometimes she does."

"And you said you get the money through questionable means." Melissa feels a grim smile form on her lips.

Seth makes a noise, like a cough or a grunt, and stands quickly and goes to the counter and turns on a little boom box. Did she hurt his feelings again? Strangely, the idea sits pretty well with her, she's been hurt too, and pretty badly. Her brain starts to list all the things Seth has confessed to—petty burglaries, carjackings, let alone the goddamn murderous home-fucking-invasions—but stops herself there. If she goes any further, she'll start shaking and maybe break down and fall apart.

A heavy, screechy song starts playing, low in the room, a slowed-down version of "Love Hurts," not drowning out the highway but accompanying it. Maybe they're in the same key. It's a song Melissa used to like, the original Everly Brothers is better, and also the countrified Gram Parsons remake, but this hard rock version is just stupid and macho and dumb and unoriginal.

"I got a little sidetracked," Seth is saying. It sounds like an apology. Melissa's forgotten what they're talking about. He starts swaying around the room in a faux tango. "Let's dance," he says dreamily. When Melissa only stares at him, he says, "But wait. First you do me, then we'll dance."

He falls into the seat next to her and grabs the rubber tourniquet half-hanging out of her purse, and knots it expertly around his arm. He's done this many times before. But a sense of dread starts to rise around Melissa now, frightening and cold, a flood of it, like enough water to close above your head and drown off your air. Seth doesn't notice and takes her hand and puts it across his inner elbow. The vein there is blue and beautiful, just like before—a phlebotomist's dream, perfect access to someone's inner tubes, Seth's private, personal interstate thoroughfares. With her small hand covered by his own, dirt under his fingernails, scars on his knuckles, he leans in again and kisses her, for a long time. He tastes of beer and peppermint and something else, something smoky and sweet.

"You never told me who you work with," she says when they're done and lean apart again. "Or work for. I can't do it until you tell me."

"*Who I work for*?" Seth pulls away, irritated now. "Goddamn. Why do you wanna get in on that? You know I ain't gonna tell you that."

But she won't let up. "Who do you go off and—and do shit with? I gotta have it, Seth. We can't proceed without it."

He takes a long drink of beer and lets out a quiet belch. An odd, impenetrable air has sealed itself around him now, defensive and almost frightened, and he seems to be weighing several factors, multiple competing cruelties in his life of crime. She waits on a knife's edge, this is it, she knows, either he will or he won't.

"Do shit," he says after a time, "or go into peoples' homes?"

"I guess…go into peoples' homes."

"If I give you one name," he says, "will you kiss me again?"

Feeling the dread, but strangely dulled now, Melissa nods.

"Okay. Okay. See, once in a while I run around with these boys from Newbury. We get hired to go into people's houses. Get shit. Break shit. You know. Rough people up, toss 'em around."

The smell in the trailer—feet, sweat, bacon, rotting trash—turns Melissa's stomach. She sees Mrs. Poulson's daughter's fridge again, the slimy molds crawling and writhing inside it, tentacled horrors searching blindly in the hot dark for prey. "Boys? Which boys?"

Unexpectedly, Seth cracks up. "Jeez, fuck, you are one muthafuckin' tough-ass cookie, Sweet Melissa, you know that? One name, right?" When she nods again, he says, "Bleiler. Teddy Bleiler. I call him my tater from another mater. He introduced me to the boys."

"Boys," she says vaguely. "What boys?"

"You said one name. I gave you one name. Teddy Bleiler." He leans in and kisses her again, and she takes it again.

"How do you spell Bleiler?" she says when they pull apart.

"Aw, fuck this. Shut up and do me."

Melissa surrenders. She uncaps the syringe, finds the big blue vein again, like a snake in the crook of his elbow, and after a moment's hesitation, plunges it into his arm. She takes a deep breath, closes her eyes, and pushes the liquid into his veins.

I'm sorry I'm sorry I'm sorry, the highway seems to whisper from outside. *No you're not no you're not no you're not*, comes the distant reply. The sibilant hiss of the cars and trucks lays under the music like a synth, and the screechy-voiced lead singer serenades them about how love is like a flame, and Melissa realizes with a distant detached curiosity he's right, it *is* like a flame, it really does burn you when it's hot.

"Let's dance," Seth says, watching her remove the needle and cap it. She drops it in her purse. He reaches over and tugs at the edges of her rubber gloves, but she pulls away.

"Nope, I wanna keep these," she says. "You might want to sit with me, Seth."

"Aw, come on, Sweet Melissa. I'm gettin' a house call from my favorite new nurse, who just happens to be sitting on my lucky couch!"

Seth stands, and pulls her up too. He leads her in a slow, clumsy dance—the "Love Hurts" song is over now, and some other song has come on, some slow song with a slide guitar that wants to be sexy but just ends up only being a teen boy's idea of it, they sway there in the trailer for a time, arm in arm, chest to chest. It's almost sweet.

After a moment, Seth throws his head back and laughs. "Oh shit!" he says.

"You okay?"

But now Seth's legs are giving out under him, and he sits hard down on the floor. "*Oh shit...*" he says. "That one...did me right."

"You okay?"

Seth looks up at her with an odd expression, his eyes go wide, as if he's witnessing some kind of inner horror, or wonder. His head falls back, his breathing goes shallow and slow as she lets him sink to the matted carpet. A little green wire twist-tie is on the dirty rug right next to his ear, almost in his ear, and Melissa bends down and gently flips it away.

The song with the slide guitar is still playing as she goes around the room and wipes down anything she may have touched, her brain humming quietly to itself, and she finishes the beer and puts the bottle in her purse. She leaves the lights and the radio on and makes it almost halfway home before she throws up.

teddy

1

In the shower it hits her, *Holy shit holy shit Mel you did it you killed somebody.* Her legs tremble and she has to put her hand against the wall or she'll fall, like some old biddy in the bathroom. Her toes are pale grub-like things with badly chipped red polish on them—*Candy Apple Wed* it's called—and she thinks *Holy shit holy shit holy shit.* But the water is good and warm and firm, that's what she needs right now, Jack put a new shower head on last winter, just like the one her mother has—oops, *had*—in her house, it's the best shower head she's ever owned.

But Seth was just a kid. A cute, innocent kid, with a daughter of his own.

Innocent? Eh, maybe not so much. Seth may have been cute, Seth may have been a loving young father, but Seth was no innocent. And the King Kong tattoo—the snarling, the planes, the building, it's all too perfect. Nope, Seth deserved what he got, Seth asked for it and Seth got it.

But something inside her has shifted, the tectonic plates of her soul have rearranged themselves, she's a killer now—on purpose. She's willfully taken a life. She'll have to live with it for the rest of her own.

Ha. You were a killer before, hon, don't you remember? What about little Joshua James, doesn't he count?

Well, technically she did take a life before, a little boy's life, that much is true. But that was an accident, if she knew what was happening she would have changed course immediately. And really, if you want to get technical, she didn't kill Seth, rather it was his own vascular system, that internal turnpike of toll roads and thoroughfares, that distributed the stuff to his brain and his lungs and his heart. He wanted it, all she did is bring it to the entrance and set it just on the onramp, he did all the rest. She puts her face fully into the spray of water and turns up the hot, it feels good on her skin, she starts scrubbing and scrubbing, she wants to get clean now.

2

Melissa has no idea what she's doing. She sits at the desk in her mostly empty second bedroom, which neither she nor Jack had any idea what to do with other than turn it into a bare, depressing pretense of a home office. Against the wall there's an old presswood desk they poached from her mom's basement—Jack manhandled it in here almost all by himself, walking it corner to corner across the driveway as it threatened to split apart into a pile of sawdust and glue—and now she's sitting at it and opening the White Pages and thumbing through the endless tiny hieroglyphs of Ma Bell. She keeps a laptop computer, she bought it third-hand a few years ago to help her through nursing school, but now it functions more like a paperweight, it's been a dead thing since *That Day* and the news sites and the crime blogs started posting horrible photos of her taken from across the courtroom, her body slumped and hollowed-out, a lipless slash of a mouth, more haunted eyes and waterfall hair than anything else. Because of this, Ma Bell and cable TV are the only way to go.

Though she didn't have a chance to write it down, she's sure Seth said *Teddy Blyler*. It wasn't *Bloeler* or *Blueler* or *Blayler* or *Blaylor*, but *Blyler*. Or *Blieler*. Or maybe *Bleiler*, one of those three. The name sounds exotic somehow—Dutch or Czech or Yugoslavian, *Blaler, Blayler, Bleeler, Bleiler, Bleyler, Bliler, Blieler, Bloeler, Blockler, Blowler, Bluler, Blueler, Blyler*, she scans all of these names until they swim in her vision. A ripsnorter of a headache is beginning just now at the base of her skull, like some old ghost's fingers tightening around her neck. She sips her coffee—she's drinking it sweeter lately for some reason, so much sugar and cream it's the color of sand—and with her pencil she circles several of the names. The addresses next to them are vague and unrecognized. *Signal Hill. Oriole Acres. Chestnut Meadows.*

"Sweets?" Jack's voice floats in from the other room. "What happened last night?"

What happened last night? Melissa tries to remember. *Oh, not much. Just a little thing I've never done before, something terrible and horrible but maybe also pretty okay. Overdue and quite horrendous but also not so bad, how're you?* Whatever it was, Melissa slept better last night than she has in days. No weird noises, no roaring jumbo jets or slamming doors, no nocturnal bogeymen creeping around the rental house. After her shower, it was head on the pillow and lights out.

She keeps searching through the White Pages and distractedly calls back, "Nothing, I worked late." Her finger traces down the names and the addresses. *High Forest. Skyland. Indiana. Merrywood.*

"What?" Jack's in the kitchen. He's making food, always making food.

She lifts her gaze again, realizing now she'd actually said *Nothing, I lurked wait.* Idiot. "I mean, sorry—I worked last night."

"On a Friday night?"

"Yes. Yes. Right." Despite her shortcomings as a liar, even after *That Day* and all that preceded and followed it, she still believes she can learn to lie as good as anybody. People get better when they work at things, right? "There's a study monitor coming on Monday," she says, "lots of paperwork to get ready. It's called working for a living, Jack. You should look into it."

"Ha." Jack cackles to himself. "You want breakfast?"

"I'm not hungry." This is true. Last night her stomach twisted itself into knots and has yet to unclench. The nausea, which came in waves in her belly, bringing cold chills and sweat, has mostly subsided now, but it's not gone. Ending someone's life, it seems, is maybe not the best thing for digestion.

But suddenly Jack is there, behind her in the doorway poking his shiny bald head around the corner. "You okay, Mel? You sound…odd."

She spins around in her chair, blocking the phonebook. "I'm doing something here, Jack."

"Sorry, sorry," he says, and disappears. She opens the bottom drawer of the desk and digs inside and pulls out an old map. It's a map of her adopted hometown: *SELLEFORD, NORTH CAROLINA*, it says, *INCORPORATED AUGUST 11, 1886.* With one finger on the phonebook and one on the map, she starts matching names and addresses.

But then Jack's in the doorway again, coming into the room now with a plate of food—pancakes, a fried egg, a few sausages swimming in syrup. "Food is love," he says. He sets it down on the desk next to the phone book, with a fork and a napkin and an awkward little flourish and looks at her smugly, as if he's the best fiancé ever.

"Aw, Jack." She does her best to hide her irritation.

"Oh yeah—the police guy, the detective. He called me last night."

Melissa's headache tightens again. That hand on her neck. "Yeah?"

"Those are veggie sausages, by the way. It's my new thing. Not digging the pig these days."

"What did he say, Jack?"

"That guy's such a dick. But not much. No developments. No leads. He sounded weirdly okay with it. I tried to ask him a few questions, but he hustled me off the phone." Jack returns to the doorway. "So, sad to say, *nada*. At least for now. Enjoy," he says, and shuts the door behind him. Jack has a weird way with exits.

Nada. Terrific. Just great. Those two cops inspired *nada* faith in her before, and even less than *nada* now, negative faith. Melissa picks up one of the syrup-sticky sausages with her fingers and munches on it as she goes back to comparing names and addresses. There's a T. Blyler on McArthur. On the map she searches for McArthur, and finds it in a nicer part of town, on the hills across the highway, behind the big construction area where they're building the new mall. Huh, new money. Melissa doubts one of Seth's home-busting buddies lives in that trendy neighborhood, it's full of doctors and realtors and corporate salesmen. So, T. Blyler is out. There's a Timothy Blieler on Ellis Street, which is toward the south end of town, not far from the highway, back toward Seth's trailer. This is a decidedly *not nice* part of town, Dogtown, the locals call it, boxy cinderblock and tarpaper homes, government housing with abandoned clothesline posts loitering between the buildings. It's mostly a black area, which throws an additional element into things. She doesn't figure Seth for a racist, for a KKK kinda guy, but best buds? Maybe not.

And then there's Theodore Bleiler, this one in Oriole Acres. *Theodore, Theo, Teddy, Ted, T-man.* On the map, Oriole Acres is a trailer park near the river, the tiny diagram of the lanes like little vascular beds curving in on themselves. Now *that* might be a place where one of Seth's friends would live. Oriole Acres. A trailer park on the river. It sounds exactly right. *My tater from another mater*, he'd said.

And then that name: Theodore Bleiler. Teddy Bleiler. Not Blyler, or Blieler, but Bleiler. Melissa picks up the other sausage and ignores the ketchup but swabs it in the syrup and eats half of it in one bite, it's good.

3

The trailer park near the river—Melissa's driven by it about a million times because it's off Scott River Road, which is how everyone accesses the little park that edges the river for a half mile or so. In the park there's an overgrown riverwalk where men sometimes meet other men for sex in night parking lots, and an old rusty playground and carved-up mossy benches along the way, and used needles and goopy condoms on the rooty, eroding banks of the river. Melissa dips her Subaru down the slope of the drive and into the trailer park, and putters along for a better view. She's looking for 146, where Teddy—sorry,

Theodore—should presently be living. Occasionally there are numbers on the sides of the trailers, the cheap metallic stick-on kind you buy from a hardware store. Melissa's no stranger to trailer parks, she spent several months after high school as a den mother to a trailer full of shirtless, chain-smoking dropouts, but this isn't the sort of park she experienced then—happy, with retiree neighbors and little wire fences bordering the grass. No, this is one of those parks where life itself seems to have taken a terrible turn and you can smell the desperation—half the units empty, mold sprouting along the sides, driveways and yards cluttered with dismantled motorbikes, kids' toys, and empty cardboard flats half-disintegrated from the rain.

Finally there's 146, and Melissa slows to a stop. It's a slightly tilted, crumbling single-wide, once an avocado green but now moldered to a fungal gray. A stack of cinderblocks form stairs out front—not even a porch for Ol' Teddy Boy to drink beer on. Melissa U-turns around and circles back to get a better look. The oil-stained parking spot in front is empty, and the uncurtained windows are dark. If he still lives here, it feels like Teddy is not at home.

She cruises back up to the main road and heads to the nearest convenience store, a little place just off the river that, from the dusty, land-that-time-forgot look of things, sells more bait and fishing tackle than it does beer and lottery tickets. Melissa gets a Pepsi from the cooler—stored next to the bait worms, which wrap around each other like a ball of intestines, but she supposes there's no way for them to befoul her factory-sealed soda—and a small, dusty package of Fig Newtons. As she moves up the aisle there's a sunglasses rack, and impulsively she stops and lifts one from it and puts them on; in the little spotted mirror there she looks more than anything like a little girl trying on mommy's glasses. That's all right—young is good, even at her tender age, time is not her friend, time is nobody's friend. She takes everything up to the counter and without a word pays for it in cash.

Back at the trailer park, she finds a shady place under a tree about thirty yards from Teddy's place. She backs in so there's a clear view and munches her Figs and sips her Pepsi. No activity. When the food is gone, and half the pop, she leans her chair back, adjusts her glasses, and prepares to wait for the long haul. She feels like one of those private detectives on TV, she grew up on all those dumb shows, the endless reruns, watching them and feeling jealous of their certainties and their clear goals and their sense of righteousness as they raced here and there around those scrubby LA roads. Maybe that was her problem—there was never a mission, never a thing to solve, it was all just a tepid day-in-and-day-out, formless and hazy, an endless scratching at her own primitive itches. And the TV cops' life of watching, observing, spying, surveilling, it felt good and easy to look, to snoop, to stare, to pry. Nancy Drew was a great pryer into things, and the Hardy Boys, and Melissa felt it might be second nature to her too, she was a born wallflower, a perfect observer, sometimes it felt like she even stood apart and observed herself.

But hey, wouldn't you know it, maybe luck is with her today—*or maybe not, too early to tell, ha ha*—a car pulls in from the main road and goes straight to Teddy's trailer. It's a stubby little Ford of some kind, Melissa sits up, cars aren't her thing but it certainly doesn't *look* new. There are two guys in the car, youngish, a white guy and a darker-skinned guy, maybe Latino or something. Chatting. The white-guy driver has a kind of starving-artist, heroin-chic vibe, with a swept-back cascade of greasy brown hair, and the other has the thick neck of a football player, with a boxy face and a *cholo* chin-beard. They certainly *look* like they're up to no good, but then again maybe they're just construction workers on a lunch break, who can tell anymore?

As the white guy gets out—thin and sinewy in a purple t-shirt and black jeans—he gives Melissa's car a quick glance. Startled by the sudden clarity of his gaze, she resists giving him a nod or a wave, but only turns away, pretending in her head she's waiting for someone else. *Noah, Noah, I wonder if Noah is ready yet*, she thinks idiotically to herself, as if the man can see her thoughts, and then feels a cold slosh of dread and sorrow at Noah's terrible fate. *Shit.* Why did she have to bring Noah up at a time like this?

Unheedful of all this internal drama, Teddy—if that's who he is—hops up the cinderblock stairs and goes inside the trailer. The other guy waits in the car.

Melissa uncaps her Pepsi and takes another swig. By now it's warm, but the sugar is good and brings her back to herself. "C'mon, c'mon," she whispers, her breath whistles in her nostrils as another car, an old brown Buick, floats into the park and putters past 146 and toward her, but she resists sliding down in her chair for this one too. *Try to look like you belong here, honey*, she tells herself, and glances away as the car approaches and then passes. It's an old woman, wearing a wig like a silver helmet.

Just then the door to 146 opens, and the guy, Teddy—maybe, *maybe-baby*, or maybe not—hops down the stairs and slips back in the car. He starts it up, and he and the chin-beard guy pull away. After a brief pause at the main road, they pull out onto the county road and head east. Back toward town.

Melissa starts her car and follows them up the drive and into the road, keeping several vehicles between her and Teddy-boy. Those cop shows do it all the time, but it isn't easy because Teddy-boy seems to be a terrible driver, or at least reckless, he darts in and out of traffic and drives so aggressively he almost causes at least three minor fender benders. Offensive driving, Melissa remembers her father calling it, and he was right because it is quite offensive. She's still with them as Teddy and his buddy speed past the rail yards and the warehouses, skirting the edge of town on the outlying road that edges along the river. Then he turns left, headed toward the northern verges, past the Dairy Queens and the taquerias and the sex shops and onto a tree-lined two-lane that leads them through neighborhoods and pastures and into sun and shadow and woods and eventually to an old car wash.

The car wash is one of those do-it-yourself setups, the kind with several bays and huge brushes and hoses. One of the only developments out here, it's surrounded on three sides by stands of scrubby, malnourished poplars. Across the street is an out-of-business lube shop, next to another lonely building that says *Wren'z Hair*. Below that, a handwritten sign proclaims *CUT COLOR WAX WE CUT YOU STRUT*. The parking lot's empty and the curtains are drawn, nobody home and evidently haven't been for a while. Lots of failed dreams on this side of town.

Melissa pulls into the car wash and watches as Teddy-boy hops out and the other man—*Teddy-pal*, she supposes she can call him, and why not—slides into the driver's seat. Teddy squirms out of his t-shirt and into what looks like a dark blue car mechanic's button-up and says something and nods as the other guy pulls around and drives off. As Teddy heads toward a little brick building in the far corner of the parking lot, he deep digs in his pockets for something—keys, it turns out, a ring full of them, and unlocks the door. The building is tiny and windowless, like a troll house in a fairy tale. He goes inside and the door slams shut behind him.

Well. Wasn't that exciting. Melissa has no idea what to do now. She's already spent more time than she expected stalking this guy around the peripheries of town, but it doesn't make sense to drive away now and let her efforts go for naught. Before she can get cold feet, she pulls her car around into one of the bays—the farthest from the little troll house—and turns it off and lets it settle. Takes a moment to psych up her courage—*Do it do it do it doitdoit*—and gets out but immediately gets back in, having no idea, not a single solitary one, of what she will say to him. Is there a plan, or is the plan just not to make a nuisance of herself?

She stands up again, and that's when Teddy comes around the corner.

"Hi. You need something?" he says.

Suddenly white-hot, Melissa only stares at him, unable to respond. Teddy needs a shave and a good meal, but otherwise he looks a little like that comedian guy who played the drug-dealing but still admirable hero in that one movie, if he had let himself go a bit, and also with his hair swept back, a dimple-jaw and a lopsided scar below his smile. His shirt is indeed an auto shop shirt, oil-blotched with short sleeves and plain as day it says THEO right on the stitched name-patch on the left breast.

Melissa waits as he approaches and extends a somehow already-dirty hand. She has to work to keep herself from running away, from sprinting out into the empty road and all the way back home, and he wants to shake her hand?

"Here's how you do it," he's saying. She blinks at him for a moment, stares at his outstretched palm, then realizes it's not a handshake at all, it's a request for the funds she'll need to operate the machine. She digs numbly in her purse, snaps open her wallet and pulls out a five dollar bill. Theo—*Theo Theo Theo means Teddy*, a taunting little voice chants again and again in her thoughts, *Theo Theo is Teddy, darling*—Theo takes the money and feeds it into the change machine. "You put your money in here," he says with complete disinterest, "and see, your change comes out here."

With a musical clinking, the change cup fills with quarters. Melissa stares dazed as Theo takes them all and tries to pass them to her, but it's as if her brain and her eyes aren't connected, she can only watch in amazement.

His eyes give her a bored once-over. "You ain't never done this before, have you?"

She shakes her head. Of course she has, she's washed her car many times and Jack's too, not here, maybe not at this place but at others, there are more than several of these shitty little car wash joints all over town.

"Here," he says, impatience growing in his voice. Melissa watches as he pumps four quarters into the machine and turns the dial to RINSE, then lifts the long pole of the hose from its hook on the wall and begins spraying her car. "We cain't do the whole car for you," he says. "Wish I could, but..." When he finishes rinsing the car, he turns the dial of the machine to *SOAP*. A gushy mess of suds oozes out of the brush, Melissa watches hypnotized, her purse clutched to her breasts, as he begins soaping up her car. He washes the hood and the grill, and then turns to her.

"This is far as I go," he says. "We do it for anybody, we gotta do it for everybody." He pushes the pole at her, and she sees herself as in a dream taking it, it's cold and wet and the suds wash down over her wrist. With one hand she starts mechanically brushing the hood of her car with the long pole.

"You may want put that somewhere outta the way," Teddy says, nodding at her purse. "You're gonna get it all wet and ruint."

Like a sleepwalker, Melissa sets her purse on the dry cement and takes the pole with both hands. Her knuckles are wet and bloodless with strain, her chest throbs with her heartbeat and the blood pushes itself through her veins, through her shoulders and arms and all the way down to her cold fingers. When she looks up, Teddy's gone.

4

A pot of autumn simmers on the stove, but the sticky and cramped feeling from sitting in the car all day twists and flops in her gut, the last thing her stomach needs right now is hot spicy carrot soup. And that paralysis from meeting Teddy or Theo or whatever he calls himself—in her mind she keeps seeing his wheat-chaff hair, that scar below his lip, that cold smile that says *I'm here to help but not really, really I just want you to leave me the fuck alone.*

Jack steps in from the back, dressed only in a towel wrapped around his waist. "Whoa!" he says, surprised, and retreats down the hall. "I didn't hear you come in."

Melissa hardly notices, but she recoils from the soup as if it had insulted her. "What is that?"

"How's it going?" Jack calls from in the bedroom. "I been cooking all day, in between grading papers and writing my own."

"It smells...*orange*."

"*West African Peanut Butter Soup*. I found it in one of those flower-power cookbooks my aunt gave me, it's what they eat in Mali or Senegal or wherever, lotsa peanuts over there, goobers and groundnuts, that kind of thing." The sound of various drawers opening and closing comes banging up the hallway, Jack keeps some of his clothes here for times just like this. "Matter of fact, that's where the term *goober* come from. *N-Guba,* they called it. *N-Guba*. Goober peas. It's African."

Melissa doesn't answer, instead she's turning to take in the house, the pattern of light fading down the hallway, growing in unease as the shadows gather toward the back of the house, it's unnerving how the night comes on, strolling like an old man from room to room. Or it could be the house itself, she's never liked this place, its inadequacy only revealed itself to her after she'd had several weeks to get used to it. The high ceilings were fine, but to dress up the dining room the landlord installed rustic stones around the fireplace all the way up, and the weight of the rocks caused that part of the house to sag, and now the floors all slant that way, if there'd been hardwoods instead of cheap-ass rental carpet she could have poured out her coffee and watched it runnel its way toward the fireplace. It's a little thing, but it sets off her sense of misproportion, and nags at her every time she sees it. Now every angle in the place leans wrong.

Jack comes out from the bedroom, smelling of shampoo and sweat—and just like that everything's a tiny bit better, Jack has that touch, he was the one, he'd stood by her even during the darkest days of the trial, the moments that seemed to void themselves out, so terrible were they she can hardly remember them, blank spots on the map, *Here Be Dragons*. But she does remember him sitting with her at many of her hearings, so tall and shiny bald and his ridiculous turquoise pants, and still to this day he defends her to anyone who'll listen, his own surly backwoods family included. Jack isn't perfect, of course, back when they met, in bars and places like that he sometimes stared at other women a little too long, more than just a glance, a full drink of water, maybe not understanding how obvious it was or not thinking anyone cared. And Melissa understood some of his assumptions about society could be, well, somewhat *naïve*, as he could be, let's face it, sorta simple and straightforward, you can read mama's boy all over him, not that Melissa knows very many to judge, really. Worst of all, there are no mysteries when it comes to Jack, he has no contradictions, no hidden rooms or secret gardens or far closed wings in the castle. There's just...Jack. In his turquoise pants. Cooking.

They met when Melissa was at the intermediate-care facility—that filthy place, the one with the residents' snot and poop and earwax smeared on all the door handles, and Melissa kept a box of tissues with her wherever she went—and Jack was there to make a delivery of coffee and tea and various client hydration supplies, he was the guy dollying in the bottled water and setting up the plastic straws and stirrers, an in-between gig for him, still a trucker but the local delivering kind then, and Melissa alone in the kitchenette. He'd looked cute in his uniform—his T-top smile and his schlubby ass a breath of fresh-air among all the other medicated zombies wandering the halls. But when she tried to slip past him, she bumped a box from his dolly and they both watched in slow motion as it fell and exploded into thousands of red plastic drinking straws scattered across the sticky-footprint floor. Melissa was all apologies, but Jack thought it was funny, and together they picked up the straws and put them back in the box for use later on, no one ever had to know, it was their little secret, and that was that.

After *That Night*, when Melissa was out of observation but still suspended without pay, Jack brought over groceries with his own measly salary, which is one of the reasons she's hoping to help him through school now. When he started long-hauling he was gone most of the time, and for a year and a half this created a certain dynamic for them both, Jack gone and on the phone and working, Melissa finding her way out of her little labyrinth of grief at home. But then he quit trucking and was home now and starting in on his student teaching, and she worried that like two negatively charged electrons their delicate arrangement would slip—his ubiquity would create rifts and disappointments and unspoken grudges. But it didn't. They got along. Not perfectly, not the ideal couple, but one they both could manage. And slowly, over 36 months, with his help she began to unrumple herself and become a person again. She's seen his heart, she's held it beating in her hands, and more often than not nowadays she gives him the benefit of the doubt.

He ladles the soup into two bowls, and carefully without spilling brings them over and sets one of them in front of her at the table. "It's a smidge spicier than maybe you like it," he says, sitting down, "but be careful with the salt." In the overhead light, the soup is a garish, lifejacket orange, the color of misadventure and risk.

"So, this weekend," he says. "If you remember, I was gonna step out and go camping. Just Friday and Saturday. A group of the dudes are getting together and heading up to Woodbury with—" He stops when he sees the look on her face, which is not in pain, but not entirely at ease either. "You okay?" he says.

"I'm sorry," she says, putting a hand to her forehead, the way her mother would.

"I can cancel, Mel. If you need me to."

"No no, I'm just…" A strange feeling now, maybe a histamine fever coming on or the beginnings of a cold, she seems stretched to a limit of something or other. "I need to get my such together."

The room is quiet. Jack studies her, alarmed. He says, "Your *such*? Did you hear what you just said? You need to get your *such* together?"

It seems like a good idea to try the soup, Jack's worried and he'll like that, she makes a show of sipping loudly from her spoon. "No, this soup is *interesting*," she says, trying not to think of the color of it, nor of being alone. "Complex. I think it's really good."

"Look," Jack says, sitting back in his chair and wiping his face with a big-knuckled hand. "Can I ask you something?"

Melissa takes another noisy sip from her spoon. "Of course."

But then, before he can say another word, a muffled blast of noise—music, allegedly—comes booming in from next door. It shatters the quiet with the force of a kick, harsh and hammering and crackled with overblown speakers.

"*Motherfucker!*" Jack shouts and bolts up. He stomps to the door and throws it open, pausing there for a moment before disappearing from Melissa's view as he stalks out onto the porch and into the yard. Through the window in the foyer she sees that next-door kid out there in the driveway, *whatshisname,* Gordie, washed in the harsh floodlights of his house.

"*Dude!*" Jack is yelling. "*Hey!*" Melissa moves over to the kitchen to get a better view, watching Jack and the kid now through the open front door. "*Your fucking stereo! Turn it down or I'm gonna do it for you!*"

Melissa's hand knocks something that skitters away and threatens to roll off the counter, and she snatches it and looks down to find an icepick in her palm. An old icepick, ancient and bent but still strong, an icepick worthy of a grandfather, the needle shaft spotted with age and the wooden handle stained by years of fingers and sweat and use. Jack must have brought it over. She's never seen it before.

"*Turn it down!*" Jack's voice comes again from outside.

The music gets suddenly quieter, and a venomous nasal bleat comes across the yard and into the house—"*Queer!*"

After a moment, Jack huffs back inside, his bald head flushed now and his face blotchy, but he stops short when he sees her, no longer at the table but leaning against the counter. Her face guilty but not exactly sure why.

"What are you doing?" he says. His eyes take her in, wary in their knowledge of her and the ways of her body and how it communicates.

"I need a day off." Melissa hugs herself, as if she's cold. "Maybe I'll call Angie and tell her I'm not coming in tomorrow."

Jack's eyes remain worried, he takes a moment, maybe still perplexed at her and her behavior. Then he says, "Can we finish our dinner first?"

Melissa takes her purse from the counter and goes over to sit at the table with it in her lap, cradling it like a favorite cat. She leans over it and takes a showy slurp of thick orange liquid. It's cooled down just a bit. "This is damn good soup," she assures him. "*Nguba.*"

5

The next morning, the car wash is empty. Not a single customer, not a single sign of Teddy, Teddy has both *CUT* and *STRUT*. Melissa considers waiting around for awhile, loitering in the same farthest bay away from the road and seeing what happens, but the thought of it makes her feel sad and rudderless, like a homeless person with nowhere to go. But there is somewhere to go—to work. Not that she's actually going there today, she's planning to call the clinic and tell them she's too sick to come in.

About a mile and a half down the road there's a little pastry shop—*Red's Velvet*, it's called and indeed, the interior is deep red, lipstick red, sexy heels red. The shop is in a converted old house and the floors creak, alerting the room to every step Melissa takes, and the tables are crowded a little too close together, but out back there's a patio that sits under shade trees and gives customers a relief from the overpowering color scheme and a little privacy. So she gets some coffee—in a scarlet paper cup, of course—then comes back outside, digs out her cellphone, and dials the clinic.

It's Grace who answers, in that weirdly adenoidal tone she seems to reserve solely for phone conversations, Melissa doesn't remember her voice being so pinched, but phone lines do weird things to voices. "Silver Star Treatment Center."

"Grace?" Melissa cradles the phone and turns away from the road, to minimize any traffic noise. "Hi, this is Melissa. Hey, listen, I'm a bit under the weather and, uh...I was wondering if you could tell folks that I'm staying home today, I'm just not up to coming in right now."

"Oh no! What's wrong?" The fake concern in Grace's voice is depressingly plain, no doubt it's the same tone she uses for lost pets, hospitalized grandmas, persecuted church groups, and nieces who've skinned their knees.

"It's, um, it's nothing. It's just, you know, I had a bad night and...and I think I might be catching. It's—it might be contagious."

"Oh, that's terrible! Here, let me patch you in to Dr. Larry."

"Oh, that's okay, I don't want to bother him, I just—"

"Holding for Dr. Larry."

Too late. The phone gives her a couple of clicks and then a hum, she considers hanging up and moving on, but something tells her it's better to go ahead and bite the bullet now rather than deal with it for days. She takes a seat on the leaf-strewn top of the picnic table and tries to bring up a little phlegm in her throat to sound more sick.

Then there's Dr. Larry's melba toast voice on the other end, "Melissa. How you doing?"

"Uh, not bad," she mutters weakly, feeling like a middle-schooler again. In the glass she gets a doubly exposed view of both the inside of the cafe and the reflected passing traffic behind her, the transparent ghost cars slide back and forth, and she tries to sound sick but not *too* sick.

"That's good," Dr. Larry says. "I ask the girls up front to let me know when someone's not doing well. I get worried for my team, you know. Is there anything I can do?"

"Um. Do? About what?" Out on the road, a particularly loud truck farts past, and she cradles the phone in both hands. "I'm just a little under the weather."

"Well, I'm just making sure everyone's been easy with you."

"No, I'm fine." In the window, the reflection is bright—the morning sun on the hill across the road, and the green grass seems to roam all the way up the slope. Through it, beyond it, the transparent red-shaded ghost of a waitress flits here and there, carrying trays, talking to customers. "I'm just…tired. Bad night, and all that."

"Well, I get worried that the girls aren't as, you know, *supportive* as they could be. They can be hard on the new kids. Seeing how far they can play you."

In the rear of the cafe, something else catches Melissa's eye—an older woman sitting in the corner, back near the bathrooms. Munching something, maybe a bagel or a donut or a muffin, hard to tell through all the refractions. Eating with two hands, like a man with a hamburger, when she looks at Melissa over her food their eyes meet solidly, until Melissa finds herself glancing away in self-consciousness. Maybe the woman can't see through the plate glass window, or maybe she can and just doesn't care. "And you heard about Seth," Dr. Larry says.

"What?"

"The young guy? Seth Rainey? OD. Found in his home."

"*What*? Oh *wow*," she hears herself saying. A dread, coiled and quiet, stirs inside of her. She sees Seth's dirty carpet again, that mostly empty fridge. "Oh no. I'm so sorry to hear that. He was a…a good kid."

"It happens. We see it sometimes. Comes with the territory. I saw he was one of yours. Not as tough as with your family, but still. Hurts when we lose one of our own." Melissa doesn't answer, her eyes have found the woman in the corner again, who doesn't even attempt to hide the fact that she's watching Melissa. Eating and chewing and watching. "Well, I know you're worn down, so no worries. If we don't take care of ourselves, we can't care for others."

"Yeah."

"And please. The girls—don't let them play you, they'll fucking kill you now."

"What?"

Dr. Larry's voice is tinny over the phone, making his voice sound as thin as Grace's. "I said, don't let them play you, because they will, you know."

"Right. Right." Melissa glances at the chewing woman again. Still there, hemmed in by the refractions of the glass, her face in the window seeming to loom out from the mirrored hill across the street, still staring, still chewing, still watching. "Yes, yes," Melissa says. "Okay, thank you, I will. I mean, I won't."

6

She drives by the car wash three separate times, but Teddy isn't there. Three times she circles the parking lot, pausing in the same bay, and pulling away when she sees who's working there instead. It's a girl, her hair looped in braids that hang over her shoulders. Melissa finds it strange that Teddy works at a car wash anyway, she didn't know that was a thing. She cruises by Oriole Acres to find Teddy's trailer dark again and hollow. The only place left to go is home.

Each time she comes in she feels scraped out, disgusted by her own needs. She lays down on the couch with a damp rag over her eyes, maybe all this talk of feeling under the weather is starting to bring it about, because she really is feeling sick. Another pounding headache blooms in red and black flowers behind her eyes, her own retinal laser-light show, and a kind of torpor has taken hold in her arms and legs. But then—*no rest for the wicked*—she makes herself get back up and drive out to the car wash.

By now it's almost evening, and the waning sun smears the west with watercolor pink as her car pulls into the place one last time. If Teddy-guy isn't here now, this is it for the day, and probably for forever. This grudge, this pull or yank or need or whatever you want to call it, it's eating her alive, time to be done with it.

She coasts around the deserted lot and pulls into her usual bay and turns off the car. It kicks a moment, grumbles a bit, then settles into sleep. Melissa grabs her purse and gets out and pauses against the trunk, there's no sound other than the occasional hiss of a passing vehicle out on the road, even the birds are quiet, it's as if the world dropped away just outside the borders of the car wash. The pavement in this bay and the other ones are bone dry—hardly anyone has been here all day.

She works up her courage and leaves the bay and goes across the parking lot to the little troll house, to find the door closed. She takes a deep breath and knocks. No answer. Rattles the knob, but it's locked.

Well. Maybe this is best, maybe we should just forget the whole goddamn—

That's when footsteps echo behind her. She turns to see Teddy approaching.

"Help you?" he says. His voice is deep and toffee-thick, richer and heavier than she remembered. A weird thought comes to her—*He should've been an actor or a late-night radio DJ*—but she can't answer him now, her throat is constricted, it's all she can do to keep breathing.

"You're back," he says, oddly cheerful, recognizing her. Her mouth opens, but nothing comes out. Teddy breaks into a smile. Fierce brown eyes, Apollo cheekbones. That hair, like a photo she once saw of Stalin as a young man—beautiful, haunted, driven, big plans to come. He sees her looking and something registers in his face, some secret confirmation grows in his eyes. "You ain't here for a car wash, are you?" he says.

Melissa shakes her head. She's shocked at her own exposed grief and bared intentions. Her throat eases up a bit and she manages to say, "Not really."

Teddy's eyes drop from her face down to her breasts and back to her face, and Melissa becomes aware of the loneliness of this place—trees everywhere, dark, broken window storefronts across the street. *We Cut You Strut,* an occasional passing car at best, if things went wrong out here, there would be no one to help.

"You gotta tip for me?" Teddy asks. Slowly, feeling as bashful as an adolescent, Melissa digs in her purse and pulls out a twenty. Teddy's shirt still says THEO, she notes with distaste, it's the very same one as the day before, *These boys need girlfriends, somebody to take care of them, do their laundry.* Teddy grins and, stepping a little too close, takes the money and stuffs it in his hip pocket. Then he strolls backwards, still smiling at her, to the far bay where her Subaru sits parked and ticking to itself. He has a weird little metallic key, he inserts it into the coin box and twists it on, and no dollars, no quarters this time, just Teddy—Teddy works here, Teddy is the man, Teddy has the inside scoop, *the more he has the more he wants.* He spins the dial to RINSE, then picks up the big metal pole and starts spraying her car.

Melissa, flat-footed in her nurse shoes, watches transfixed, purse in hand.

"Want me to take my shirt off?" Teddy says. He seems to be enjoying himself, he knows his power over women, has known it for a good while apparently. His young girlfriends no doubt told him how beautiful he was, how Adonis himself would seem dull and ordinary next to him. Melissa nods, and he laughs, pleased with his power, his unearthly beauty, and pulls his shirt over his head and tosses it onto the pavement in front of the bay, out of the water's reach.

As he goes to work, the muscles rolling in his back as he grooves to some internal melody only he can hear, Melissa slips her hand inside her purse, she takes a deep breath, he really is a fine specimen, the kind of virile older boy teenage Melissa would touch herself in bed over, think swampy thoughts about in the loneliness of her room, even now her breath comes quicker, and she takes a quick step toward him, but then he turns and stops her in her tracks.

"If my boss knew I's doin' this," he warns, "I'd be in pretty deep dog shit. I hope you're grateful for this. And I hope you gonna up the tip a little too."

When she doesn't answer—Teddy seems weirdly attentive to her state, maybe he really is a smart guy after all—he takes a moment to look at her, to really see her. His eyes are dreamy but cold and guarded, and a hint of doubt has crept in there too. "You don't talk much, do you?"

"Only when I have to," Melissa tells him.

Teddy goes back to his scrubbing, she stands there for a moment more, feeling her breath move in and out, she glances at the lonely road, the hair place is dark, has been dark for a long time, *we cut you strut,* she thinks, and then drops her purse and steps up behind Teddy and with the ice pick in her hand, she pumps it hard—*onetwothreefour*—into the left side of his neck. She was aiming for his ear, but he moved. Quickly she steps back.

"*FUCK!*" he yells. He drops the soapy brush, still oozing suds, and reaches up to the dark blood welling out of his neck. "*What... what za fugg?*" he cries. He looks at his hand, slick-black in the fading light, eyes wide in disbelief.

He turns to her, mouth open, still wondering if this is really happening. Then he comes at her, but she holds up the icepick, threatening him, and he stops.

"*Wha're you doi?*" By now blood splatters on his shoulder and drips down his bare chest.

"Who hired you?" Melissa growls through clenched teeth. The ice pick wavers in front of her.

"*Hired me?*" Teddy comes at her again and she jabs at him but misses, and he snatches her hand and tries to pry the ice pick away, his fingers are firm and painful on her wrist as they grapple. And then with his free fist he must have punched her because the next thing she's standing five or so feet back, the world tilted, with fireflies blooming in her vision. But the ice pick is still in her palm—it feels good and warm and familiar, *Jack,* she thinks, *Jack used this, Jackjackjack,* and when Teddy rushes her, she slashes at him with it.

He takes the slash and punches her again—a solid blow, a familiar feeling now, an old friend, and then she's on her ass in the wet pavement. Her face is wet too, and she reaches up and touches her nose, it's numb and dead, not a part of her at all, more like a mask, but her fingers come away dripping black in the gloom.

Teddy's neck, on the other hand, is a fountain. He comes at her again, but before he reaches her he slips to one knee, she scrabbles back in the wetness on her ass and pulls away from his reaching grasp as he holds his neck with his other hand. He's crying.

"*You s'ab me, you bish? Wha're you doigg?*" Not so handsome now. His voice is weird too, and airy, not at all the same cocoa baritone of earlier. *We cut you strut, Teddy old boy,* she thinks again, and for a suspended moment they stare at each other, a car passes out on the road, a hiss of air, another life sails by innocent and unworried about home invasions and night terrors and Jack's old icepick.

"Who hired you!" she hisses.

The ground beneath Teddy is dark with his blood. He looks at her with genuine sadness. "*Wha*?"

"To come into my house? Tell me and I'll call someone to help you."

Painfully, like a toddler Teddy climbs back up on his knees, every movement now is demanding, requiring strength, he spits blood. Melissa stands stiffly up and, though he tries to block her, she feints—*once, twice,* somehow already good at this—and then jabs him two times again on the other side, little vampire bites in his corded neck.

"*Urhh! Urhh!*" Teddy gasps and snatches for her, but she's already back out of his reach. She watches as he lists to the side, a ship going down, hands now as if somehow his head had come off and he's holding it on. He's crying.

She moves closer and stands over him. The car wash and the woods and the road are quiet. Then the hiss of another car approaching, lights edging up on the hair place across the street, and then past and away and things are quiet again.

"You're right, Teddy, I don't have much to say," Melissa says in her calm but peppy nurse's voice, it's that chipper neutral tone she uses to talk to her patients, rich and poor, young and old, sick and healthy, it helps to put them at ease and makes her feel slightly superior, just a little in charge, as though she and they, their problems and her problems, their sickness and her sickness, were entirely separate things.

jack

1

When Melissa pulls into her driveway with smeared blood on her face, with even her clothes ragged and bloody and on the far side of being ruined, she says a silent thanks the kid with the hair isn't out there, there'd be no way to get past him looking like this, the house could use a garage or even a carport, but nope—not in this neighborhood. She opens the front door and creeps quietly, gently, inside and pauses in the foyer. The TV loud in the other room, a game show by the sounds of things, hints of rustling and Jack surely sitting at the table grading papers and lost inside his new life of school and lessons. She tries to be a ghost while sneaking down the hall, but then his voice calls out: "Sweets! You're home! How's it goin'?"

She stops in her bloody blouse, considers the cracked and swollen face that grimaced back at her in the rearview mirror on the way home. Jack can't find her like this, his heart couldn't take it. She darts for the bathroom.

"What are you doing here?" she calls out from the hall, making her voice sound casual and unconcerned about anything, just an average day, and of course overshooting it. "Hang on, I'm feeling a little, you know, odd." She shuts the bathroom door and locks it.

Heavy footsteps coming down the hallway, Jack's wearing his shitkickers, size twelve, and it sounds like a platoon of tanks crunching down Main Street. "Just looking over some papers," he says, outside the door now. "Everything all right?"

In the mirror, Melissa stares in dark wonder at herself. The bottom half of her face is swollen and red, and there's a finger painting of dried blood across her neck. Everything is definitely not all right.

"Wow!" she says. "I'm just—yeah, I've got diarrhea. But it's okay." Frantically she starts undressing and splashing water on her face and scrubbing the blood away from her chin and her arms. There's a lot of it, and in a moment the sink below her is pale pink, with little watercolor spots here and there on the counter. Where her clothes have fallen, red calligraphy stains the tile floor. *Shit shit shit.*

"Diarrhea?" Jack says through the door. He's just outside, mere inches away, she's sure he can hear her bumping around in here. "It wasn't my soup, was it?"

"I think I had a small accident," she says. "I hit my nose."

"Your nose? *What?*" When Melissa doesn't have an answer, he says, "You're scaring me, Mel." The knob rattles as she splashes her face one last time, and she yanks the towel over her breasts and fumbles at the door and opens it just a crack.

"Jack, relax, man, just trying to clean myself up here," she complains, hoping the shakiness in her voice comes off more as irritation rather than the aftermath of deadly violence. "I'll be out in a jiffy."

Jack is standing in the hall, backlit from the light in the dining room, and his eyes grow wide when he sees her. "Oh *fuck*," he says. "Mel! You look terrible, your eye's swollen! *What the fuck, Melissa?*"

"It's not that bad, I promise," she says, and slams the door in his face. She locks it again and looks at herself in the mirror. "I banged my nose on the door at the clinic. It looks worse than it is, I promise."

"*Shit!* Are you okay? I thought you didn't go in today?" There's a shuffle of steps outside as Jack tries to take it all in. "Can I get you anything? You need some ice? Ibuprofen?"

"Uhh…yeah, that sounds good," she says, just wanting him to go away. "Go get me some ice. And some aspirin, that'll help."

She hears Jack move off and takes a moment to breathe a bit easier. The worst of it's over now, the rest is just coming up, and following up, with the lie. *Hit my face on the door, you know, one of those stupid times when you're talking to somebody and not paying attention and you open it only to whack yourself right in the nose. Ha ha.* Jack, God love him, is a bit suggestible and gullible, he'll believe her, it'll take some doing and it'll probably be the only thing they talk about the rest of the night—how a moment like that could play out, again and again—but she can make him believe her, she's sure of it.

With that out of her mind, it's back to the real crisis—Teddy. He was there in the car wash bay, face down, surrounded by pink soapy blood, the same color of the blood now in the sink. She lets the towel across her chest drop to the floor and looks at the figure in the mirror. Swollen face, cut nose, fat lip. Like a mugshot. Blood smeared along her collarbone in an almost perfect four-fingered hand wipe, in attack or appeal, hard to tell which is which anymore.

2

The next morning she's up early, having mostly slept well aside from some painful tossing and turning. The hours haven't been kind to her face. Her right eye, where Teddy caught it—allegedly, there's no memory of the punch now at all, just a white blot—is swollen both above and below the eye, and her left eye is bruised, just a little bit underneath, nothing a little concealer can't fix. There's also a cut along the left side of her nose, not large enough to need a Band-Aid, but there it is, scabbed ink-black in the harsh morning light. She cleans it as best she can, rubbing the dark encrusted parts away with a spitty ring-finger. Not too bad—as an official picker, an old scab-scraper from way back, she can attest to the fact that getting rid of the scab often helps more than you think it would. Not that she would advocate that to anyone.

Next is foundation on her face and neck, way more than usual, maybe a little too much even now, judging by the unnatural tan of her skin in the mirror. No point in risking it though—better to wear too much than not enough. While she smoothes it on she practices her story—*hurrying to meet an old friend at Pinkie's Pub, yes yes sick as a dog but I still had to make the appointment, lawyers and all that, a little out of it and not looking where I'm going, metal door into face, bang, ouch!, much grimacing and laughter and a few aspirin and Band-Aids from the waiters*—and hoping that'll be the end of it.

She pulls into the employee area of the clinic parking lot—a little too quickly, she's staring at her own name stenciled there and not at where she's going—and with a ghastly scrunch her car runs aground on the concrete parking block. *Great,* backing up and over the wheelstop, *muck it up, girl, before it gets a chance to look good.* She gets out and goes around to inspect the damage. The *Reserved for Melissa Sweet, RN* is scratched, looking somewhat less new now, the words with a conspicuous black shoe-polish swipe across the left side. Maybe that's for the best, it fits, scratched and scarred is kinda how she feels on the inside too.

But something catches her eye. In the high grass just beyond the bumper is a little black box. A little black plastic box. She kneels and picks it up and sees it has a pair of magnets on the back. It rattles with something inside, and on one edge of it there's a little slot you can slide open, and sure enough, there's a key and a keychain in there.

It's one of those contraptions that people use to hide extra keys in case they get locked out of somewhere, under the fenders of cars, behind birdhouses, tucked away on porches, or under fake rocks in the garden. The key is brass, simple, no nonsense—a Home Depot special. And there's a keychain, a wooden carving of some sort, not much bigger than a walnut. It's a monkey, a small monkey, red-rust brown, tail curled around itself, cheap ruby rhinestones for glittering eyes. Carved from a peach pit, of all things. It must have fallen from someone's car, or purse. Maybe the guy who painted the parking space. Or maybe Jack put the box carefully inside her wheel-well and forgot to tell her about it, and her parking block maneuver knocked it loose.

In the clinic, Dr. Larry's office door is closed, as it usually is, and she knocks and waits for a moment. But there's no stirring inside, and no one comes to open it. This makes her feel better, *hey at least she tried.*

Close by is Wilston's door, and she knocks on it too, just for completion's sake. As she waits, there's movement at the very end of the hall—an aide stepping into an examination room, and when the door opens, Melissa catches sight of a woman in there, dressed in one of those horrible ungainly clinical gowns and sitting on the exam table, her hair's a fright, she looks like she's just woken up from the worst night's sleep ever, but even worse, her left eye is shockingly horribly gory, a terrible gaping mess—the cavity itself is empty and tissue has spattered up her brow and down her cheek, from a distance it looks as if the remnants of the eye itself, bloody and boiled egg-white, are on her face. For a terrible moment, she and Melissa catch each other's eye, then the door swings shut.

Before Melissa can fully process this, Angie turns the corner of the far end of the hall and saunters down it. As she passes, she gives Melissa a quick wink.

"Is everything all right?" Melissa stammers, with another stunned glance at the closed door down the hall.

"Sure," Angie says. "Why wouldn't it be?" And then she's past, headed toward the front of the clinic in her casual life of assurance and clarity. Melissa, her pulse beating hard in her temples, goes into the L-shaped nurse's station near the corner and shuts the door.

The little box *click-clacks* in the pocket of her lab coat, and she pulls it out and opens it. The monkey smiles at her, its gemstone eyes sparkling in the flat wash of the overheads. Now that she has a moment, she realizes she's seen one of these before, a long time ago. There was a Sweet family vacation once, just the four of them somewhere in the Smoky Mountains, a long time ago when Noah and she were kids and Big Noah was still around. A cheap roadside tourist trap convenience store on the edge of a ravine, a late-afternoon sun flaring through dirty store windows. Melissa, wearing that cheap souvenir Native American headband with feathers sticking up from the back of her head, her parents bought it for her at the start of the trip and she refused to take it off except for bathtime and sleeptime, and little Noah got the cardboard angel's wings that folded up just so. Inside the store, she'd wandered over to a circular spinning kiosk which had all manner of dollar-store trinkets and sunglasses and candy necklaces, and on the opposite side of the kiosk was a little monkey keychain, exactly like the one she has in her hand right now, its tiny fake prism eyes manic and somehow sad at the same time. A shadow had fallen across her and she looked up to see Noah outside the dusty window, he had his wings extended out and he cupped his hands against the glare and grinned in at her, and though his face was mostly obscured by smears of glue and old tape and whatever else they'd put on those windows and never scraped off, his eyes were clear and he looked right at her, they made faces at each other. Noah was healthy then, and Big Noah too, that was back before any family nonsense or *linger-long something wrong* had come down on them like some plague from the—

The intercom buzzes. "Melissa?" Grace says. "Call on line two."

Melissa stirs as if waking from hibernation. Memories of her family—they will be with her, and mess with her, for the long haul, the rest of her life, might as well get used to it already. "Thank you," she says, and blows out a breath as if to dispel these thoughts and picks up the phone. Most likely it'll be Jack, he's the only one who calls and in fact is the only one left to call.

"Hey, baby, whatcha got?" Jack's voice is boomy, as though he's in a closed space, a locker room or a bathroom or something.

"Hi, Jack." Her own voice is strange and flat and hollow and weak, a puny feeling has settled in, maybe she should eat something to get her strength back.

"How you doing?"

"Ah." No point getting into it.

"How's your face? Boy, you were looking rough."

"Yeah, it's, uh…it's better. What's going on?"

"Hey. I wanna take you out tonight."

Melissa swivels on her stool, feeling the antiseptic dreariness of the nurse's station around her. It's bland and bright and way too cramped, and that nauseating overhead light. Strange how doctors study for so many years, go into debt for their educations and their lives of healing, just to spend their time in airless windowless cells like this, if she'd gone to school for that long it would have been to be outside, feeling the fresh air and wind on her face, a life inside under these fluorescents is no life at all. "I don't know," she says. "I'm not feeling too social these days."

"We're getting bonuses," Jack says proudly. "They told us this morning."

"Hey. Nice."

"Maybe we can catch a movie, get outta the house. It's good for you, Mel, you need to get busy."

"I've been busy," she says, with an unexpectedly grim tone.

There's a pause on the other end of the line. "What does that mean?"

She shakes her head even though he can't see it. "Nothing, I'm sorry. Forget it." The office door is closed, it would be nice if someone would interrupt her and get her day started. Maybe she can lose herself in the hustle of everything to do.

"I'm serious," Jack says. "Chinese buffet. All you can eat. Or if you don't want to get honeyed up, I can swing by and go for takeout."

"I can't get honeyed up, Jack—my face." She realizes she's inspecting the peach pit monkey. If you turn it one way, it has an expression of joy, another way the grin becomes a grimace. "Listen," she says, "did you happen to put one of those hidden key thingies under my fender?"

"What?"

"I found a key in one of those magnetic key boxes just now. The kind where you hide the key somewhere? In case you get locked out of your house or whatever? It fell off somebody's car. Maybe my car."

"Jeez. Um, no. I mean, I baby you but not *that* much. If I do something, you'd better be sure I'm gonna tell you about it." On the line there are voices behind him now, maybe in the hallway, boy's voices. Laughing. Happy and distant, a lifetime away.

"Let me think about it," she tells him. "But, oh hey—they need me, I gotta run." Before he can respond, she hangs up the phone.

3

After work, Melissa has an appointment with an old high school friend of her mother's. He's a lawyer, a man in his early 60s named Andy Mair, who has only recently gotten his license to practice—a late *late* bloomer, Sandra joked just weeks before the top of her head was blown off by a quartet of masked strangers. Melissa isn't completely sure of the particulars there, but it seems like the usual depressing tale—broken marriage, broken spirits, broken promises, broken luck. Whatever it is, Andy's almost guaranteed—even at his relatively advanced age—to be inexperienced at practicing law. But Jack's reassured her that things like this, the handling of uncontested estates, aren't too complicated, besides, he said it would be only fitting for her to trust the legalities of her mother's and brother's affairs, such as they are, to an old friend.

Not that there's much left. There's only the calico-bricked rancher and the sad little bare yard around it, not even paid off. But hey—there've been eight years or so of regular payments, so there's that. Still, it's tough for her to think in these terms, her family's tragedy, the terrible situation and the brutality and the blood of it, because it all feels unreal, synthetic, one step removed from real life. Like any moment her phone will ring and it'll be her mother.

The apartment building is on the low side of a hill, with parking above and steps that angle down into the bowl, so that as you descend the stairs you get a weirdly intimate peek into the building's second-floor apartments. Most of them have closed curtains just for this purpose, and the draped, sunlit windows watch her like a wall of eyes. Following her mental notes, she goes down the stairs into an open corridor and down a short hallway with doors on either side until Number 114 comes up. Before she can knock, the door swings open, and there stands Andy Mair.

He still has hair, does old Andy Mair, Melissa thinks nonsensically, like a verse from a children's book, and indeed he does, a great shock of white hair, a beautiful head of hair, tangled and wild as if it has been moussed and primped instead of merely slept upon. He's wearing a frayed sweater and a pair of jeans with holes in the knees and a pair of dollar-store slippers that might be older than Melissa herself. But even here, in his own apartment, a sense of disappointment hovers over him, an air of wrong turns and stubborn setbacks.

"Oh my gosh," Andy says in his old man's voice when he sees her swollen eye. "What the heck, Melissa, what happened to *you*?"

She gives him a sad smile and a loose *just friends* hug. "You should see the other guy. How we doin', Andy?"

Melissa's known Andy for most of her life. For years he was a fixture around their house, his hair white and gorgeous even then, dinners on Friday nights or stopping by for a drink or two after work, beers and football games on the living room TV. Fixing up the back deck with Big Noah on Sundays—the two of them clattering and yelling, with a *Whack whack Crap! Whack whack William SHATner!* drifting into the house every so often.

When her father fled, Melissa was surprised that Andy kept coming around, she'd always thought Andy was mostly her dad's friend. It didn't take her long to understand that Andy was now her mother's friend, and since Big Noah was out of the picture, *ol' Andy Mair-with-all-the-hair* was seeming to take quite a close interest in Sandra. That didn't last long. Sandra set him straight and let him know in no uncertain terms that she and Andy were not *simpatico* in *that way*, and that she liked him as a friend, but not as a partner. Now, as much as

Melissa's glad not to be related to him—*Ewww,* she thought back then, *Oily Andy, I do NOT want him for a stepfather*—Andy still deserves to be the one to handle these legal affairs.

Inside, the apartment is every bit as dull and depressing as she guesses the interior of Andy's brain might be. Discount furniture pointed at a cheap flatscreen TV against the wall, last year's bikini girls calendar and a blue Scottish flag sagging from the walls. And a spartan little breakfast bar that opens into a spartan little kitchen, with only shabby birdwatching books on the counter, their spines labelled with peeling library stickers, to give it any sense that someone lives here at all. *Hey, at least it's clean*, Melissa thinks, not a crumb anywhere in sight.

"Can I get you anything?" Andy asks. Just over the TV, his law degree hangs framed on the wall. It's the newest thing in the place. Maybe Andy likes looking at it when the game is on.

"Glass of water?"

Andy nods and slumps into the kitchen. The couch seems to be Andy's territory—there's a peculiar Andy-sized slump there on the right-hand side—so she finds an awkward seat on the only other piece of furniture in the place, a dusty papasan bowl chair in the corner, facing away from the TV. She lowers herself into it with her purse in her lap and her sensible nurse's shoes stuck foolishly out, like an oversized kid on an ill-fitting amusement park ride.

"Hey, listen, Mel," Andy says over the sound of tap water from the kitchen. "I'm so sorry about your mom. She was an amazing gal. I know you miss her terribly. And Noah. What the jeez, man?" Through the gap in the breakfast bar, he leans low and catches her eye, and when the quiet grows long, he just shakes his head and comes back around with the two waters. He hands her a wet glass. "Have they found the...you know, the people?"

"No. They're not anywhere that close or that competent." Melissa raises herself up to sip from the water, and looks for somewhere to set the water down, but there's nowhere, so she ends up holding it in her lap. "We're just, you know, still waiting to hear any news."

"Darn. That's rough." Andy takes his spot on the couch. "I'm not surprised. 'Round here the cops are mostly zipperhead lobotomy types. Anyone with any sense has already moved to Charlotte or Winston. The ones that stay, soon as they get their pension, it's just cruise control 'til retirement."

"I knew this town was mean, Andy. But nothing like this."

"This business with your mom and your brother is nuts. Who would have thought, this little town, right? Matter of fact, I have a friend," he says, adjusting the couch's pillows, sitting back, getting comfy, he looks relieved to have a visitor, even in a semi-official capacity like this, "a professor of mine who writes op-eds sometimes for the papers. One of the biggies up north sometimes sends him down to parts of South and Central America to write about the legalities there. He's seen some shit, let me tell you—assassinations, guerrilla warfare, torture in Nicaragua. But somebody once asked him where the scariest place he ever went was, and believe it or not, he pointed right here." Andy's index finger jabs at his denimed thigh, like a pin on a map. "Right here in Selleford."

"Why?"

"He said it's the only place he'd ever been where you can get someone killed for two hundred bucks." Andy shakes his head of hair in the ghoulish wonderment of it all. "This fella's covered cocaine, war, famine, corruption, drought, you name it. And Selleford's the single scariest place he says he's ever been."

Melissa's hands are shaking slightly now, so she needs them both to take a sip of water. Fractured images spring at her—masked men arguing in her mother's living room, Teddy's rough hands, blood rimming his nails like grease, holding in his precious fluids as they spill from the perfect little holes in his neck.

"Anyway," Andy says in the silence, moving on, maybe seeing how pale her face has become. "How you holding up?"

"Ah. Today was hard." All day, meeting peoples' gaze like digging a grave. And her body, sore from yesterday. Whether it's some kind of combat fatigue or a traumatic need to ball up into herself, she can't really say, it was lethargy and torpor all morning and afternoon, and even now it would be wonderful to lean back in this papasan bowl and just go to sleep, to make the world go away.

"Yeah," Andy says sympathetically. "Well, I have some good news. I looked into your mom's affairs, and you'll be happy to know that everything is clean. All legit. No liens, not much debt other than a little credit card crap and the house. You're the sole…um, survivor. Legally, I mean. I can't imagine the probate court will give you any trouble. So, there should be no complications."

"What about a will?"

"There's no will, not that I know of. You may know different. Obviously, the house and the assets haven't been fully tabulated—that's on you, of course, when you get the chance, let me know if you need help, I've got people I can call. But the papers I have make me think she hasn't drawn up a will. And that's good for you too."

"What if they were, you know, mentally incapacitated? Would that complicate things?"

Andy frowns. "You mean, like, what? In a vegetative state?"

"More like mentally ill."

"Ah." Andy crosses and recrosses his slippered feet. He's well aware of her family's issues, has been for years. "I mean, that does complicate things, but not as much as you'd think. I can't imagine your brother had much to leave behind anyway."

He's right. Noah's room was as bare as this apartment. As bare as his life itself had become in those final few years.

"But mental illness is a tough one," Andy goes on. "My ex-wife's mom had some trouble with this, so I know about it a little bit. Late onset is even harder, because it's so amorphous. Hard to pinpoint legally, hard to get a diagnosis. Most doctors I know would rather teach people how to deal with it rather than medicate them to death, the drugs can be almost as bad as the disease. Many times they're still considered by the courts to be, you know, of sound mind. Unless proved otherwise."

"Why wouldn't they want to help them with medication?"

"It's weird. I'm not a doctor, of course. But drugs—Thorazine, for instance—they only help so much. Schizophrenia's as much a case of too much dopamine in the brain, or a misfiring of the synapses, as it is anything traumatic or a type of brain malfunction. It's like a genetic instability, you know?"

Melissa's hand is magnified by her glass of water, and the whorls of her own fingerprints catch the light coming in from the blinds. "What's so difficult about that?"

"Well, lots of times, the symptoms present themselves only negatively. Like recessed symptoms, diminished emotional expressions, flat affects, that kind of thing. It's hard to treat, and even harder to build a legal argument around. They don't even agree on how to diagnose it. The most common is just when someone has two or, God forbid, more than two symptoms. Delusions, paranoia, hallucinations, that kind of thing." He runs a hand through his luxuriant hair, absentmindedly flits at it until it's perfectly imperfect. "All in all, schizophrenia's just a big legal mess. Thank goodness you missed out on all that."

"Yes. Huh. Thank goodness." She gives a showy sigh, exhaling the phantoms. "What a weird thing to call it. Schizophrenia."

"Why do you say that?"

"Well, *schizo*. Noah didn't have a split personality at all. He was just Noah. But broken."

"No no," Andy says, "it's not a split personality, that's a myth. My wife and I thought that too, but the doctors told us it's more referring to a schism between someone's internal and external lives. You know, what they *think* is happening and what's *really* happening, perception and reality and all that. It's not two personalities in the same brain, it's sort of living in a different delusional space than everyone else."

"Ah." Melissa's eyes wander to the window, she doesn't want to look at Andy, for some reason it feels better not to. Eye contact lately feels like rubbernecking at the scene of a car accident. "But let me ask you something else. Off topic."

"Sure."

"Is…is it, uh, genetic? Does it, you know. Travel in families?"

"Schizophrenia? From what I understand, yes and no. There's a greater chance, but the genetic combination that leads to mental issues is not a guarantee. Like I said, it's complicated. I mean, Joan of Arc heard voices, who's to say who's crazy or not?" Andy takes a sip of his water, thinking about this. "Clearly it travels in families. If I remember, it's like we can inherit a predisposition for it, but that doesn't mean we'll definitely get it. We only inherit the favorable conditions. Whether or not it actually happens is something else."

The room gets quiet. Melissa thinks about all of this, genes and wills and sudden violent deaths. When she makes herself glance back at Andy, he's looking at her with concern. "If someone dies," she says, "who gets their assets?"

"What do you mean?"

"Like, for instance, if I died. Would my boyfriend get my stuff? Not that I have much of anything."

"Oh. Well, that depends. Usually it goes to family."

"Can I draw up a will?"

"A will?" Andy pauses. "I mean, yeah. Sure. Anybody can."

"Is this something you can help me with?"

"Of course. But, I mean, is this something you're thinking about because of your mother? Because you're—you're strong, Mel, you're young. The odds of this kinda thing happening again are…I mean. Not great."

"It's nothing specific," Melissa says vaguely, not able to meet Andy's eyes again. "Not really."

"If you're asking can I do it? Yeah, I can do it. I can draw up a will easy. It takes, I dunno, couple hours." Outside now, in the parking lot, a car revs its engine—*roooom roooom*—and Melissa has a sudden wrathful vision of swinging at it with the crowbar she keeps in her trunk, spider-webbing the windshield with the violence tangled up inside her.

"Oh, you mean you want to do it *today*?" When Melissa nods, glassy and distant, Andy says, "Yeah, no, I'm not quite ready to do that now. I mean, I'd have to learn how to do it. For your sake. I wouldn't want to make a mistake or…" He drifts off. The car's gone, and the room gets quiet again. In the kitchen, the freezer's ice maker clumps a batch of ice into the receptacle. Finally, he says, "I'd feel better if you gave me a little time to…to fix it all up."

"Sure," Melissa says. She leans over and sets her glass of water on the carpet and starts the awkward process of levering herself out of the papasan chair.

"So," Andy says, now with an odd, unsettled tone in his voice. "You've got time to figure all this crap out, Mel. It's obvious what happened to your folks and it's all well-documented by the authorities. You'll have no problems claiming any of it. What there is to claim, anyway."

Melissa finally hoists herself out of the bowl chair and stands up. She waits for him, ready to be led out.

"Look," Andy says. "Is there something we need to talk about? I mean, you're all…"—eyes flitting across her body, her chest—"grown up now and everything. I was more pals with your folks, obviously, so I'm not sure where your head is at. But…are you feeling okay?"

She isn't feeling okay. She's stuck in time, suspended in amber, a fossil of herself. "It's just all this death, Andy. Kinda messes me up, you know? Things happen fast."

"You mean your mother and your brother?"

Visions of Seth helpless at her feet, like a projected film, jerky and faded, a movie of a memory. And then her childhood room at home—magazine pull-outs tacked to the walls, blacklight posters, the *click-clack* curtain of plastic beads in the doorway that were kinda neat at first but quickly got annoying when you had to duck every time you came and went. If only she could go back there now, go back and warn her family about the terrible things that hid in the future, waiting for them.

"Yes, well," Andy says in the silence. "Okay. Yeah, okay. Let's do it. I'll study up on it."

"All right," she says, and shoulders her purse. Produces her best fake smile. "Thanks, Andy. So…when do you think we can make it happen?"

"Your will? Um, can you give me a week?" She nods faintly, and he runs his hands through his hair again. "Great, great. I think by this time next week you'll be feeling much better, and you'll be a completely different person. I've seen it, believe me."

4

The sunset's a ragged wound in the sky as Melissa pulls into the driveway next to Jack's pickup, which is parked thoughtfully—almost annoyingly—off to the side, so her car can have the A Number One spot. Jack's good like that, he's a good guy, but he's also, she thinks with a tinge of guilt, kind of a wimp.

Pussy, that's the word you're looking for, isn't it, Mel? He's a pussy. That's true, but she likes him anyway, maybe likes him more because if it. Pussies are sensitive. Pussies take account of other peoples' feelings. Pussies don't go into peoples' houses and murder their families. No, Jack's being a pussy is *A Number One* with her.

But when she opens the car to get out, she's assaulted by the serrated sounds of industrial doom. For a moment she sits with the door open, listening as the song—if it is indeed a song; it sounds more like a machine shop with all the loudest tools going at once—grinds on. She wants to be game, she tries to make out a chorus or a melody but it's only shrieking and growling and sawblade guitars, and she climbs out of her car to see the kid, Gordie, kneeling half in and half out of the front seat of his GTO as he works on something underneath the glove compartment, his shirt's ridden up in the rear, exposing the pale pink moonscape of his pimply back. The music is way too loud, a boom box right up to her property line, in the little strip of grass separating her driveway from Gordie's own, speakers aimed at her place.

"Gordie!" she calls over the blare of the music. She wonders how black her eye looks in the dusk, she hasn't glanced in a mirror all day long, and judging by Andy Mair's reaction, the concealer wore off long ago. When the kid doesn't answer, she tries again, louder: "*Gordie!*"

He extracts himself from the passenger seat and looks over, and his face falls into a mask of scorn. "*Get off my damn yard!*" he hisses, then he stops, seeing her more clearly in the fading light. "Holy shit. What happened to you?"

"Gordie, look, I know—"

"If you don't get off my yard, I'm gonna call the cops!"

The strip of grass between their driveways is five feet wide, if that, and if she's in Gordie's two and a half feet, it's by mere inches. Better to try the sensible route. "Come on, Gordie, we don't have to—"

"If you don't get outta my yard, it's trespassing. You'll go to jail!" He stands up and swings the smooth dark curtain of hair out of his face. It's glossy, catching the last of the light in the sky in a smooth canopy of lustrous brown.

"Gordie," she says, her babysitter years coming back to her now, dozens of nights of appealing reasonably to preschool maniacs and bedtime lunatics. "Please—"

"You're killin' my grass! That's at least a misdemeanor right there!"

Melissa only stares at him now, her eyes dark in the dusk, and something in him seems to take stock, to slowly shift into...what? She isn't sure if she looks scary—her face swollen and bruised, maybe even monstrous in the right light—

or if there's something else, some unexpected strangeness in her gaze. Whatever it is, Gordie takes a nervous step sideways, tightens his fist around his screwdriver, and, looking more spooked than anything else, without a word he turns off the radio. Melissa points at him—*Excellent choice, kid*—then traipses across the driveway and goes in through the front door of her house.

5

"Hey hey," she says, and shuts the door behind her. The house is dark, which is odd because the smell of Chinese takeout hangs heavy in the air—sesame oil and ginger and something sour and cloyingly sweet, ketchup and pineapple, maybe, or corn syrup. She goes into the kitchen and turns on the light—and then stops, feeling a sense of numb unreality. A displacement of intent in the air, palpitations of leftover rage, the kitchen looks exactly as it usually does, her mind instantly catalogues its tiny various details—dishrag in the handle of the refrigerator door, faucet dripping on the ceramic sink divider so it doesn't *plop plop plop* you into madness, kitchen rug still at a perfect obsessive-compulsive 90 degrees to the counters. Everything almost exactly in place.

Almost. On the counter, a white take-out bag sits upright and a little lonely, but a brown liquid—garlic sauce, by the smell of things—has leaked out from the bottom of it and is amoeba-ing across the counter. Still spreading, in fact—it hasn't yet reached the edge, but in another 30 seconds it will, unless it slows to a dried film first.

"Jack?" Melissa lifts the bag out of its own mess and starts to wipe away the sauce with the dishrag, but that's when she gets a better view of the living room. It's a different scene in there—that part of the house is a disaster, bookshelves overturned, vases and empty drawers and couch cushions jumbled across the floor. Wall photos cracked, broken glass littering the dark carpet like raindrops.

All of this is absorbed in the blink of an eye, her gaze flickers from point to point, seeing but not seeing, comprehending but not really, the only thing that moves is within her—a giant sense of doom, lifting like a leviathan storm on the horizon.

"*Jack?*" she hears herself say again, her voice trembling now and uncertain. She goes into the living room to get a look down the dark hall. Nothing—no light, no sound, no movement.

Then—something in her peripheral vision causes her to let out a wheezing, punctured-tire hiss of air:

Above the TV, the words spattered across the paneling in a scrawl that looks disturbingly like—well, in her sudden blaze of stupefaction, no use thinking about that.

"*Jack!*" Her voice is loud and shrill in the empty spaces. Pounding in her temples. She takes in the room again, quicker now, wiser eyes. Nothing, no sign of anyone.

She drops her purse on the floor and, her brain burning so hot lava should be pouring from her ears, she runs down the hall and into the bedroom. It's dark in there. That sooty smell of sesame oil and soy sauce again, and a wild thought pops up—*You'd better not be eating in my bed, buster*—as her hand finds the light switch and flips it on.

And there's Jack, lying in her bed. His bald head tilted back, as if asleep. But a motley collection of icepicks—some plastic-handled, yellow and brown and red and black, but the great majority of the handles are made from wood, there must be 15 or 20 of them—poke out from various bloody points in his chest. Two of them directly in his eyes, left and right, imbedded down to the handle, like a bizarre optometrist's gadget. Two more in his ears. His fingertips are black with blood, as though he'd been fingerpainting.

"Jack?" she hears herself say in a fever dream. Another thought comes to her from faraway—*what's he doing he's trying to scare me will he jump up with cheap bloody vampire teeth and chase me?* But Jack stays maddeningly, impossibly, terrifyingly still.

There's a squeak and a click then—the closet door, she's heard it a hundred times, she's even asked Jack if he could get some WD-40 and take care of it but he never did—and in a searing panic she turns and sees a man stepping out. Grinning.

"Paging Nurse Melissa," the man says. His voice, deep and grainy with mucous and food, needs to be cleared. "White courtesy telephone, please." And then he does clear it.

It's the guy from her mother's house, the big guy, the burly guy, the one with all the hair, the one who killed her brother and her mother, he killed both of them. For the first time Melissa gets a good, close-up look—he's big and broad, with a belly and a bad haircut and what are surely emotionally painful acne scars, and his sociopath's dispassionate glare and a psychopath's bright, gleeful smile—business up top, party down below. He wears overalls, stained and sagging like he just came from the farm, the dark smears along the front and down one leg which Melissa at first takes to be blood, but most likely it's oil or brake fluid, the spots are old and dried. He's spearing lo mein out of a take-home food carton with a red plastic fork.

"Those fuckin' things are cheap, dearie, but they add up," he says. "Cleared out the Wal-Mart of every one. And I won't get reimbursed for those, by the way, no petty cash for me, so as I see it you owe me close to seventy bucks. I saved the receipt, in case you want it." He takes another messy bite of lo mein. Through a full mouth he says, "But hey, I give you points for imagination, there ain't been a true icepick aficionado since Abe Reles in the 30s and 40s, he was a little guy, you know, one of those Murder Inc. types. Used to stab his victims in the ear because it made the cops think they'd died of a cerebral hemorrhage. He was a pro's pro, not some messy, sloppy fat bastard like me. So I see a lotta potential in you, honey."

Without thinking, without a single coherent spark of a thought in her head, Melissa dashes to the bed where Jack lies motionless and digs under the mattress for the knife. It's firm and hard and good, all those things at once, and she pulls it out and with two trembling hands wags it threateningly at the man.

He grins that charnel house smile. "Thought you'd start a war with us?" he says. He takes another forkful and stuffs it into his mouth, the noodles swipe along his beard like a dirty mop. He advances, steps into the center of the room, chewing mightily, and Melissa backs away, back around toward the door, toward the hall.

From the corner of her eye there's a flash of movement—someone else out there—and she turns and sees another guy, a ghost in the hallway, in the bathroom, musta been in the bathroom, *those fucking blue curtains,* then he's on her, his hands hard and painful around her wrist, and he twists the knife out of her grip. It falls to the carpet as he wraps his arms around her torso in a bear hug and drags her squirming up the hall.

They end up back in the torn-apart living room. "Not sure why," the big man says as he ambles out of the darkness and into the light of the kitchen. There's an odd, diplomatic calm in his voice. "We know who you are. We know where you live. It's so easy. Where you and your honey-bunny work."

Melissa fights against the guy behind her—it's the same chinbeard guy who was in the car with Teddy, she's sure of it—and he clasps her wrists and twists them painfully behind her. The big man steps up and leans close in her face as she fights and grunts like an animal, he has a lazy eye, one bright hazel pupil staring off just slightly.

"Might as well be neighborly, know what I mean? Since we're old friends and everything. So. I'm Moreau, and this here's Garza. Pleasure to meetcha." In the half-light, his yellow, tobacco-stained teeth glisten. "You took out Seth and Teddy and they didn't do nothin'. Seth's a good kid. Now his little girl's got no papa. And Teddy... Well. You're just lucky he never got proper hold o' you. Woulda ripped your fuckin' head off, blondie, and fucked you right in the neckhole."

A guttural wordless moan of rage and despair rises from somewhere, Melissa realizes it's her own, and she fights and scrabbles against the guy behind her.

"Take a look there," the man says. He's pointing at the writing on the wall. *SHADOWDAYS*, it says, the dripping dried now to a black crust. "What do you think? Too on the nose? I told Garza it wouldn't work, sends the wrong message, too obvious, it gives away too much. But he was right as usual, I'm startin' to like it, it's growin' on me." He tosses the lo mein away. "Your boy wrote it. Or was made to write it. He asked us why that word, and I told him, welp—today's the day everything gets really fuckin' dark."

Melissa uses this moment to kick at the man behind her, and they step-stagger a few feet into the middle of the room.

"I was hoping you could read it to me," the big guy's telling her now. "What does it say?" Melissa doesn't answer, only a feral grunt as she tries to free herself—but the big man steps up and punches her in the face.

The sound is flat and unsentimental, dead water slapping the deck of a boat, and the feel of it's oddly familiar and for a moment everything goes white and cottony, the edges irising in like the closing of a lens. They must have reeled back, senseless for a blanked-out moment, because when she can feel anything again—it had to have been instantaneous, but it feels like minutes have passed, there's a time when the world just isn't *there*—a dampness washes down her face now, a dripping from the ridge of her brow.

"*WHAT DOES IT SAY?*" Moreau yells in her face. Spit and particles of food spatter across her nose and cheek and the man behind her yanks her around to face the words on the wall again. Her legs sling against the counter, the breakfast bar that Jack always wanted to put chairs at so she could sit there and talk with him while he cooked, but all the chairs they found on their few shopping trips were the wrong kind, or too tall or too short, so they never did end up buying any, and without thinking she lifts up her feet and pushes against it with everything she has.

The guy behind her—*Garza, Garza, that's his name*, Melissa thinks insanely—stumbles backwards, over the metal and glass coffee table that Jack bought from Goodwill, the one she hates but there was no other table, so they lived with it. But now Garza loses his balance and takes her with him, and the table collapses under their combined weight, splintering glass and making a loud crash in the room, and Melissa feels her hands go free. Garza is tangled up in the table with both of their weight and now he's crammed into it, snarled like a nerd stuffed in a trash can.

Without a pause, she skitters over to her purse and thrusts her hand in it. Before the big guy can reach her, she comes up with the little can of bear spray that Jack got her. She flips up the cap and squirts it hard in his face.

He's quicker than he looks, he sees it and manages to mostly cover himself with one beefy forearm, but Melissa doesn't wait—she sprays it at the other guy behind her, still struggling with the coffee table, he does get a full blast, an aerosol jet of caustic liquid which immediately chokes his eyes. As the two men curse and kick and grope painfully in her general direction, in a heartbeat Melissa's on her feet and out the back door.

6

The best she can manage is a kind of limp-stumble across the weedy backyard—something tender in her ankle, it must have twisted somehow in the fighting—but before she's halfway across, the back door bangs open and behind her comes the big guy, face wet, eyes red and swollen under his beard, lurching like Frankenstein's monster through the doorway. A rush of breath escapes from her, a panicked moan or a burrowing behind her eyes that pushes her to run harder, and at the chain link fence she steps up and swings herself over just as the big guy snatches at her pants leg.

She lands hard on her ass. The man begins to vault himself over, his bulk dark against the night sky and the branches of the big oak half-dead in the backyard, a black shadow glinting in his hand, its straight-edges and curves delineated more by the darkness than anything else, and she scrabbles up on her feet and flees for the nearest house. There's a light on there, and the back door is stupendously, miraculously open. A metallic shivering clink of wire and chain as the man clears the fence and comes running at her, and she slips inside just as he gets there, she slams the deadbolt closed and, sobbing now, goes limping into the living room as the back door window explodes.

The living room is bright, the walls stark and bare. Cobwebs drip like party streamers from the ceiling, a slanted crucifix on the wall, TV chattering with some kind of game show rerun, *Match Game* or the *$100,000 Dollar Pyramid*, whichever one it is that has that grinning fellow—whatshisname, Gene Rayburn, the one with the weirdly long, thin microphone. And an older woman, lumpy, her face like a withered mask, gaping at Melissa from her recliner, and also that kid, the kid with the car and the hair—*Gordie*—shocked, leaping up from the couch. "What the *fuck!*" the kid says.

But now the big man bursts into the living room, his heavy presence shifting the air like a wind, bringing with him the white-hot terror of panic and an icy dreamlike need for him to be elsewhere, to be gone, *begone*—and Melissa swings her arm around and surprised to find she still holds the pepper spray jets him point-blank full in the face.

He screams and grabs his eyes. "*FUUUUCKKKK!!*"

The gun wavers in his hand but Melissa can't take it from him, she'll just end up getting herself killed instead. And this house is a trap, of course it is, it's a dead end here just like the last house. The only choice is out—out and away.

But the big guy has stepped forward now, blocking the rest of the house, his gun waving blindly around the room, Melissa sees it fire before she hears it, a little explosion of force and percussive fire, *BOOM!* and the wind of it brushes her face and instinctively she ducks to the floor. She slides over and stays low and still and not breathing against the wall. Moreau's eyes are swollen shut, weepy and red as he blind-waves the pistol here and there. The barrel wobbles over her head and she holds her breath and closes her eyes, tears leaking as the little black hole, its deadness reaching down and tapping into the dead cosmic void itself, searches back and forth above her.

A strange stillness comes over the room. The big man snuffs, the kid standing there, frozen. The old woman hasn't moved, if she ever did. For a surreal moment, they all listen as the whisper of a car passes outside.

Then the old woman lets out a mouse squeak of fear—"*Awwwpp!*" is what it sounds like—and the big man spins and fires blindly again—*BOOM! BOOM!*—twice this time. A great red Jackson Pollock appears on the wall behind her.

In a fit of desperation, Melissa scrabbles past the big man, past his leg—centimeters from his work boot, the frayed orange stitchings of his overalls, a smear of red mud on the cuff—and crawls back into the kitchen.

She starts to head back out the door, and then stops. A keyring on the counter, with a key. A car key. Her own keys are back in her house with her purse, too far away and lost among the rubble of her things and that other guy, what's his name. And this key—it's only one, one car key on a keyring. But attached to it is a teeth-baring, jewel-eyed peach pit monkey.

"*HEY!*" the kid cries from the other room, and there's another *BOOM! BOOM!* muffled now by the walls. Melissa snatches the keychain and slams out the back door.

But the other guy, the dude—*What is his name?*—is mounting the fence, he can hardly see, gauging by the clumsy, grasping manner of his climbing. Melissa sprints around the far side of the house, through the little metal gate there, which is open, *thank God for lazy-ass people*, and around the side of the house and into the front yard.

The neighborhood's just as she left it less than five minutes ago, hushed, not quite full night, still a scar of maroon in the western sky—

—and she stops suddenly, wondering if any of this has happened at all. Is it a dream? Will she wake up, sit up thrashing? She feels unmoored from herself—there's a stumbling sense of disorientation—*And wait*, she thinks, *what am I doing? I'm so stupid, Jack's gonna find this so goddamn funny*, crickets ratcheting up and down all around her, the air cool, a gorgeous and pleasant autumn night. And Melissa, lost in reverie.

7

There's no one but her and the little baby, the incubator, and two empty sleeper chairs, their footrests kicked mysteriously back. The window, gazing out on rooftops, gravel, hot cars arranged in rows, far distant hazy hills. It's cool in here. The baby sleeps, half on his side, little Joshua James, full of tubes and seeming stillborn, the rise and fall of his tiny chest only noticeable if you look for it. The synthetic wonder of science all around him, modern medicine, miracles and wires and a wall of red-socketed electrical outlets, waiting for some arcane and mysterious purpose. Outside in the hallway, voices pass, laughter and a smoker's cough and more laughter, Melissa approaches the incubator, tiny blue bottle in her palm, her fingernail pries off the little safety cap and there's the IV—

8

Then another shot—*boom!*—not quite as loud, and she blinks. She's back.

The car, the kid's goddamn muscle car, parked in the driveway, its nose pointed wonderfully out to street. She sprints across the lawn and opens the door and jumps behind the wheel. There's a glint of something in her peripheral vision, and in the side mirror she sees the front door of the house open and a dark shadow dashes out. "*Wait!*" the kid shrieks. He lopes across the yard and opens the rear door to the car.

Garza—*That's his name, Garza*—is coming around the side of the house as the kid leaps into the back seat. "*Fuckin' go!*" he bawls.

Melissa jams the key into the ignition and the car starts with a glasspack roar and the mirror catches the big man lurching like a ghoul across the yard toward them. Garza's furious face scrabbling at the window as the engine roars and the car fishtails across the yard over the gutter and into the street. The tires catch pavement and Melissa and the kid in the back jerk as they burn rubber and peel off, in seconds they're down the road and careening through the electric night, dark rows of dark houses, small blue and yellow smears flickering in the twilight geometry of black.

gordie

1

Suicide has called to her before. It's her siren on the rocks, her safety hatch, her contingency plan if all else fails. It doesn't matter how, it's all the same, she's kept it ever since she was a little kid, holding it delicately in both hands like a shoebox with an injured bird inside. She would lie in bed and think how delicious the world would be without her—a better place, simpler and more at ease with itself. She was always different, always weird—off, out of bounds, loony, loopy, unbalanced, whatever the hell you wanted to call it, everyone knew it even in elementary school, the other kids so simple and full of places to go with their bright futures and laughing dinnertime families, while Melissa showed up to school in checked pants and striped tops that didn't quite fit, and sat at the back of the classroom and went home to a house full of dread. She accepted it all, but the reasoning behind it could never be found—it just was. Her mother, Sandra, was certainly boringly normal in all the usual ways, almost maddeningly so, it wasn't her fault. It must have come from Big Noah.

When her father left, and her palpable darkness was within reach, young Melissa became an outcast, not the lowest of the untouchables at school, not the bottom of the public school food chain, but low enough for the other kids to treat her as if her condition was catching. The worst part of it was that they were right, they all knew it was true, even her. Time and again she proved herself different from the others—she muddled simple instructions that everyone else somehow got right, mixed up dates, showed up underdressed to school parties and overdressed to softball practices, she skirted rules and took detours and shortcuts the other girls wouldn't dare, she told lies, skipped school, shoplifted, lived by her own broken accord. Aside from being an outcast and untouchable, she mostly got away with it. Even with her crappy grades her teachers were nice to her, maybe sensing some untapped potential, but unwilling to work hard enough to wheedle it out. That was okay. The stupid little Stanford-Binet IQ test told her she was certainly smart enough, so poor scores didn't bother her in the least, she was bright so she didn't need to play by the rules and actually *be* bright in those silly performative *pleasing your master* kind of ways. It was a silly dance—you went to school, you did your best to impress others, a few of whom were paying attention but most of whom weren't, and then you used those codified conquests to attend other schools and impress *those* gatekeepers, and the hamster wheel turned all over again. The supplication of it was the worst part. Certainly there were a few friends here and there, other blunted souls, and some of those were, believe it or not, even odder and more damaged than Melissa, and where are those sad souls today, some of them are probably dead.

She dabbled in the usual food service-slave gigs, but in her third year of high school her reclusive tendencies seemed to fade out all by themselves. Enough with the bell jars and the bad attitudes, now certain selected boys were allowed to visit her compact little universe, nice boys, polite boys all of them or they wouldn't be there otherwise. The first when she was sixteen—Billy Dickey, his name was, not that he ever got a chance to live up to it. But Billy had a car, a red little snubbed-butt '80s hatchback Toyota with a Blaupunkt stereo that was his pride and joy, he talked more about that stereo than anything. Billy was a year older and from a well-to-do family, he always had gas money and beer money and movie money, and Melissa liked cruising with him on balmy nights after work, windows down, her fingers drifting along the seam of his denimed thigh. But Billy was a *Nice Boy*, which meant that Billy was *Headed Elsewhere*, legacied to a *Good College*, so their romance lasted only a summer. After that there came a queue of boys, some richer, some poorer, most of them only briefly able to distract her from her loathing of jumping through the hoops, as her father had said it, doing the eternal brown-nose boogie.

She wasn't university material, she knew that. Despite her smarts, sociology and politics didn't interest her, Algebra Two or Pre-Calc seemed made entirely of hieroglyphics, and when a car of her own came along—a third-hand Chevy Impala, a rusted-up metallic green yacht—it was all over, she became a child of the roads. This led only toward more opportunities to stray—cutting classes to nap on the car's wide bench seats, coming in mid-class with a pocketful of creative excuses, charming a report card from her homeroom teacher and then carefully filling in the grades to make it look like they were better than they were, it was all the same. Her mother would sign the counterfeit card, and then Melissa carefully copied the signature, slope for slope, curve for curve, onto the real one.

Despite this dark aptitude, her link to suicide lived on, it was the safety valve which lowered the pressure of everything else. Being at peace was part of her defiance.

At last there was a stab at college, a hot, treeless state school with zero prestige and fewer requirements for entry, and at that college there was a boy named Michael Morton, and it was with Michael Morton that Melissa's future revealed itself.

Gannet State wasn't terrible, but it seemed to attract the students no other school wanted. Michael Morton was one of those, a wary, dark-headed boy with bad skin, bad posture, and a lazy eye, who everyone in their collective genius for cruelty called Michael Morbid. Melissa first noticed him during her freshman year, he was always scampering down the hill near her dorm, feet slapping the concrete and making echoes that bounced up against the brick walls of the building, causing a hundred eyes to look out the windows to see the running young man who seemed ill-matched for the challenges of state school, not to mention real life. No one had to say it, everyone understood his upbringing and his family were somehow sad, or strange—deeply religious maybe, or at least very odd. But that bewilderment endeared him to Melissa, there was a kinship, she wasn't as pitiful as he was but they were similar in quality if not in kind, and she made a point to be nice to him. She sat with him sometimes in the cafeteria, wrote terrible heroic verse poetry with him in the library, smiled sweetly when he marched past her in the halls. Because of this kindness, he started to look for her around campus, in the cafeteria, he would sometimes wait for her outside her classrooms and people thought they were dating, which was awkward but mostly who gives a shit, she'd already accepted her life in exile while he still struggled with his. No one knew what he studied, nor did he ever bring it up, nor did he ever discuss his other friends, if he had any, he was just there. Always close by, always radiating an aura of abandonment, deterioration, and need.

Once he and Melissa went to see a movie together, cruising the highways and rural backroads to the distant strip mall theater in her big green boat, to see *Orlando*, which she found interesting but a little confusing, though Michael gushed about it on the way home in surprisingly insightful terms. But when she pulled up to his dorm to let him off, he dawdled in the passenger seat, breath whistling through his nose, while Melissa stayed quiet due to the sense of distress in the air that she didn't dare acknowledge or disturb, he was trying to work up his courage to kiss her and failing. It was as painful as if he really had kissed her. Finally the desperation broke and he opened the door and got out. He said, "See ya later," and disappeared from the pool of light inside the car, and also her life, except for one last time—the whole regrettable business with Kevin Schiemann.

Kevin Schiemann was one of the school's BMOC's—a frat boy, once president of the student council, a young Republican who would later skate off to law school and an internship with a state senator. Despite Michael's shyness, Kevin noticed him, and in his casual cruelty made a point to make him miserable every chance he got—taunting him on the sidewalks, mocking him in Economics, jeering at him as he lumbered across the stained carpets of the science building. It got so bad people said they could see poor wall-eyed Michael Morbid visibly trembling when he saw Kevin coming. To Kevin, of course, that was all part of the fun.

At the time, Melissa had taken to trekking around the small college town in the evenings, past sleeping houses and down the dark Main Street, and on weekends she took longer, extended walks that led her into the surrounding neighborhoods and suburbs. It was her way of keeping fit, mentally and physically, and on her way back, particularly when it was late, she would thread up Fraternity Freeway, the bare lane with large crumbling houses on either side, which led right into the gated main entrance to the school.

This one night—it was a chilly Friday early in her second year, because she was wearing her too-big bright yellow jacket, the fitted one that made her look like a giant bumblebee—she'd been hurrying past one of those shabby mansions when a crowd outside caught her eye. It was a party, there was the usual throb of bad music, the splatter of voices, but these partiers weren't just reveling, they were clustered around two people, college boys who were fighting with fists. As she got closer, Melissa saw that one of the boys was Kevin Schiemann. The other was Michael Morbid.

Even from the sidewalk, it was clear Michael didn't have the upper hand. Melissa would find out later he'd passed by here and was lured over by false promises of new friends and free beer, she couldn't imagine what idiot state of mind had caused him to think he'd be safe among these privileged pricks and prickettes, but now he seemed to have lost his nerve and was trying to get away, sometimes cowering, sometimes attempting to hit back, he was pushed back into the fray by the mob of college kids surrounding him. Kevin's fists flung out to connect with Michael's eye, his ear, his temple, his cheek. In the harsh floodlights, Michael's face was red and swollen, and even from where she stood it didn't seem like he had much left in him, if he ever did. One hand held out for mercy, the other pulled in to shield himself.

Melissa didn't know Kevin Schiemann, only his reputation—kind of a dick, popular and handsome, a child of entitlement—but she did know Michael Morbid, they were friends, and it was as if her mind completely shut off, the grievance of it made her see everything in strobing flashes of red. Looking back, there were only glimpses, like blurred Polaroids, of what happened next.

Her shadow led the way as she went unnoticed along the edge of the property and around the side of the house, looking for something, not sure what, but when she found it and resurfaced into the light with it in her hand, the crowd of people didn't react—or if they did, they didn't make any attempt to stop her. As she approached the fighting boys, it might even be said the group parted around her, in her memory there were glimpses of laughing faces turned her way, teeth bright and wet, glossy hair and cherry mouths, blush-cheeked boys with loosened ties and dull malice in their gaze.

Kevin Schiemann didn't notice, he was too busy mooning for his friends, success already at hand, not that it ever was in doubt. Melissa wove her way toward him, calmly stepped up behind, and—with a smooth stroke that was the talk of the weekend—broke the mallet putter she'd found behind the house across the back of Kevin's skull.

This was, not surprisingly, the end of her college career. Kevin went down in a pool of blood, suffering a concussion, hospitalized overnight, mostly for observation. Michael Morbid slunk away into the shadows, nursing a sprained hand, a broken collar bone, and a fractured supra-orbital ridge. He dropped out of college four days later. Melissa never saw him again, but then she never saw any of them again—the school expelled her, never to return.

In the end, after all the failing and flailing, she did only what she was destined to do—fell into a depression, dawdled again with suicide, and then enrolled in a community college and got her nursing degree. Mother and daughter ever the same. With her Associate's in hand, she and Sandra found a place for her an hour away in Birmingham, and while waitressing and cleaning houses for money, someone rang her about a job, in Baptist Medical's neonatal ICU.

2

But now she drives in a frenzy—screaming and shrieking and crying as the violence in her head rewinds and unsprings itself again and again. Blood on the wall, blood on the floor, blood on Jack, blood in her head. There may have been a shriek at the dashboard, a hard-knuckle crack at the windshield, an elbow jab at the window—who can be sure, her brain is white hot, a blizzard, a void, for a time no one's there, the world merely an insensate mass of blind impressions. And then she's back—slowly, rising from black water, she feels the world returning, stoplights sailing overhead, flickering and stuttering as in a dream, streetlights just tracers on the edges of her vision as they pass, fast food places like Christmas trees, promising peace and pleasure and gustatory diversion, a carnival of earthly delights. Lucky she didn't cause a wreck.

Behind her, the kid sits upright now in the middle of the seat and stares numbly ahead. Eyes wide, hair in his face, but he doesn't seem to care, they drive silently now, going nowhere, just driving down wide streets and then into neighborhoods, dark houses like wallpaper along the sides of the road, bridges over black rivers, their hollows full of menace, trees sweeping overhead, and the stars beyond, unmoving and cold and hostile. Melissa has no idea where they're going. Until she does.

3

They park on a side street in a nondescript neighborhood. Surrounded by dark ramparts and fortifications, apartment buildings where—in another age, another life—Melissa visited a hundred times with hope and possibility brightening her fractured heart and showing her the way, not seeing the true shabbiness, the dearth and dirt of it. It's Jack's neighborhood, where he lived when he wasn't staying over at her place. It was always meant to be temporary, but it turned out to be years.

The kid, still in the back seat, stares wordless into his lap. Curtain of hair in his face, eyes recessed in darkness. Melissa lets out a shuddery breath, even sorrow's gone now, sorrow would be nice, at this point it's just the void of emptiness, a razed-out vacancy. "I'll be back in a minute," she tells him, and gets out. She takes the ape keychain with her.

In the moonlight, her blouse is soaked black, mostly on the left side. That table in her living room caught her just so, and now in the chill, the cut's wet and sticky against her skin. On the sidewalk two older people walk their dog—a little shar-pei, old man wrinkles and a muzzle sniffing up at her through a face like a loaf of bread—and they gape as she limps by, there's someone else further away, across the street, a dark presence more felt than seen, but Melissa ignores everything and wills herself to painfully mount the stairs, one by one, pulling herself along by the cold metal handrail up to the second floor, down the dark hall to the rear, to a door just like every other door. There's a withered little potted palm, one she gave Jack almost a year ago and he killed it immediately like he does all of his houseplants, but she digs in the dry soil and finds the key. No monkey keychain this time, not like the one in her purse nor the one in her jeans, just a flat piece of cheap brass from the hardware store down the road from Jack's school.

She opens the lock and steps into the apartment. The smell and even the feel, the *mood* of Jack, hits her in the darkness. Her hand finds the light switch, and then there's that same old undergrad suite where Jack slept and ate and shat—shoes and clothes everywhere, Ralph Waldo Emerson and William Blake posters on the walls, their old eyes shaming her from centuries back. Crusted plates in the sink and fruit flies dogfighting over the trash like biplanes. The layout of the place is not unlike Melissa's—small kitchen, attached living room/dining room, hallway leading into shadow. Maybe most apartments are like this. A photo in a clear plastic case on the countertop—she and Jack near sunset water at his parent's house down on Lake Samuels. It gives her a new gash of dread and sorrow to see him here—so happy and smiling, his bald pate glossy in the evening, she feels underwater again, everything in dreamy half-motion and submerged by cold rolling waves of shock. Memories of his hand around her shoulder, his fingers, his thumb digging into her, the grip like Big Noah's, like a guardian golem enchanted to keep her safe. She felt good with him—he was big, he had that paladin's vibe, the feeling when you're with him that everything's going exactly as planned, even when it wasn't.

She leans on the counter, breathes hard through her nostrils. *Well.* Everything isn't going to be just fine anymore, that's pretty much a given.

She digs through the utility drawer, past the hammers and the screwdrivers and the Allen wrenches, under the Band-Aids and the box cutters, and finds an old wallet where Jack keeps his spare credit cards he's paid off but hasn't yet closed. Jack was good like that—always planning, always saving stuff for the future, just in case. Money freaked him out, and so whenever he got some credit or a little something extra he put it away, saved it for later, there must be five or six cards in there. In his young years he had money troubles, grew up poor and even a little desperate—tales of filching dinner, of cold, kerosene trailer nights, delinquent phone bills—and he made an effort not to let it happen ever again. She stuffs the wallet in the back pocket of her jeans and goes around the counter and down the dark hall to the bedroom.

Here the walls are bare and somber, even with the overhead light. There's a feeling of absence, of Jack just having left, just stepped away, the reek of his shoes hangs in the air. A single mattress and box spring pushed up against the far wall, sheets tangled across the mattress and, well, not that clean, Melissa never really liked this bed, this room, this apartment, there's a reason Jack spent more time at her place than she did at his.

The closet door is almost closed but not quite. She half expects some bogey to jump out, the big guy, or Garza, but then she's up on tiptoes, her hand searching on the very top shelf. She feels around up there among the boxes and photo albums and finally finds it—the leather holster with the handgun he's tried to get her to target shoot with him on several occasions. She never did, it scares her. She has no idea what kind of gun it is or the company who made it or who was famous for using it, it's stubby and black and heavy and that's all that matters. Her fingers unsnap the holster and she takes it out and fumbles open the cylinder, something she watched Jack do time after time. Every chamber is full. Shiny and oily slick and full, it reminds her of little wasp larvae squirming in their nested cells.

She turns off the light and goes like a sleepwalker back down the hall. Standing in the living room, looking around, waiting for something to make her feel like things will be okay, she's embarrassed by the intimacy of being here in Jack's living room alone. Many nights, many laughs, on that lumpy couch. Melissa hates that couch. When you sit, you're either on one of the wooden slats underneath or you're off to the side, sitting at a tilt—horrible, inhospitable, that couch. It would be so fucking nice to cuddle there now.

Outside on the sidewalk, the old people are gone, the street empty of everything but parked cars and things she'd rather forget. Gordie's in the driver's seat now with the front door open. As she approaches, he turns to look at her with his thunderstruck eyes. "What about—what about grandma?" he says. "What about Lucy? What about her?"

Lucy. Boom, splat, that abstract expressionism on the wall behind her, that bloody Basquiat. What can she say? She doesn't know the people who attacked her either, she knows *of* them, that's all, has seen them before, but they're mysteries to her too. Especially the big guy, the one with the hair. Melissa wipes her nose on her sleeve and says, "I'm sorry, Gordie."

"Cops. The cops can help us." His voice shudders just above a whisper. It sounds odd, and his face is puffy with tears in the light of the streetlamps. "I mean, what the fuck? These assholes. The cops'll know what to do and—"

"Move over, please," Melissa says. "I'm driving."

"What?" His eyes scan her again, doubt crowding doubt, nothing too strange for him anymore. That's when Melissa pulls out the stubby gun and shows it to him, presents it to him. The barrel slick in the glow from the streetlights. For a moment the kid is silent, still as a photo, maybe not sure of the intent or the subtext of her message.

"Are you fucking kidding me?" he says. His voice, still quiet, has lost its hesitance, now it's solid and firm. "This is my car."

"I'm really sorry," Melissa says. And she is, she really is. "Move over or get out."

For a moment Gordie turns to glare out at the faceless apartments across the street, their dark edifices and angles, the lighted windows, petty fires burning against the unknowable night. He lifts his skinny body over the console in the middle and slips into the passenger seat. Melissa climbs in, and that's that. She jabs the ape keychain into the ignition and turns it, and the car roars to life.

4

It feels good to drive, to pass over the pain, to stay in motion, the hateful landscape never the same, all of it unable to reach her, to get hold and keep her captive. The world of pain and the world around her are sometimes the same, sometimes different, they meld and align and separate, but if she keeps going maybe she can outrun it all, outlive it all, everything feels so caustic how the world is conspiring to destroy her in these moments of weakness. But the freedom to head somewhere and then to get there, that part still feels fine—like a shark, she must keep moving.

They're on the industrial side of town now, truck stops, prefab buildings of indeterminate purpose, paint-stripped doorways and cracked windows where who knows what happens inside. Beyond that are railroad tracks and bridges, broad flat empty parking lots broken by kudzu gorges and blasted urban-waste creeks with trickling black waters hidden under weeds and bricks and trash. Melissa cradles her side against the blood and the stinging pain, it's really starting to hurt. There's only now the exhaustion, the bone-weariness, how good it would be for sleep to come to her and take everything away for awhile.

Gordie, his eyes flat and emotionless, like a doll. Staring out the window.

For the first time Melissa is able to look at the car. It's a GTO—leather seats, turbo gauges, a speedometer up to 160. A shit-fire, bad-ass ride. No wonder the kid's proud of it. Wasn't there a movie with GTOs, some old thing with James Taylor of all people? Maybe she dreamed it. The radio is an original model with silver knobs and punch buttons in the middle, *AM all the way, baby,* none of that clanging shimmering growling crap the kid listens to. She turns it on and a soft number comes on—*Gerry Rafferty, now that name is easy to remember*—the song with the sax, something familiar, it gives her something to cling to. There's a gas station up ahead, flared lights in the night, a satellite drifting in the outskirts of a planetary orbit. Jack used to make her watch those cheap Friday night spaceship movies—*used to.* These new thoughts shiv hard in her ribs, she pulls into the gas station and up to the pumps, it'll help her get her focus, who knows if they need gas or not.

Gordie seems utterly deflated, his profile sharp from the light of the pumps.

Melissa coughs phlegm. "You don't have to stay," she says. His pain is obvious, his perplexity and despair about what's happened, he's aware too that it's entirely her fault. If she had never run there, his grandmother or whoever it was—*Lucy*—would still be alive. For this, there are no words. "I can let you out and you can, you know. Get outta this mess. But you're welcome to stay. Or...or go, either way, I don't know. It's up to you, man."

Gordie stares into the floor between his feet, there's an old fast-food bag stomped flat under his sneakers and a lone french fry emerging from the paper like it's waving for help. Without a word or a glance, Gordie gets out of the car and slams the door and slouches into the station.

Beyond the car, beyond the lights, it's a void out there—a great solid emptiness, warm and soft in its nullity. The abyss calls to her, anything that doesn't have feelings and gnawing pain and memories and clenched-gut nausea, she should take off right now, that'll make it better, ditch the kid, leave him to whatever mess he'll inherit from the cops and from his poor old grandma, let him sort it all out.

She gets out, goes around the car and starts filling the gas tank. A shiver flits across her back—could be the night chill or could be she's in shock. The dirty plastic numbers of the gas pump tick higher and higher and higher—turns out they did need the gas—and in the back seat there's a jacket, camouflage by the looks of things, the rear door creaks as she opens it and lifts the coat to give it a look—size L, obviously meant for Gordie, who isn't fat in the least but will be tall when he's finished growing out of his lean-teen years. Meant for hunting, maybe. Across the back of the jacket are the words "Peace, Love, and No Mercy," decaled in a kind of Germanic, heavy metal lettering—all sharp points and Gothic fence-post menace. She slips into the jacket as the gas pump clicks off, all done, she replaces the nozzle and puts the cap back on, and with that great black bottomless hole inside her, she goes across the parking lot and inside.

It's bright in there, a greenish glow washing over everything. An old woman behind the counter, her hooded gaze catching Melissa's every move, and Melissa knows that her blouse is soaked with blood but the jacket hides most of it. Gordie's nowhere to be seen. Perhaps he ran out the back or hides out from her in some storeroom somewhere. *Just let him go, it's better that way,* he'll slow her down and keep her from filling that bottomless hole back up.

Melissa limps down the aisle and clutches a loaf of bread to her breast, then moves over to the refrigerated area to get a soda. On her way to the front, she swipes a package of cashews and a bag of chips, *Ranch-O* flavored, and a couple of chocolate bars. Goes to the counter and places her food carefully, delicately, onto it. Now that she gets a better look at the old cashier, it's hard not to recoil—red splotchy sores down her face, oozing suppurations which seep and glisten, that awful torment between a pain and an itch. The woman needs to be treated, to wash the wounds with antiseptic, cover them and keep them clean and moist, she should be in someone's care. "Is this everything?" the woman says.

Before Melissa can answer, there's a *bang!* from the far end of the store, and she spins, her nerves sizzling, ready to see a cop or that big guy rumbling toward her from down the aisle. But it's only Gordie, dawdling out from the bathroom in his heavy metal t-shirt—*Skuggämän,* it says, white on black, in some ragged scratchy font—and snatching a couple of bags of jellybeans as he circles back around. Without pausing or even meeting Melissa's eyes, he drops his candy next to her items. Then he goes outside across the parking lot, in the long silence Melissa watches him, he has an almost feminine grace, a natural athletic ease with himself, lithe as a dancer or a big cat, and gets back into the passenger side of the GTO.

"Is that everything?" the woman asks again. Melissa turns back around. The woman's sores are angry, mottled, infected, she really needs a doctor.

"Yes, ma'am," she says.

5

Who can say when the murmuring started? It just seems like it's been there all along, far in the background, the radio low, a whisper-voiced late-night DJ with the signal coming and going. And the voices are quiet, maybe it's all the interference from the electrical wires that rise and dip as they pass, the non-ionizing electrical fields and low-frequency magnetisms as the GTO rumbles over railroad tracks and down endless frontage roads. The no-man's land of streetlights and sidewalks and vape shops has opened its arms to them, the tattered fields and chainlink fences and cellphone towers have taken them in as one of their own.

There's a little flat-roofed motel out this way where she and Jack spent a lovely lost afternoon, and there it is—that old place, the Red Lasso, looking worse for wear now in its dotage. She pulls into a far space around the side, near the cracked dry pond of the empty swimming pool, and after a wordless moment with Gordie, she gets out and goes into the lobby.

It's dim in there, which puts Melissa more at ease. The young man behind the counter with a hump on his back like an old woman's, crooked and ridged even through his flannel shirt. Faded images of vacation destinations on the wall—Machu Picchu, the Scottish Highlands, the Leaning Tower of Pisa. A stuffed hawk glares down at her with dusty eyes.

She pays with Jack's card. Suspiciously, he studies it, the signature on back. "Where's Jack?" he says, maybe half-joking. He nods toward the far GTO, where Gordie sits staring at them with haunted eyes. "Are you Jill?"

"Jill's dead," Melissa says. All frame of reference is gone now, she's still adrift or at least not sure what's funny and acceptable anymore and what's horrible. Not that it matters.

"*Whoa*," the hunchbacked man says, stepping sideways, appreciating the dark humor.

She signs the bill and collects her key—no monkey this time, just worn silver metal and a plastic key fob. The rooms are exactly like when she and Jack were here, small and bland, with dark wood paneling that suggests another age, another optimism. But the blandness is helpful, bland is good, she needs bland right about now. Gordie's quiet, sitting on the chair in the corner and leaning back with his eyes closed, the stillness of affliction, the trauma of loss wafts around them both. She tosses the snarling monkey keychain on the dresser and goes into the bathroom.

The lights over the mirror are horribly bright, but that's okay, she pulls off her blouse and inspects her side. The cut isn't too bad—it's messy but it will heal fine, a few cold water splashes and it's already looking much better. The lavatory drawers are mostly empty, but one of them has a few old, discolored Band-Aids, which she carefully puts on. In the mirror her own shallow eyes stare back, night jewels sewn into a voodoo doll, she's never looked worse, not even after the death of little Joshua James. Aged half a decade in a day. Seeing your boyfriend with icepicks like goggles on his eyes does funny things to you.

Back in the main room, Melissa goes to the bed near the wall and sits. In the chair, Gordie seems asleep. "You okay, honey?" she says. He doesn't answer. She stretches out on the bed, it feels good even with this shitty mattress. Her bones ache. How can she go on without Jack? He's been her lifeline, her pillar, her port in a wicked sea, he saved her but she wasn't able to save him. She wonders if the blame of the whole thing will be its defining feature, like it is with Joshua James. She knows that she will—it already is.

But right now, her feelings—at least those on the surface, there are other ones, murky and half-felt, massive bodies only shadows moving in fathomless depths—are more about hatred. Now the plan is to kill, to strike out, to slice that man—*Moreau*, her mind spits at the word—into cat food. Melissa ate cat food once, on a dare, the wet, chunky stuff, it came apart in her teeth in a mealy mess and she gagged, it was horrible, a sour potted-meat roadkill smell. *That's* what she'll pulverize him into, not even chunks but turn him into a gritty, granular mess. Blood pudding.

The nerves ebb and flow with her breath, she's wondering how not to think of Jack—how not to think of anything, really, not Jack, not Joshua James, not even that Moreau fellow, that monstrous hairy lumbering Sasquatch. As her body slips beneath the soft murmur of traffic coming from out on the road, the occasional creak and slam of a car door opening and closing out in the parking lot, she starts to drift, to wonder in the far peripheries of herself if maybe confusion has come upon her again and this really is all a dream, a nightmare, maybe she's still out on the lawn lost in reverie, or maybe Jack's still here, still alive, it's the night terrors again. They could be on vacation, the two of them, he could be at the ice machine around the corner this very moment, fussing with and then tossing the little plastic liner away and simply filling the plastic ice bucket directly from the spout. Returning now down the sidewalk, under the awning's flickering bulb and around the corner, pausing outside the door—

6

—and she can't stop admiring his pale impossibly tiny hands, his perfect little fingernails, the tented vein where the IV goes in. His eyelashes. Her gaze lifts up the IV tube to the drip solution bag. The syringe in her hand, the fluid in it clear—so innocent, so harmless. Like water, a clear elixir, a fountain of youth. You could almost drink it, like a shot of tequila, except this wouldn't even burn. How is she supposed to—

7

She wakes with a start. Still in the motel room. Still on the bed. Still in her clothes, in the same position, like a corpse in a coffin. It's dark out, but a cool sigh of air across her skin tells her it's hours later. It's early. Maybe even getting toward dawn. She wipes her eyes and sees the room is just as it was. But Gordie's gone. She's alone.

Maybe he's on the pot. She licks her lips and thickly calls, "Gordie?" but knowing already he's not here. The room just a cavity, crowded with empty space. Even she's hardly there.

Stiffly, she rolls out of bed and gets up and pokes her head in the bathroom. Pushes back the shower curtain. Nobody.

Like a storm front, a panic comes upon her, it practically blows her hair back, the kid has run, gone to the cops, and now they're outside setting up, surrounding the hotel, pistols and shotguns raised and ready, men in riot masks signaling each other with silent inscrutable hand motions.

Aw, sheeit, a voice says from nowhere, maybe from inside her head.

She edges into the main room and peeks out from behind closed curtains—a mostly empty parking lot, bracketed by two bulldozed fields in the pre-dawn gloaming. Scrubby trees fight for life here and there. Across the road and farther off, a storage facility huddled in the gloom, lonely and forgotten and orange. The GTO where she left it, down at the far end near the pool, out of sight of the road.

The pool. Melissa lets the curtains close and takes a moment to breathe. Something sparks in her weary brain and she opens the curtains again, and sees again what she already saw—someone sitting out near the vacant pool, facing the cracked bowl of empty concrete. That bad posture, that shiny drape of dark hair is recognizable anywhere.

She opens the door and, feeling the chill, tiptoes barefooted across the parking lot. She navigates the chain link gate and enters the pool area to where Gordie sits at the edge, fully clothed and staring off, the far bright dawn just now firing up low in the sky. He's balled up, not even hanging his legs over the side, his bare feet bony and impossibly white in the half-light.

"Gordie?" He doesn't answer. Melissa circles around to the edge of the pool to see his red eyes and teary cheeks catching the light. In this weird liminal glow he's almost pretty, with a profile like that of an actor she had a crush on when she was a kid. Weirdly, the name comes to her from across the years, *River Phoenix, he looks like River Phoenix.* Cheekbones for days.

If there was anything left in her heart now, it would crack all over again, just for Gordie. He didn't deserve this. He has no part in any of this, his share of things is merely bad luck, he lived next door to a psycho chick, that's all, his light was on and his back door was unlocked, that's it. She lets herself down beside him and scrunches her knees to her chest in unconscious imitation of him. Birds chatter in the fields, calling to each other, and the breeze is cool but hints of even cooler breezes to come.

"Look," she says finally, quiet, almost a whisper, she feels yanked from that terrible dream she's still somehow in the middle of. "Why don't we ride you back into town?"

In her mind there's Gordie's grandmother, gaping at the burly man as he fires, and now a vivid red bouquet of June roses bloom out of her head. Not a painting, and not the dark rusty blood of reality, this color the most vivid thing imaginable, it threatens to overspill into other memories and intrude like a virus where it doesn't belong, onto remembered dresses and boyfriends' cars and her favorite barrettes when she was ten years old.

When he doesn't reply, she says, "I'm sorry, I made a mistake. Lots of mistakes. It's not your fight, it's not your thing." She works to get rid of it, the monstrous regret, she digs her knuckles into her eyes. "I'll just...drop you off. I'll get you out of it, I'll go and I'll tell them that you're not involved, that you're not—"

"I want to kill those *fuckers*!" Gordie yells. "I want to blow their *fuckin' heads off*!" His voice is shockingly loud in the morning. "They'll be sorry they ever—*ever*—fucked with me!" His jaw and temple work, in and out, his fists pump like he's gonna punch somebody. Then one index finger extends and jabs, he's confronting an imaginary someone standing in the depths of the empty pool. "I want to— I wanna *fuckin'*—"

He trails off into a cough of tears. Sad for him, and sad for herself too, Melissa takes him by the shoulders and squeezes him as he bawls harder now, lost in the hardship of missing pieces, absent family, orphanhood, or whatever his version of it was. She understands being alone, she knows survivorship. The pink sky unfurrows itself above them. He leans into her and partially unfurrows himself, and one of his bony white feet drops into the empty concrete bowl as his cries bounce off the hard planes of the hotel courtyard.

8

She tells him everything. Well, almost everything—every little bit of it she can spare, the break-in, the double murders, Seth and his payback, Teddy and *his* payback, and then the terrible retaliations. It's been such a grim series of events, they've earned their own title in her thoughts and are filed along with the others, a quartet now of terrible melodramas: *That Day. That Night. The Requital. The Retribution.* No need to tell him about little Joshua James, though it's hard to say why, the reasoning stayed below, down in the murky depths. But Gordie, after his bout of grief has passed, seems to come alive in the awful telling of things, his eyes bright with hatred and desire, he keeps asking questions, digging deeper, going beyond what she expects, he seems to have a zest for misery, a zeal for malfeasance, his concerns eddying around the very same things that made herself nervous—*Who the hell are these people? What were they doing at her mother's house in the first place? What were they after? Who is that crazy big guy, whatsisname, Moreau?*

Moreau. The only Moreau Melissa's ever heard of is the weird doctor in that old book about people being turned into animals. Somehow it fits, because that guy *is* an animal, a smart but vicious and violent animal, like a hyena or a jackal or a goddamn grizzly bear. Gordie doesn't automatically take her side in things so much as question her and her choices, second-guessing her opportunities and also the lack of them, but from what she knows about him it sort of fits, no doubt it feeds into his teenage genius for strategic and tactical hostilities. For now, feeling more alone than she ever has in her life, it's better than nothing.

And that's when the phone rings.

The phone is a smudged and battered thing of indeterminate age, as squat as a maroon toad on the little banged-up table between the single beds, and its antique ring clangs in the room with the bland distress of a civil defense siren. Melissa stops mid-sentence and stares at it, worried.

"Don't get it," Gordie says.

"It could be Jack," she says, knowing immediately this is wrong, but there's a little crack, a fracture in her thinking, that allows for any possibility. Maybe, just maybe, this entire series of events has been mistaken, misinterpreted, a mirage, a terrible distortion, there was an error somewhere and if there's one error there could easily be two or three, a whole string of them, maybe things are not at all what they seem, maybe Jack is alive and somehow she missed it, you just have to consider that.

"Listen, lady," Gordie says, his words coming slow, as though he's talking to a child, "I don't know what's going on inside that banged-up head of yours, but it ain't your guy."

They watch the phone ring and ring, and Melissa is one delirious heartbeat away from reaching over and picking it up.

"It ain't the cops, neither," Gordie adds. "There's no way the cops know where we are. Or them other guys. Has to be the front desk. Just the front desk, that's all. Maybe there's something wrong with your card or something."

Finally, the phone stops. The sudden quiet make Melissa feel dizzy, as if the very things she's taken for granted—gravity, air, wind, sunlight—are proving themselves at last to be false. She pulls off the plastic wrapping from the little cup on the bedside table and goes to the sink and fills it. She drinks, staring at the wall. Her face feels like a mask, like someone's made a cast of her face and put it on her.

"Okay," Gordie says. "I have another question for you." He's lying down and spreading out on the bed now, gazing thoughtfully up at the ceiling. Across the room, the blank grey eye of the TV stares back at them both. "Feels like I'm not getting the whole picture or something, like there's something very fucking crucial you're leaving out. Why were you off work for so long?"

She doesn't want to look at him; his eyes are too aware, too full of things it's better to forget. In the dim windowless corner there's a little table and a chair, and Melissa goes over and sits down. Across the room, near her bed, a beetle is traveling up the paneling, past a crooked print on the wall, two white owls perched on the branches of a tree. Their little yellow eyes gaze off worriedly, they know about predators and prey.

"There's one more thing I…I should tell you." She wipes a palm across her forehead, and then dries it on the thigh of her pants. It helps, for some reason, to keep her hands moving. "There was a…an incident. Long time ago. I…made a very very stupid mistake. I'm still sorry about it today." She tries not to cry, because if she starts she'll never stop.

Gordie's taken off his pants and sits under the covers with one hairy leg poking out, and now this gesture of comfort, this tiny sense of home, makes him look more than anything like a little kid, a sad lonesome child who's just lost his family. She takes a preparatory breath, and then she does tell him, everything now—her first job after college, little Joshua James Newcombe, how the medications were mixed up, *That Day*, the investigation, the firing, the three years of staring at the wall at home, everything—she at the table in the corner, the boy listening on his bed, as the windows behind the curtains brighten and the room gets hotter. It takes her a while to get through it all, her voice halting and catching, and coming on the heels of where they are, of what's happened, it feels as if nothing can get any worse, as if her life has become a long waking horror, a mudslide of bad dreams, and she can't seem to wake herself up.

"Holy fuck," Gordie says when she's finished. There's a long pause, and then he says, "That's some shit. You've got some bad juju in your life, lady."

Melissa nods distantly, thinking as always of that little boy, sad little innocent Joshua James. And also of Jack, sad little innocent Jack.

"But it all makes perfect sense to me now, you know. Don't you see? You're not seeing it."

She looks up at him. "Seeing what?"

"This little kid thing. It happened in Alabama, right? Birmingham? I didn't tell you this, I didn't think to mention it, but I saw those people drive by. A few times around the block. Then they rolled up and stopped. Those dudes, I thought they were friends of yours. A car let them out and then kept going."

Melissa shakes her head. "What?"

"But listen, here's my point. It had Alabama plates." Gordie lets that hang in the air for a moment.

Melissa's thoughts are thick, they can't untangle themselves, they lay heavy in her brain. "What do you mean?"

"Their car, I saw their car in the neighborhood. Casing the place. Didn't think anything of it at the time. But I know plates, I'm a grease monkey, it's a thing I do. In Alabama they number their plates by county, the biggest is number one, *numero uno.*" When Melissa stares at him blankly, he says, "It's gotta be Birmingham."

"Wait. You studied the Alabama license plate system?"

"Well, I mean, look—I was a kid, all right? Some kids do models, other kids collect stamps, first I learned flags, and then I learned plates. There's a handful—Alabama, Montana, Nebraska—that issue tags from population numbers, and I'm tellin' you, plain as day, lady. Somebody back there's pissed at you. In Alabama. Somebody with a score to settle."

"A score to settle?" She tries the idea out, tries to make it work, to make it fit. "For what?"

Gordie straightens up on the bed, excited to be contributing, his back against the headboard. It isn't attached to the bed at all but nailed to the wall, a pseudo-headboard, and his white hairy knee pokes out from under the covers even more, looking pitiful and gaunt, the limb of a prisoner of war. "Somebody's got a score to settle. With you."

"Like who?"

"Goddammit, lady. Think about it. Follow the pain. Who got hurt during the incident with the kid?"

"The kid's parents?" A weariness like a delicate silk scarf has wafted over her. She needs sleep, she could curl up right here and never resurface ever again. "I met them, Gordie. They were nice. Sad, but nice."

"People change, lady, you know that. I mean, fuck, look at you." He shrugs then, trying to soften his tone. "I'm not saying it's them, exactly. But *somebody.* Somebody down there doesn't like you, I'm tellin' you." He looks around the room and sniffs. "Hey, I'm hungry," he says. "I need to eat something."

Melissa nods at the little fridge near the bathroom, which she stocked from their convenience store haul. "Food's in there."

Fuck that! a voice says from somewhere, maybe from the TV. Melissa turns and looks at it, sees that it's off. Its dead blank eye reflects the white owls on the wall.

"Why can't we just go get something to eat?" Gordie says. "Something real?"

"We're in hiding, man. We can't have anyone see us."

The kid's hands are flat on the bed. Even from across the room, Melissa can see his knuckles are red and scarred—old man's hands. Mechanic work must be hard on the skin. His lean, angular face, half-hidden by his sleek hair, a boy not yet coming into manhood.

"Did you really kill that kid?" he asks again, as if just to make sure. "The baby, I mean." Melissa doesn't answer. "Look," Gordie says. "If you think about it, that's almost worse than the other stuff. The stuff from last night. This is a baby we're talking about, a *baby*. Something like that doesn't happen without some kind of…you know. Ripple. Repercussion."

"There were repercussions. I lost my career. My health, my mental health."

"But they lost their *child*. And then you lost your family. See how it stacks up?" There's a silence as Gordie contemplates all of it. "And why did you think these guys are after you again? This, what—this fucking *key*?"

"I don't know," Melissa admits. The monkey keychain is on the table. It's screaming now, its fangs glinting in the half-light from the curtains. "I honestly have no idea. I was hoping maybe you could help me figure it out."

"Seems pretty cut and dried to me. You made a big-ass mistake, some kid died. Some*body's* kid. Them people heard you're back on your feet, found some other people to come up here and make you pay and put you back down in your place. It's the only thing that makes sense. I mean, I saw it myself."

From beyond the window, the sounds from the road are picking up now, nine-to-fivers headed to work. "So what do I do?" Melissa says.

"It's not just you, lady, it's me too. They killed Lucy. So I'm in this now, and they're gonna be sorry. So fuckin' sorry." Gordie's face is ashen and sweaty, almost ill. "Okay. So, here's what we do." He gets up and in his underwear goes across the room and turns on the TV. It starts droning, volume low, almost a murmur, some cop show, some sandy location, scrubby brush, men in polyester suits with guns running down a beach, seagulls scattering from their approach and landing again after they're gone.

"Like any good movie," he says, staring at the screen, seeming to take inspiration from it, "we take charge. They're the hunters, right? We're the hunted."

I'm not touchin' it, a voice from the TV says, causing Melissa to glance over again. None of the characters had spoken.

"They're fuckin' with us, right? So, the question is, what are we gonna do about it?" He returns to the bed on his knobby-kneed little stick legs, and settles in again and tosses the covers over himself. "We know they're coming after us. They're still out there, looking for us right now, in fact. So we need to be ready."

"How?"

"I dunno. But see, we let 'em know *we're* ready." He pauses, considering. "Maybe we should scare 'em'." He digs in the table drawer and removes Jack's handgun from it. He slips off the case and aims the gun at the TV. "We gotta do something they won't expect. Set a trap. Go after them. It's the only way. You gotta bully the bullies, see. Let those fuckers know we're gonna make 'em pay for what they did."

Melissa leans back and closes her eyes. She feels magnetized to the chair. "How do we do that?" she says from somewhere distant.

"Well. We fuck with 'em. Maybe we surprise 'em."

He don't know nothin', a voice on the TV says.

"How?"

"Well, it all goes back to the kid, right? The kid in Birmingham."

"I...I dunno." She's barely keeping herself afloat. "I guess so."

But the manic energy in Gordie's voice won't let her sleep. "Look, it works in the movies. Like I said, surprise 'em. Bad guys waiting for Plan A, good guys go with Plan B."

Someone passes outside—Melissa senses it even with her eyes closed—and she makes herself open them, and she struggles up off the chair and goes to the curtain. Outside there's an old woman in the parking lot, her skin like shoe leather, shuffling along in bright polyester and dragging a leashed puppy along the pavement.

"They'll track us down eventually," Gordie's saying. "But if we catch 'em off-guard, we'll have an edge."

"So what do we do?" Melissa says, looking at the old woman. The sores on the woman's legs seep and glisten in the bright light.

"We trace it back. Obviously."

"Trace it back?" She closes the curtains and turns to see Gordie still admiring the gun. It's small but sleek. Sexy, in a way. "Back, how?"

"Back to the source. Back to Birmingham."

Birmingham. Melissa hasn't been there in years. She planned on never seeing that goddamn town ever again. "But they'll think of that. Won't they be waiting for us to do something like that?"

"Not like this," he says, and points the gun at the TV again. He closes one eye and sights along the barrel, aiming at one of the polyester cops. His voice is quiet, full of squashed-down rage. "Not savage. Not with a gun. Not with me. Not ready to blow their fucking heads off."

9

They need food—hot food, not the shitty, stale convenience store snacks Melissa bought, but something real to give them strength for the trials ahead. Protein.

While Gordie takes a shower, she gets dressed to go out and find them some breakfast. Bacon and eggs, Gordie insisted before he disappeared into the steamy bathroom, the towel wrapped around him like a kilt, with hash browns and toast and a couple of those little plastic jelly boats—strawberry, if possible, grape if not. But definitely not apple, apple jelly's disgusting. Melissa has no opinion on this.

The cafe's close, a mere quarter of a mile up the road and on the same side of the highway, so she ties her hair up and slips into the *No Mercy* jacket, which she realizes stinks now with Gordie's funk and also gasoline, and slips out the door and braves a walk down the gravel shoulder, hiding her face and wary of passing cars.

It's a little place, long and thin, with an old sign outside says *Deano's*. Melissa opens the door, and the air itself in there is oily, she can feel it on her skin. The inside is bigger than it seemed, and brighter, which is a little freaky after the literal and metaphorical darkness of the long night and her conversation with Gordie. It's mostly empty except for a few grizzled men, truckers no doubt, stumbling in for coffee and salty meat, they sip coffee in their solitary booths, each a ruler of his little kingdom. She checks the faces for anyone familiar. In the far corner booth, a lone woman sits, a black woman turned away, and a waitress flitting here and there, a tiny thing, she might have been pretty less than a decade ago, but that was before hard luck settled permanently into her features, and as Melissa sits at the counter, she comes over as though wafted by the oscillating fan.

"Help you, honey?" she says. Up close, Melissa sees her face is pocked with blackheads, she could use a long morning in front of a mirror clearing those things out. Melissa's aware that the only female in the place who looks rougher than this woman is herself. She tells the woman her order—two full, fried breakfasts, with two milks and two orange juices, to go. And lots of jelly, any kind except apple. The waitress writes it down and puts the order up on the metal wheel for the cook in the kitchen, all Melissa can see of him through the window is a bobbing, greying afro.

Birmingham. She hasn't been back since the charges were dropped. She moved up to North Carolina to be closer to her mother, to get away from the ghost of young Joshua James, and that shitty town was supposed to be in her rearview mirror for the rest of her life. But now that she thinks about it, maybe Gordie's onto something, there's a sick sort of logic in it now that somebody down there is pissed—*very* pissed—and is taking it out on her. Wanting some payback, maybe. Certainly, she's made no enemies up in Selleford, for the first year it was practically house arrest, a shut-in's life, her mom went and got groceries and medication and whatever was needed while she stayed in and slept, her world a sad circuit from couch to bedroom and back again. *Depressed* wasn't the right term, it was more like *obliterated,* she could hardly brush her teeth until Jack came along. But somehow, these people—these men, these oversized, hairy-assed wildlings—they were pissed at her since Alabama?

Or were they? There's that key, the screaming ape. What was that? Maybe somebody put it up in her wheel-well, in that magnetic key holder, stowed it on her without her knowledge. Did Jack put it up there? Angie? Grace? Maybe one of the doctors? What could they want with her? Her troubles had been settled three years ago back in Birmingham.

And then the ring her mother was going to put on Craigslist, but she remembers the men asking about a *key,* not a *ring,* a *key.* They were looking for a key, and she found a key, up inside her wheel well. The screaming ape key. What the fuck? The more she thinks about it all, the less sense it makes.

They vant for to keel you, a voice like a bad Dracula impression says from somewhere.

The waitress comes back and places two greasy carry-out bags in front of her and leaves with Jack's credit card. Melissa peeks inside, food on paper plates and swaddled in plastic wrap, the grease orange and already pooling, delicious and terrible for you. But her stomach growls—*hunger's good, right, hunger's healing*— and she reaches in and carefully removes a plate from one of the bags and sets it on the counter. Unhealthy or not, the food's fresh and hot and glistening, and she tackles the bacon first in huge, sloppy bites. Then the eggs. Then the toast— dry, no jelly needed, it crunches in her bulging cheeks.

Birmingham. What are the chances these people really are from Jefferson County? Maybe it's not about a ring or a key at all, maybe there really is some kind of payback project going on? There was a boy when she was little—Stanny Fletcher, his name was, a tan little hay-headed boy who always seemed to be in the wrong place at the wrong time. And then Stanny had finally done it, had gotten himself killed in their neighborhood when he ran out between two parked cars into the oncoming path of another. *Splat, whoosh, scrape, scrub.* Right on the pavement. It was a tragedy, everyone in the neighborhood felt it. But then the parents—who Melissa knew as mild, moderate, even kind people, the dad a baseball-loving middle-manager at a beer distributor, the mom a cashier at the grocery store—they changed, they became cold and hard and bitter. At first the dad was strangely calm and agreeable about the whole thing, as though under a spell, accepting of the generally held narrative of events and even hugging the driver of the car, a wide-eyed 17-year-old with his first vehicle. But he weakened under the grief of things, now he said he was gonna sue the kid, even though the accident was plainly little Stanny's fault. *I'm gonna teach that kid a fuckin' lesson,* the father had growled on Melissa's back patio, his face drawn and white, his fist clenching and unclenching. They took the young driver and his family to court, and lost, but the leftover anger, the backdated outrage, had stayed with Melissa for years.

She's still hungry. She peeks into the other sack. Another paper plate, more bacon and eggs, more toast, more grease. Feeling a little naughty, she lifts the plate from the bag, peels off the plastic wrap, and starts in on Gordie's breakfast too. If anything, it's better than the first—the eggs slightly cooled now and deliciously runny, the salty bacon undercooked a tad, just the way she likes it, crunchy toast with plenty of the little plastic jelly boats. Concord grape, of course.

Birmingham. Could that be possible? Could someone—years after the fact—be hired to come up and harass people—to fucking *kill* people over it? There'd been investigations, *That Day* was officially ruled a mishap. The courts said so—the law's behind her all the way. Melissa remembers seeing Joshua James' parents across the room as they came into the courthouse. A young couple, quite normal looking, even bland, sorta sweet though obviously traumatized. Joshua James was their first child, a beautiful boy with a full life ahead of him. They didn't notice Melissa as they passed by her, or she doesn't remember if they did, and in the courtroom when she was found innocent of manslaughter, they didn't make eye contact. When it was all over, they were among the first people, arm in arm, filing from the room.

Melissa finishes the other breakfast, bite for bite. Maybe the best breakfast she's ever had. But now there's rolling thunder in her stomach, a seasick listing and tilting, and when her stomach clenches again, announcing its intentions, she stands and goes around the counter to the bathroom. She just makes it into the women's room, empty at this hour, before the dueling breakfasts come back up in a lively mix of yellow, red, pink, beige, and orange. She retches again, stomach straining, neck pulsing, and mouth gagging, a globby mess stringing from her mouth and bobbing chunks in the stinking bowl.

She flushes, rolls off some toilet paper and wipes her lips. Leans against the cool of the wall like it's her boyfriend.

Birmingham. The car had 'Bama plates—Jefferson County, in fact. As plausible as anything else, but the more she thinks about it, the more it settles down like a skull cap onto her brain. It *fits.* But what about Seth? What about Teddy? They lived here in Selleford, in North Carolina, not Alabama, that's a fact. But also it's ridiculously easy for someone with resources to come looking for a certain kind of help up in these parts, and then find it. She rolls off another mitten of toilet paper and wipes her mouth and sits on the toilet seat with her eyes closed. The big man, Moreau, and the other guy, Garza. And Seth and Teddy. It's a game of retribution, of course. A retcon from three years ago. They looked for it, and they found it.

10

When she gets back to the room, Gordie's out of the shower and watching TV again. The chatter of it hurts Melissa's brain—interspersed with the usual television nonsense, the voices are no longer murmuring but saying *Stomp it!* and *Dumbass!* No point in asking him to turn it off—it seems to be what he needs, some game show now, the faces are smiling but the voices are clipped and angry or confused and bewildered. *Get back!* they say, loud and full of fear, or *You'd better not,* in low, pleading tones.

She puts the new bag of Gordie's breakfast on the table. "What took you so long?" he says. "Where the hell you been?" Melissa shakes her head, not sure how to tell him what she's been thinking. "What is it?" he asks, sitting up, worried now. He can see it in her eyes. Something's different.

And she doesn't want to hold onto it, shouldn't be required to, she wants to get it out of her and away from her. She tells him, "Gimme an hour and I'll be ready to go."

mimi

1

It's a simple drive, just a several-hour jaunt down I-81, with a westward merge onto I-59—most of the ride, once you're down off the mountain, as frictionless as a puck on an air hockey table. The road's mostly furniture outlets and firework depots hugged by gravel parking lots and weedy banks, red clay ridges with the sides blasted away, evidence of some long-ago war. Melissa's anxiety about the car being spotted is in constant churn—in the bright sun, a souped-up GTO is too easily noticed among the sober Hondas and gutless Toyotas, but Gordie assures her it's hardly the only muscle car on the road, in fact as they head west now toward Birmingham, the yard chargers grow like weeds, one in every ten almost, the South does love its Detroit muscle. Still, she drives tentatively, hesitantly, just plain slow, like her mother would.

STOP IT! a voice from the backseat shouts.

The kid's asleep, leaning against the door with a blissful, beatific look on his face—if angels had peach-fuzz mustaches and wore their hair shiny and long, that is. He *is* kind of appealing in his own way. Certainly, he's smart. He'll grow up to be a good-looking man, if he lives that long. She can't help but be grateful for his company, and regret deeply what's happened to him, for what she caused to happen to him, the kid's a bit of a question mark but he seems to not have much family other than the old woman—Lucy, the one who had her brains turned into baby food. Melissa knows from personal experience how shredded up it makes you feel inside, how you can hardly go on living a normal life after something like that. The simple answer is that you can't. Jack's death has cauterized her own life into one huge scorched-black trauma, there's an empty place in her now—a bombed-out crater where Jack used to be, like the red clay wounds on the side of the road. She wants to turn away from it, from this battlefield of her life, but she can't, first there's this situation, then she'll mourn for Jack.

"Left my goddamn music at home," Gordie says suddenly, sitting up and looking out the window. He sniffs and wipes drool from the corner of his mouth.

"What?"

"Music. I like to listen to music in the car."

"Yeah. And also when you work on your car at home." Melissa feels herself grinning, bleakly kidding, good buddies now, murder will do that, she supposes, make comrades of misfits.

"*Skuggämän,*" Gordie says.

"What?"

"The band. *Skuggämän.* They're Swedish. They fuckin' kick."

Melissa nods, mostly to herself, surely they do. "You like metal? Like Whitesnake, bands like that?"

Gordie lets out an impatient scoff, as though it had been trying to get out of him for some time. "*Fuck no.* Pussy bands. I like the bands with teeth, the ones who'll bite your head off if you look at 'em wrong. *Skuggämän,* they spew blood. Viking metal."

"Jack liked metal."

"Jack?"

"Boyfriend." Jack, with his icepick goggles. Blood on his fingers. That stupid word scrawled on the paneling. She watches the blue-roofed Stuckey's hurry by, sees a man and two girls going inside, and is oddly cheered. It's good to stay close to the real world, the actual world of everybody else, the world of families and pecan logs and good easy deaths.

"Oh. Shit, right." Gordie's silent for a moment, giving it a breath of respect. "I doubt he would have liked *Skuggämän.* Nobody likes *Skuggämän.* They want to make people hate them. They dare you to turn them off. They toured and slung pig's blood at every show and it was cut short because places kept getting shut down."

"*Pig's blood?*" What sort of problem did they hope to solve with such an act? She imagines them slinging it, shiny dark liquid arcing in frantic, smoky lights.

Gordie turns to her, lips thin with the depth of his conviction. "They're not playin' around, see. And we aren't either."

This makes her quiet. There's been enough blood for now, pigs or not. But Gordie speaks up again, "So, who are these people anyway?"

"What?"

"These people. The ones we're going to see?"

"The Newcombes. Uh...Cary and, uh, Mimi. Parents of that...that little boy."

"Carrie?"

"Cary. Like a guy's name."

Gordie sits against the door. "And what was his name again? The little baby?" There's a weird, unexpected softness in his voice, Melissa didn't think the kid had any empathy in him after his driveway antics but here he is, getting a little touchy-feely over a little baby's life cut short.

"Joshua James. Cute little guy."

"All babies are cute, right?"

"Eh. Not really." Melissa considers this, happy not to have to think about one particular little tyke anymore. "Some of them have pointy little heads, some have flat little heads. Bunched up faces, little old man faces." A memory comes to her, gazing into the NICU, all the infants sleeping in their hi-tech cribs. A matronly nurse drifting among them, making sure they're all breathing peacefully and their signs are strong, the window glass smudged with fingerprints from all the parents and family and friends who came to fret and admire.

"So, we're just gonna… What? Go talk to these people? Bring over a six-pack?"

"I was thinking that's kinda your territory." This thought brings a smirk to her face. "You're the one with the devious teenage anger issues."

"Hey, what can I say, I don't like assholes. But I don't think I'm anywhere close to you in the anger issues department."

A road sign that says *Birmingham, 91 miles* passes them by. They crossed into Alabama from Georgia about a half hour ago. "Seriously," Melissa says. "What *are* we gonna do?"

Gordie gets pensive, his thoughts seem to point inward, all the possible plans and schemes and machinations. "Well, I dunno. I suppose we should…you know, check 'em out. You've met them. Could you identify them?"

"In the courtroom when I had my hearing. We didn't say anything to each other."

"Would they recognize you?"

Melissa's memory—admittedly not very good, trauma will do that, it turns everything into hazy old photographs—it was mostly of them staring stoically ahead, not even looking at her. But there was one time, one single, searing glance the woman gave her across the courtroom before she'd left the chamber. Her wounded eyes peeking out from under dark, prematurely greying hair—a bleak, vindictive glower that plainly wanted to nail Melissa to the wall. That was one of the worst parts of the whole affair, the woman's grim hatred suddenly revealed.

"What would I have told them?" Melissa says. "*Sorry I killed your son? Oops, had a bad morning?* There's not much you can say at that point. They don't want to see my face, let alone talk to me."

"But see, what I'm getting at is, if they know your face, we can't let them see you. They would just call the cops." Gordie wets his finger with spit and tries to smooth a sun-wrinkle out on the GTO's old vinyl dashboard. "We'll have to sneak up on them. Spy on them."

"Spy on them?" This idea seems so outlandish Melissa has trouble picturing it. *Spy on them.* It seems like something a kid sleuth would do—Nancy Drew with a flashlight, vast moonlit mansions, staircases and shadows and creepy gothic gardens. "Why would we do that?"

"I mean, they're not gonna tell us anything if we just fuckin' *ask*. They hate you. Trust me. And the only way we're gonna learn who did it is if we do it carefully. Do you know where they live?"

Ahead, a bridge across the interstate floats toward them. The sign says *Trooper Richard Lee Riley Bridge*, the cop must have gotten himself killed to earn a bridge, Melissa thinks of a family, a young wife, a fatherless baby squirming in her arms. On the bridge a lone figure stands, slight and slender, a woman, could be Richie's wife staring down at the cars. The sun in the west, making her a silhouette. Then she passes overhead and is gone.

They hate you, they're dead, everyone's dead, a voice from the back seat says.

Gordie clears his throat. "I said, do you know where they live?"

"Oh. Sorry. Where they live?" Melissa lowers the sun visor against the glare. "You know what, I actually do know where they live. I went by there one time, drove by just to see it. It's nice. Big. Joshua's father, Cary, he's an accountant, it's in one of the town's older neighborhoods."

"Well that's—ah, shit. Look behind us."

Melissa glances into the rearview mirror to see several cars back there. One of them is a newer model, shiny and sleek, with a complicated front meshwork bumper. Lights up top. A state trooper. "Oh shit," Melissa says. "Is this bad?"

"Could be. I never got an inspection." Gordie draws a deep, uneasy breath, it's not a breath that sets Melissa at ease. "And I wouldn't doubt that they're on the lookout for a car just like this one. They communicate, you know, they talk."

Melissa's heart has already seized up, the panic will follow the waves of fear, it will come upon her gradually and then suddenly if she doesn't do everything to calm herself down. They'll ask for her license and with shaking hands she'll give it to them. And if she does that, they'll know her then, they'll slip cold steel around her wrists and haul her to jail, and for the rest of her life too. But that can't happen—there are things to be done, truckloads of things to do.

Behind them, the trooper's car moves into the other lane and slowly advances.

On the steering wheel Melissa's knuckles are bloodless and white, a strange cocooned feeling is coming upon her, a shroud of dread so complete it's almost comfortable, like the rest of the world was once a dream but now she's awake. "I'm gonna run, Gordie," she says. "I'm gonna outrun him. I'm sorry."

"*What?*" The panic has switched—jumped over from her to Gordie. "*No you're not!*"

There's a sound in Gordie's voice she hasn't heard since his house. "I can't let them take us in."

"You can't outrun this guy, lady! He's a trained cop. You're just a—a fucking pillow fluffer! Calm it down. The best thing we can do is to let him stop us and give us a ticket for the goddamn inspection."

Glancing in the mirror again, the trooper's closer now, he hasn't turned on his lights yet but that will come, she knows with a pounding in her chest that the lights will spark up any moment now. It was stupid to try and drive this far in such a conspicuous car in the first place, they should've hot-wired some ordinary wheels back at the motel, some Honda or Subaru, surely Gordie could have done it with his eyes closed. She wishes she could close her eyes, there's a whirling sense of vertigo in her head, she wishes she could lie down somewhere, pull the covers over her and will herself into a better dream.

He's gonna get ya get ya get ya, a woman's voice sneers from the backseat.

The hallway of trees—more pines, by the lean limbless look of them—it seems to ripple now, to close in, the highway is a quartet of stark, flat lines converging into a single point. In the mirror Melissa keeps her eyes on the cop car as it noses up beyond the others, the little cluster of vehicles like a school of fish all going the same relative speed, now they're all nervous to drive along any faster than the trooper, just like Melissa. The police car drifts out from the crowd and changes lanes again to get directly behind the GTO. In the mirror the cop's form is only a grey blob, darker than the road behind him, his sunglasses darker even than that.

Gordie sits in the passenger seat as though in church, eyes fixed straight ahead, hands helpless in his lap, and Melissa stares forward, still as a mannequin herself now except when her eyes flit up or over to the mirror without turning her head, the nerves in her face and on the backs of her hands itch, they tingle, her heart pulses in her ears. If the trooper stops them, it's over—*Jail or the rubber room, baby, for the rest of yo life!* says a voice. Her scalp prickles, sweat oozes, she feels frozen stiff, of course she'll confess to kidnapping the kid and the killing of sweet young Seth and handsome Teddy, she will tell them everything—even the fight and the chase and the killings in her own neighborhood. It's insane and unbelievable how quickly everything's changed, flipped upside down, somehow now she's the bad guy, but it's her own story and she will tell them everything and in her own way.

Behind them the trooper's car stays a steady but somehow sinister distance back, as if menacing them, taunting them. "If he sees the inspection he's gonna nab us," Gordie says. "And if he does—now just play it cool, be cool, we'll be fine as long as we're cool."

Melissa can't answer, it's hard thinking through the terrible chain of events—the trooper stopping them, collecting their information, radioing for a check, the check'll come back positive for shootings and kidnappings and icepicks. *It's her*, they'll whisper with a chill in their voices. Her thoughts go to the gun in her purse, and a vision of herself stopped along the roadside, waiting for the cop to get out of his car and make the long journey to her own, reaching down gently with her right arm and taking the gun from her purse without alarming his approach, and when he appears next to her in the window and asks for her license and registration, she will raise it and shoot him in the face. Very simple. A loud noise, a slight recoil, a tiny black hole under the trooper's eye before it fills with a rush of red.

"Steady, keep it steady," Gordie says, his voice a drone in an attempt to calm her. "You're doing just fine."

A hissing makes itself apparent now, sinuous and low, like wind or sheets of rain on the pavement and in the trees, but there's only sterile shadowless sunlight and the straight pines all around, it doesn't sound like her own breath hissing in and out, nor Gordie's.

Goddammit! a voice yells from the backseat. *You're messing it all up!*

The trooper's car drifts out now from behind the GTO, starts to come around them on the left.

"All right," Gordie says, his knee bouncing, "good, this is good. Keep looking straight ahead. Chill. Don't look at him." But that's almost impossible—the cop's presence pulls on the shredded periphery of her attention like a bomb about to go off, his car getting closer, coming up next to them, and then the impulse to turn and look is too great—with both hands on the wheel, Melissa gently, deliberately, twists her head and glances over.

It's Jack. It's Jack behind the wheel. A soft moan pushes itself from Melissa's lips.

"What?" Gordie says.

"Jack! Oh my God! It's Jack!"

But it's also not Jack—it's Jack *burned*. Face mottled with scorched flesh, his skin red and suppurated and seeping, behind the wheel of the cop car Jack drives calmly, hands at two and ten, staring straight ahead. He's wearing his usual ridiculous sunglasses that Melissa always makes fun of—they're big and bulbous like women's shades, he thinks they look cool but they just look stupid—and his collar is buttoned up all the way to the top, which is weird because he hates that, hates the confinement and the need to impress, there's even the red bothered fold of flesh he gets when his shirt is too tight at the neck. During his student teaching, his aversion to ties and tight collars got so bad he bought cheap clip-on ties, because the other kind made him feel constricted and strangled.

Gordie looks around her at the cop car. "It ain't him, lady."

Then in the car next to them, Jack turns his head, pivots to look at her—his round bald shining head glistening with pus or purulence, his eyes unknowable in their concealment behind his sunglasses. It's him, all right, and another moan pries itself out of Melissa, a pain she thought had been put away, digging a hole out of her.

"Keep it fuckin' steady!" Gordie yells.

Come on, you idiot! the voice in the backseat shouts.

Melissa gives another quick nervous glance over—the police car pulling slightly ahead now—and there's the side and back of Jack's knobby bare skull, the ears poking out from his head little round fish fins she would playfully grab from time to time.

"*Oh my God*," she moans, feeling buried by her grief. Her fingers are glued to the wheel, which is itself locked, if the highway turns or swerves to one side or another who knows if she can make the veer, the car might barrel off the road and into the trees. "I need to pull him over," she whispers, only to herself. "I need to stop him and talk to him."

But Gordie turns fully sideways in his seat and plants himself against the door. "Do *not* fucking pull him over—if you have any sense left in your goddamn crazy head, do *not* pull that cop over."

"What do I do then?"

"*Keep fucking driving!* Don't worry about that guy! It ain't Jack."

Slowly, Trooper Jack's car pulls ahead, and Melissa spares a glance at her speedometer. They're going a polite 61 miles an hour, the trooper must be going 65 or 70—not fast enough to leave her in the dust, but enough to get up in front.

"Keep fucking driving, lady. Let him go." Melissa watches the pale strip of road ahead, nothing but solid pines on either side, and it's easy for a person to lose themselves in the featureless corridor of the highway. Are they actually moving and traveling, or sitting in place? The dizziness swirls now around in her head, little curlicues of faery dust, as though someone's drugged her. "Keep it steady, lady, foot on the gas, *what are you doing?*"

Melissa looks up and realizes the GTO is drifting now, ever slower, her foot not on the gas pedal at all. Speedometer at 45 and dropping. Cars passing her now, she's edging toward the rear of the pack, going weirdly, conspicuously slow.

"*Keep it going, goddammit!*" Gordie's yelling, "Drive the fucking car! Or let me drive!"

Melissa presses the gas again and the car's speed picks back up. The trooper's car is solidly ahead now, the red taillights coming on and the cop car slows, and another squeeze of alarm from inside her. Another glimpse of Jack in his ridiculous sunglasses—how can he be wearing those stupid things, she bought him some aviators at the flea market which were way sexier than those black buggy things, but he always comes back to them—and then the cop car's pulling left, slowing dramatically onto the median and then into a dirt road turnaround through the woods to the opposite side of the highway. He's headed back west, back toward the state line.

"All right, yes yes, this is good," Gordie whispers. "Yes, he's turning. Good job."

But Melissa isn't feeling good at all. "I think that was Jack," she says. Her stomach's in knots, her face feels rashy, the floorboard is full of ice water. "I'd swear to it."

"It isn't your goddamn boyfriend," the kid says, calmer now, facing forward again. "Get your shit together."

Melissa doesn't answer, she's too busy thinking of Jack behind the wheel of that car, she wants to put her arms around him, to smell him again, to loosen that collar and ease the burned skin of his neck. But she keeps going.

"*Fuck.*" Gordie wipes his face. "If you don't get to this Cary dude and get him to call it off," he says, his voice sharp with frustration, "those two hairy assholes are gonna come around again and blow us both to shit and back. So keep it together, all right?" Melissa's eyes stay fixed on the road. "All right? *All right?* Are you with me?"

"Yes," she says, "yes, I promise. I know. I'm sorry. I'll keep it together."

Keep it together, Mel, she tells herself, her heart cries *Jack, Jack,* but she sits straight behind the wheel, puts her foot firm on the gas pedal and pushes the GTO like a riverboat headed due west, toward the port of Birmingham.

2

The Magic City—B'ham, as it's known to its residents—is a mid-sized American burg, tarnished for its past but now underrated in both its benevolence and its beauty. Laid like a blanket along the slopes of Red Mountain, under the canopies of a million trees, it fought and lost in its effort to keep up with Atlanta as the *Hub of the Central South*, which Delta Airlines supposedly sealed when it rejected the Magic City for its eastern sister, a fate which the town mostly but not entirely deserved. Despite everything, despite the years of doubt and the turmoil, despite little Joshua James, Melissa is surprised to find a soft spot in her heart for the place. But now as the GTO hums down Highway 59 on the eastern side of the city, past the airport, past the motels and the outlying borderlands toward the city skyline, it's a weird feeling, her nostalgia stitched through with tiny sutures of black dread. All her young life—school, high school, college, her first real job, all the way up to that terrible morning in the hospital—was right here.

Gordie sits staring silently out the window, hands folded primly like a debutante at cotillion. Melissa turns to him and asks, "Have you been here before?" It's as much to distract herself as it is real curiosity. Gordie shakes his head, his cloak of hair a perfect partition between himself and the world. "Not even once?"

"I haven't been anywhere. My mom and dad died when I was nine. I was raised by Lucy, and she never got out much. I had to take care of her and pretty much was on my own. This car's all I got. You won't even let me drive the fucking thing."

Melissa looks it over again. In the afternoon light, the dashboard and dials practically sparkle and shine, they're most likely pretty damn pricey, Gordie must've saved every penny he had, the depth of love and care that have gone into every detail are plain, a sad sort of sympathy comes to her and it's obvious what a tough time the kid has had of things—even tougher lately, no thanks to her, *How many lives you gonna ruin before this is all over, huh, blondie?*

"How did you afford this?"

"I used Lucy's old Buick to deliver pizzas. Three years I did nothing but save up for this car. Worked on it everyday."

"Well, it's a beaut, Gordie. I don't know much about cars, but this thing is sharp." She glances over, hoping to pry him out of himself. "But you never wanted to go to school? No college?" Gordie shakes his head. "No friends?"

"I had a friend," Gordie says in a small voice. "Kenny Martcham. But Kenny's in Brownersville Correctional now. Attacked his parents with wire cutters. He's actually kinda dumb. But we had some laughs in school, I guess."

The city skyline is closer now, a modest accretion of old buildings—once-grand hotels, anonymous insurance companies, nameless banks. Scanning them for the first time in years, Melissa feels herself pulled back into the past, the thought comes again how most of these upper floors surely were empty, their windows dirty and broken, the antique elevator doors cranking open to vast neglected square footage. No wonder Atlanta pulled ahead, Birmingham deserved to flounder, it's always been a ghost city in more ways than one, from the way its downtown empties at night, all the people fleeing to the suburbs and the strip malls, to its violent, racist past. A famous quote comes to her—*The past is never dead, it isn't even past.* Who said that? Hemingway? Fitzgerald? Whoever it was, he hit the fuckin' nail.

In the near distance the bluff of Red Mountain rises up, the high ridge of iron ore that divides the downtown from the near boroughs. The interstate bends around the city on the north side, and in a great bewildering tangle of an intersection, Melissa steers the car onto a leftward exit to another highway that leads south. Without a word they cruise as the high buildings shrink behind them now, heading through the deep Red Mountain cut, the four-lane freeway project which exposed millions of years of fossils and rock strata from back in the Paleozoic era, but hardly anyone noticed.

Taking care to mind the speed limit and signal her turns, Melissa merges off the highway and onto a neighborhood road, which leads them past a hospital and a suburban mall. Not long after, they enter into a tight cavern in a wall of trees—the late afternoon's darker here, almost evening under the heavy canopy. The houses on either side of the road are larger now, prouder, set further back into the trees. A small creek slithers through a dusky wooded area, with a path and quaint little bridges every so often, a dusky little roadside park. In another life Melissa can see herself pushing a baby carriage down these fir-shaded paths, a marriage to a cleft-chinned dentist or doctor, a plush world of babies and homemaking and lunches with the girls. Shopping in Mountain Brook in the afternoons, trying on shoes and cute, bright pants, getting her hair and nails done. It's a dream that came and went, probably for the better.

"This is sick," Gordie says.

Sicker than what?! another voice says from the back seat.

Melissa tries not to listen. "Birmingham's nicest neighborhood. Richest single zip code in America. At least that's what people used to say."

The GTO, shockingly out of place here among the dignified trees and the stately homes, glides smooth around turns and up and over small hills. "I think this is the way," Melissa says. "It's been years."

"How do you know they still live here?"

Melissa shakes her head, she doesn't, and anyway, her brain is a fertile swampland of worry and fear the closer they get, too many myriads of things yet to go wrong.

They pass two women strolling the path along the roadside and continue on until they come around a near-ninety degree turn in the road, and there Melissa pulls gently over into the gravel off to the edge. She puts the car in park but leaves the motor running. "That's it," she says, nodding at a house a block away. "There it is."

The house is huge, set on a slope back in the trees, many of its windows lit and haloing the dusky yard. It looks like a pop-up book. Stone steps, a smaller-than-expected porch, a vast wooden front door, like an ingress to an old European church. It's the kind of place where a surgeon might live, or one of the city's most affluent lawyers.

"*Dang.*" Gordie sounds impressed for once. "What the hell now?"

"You still think these people caused all this?"

"I mean, I got zero other fuckin' theories. Do you? And these people certainly can afford it. Just look at it. I'm not skeptical, seeing this."

Melissa closes her eyes, looks at nothing, her memories unreeling now like scratched home movies—courtrooms, hospital rooms, ID bracelets, metal detectors, stony-faced bailiffs, nurses and doctors hurrying down hallways, all of it blanketed by a shuddery sense of regret and heartbreak so real it physically hurts her. And beyond all that—a void, a terrible deep empty darkness.

It takes a second before she can make herself leave the car. "All right," she says. "Let's go see if they live there."

She gets out and stretches the trip from her bones. Then she reaches back into her purse, grabs the pistol, and stuffs it as unceremoniously as a pack of gum into the front pocket of her jeans.

Gordie wipes his face with his shirtsleeve. "Do we really need that right now?" He eyes her worriedly, not sure what she's capable of.

But Melissa's focused on the house eighty yards away. "It's the only thing that makes me feel better." She walks alongside the dusky road, feet crunching gravel. Gordie follows, looking around uneasily.

"Aren't we a bit…uh, conspicuous?" he says.

"Hide in plain sight, right?" They traipse through the shadows, trying not to be covert. No cars pass by. They cross the road and approach the property, the yard rising smoothly up to the citadel of the home. Tasteful, decorative lamps on either side of the porch, the exterior of the building done up in rock and mortar, looking like a castle keep in the gloom. This isn't new money, not like Dr.

Larry's fast-food affluence at all, this is royalty, or at least as royal as Birmingham's gonna get.

They leap a ditch bordering the grounds and creep across to stand in the shadow of a large, leaning oak. The house is still, like a postcard, but after a moment a subtle shape flickers inside—a woman, coming and going, room to room, the kitchen, from the looks of things, to the living room and back again. She's tall and slim, her dark hair and features more a silhouette than anything else. But yes—*another stab of shame, another messy slice of regret*—even from here Melissa can see it's her, Joshua James' mother, Mimi Newcombe, a few years older, a bit thinner maybe, but clearly the same woman.

"Where's the, uh...the dad? The dude or whatever?" Melissa doesn't answer, but her eyes follow the woman from room to room, lit here and there as she carries something back and forth, there's a strange new unrest inside her head now, a vague scratching that could be fear or disgust at herself, too many things in there, she doesn't know which is which just yet, maybe it's rage.

Tear they head off! a voice from back by the car shouts.

The house looms on the hill, a bright beacon of all the things Melissa can't have, that she'll never have—lives are different here, these people breathe a cleaner air, laughter and interior decorators and walk-in closets and florists and hairdressers and home theaters and everything exactly in its place.

"What do we do now?" Gordie says. His voice carries its own hint of dread, as if it's one thing to talk about this, to brag about it from hundreds of miles away, but another thing altogether to actually carry out this foolishness. "She's the one who hired those assholes?"

But Melissa retreats into the shadows. "Not right now, not yet," she says. Her brain is hectic, bustling with contradictory impulses, now is not the time for any of this. She steps away from the tree, down the dark line of its shadow. "There's a few things I want to take care of first."

"Wait. What?" Gordie follows her, back down the lawn now, out of the darkness and toward the road. "Why the hell did we come here? What the fuck?"

"I wanted to see if it's still them," Melissa says in her hushed voice full of contradictory things—worry and rage and dark pernicious desire all braided together. Part of her hoped the Newcombes had moved, that they'd slipped into the mysteries of time and distance and then it would be over, it would all be blessedly over. But they haven't. They're right here, they're still goddamn right here. "And it is," she sighs, crossing the road and opening the car door with a shriek of metal. "It's them, all right."

3

This motel is on the west side of town, just off the interstate and claiming a mostly abandoned shopping center for its own, except on the north end where the only places still in operation are a hardware store and a truck stop surrounded by snoring tractor trailers. The motel is called the RoamRite, and all the rooms are "smoking," they don't even ask, not that Melissa cares, she's exhausted and they both need sleep.

They check in, and Gordie takes the bed near the window, same as always. They're both quiet, perhaps with fear, maybe with dread, but mostly it's simple exhaustion—being a fugitive is hard work. They pull the bedspreads from their beds and toss them onto the floor, it's a practice Melissa read about once and now she does it every time, places like this never clean the bedspread, they just recycle it from room to room. There's a pizza joint about a mile back, and without asking Gordie, Melissa phones in an order for a large pepperoni, extra cheese, and pays for delivery with Jack's stolen card. For half an hour they lay dazed on their beds staring at the TV—another cop show, this one featuring a fat stupid cop with a fat stupid mustache—as Melissa tries to ignore the chorus of voices in the room, *Hoggie bastard* and *I'm gonna waste you, essay* and *Better give up, you gon' get yoself kilt.*

Gordie takes a shower. For a grease monkey without a single change of clothes, he's oddly, compulsively, fastidious. Melissa hears him in there, growling some metal lyric to himself. When the knock on the door comes, she pries herself up and pays the delivery girl out on the doorstep, the girl round and short and fresh-faced, her big eyes looking back from a field of freckles, and she reminds her of herself ten years ago.

"Please be careful," Melissa warns the girl, who only stares back and hands over the receipt and then leaves. Melissa sets the pizza on the little table near the window, and when Gordie comes out from the steaming bathroom, the wet towel around his waist, without a word they help themselves to a couple of slices while sitting on the ends of their beds and watching cops on TV run this way and that.

"Do you mind if I have the shower?" Melissa asks when she's done. She wipes her mouth with the little napkins that came with the pizza and tosses them at the trash can in the corner. They miss. Gordie, who hasn't looked her way in a while, nods absently, more interested in the shenanigans on TV. He gets up to grab himself another piece of pizza.

The bathroom's completely drenched and humid from Gordie's bathing.

Melissa stands in the bathtub and lets the water wash her face and neck. She keeps trying to think of the terrible task ahead—*tasks, girl, plural*—but her mind nudges back from it again and again, a magnet pushing away from the wrong pole. At this point, maybe it's better to allow things to happen rather than overthink them, to let the tide of things roll in and out as it needs, they've both come too far to change anything and there's no backing out now.

In college—before they asked her to leave—she read a chapter in a psychology book about something the author called "automatic thinking," it was a fancy idea, he said, also found in the Eastern notion of "first thought, best thought." Melissa isn't exactly sure if that's accurate—she's had plenty of shitty first thoughts in her time, her sad life is proof of that little logical fallacy—but it sounds good right about now. It means to trust yourself, to let things happen, to follow your instincts and not second-guess yourself into immobility. *Paralysis by analysis*, Noah called it, before he got sick. The only problem with that is whether you could trust the first thought—what if your first thoughts were barreling the wrong way up a one-way street, and there were no signs?

She gets out of the shower and dries herself off with the weirdly short, weirdly rough towel on the rack—or wait, maybe it's the floor mat and she didn't notice. Back in the main room, Gordie's finished eating but still watching TV, the onscreen characters spout violent, racist statements, but Melissa's able to tune them out reasonably well. Or maybe it's the voices in her head, she can't tell which is which anymore. She makes a mental list of the things they'll need for the big day tomorrow, and after a whispered, "Goodnight," to Gordie, who only glances over for a distracted moment before going back to his program, she pulls the covers over her head and in seconds is asleep.

4

In the morning Melissa's up and dressed and out of the room before Gordie even stirs, he's just a mop of silky brown hair poking out from the covers in the darkness, a shape on the bed wrapped in cheap sheets. Quietly she closes the door behind her and stands for a moment on the sidewalk under the hotel awning, feeling the morning and the city and also herself come alive—the interstate, the gentle hum of the downtown a few miles away, and birds, swallows maybe, surely with nests nearby in the crumbling roof of the hotel or the shopping center, diving and swooping and chasing each other from wire to wire. Their high spirits make her jealous. In the sky a soft whiff of air and a sullen smear of approaching clouds brings the promise, or the threat, of rain later in the day. Threats and promises. Who knows which is which anymore.

She trudges across the tundra of the enormous cracked empty parking lot, her shadow dragging behind her as if reluctant to get out this early, but the hardware store is just now open, *Hornbill Hardware* it's called, she's the first customer of the day apparently, so she goes inside where the gamy smell of rubber and plastic hits her like a dive into water. There's a man behind the counter, a lipless frown pulled across the bottom of his face and reading glasses propped on his forehead. Melissa nods to him and starts filing through the mental list she made last night before sleep. *Gloves. Scissors. Duct tape. Ski mask. A decent hunting knife.* It feels like a cliché, some stoned dorm-room joke or a shitty torture-porn movie, but it's real. She wanders through empty aisles like a lobotomy patient, the fluorescents gloomy and cheerless, the sugar-free version of electric light. Toilets, mailboxes, crowbars, PVC pipe, chicken wire. At the rear of the store, she wanders past *for sale* signs and stick-on letters and plastic garbage bins, and turns the corner toward the key-making machine—and comes to an abrupt stop.

Halfway down the aisle a figure stands. Shapeless overcoat, small and slight and tilted or slumped a bit, a long-ago spinal injury maybe. Nearly motionless. Turned away, front-lit by sun coming in the windows, the brim of the hat tilted down to block the light. The figure seems to sense Melissa there in the aisle but makes no move to acknowledge or even turn around. It simply stands there, feet planted in the middle of the aisle, turned away just so, solitary, having the air of a geriatric or a clinical patient—but a dangerous one, a homeless person or some poor soul ravaged by madness or terrible disease. The fear has reignited in her now, deep inside, so far from home, she doesn't want to see the face of this person, doesn't want the figure to turn. It might not even have a face, just a recessed inner darkness, it might turn and reveal only a hollow, it might decide it wants Melissa's face, to snatch it from her and keep it for itself.

She moves to the next aisle and steadies herself against rolls of chain-link fencing. Listens for footsteps, sensing for movement, but there's nothing. When a moment passes, she peeks back around the corner into the aisle. No one's there. The aisle is empty, and a swoon of overwhelm makes her catch herself and she wonders *How I can do this now?*

When she's gotten everything and takes it to the front, the old man behind the counter doesn't say a word, he only makes a worried survey of her inventory, it's a kidnapper's stash, an abductor's bag of tricks, his face a mask but his eyes taking in her every detail. And she knows she looks rough—she hardly mopped the sleep-hair from her face, let alone fixed it, and worry, grief, stress, and desperation have irreparably splotched her, no time for gettin' pretty these days.

But the old man rings her up and bags her items without a peep.

5

Gordie, however, is darkly impressed five minutes later when she empties her bag onto the unmade bed of the hotel room.

"Holy *fuck*," he says admiringly, sitting up among the covers in nothing but his underwear and looking at the new stuff. "This is serial killer shit." He picks up the knife, removes the stamped leather sheath to reveal a long, fixed hunting blade, and he does a clumsy riposte in the half-light. "This is a bad mama," he says.

Melissa takes the knife from him, packs up all the stuff again, twirls the plastic bag closed, knots the top of it, and sets it at the foot of her bed. The black cloud is back, that obliteration storming on the horizon worse now than ever, the figure in the hardware store aisle—twisted, stunted, leprotic— somehow drew a tarp of doom over the day and fastened it there. But Gordie's here at least, his verve is undeniably cheering, and simply having a witness, a buddy, a cohort, makes everything a little less awful. But, as always, the shadows hang over everything, even him, the air in the hotel room is thick, viscous, like a bar hazy with smoke, she goes over to the little table by the window, plops into the chair, and settles in to wait.

6

The afternoon grinds slowly, fits and starts, the sun hot and bright around the edges of the curtains, with nothing, not even an occasional human-shaped shadow, gliding by out on the sidewalk. The hiss of trucks and trains and highway cars is another presence in the room, and by early afternoon Gordie's up and finishing the rest of the stale pizza, which is just fine with her, she couldn't eat even if the pizza didn't look like a piece of cardboard with a jellied aspic of tomato and cheese on top, her stomach twisted up in knots and she's doing her best not to gag up or squirt out the two pieces she managed to get down last night. The TV blares, game shows, news shows, soap shows, but the humming in her nerves is almost unbearable, and the voices come and go—*Look out!* and *Back here, asshole, back here!*

Finally, the sky turns purple and the sun's half-hidden, low in the sky, and

Melissa glances over at Gordie, he's sitting on the edge of his bed now, restless, wearing only his jeans and still gazing glassily at the shifting mosaic on the TV screen. He seems scarcely alert, mesmerized, yet somehow he looks ready for anything—any sort of mischief. He's looked ready for hours.

"What do you think?" she says finally. Her tone is weary, shipwrecked, stillborn, she regrets bringing him along, getting him involved in all of this, but when she thumbs back through the chain of events, it's impossible to find the moment where it made sense to leave him behind. This whole trip to Alabama was his idea, he's essentially the brains of the operation and she's the muscle. That twisted idea brings her zero pleasure.

Gordie nods at her, but he's white as a sheet. "I'm ready."

"I don't want it to be too late," she says. "It shouldn't be the middle of the night or anything. I just want to talk to her. Maybe we can, you know, have a drink with her or something."

"Beer's good," Gordie says helpfully. He stands up and slips into his shirt and steps into his shoes. "Or snacks, we can bring over some takeout maybe."

They catch each other's eye, feeling the evening's descent quickening now. Maybe it won't be so terrible, maybe the woman will be sympathetic, maybe they got it all wrong in the first place, maybe these people had nothing to do with anything, that would be wonderful. Despite the walls closing in on her here in this room of despair, despite her need to be anywhere but in this place, Melissa makes herself stand, collects her stuff, and goes to the door.

"Last chance. You can stay if you want. Room's paid for another day."

Gordie hitches his pants. He's tall, despite the differences in age and bearing, his presence vaguely and reassuringly reminds her of Jack. But Jack's gone—death by deicing. By now the cops are crawling all over the two little neighboring houses, and Jack's body is in the Selleford hospital morgue with holes in his chest and his eyes and his brains cold and dead—those sweet, beautiful, considerate brains. Jack would never hurt anybody.

Melissa opens the door but pauses there, looking for some last sign of hope, something to keep her from heading out to do what she's planning to do. But there isn't anything, not even the occasional crazed chorus of murmuring voices seem to want her to stop. Gordie takes the plastic bag of hardware from her, and he follows her out into the hot September dusk.

7

The drive is quiet, both of them feeling the jitters, neither of them has done anything even remotely like what they're about to do, and Gordie keeps blowing his cheeks in and out with heavy breaths as if he's psyching himself up for something really terrible. They've forgotten about the dinner they were supposed to pick up, and anyway the night city has come alive, even in the outskirts and the rough side of town—echoes of headlights and taillights gliding across surfaces, dark figures creeping here and there on the sidewalks and across the street, sickly and ghoulishly skinny, infernal fires blooming down far-off side roads and flat streets, ghost children and women with babies on their hips. They drive through downtown, and a weird yearning nostalgia has come back to Melissa and she realizes she's smelling the burned, brake-pad stink of the steel mills. The mills were still running hot and heavy in the 70s but now they've been cooled for decades, the sooty old blast furnaces still standing, and this town will never be rid of the smell, it's like a curse, or DNA—you'll always be who you are, might as well not even try, you're gonna stink of rust and pig iron for the rest of your days.

Soon they're on the same road, plumbing into the swank wooded neighborhood, snaking around between the curves and the spacious homes, the high beams of the GTO illuminating the underskirts of the trees above them, everything now seems almost to have its own light, it looks almost artificial, like a stage set painted to look like leaves and woods and dreamy old trees. But Melissa draws a small amount of relief from the neighborhood itself, the homes, so august and so tasteful, nothing bad could ever happen here, could it?

They come to the same sudden turn in the road, the same pull-off at the bottom of the hill looking up at the house. It's just like before—lights mostly on, or at least most of the bottom floor anyway. The upper windows are dark.

"I wouldn't park here," Gordie warns her. "Too public. Looking's one thing, but I don't think we're here just to look this time."

Melissa studies his features in the green dashboard glow. "What do you think we should do?"

"The park back there." His voice has a wily certainty, a veteran thief's trust in his own tools. "We hike in." The park is about a quarter of a mile behind them, a little pull-off near a stream and one of those charming little wooden bridges. This sounds reasonable to Melissa—it's exactly the kind of prudent, practical maneuver she's terrible at—and so she does a U-turn in the middle of the road, going off into the wide shoulder a bit on the other side, and heads the GTO back to the park.

It's a just a little pull-off on the right-hand side, good for picking up and dropping off kids, there are even a few low hanging branches, so the GTO's practically out of sight unless the cops sweep the place. Melissa doesn't care either way—it's the truth that's important now, the unearthing of tangible reality, she's ready to get to the bottom of all of this, done running and hiding and worrying, time to get some goddamn answers.

She takes the plastic bag of hardware from the back seat, shuts the door, and follows Gordie up the path that skirts the road. The trees mostly screen them from passing eyes—several cars go by, but there are few worries, at least about that.

"This is nice," Gordie says, impressed. He ducks a fir branch. "I wish we had something like this up in Selleford. I guess this is what you get when you're rich."

"Yeah? I wouldn't know."

Of course you wouldn't, a woman's voice says from back in the trees.

They keep going, quiet now, until they approach the sharp turn in the road. The big house looms above them again, like a gothic castle.

Gordie pauses, looking up at it with admiration, and maybe a little fear. "How do you want to do this?" he asks. "What's the plan?" He sounds like a little boy again, not so tough, not so capable, just a kid helpless to the whims of others.

Melissa shrugs, but knows he can't see it in the darkness. "I was hoping that would be your department."

"Well, maybe we should go around back. Lotsa times people leave their back doors unlocked."

"Do they?"

"I mean, yeah, we always did, remember?" Melissa ignores the tone of his voice. "Houses this big, they've got a decent yard out back and sometimes leave the back door open."

Melissa starts walking again, impulsively, hoping to stifle the nerves that are trying to commandeer her body and steer it back toward the GTO. The plastic bag slaps and rustles at her knee. In velvet darkness they cross the road. Inside the house, the glow of the windows is empty, and the house seems weirdly vacant, if you overlook the fact that the bottom floor's as bright as a shopping mall. There's something weirdly depressing about that glow—expectant, ready for a party maybe, people with drinks, children chasing each other from room to room, but there's no one. An electrical wire thrums through Melissa's body, from up inside her brain, like a red-hot thread, along her spine and down to her crotch.

Her crotch. How Jack made that place feel so good. Lately she's forgotten about it. Sex and death are said to be so intricately linked—at least that's what they taught her in the Lit 101 class before they ousted her from school for giving a boy a concussion with a golf putter—but lately she doesn't feel anything at all down there, she might as well be a cheap plastic sexless doll. Or dead.

"You ready?" Gordie says. There's fear in his voice too in this moment of darkness, it's one thing to think about it, to talk about it, but it's entirely something else to do it.

Fuck no, a voice says behind her.

"Yep," Melissa says curtly, and pushes past him, up the lawn and around to the back of the house. The side yard is small and tight, and a tall but half-hearted wooden fence blocks their way. It's simple work to get up in one of the trees, climb out on a branch, and hop over. Melissa hopes against hope there's no guard dog—no shepherd or Doberman or pitty-pooch to come snarling at them in the dark—but thankfully there's nothing, the backyard is bright with floodlights, but empty, a little fire pit with deck chairs around it, but in the glare mold is visible on the furniture, soggy cigarette butts unburnt in the fire pit like pale grubs. The rest of the backyard is overgrown, shaggy and untended, as if no one has been out here in a while, there's an expensive sadness back here too. Making sure to stay inside the shadows, she creeps to the back door and tries the knob. It's locked, she shakes her head at Gordie, who chews his lip and glances away.

A dark second-floor window catches her eye—it's accessible, but high enough that if something goes wrong, if someone falls, there will be pain. "Do we try that?" she says.

Gordie closes his eyes and cocks his head, he looks as though he's listening to some otherworldly music only he can hear. "No," he says finally. "Some of those will either be locked or triggered by an alarm. We need an easy access point. Something they use every day and forget to lock."

The night insects rattle on. Maybe they should forget this whole thing, Melissa thinks, this is a terrible idea, maybe they got it wrong somewhere and they'll do everybody a big goddamn favor by simply giving up and crawling away before anyone else gets hurt.

That's when Gordie, making a fierce, determined face, marches suddenly back around the side of the house. Melissa follows, reluctant but without protest, over the fence again—the braces make it easier to climb from this side, thank God—and around to the tastefully lit front. The driveway's bright as a prison yard. Gordie hurries over to the garage door, fully exposed now, so conspicuous even someone from down on the road could spot him, and he gets down on his knees and then flat on the ground, he pries his fingers up under the lip of the door and lifts it just a bit. It's heavy, but it gives, slowly he keeps working it upward, quietly, quietly, gently, until it's a foot or so off the ground. Then he worms himself under it.

"Come here, hold this," Melissa hears him say, and she goes into the light and takes the garage door. It's heavy, and Gordie's fingers disappear, Melissa's left alone in the glare of the driveway for twenty eternal seconds or so, kneeling and straining, caught in the spotlight for anyone to see, no one passes down on the road, but the door grows heavier every second. And then Gordie's back. He takes the weight of the door from her. "Here, come on."

Quickly, her heart beating a conga rhythm, Melissa lays flat and scoots under, to the hard smooth cold floor of the garage. Then Gordie lets the big door slide silently back down. There's a car there—pretty big, maybe an Audi or a BMW, it's dark so Melissa can't see the color but no doubt it's pretty damn nice. Gordie's already at the door to the inside, waiting on her. She creeps over, and they give each other a dark look—*Are we really doing this?*

In the shadows, wondering what she's doing here, how far she's fallen, Melissa nods, and with the murmuring voices starting up again—*Back the fuck off!* one of them shouts, *This is a big fookin' blundah!* exclaims another in an inexplicable Yorkshire accent—they go inside.

8

The utility room is large, larger than any Melissa's ever been in, but aside from the size it's pretty much like any other—an overpriced washer and dryer, linen shelves, messy litterbox in the corner. The door at the end is closed, with a slice of light visible through the crack at the bottom, and a disturbing sense of *déjà vu* presses in. Gordie creeps over and peeks through the door, he nods to Melissa, and they both step into the kitchen.

Now *this*, Melissa thinks, trying to cheer herself up and shut out the dreadful voices, *this is nice*—a large kitchen, with a wide presentation of polished wood tones, an island in the middle, a gas range in the corner, and a standalone fireplace on the far side of the room. As if a kitchen doesn't get hot enough from the cooking alone, they need a fireplace? In Alabama? They've just taken a moment to get their bearings when the impression of movement snags her attention, a sense of vibration and approaching presence, a stooped shadow coming along a wall, growing smaller and sharper with every step, a scene from an old gothic horror movie.

Before they can react, a woman steps into the room. She stops when she sees them, eyes leaden, and her face is set in a kind of frozen mask, as if her features haven't yet caught up to the disturbing notion that there are intruders in her home. The woman—Mimi, Melissa sees now—takes a deep drag from the cigarette in her hand, then, languidly, a single phrase slips out—"Well, tits on toast."

That's when Gordie springs into action. He dashes to the woman and grabs her wrists, struggles with her, and Melissa tries to remember where she put the gun, it's in her right hip pocket, she can feel its hard, pitiless bulge—and she yanks it out as the woman wrestles herself free from Gordie.

"What the *fuck!*" the woman blurts now, the cigarette bouncing from her lips. Her other hand clutches an empty cocktail glass. Every thought that comes to Melissa—*We're here to talk,* or *Be quiet*, or *Zip it, sister,* it all seems like a line from a bad gangster movie. *Put your hands up*, *Sit the hell down*, *Get the hell out of here.* It's TV cop stuff, a shitty episode of *The Rockford Files*. Then Gordie backs away and all three of them stand there, uncertain, suspended in a rough, high-voltage triangle—one move from any of them will upset the delicate balance. But it's definitely Mimi, several years older, her dark hair still lovely, with pale streaks now, like shooting stars in a velvet sky.

Then Mimi clears her throat and, in a voice way calmer than it should be, says, "I don't know the combination. He never gave it to me. I don't even know what's in the safe."

Cut her head off! a voice shouts from back in the utility room.

"We just want to talk," Melissa hears herself say, and immediately she's appalled that she said it, this criminal stuff is hard, but she's pretty sure explaining yourself right away isn't the smartest opening move.

"Who the shit are you?" the woman slurs. She tries to sip from her empty glass, but when she finds it empty she gazes into it with childlike disappointment. That's when Melissa realizes Mimi is more than drunk—she's completely blitzed. The cigarette smolders forgotten now on the travertine floor.

A cascade of fake names and false motivations blurs through Melissa's brain, but then, knowing things have gone too far, there's no reason to lie anymore, there's only the ice-cold truth. "I'm...I'm Melissa," she confesses. "Melissa Sweet."

The woman stares at her numbly, befuddled, uncomprehending, or maybe just not listening. Then like a slow detonation, the obliviousness gradually collapses on her face, it's a terrible thing to witness—Mimi goes from intoxicated stupefaction to a neutral median of blank indifference to finding herself on the business end of a walking, waking nightmare.

"*Oh my God,*" the woman whispers. The glass slips from her hand and shatters on the tiles at her feet. "*Oh my fuckin' God,*" she moans, and backs away, her eyes wide now and clear. Melissa supposes this would be a good time to show her the gun, so she does, feebly and without much determination.

Gordie hovers in the kitchen doorway behind the woman, and gently clears his throat. By now Melissa's heard him do it a hundred times—he does it a lot actually, she's been hearing it without hearing it for several days now—but it comes off sounding more threatening than anything else. The woman takes him in—*Skuggämän* t-shirt, bad skin, cul-de-sac haircut, thug posture, in the flesh Gordie does indeed look like someone who would break into someone's house, perhaps a shiftless member of a suburban hoodlum metalhead meth gang. But Melissa has a wild, funny thought, despite his bravado, Gordie's really as innocent and unsophisticated as a child, all his bravado just that, a ruse, an attempt at seeming fierce without really being so. A bleating sheep in wolf's clothing. She's the one who's dangerous.

"*Why are you here?*" the woman yelps back at Melissa with spite in her voice. "*Haven't you done enough?*"

"I haven't done anything," Melissa says, lowering the gun but making sure to leave it in sight.

"You *bitch*," the woman spits. "You can't leave us alone. You have nothing, so you can only take away from *anyone* who has *anything*." She slumps back against the counter, helpless, not sure what to do with herself.

"All right," Melissa says, and waves her gun toward the doorway to the living room, still acting out the terrible TV programs but powerless to do anything about it. "Let's…uh, let's go in here."

Gordie steps just past the doorway threshold, and the woman gives him a disgusted scowl as she passes. This room is wide and mostly empty, with cloud-colored carpet stretching from wall to wall. Tasteful, framed seascapes—pastel skies, faint gulls, silver sand. The place has the feel of a just-vacated party, it looks newly abandoned, suddenly glum—empty glasses on the floor crowd the plush couch, which has been shoved up in front of the television. The push marks stand out in the carpet.

"Hey, just…um." All at once Melissa realizes she can't recall the woman's name, as if it's been blocked. *Marsha? Melanie? Mamie?* Then it comes, her tongue remembers even if she doesn't. "*Mimi*. Mimi, sit there."

The woman's already on the couch. "Just how crazy are you? How bad's it gotten, Melissa Sweet?"

"What?"

Reeeeaal bad, a voice says from the other room.

"I'm not crazy," Melissa says. She takes a seat across from the woman on a leather-covered rocker. Gordie props up the doorway, warily observing the two women. "Except with fear. Somebody's got to us, Mimi. They've been after us, and we've been protecting ourselves."

Mimi glances at the gun again. That soulless black eye. "You killin' more babies, honey? Playin' with guns now?"

The words have their intended effect—they feel like a slap. "It was an accident, Mimi. You know that, I would do anything to change that." Despite the half-sleep last night and the mostly quiet day today, Melissa feels exhausted. There's a caul across her face, she's staring at the world through a veil—herself on one side, everything else on the other. She glances at Gordie, who watches Mimi. He seems relaxed but ready to spring into action.

"Where's your husband? Where's—" Melissa realizes she's forgotten the husband's name too. The pistol is heavy in her hands, unyielding, she wants to put it down but knows she can't.

"*Husband?* Who, *Cary? Cary Newcombe*, you mean Cary? You forgot poor Cary?" Mimi heaves the words out in a spew, but somehow there's still a little grim humor, an edge of self-mocking sarcasm left in it. "You fucked him, girl, and now you can't get his name right?"

Ho! a voice says from the kitchen. Mimi's words sting like wasps, she's spiteful but she has a right to be, she'll say anything to protect herself at this point, to use her lies as weapons.

"Where is he?" Melissa says.

"Fuck if I know, girl. Couldn't take it. Between little Josh and you and...well, all of it. It didn't work out. He's dead for all I give a shit. Left here with most of our money and just the clothes he had on him." When Mimi pulls up her pants leg and scratches her ankle, Melissa gets a glimpse of paper white skin, varicose veins spreading out, a map of some unknown country. "Listen, I gotta take a piss. And I need a drink, can I make a drink?"

"Do you have any Pepsi?" Gordie asks from the doorway.

"We're not done here," Melissa says too loud, as if yelling above music that isn't there. She sits back against the chair, she feels jostled, in a hurry, she glances around at the big, bright house, the ghastly feel of it, unhappiness here lingering in the air. "Some people have been after us," she says. "After me. They...they killed my mother and my brother. And my...my—" She stops, unable to say it, *Jack Jack jackjackjack*. When nobody responds, she says, "So we're trying to find who...set them on us."

"*Killed*?" Mimi isn't sympathetic. "If you're asking me if I did it...did *anything*, I wish to hell I did. But nope, I got nothing to do with it. Sounds like a wonderful idea though." Mimi, it seems, has been somewhere fancy earlier in the day, her mascara's thick and sooty below her eyes, traces of lipstick that she's chewed almost all the way off. The room is quiet again, and the three of them wait there, listening to the September wind softly threading through the trees outside.

"Look," Mimi says then, her voice calmer than it has been. "Seriously, are we done here? Can I go take a piss? Make a drink? I'll make you one too."

"Where's your—where's Cary? I want to talk to him."

"I told you, chickie. I have no idea. We split up." Mimi makes a vague noise, shakes her head, thoughts turned finally, reluctantly, towards the bitter past. Melissa recognizes a deep misery in this woman's eyes. For all the money, for all the luxury and security, their lives are no happier than her own. She's ashamed to admit this makes her feel better.

Then Mimi looks up. "Look. You gonna kill me or not? You gonna shoot me? Can I take a fuckin' piss? I'll get you whatever you want, whatever money's here. My purse, you want my purse? The fuckin' briefcase, pictures of the baby, whatever you want, I don't have the combination to the safe. So can I take a piss already?"

Hell-lo no! a woman's voice says.

But something snags Melissa's attention. "Briefcase? What briefcase?"

"If you don't want money, what the hell *do* you want?" Mimi's voice is dry now, bare winter trees and dead kindling.

"What are you talking about?"

"You don't want money!" Melissa doesn't understand why she's so suddenly disoriented, but Mimi sees it on her anyway. "*Aah.* The briefcase. You sly *cunt,* you want the fuckin' briefcase." Mimi wags a manicured finger at her, *aha.* "You couldn't get enough of it in the trial. Cary practically handcuffed himself to it."

The briefcase. The word has an obscure, percussive feeling, like a depth charge far down below. She straightens up and tries to think back, worried, perplexed—and then it comes to her. *The red briefcase.* Red—not scarlet, not ruby, but red, like burnt umber. Red like rust. Like old blood. In her memory it's kinda halfway visible now—across the courtroom on the table, far away, farther away than it should be, the room wasn't *that* big, but always with Cary, always within his reach. But it's blurry, her mind's eye seeing it through layers of cellophane.

"Cool, it's all yours, how's that? Deal?"

Melissa and Gordie look at each other. "The red satchel," Melissa says, the words coming to her by themselves. It had been so important during the trial, Cary's notes and whatever else he kept in there. "It's *here*?"

"Of course it's here. I told you he left with just the clothes on his back." She taps her temple with a shiny nail. "*Listen*, girl, don't you *listen*? Maybe that's your problem."

Melissa sits back, still percussed. The briefcase. It's here. That burnt umber briefcase. The significance of it coming to her in pieces, a little more now—it had such a strong, sick power over her, during the trial Cary had it with him, always, every day. And her, never knowing what was in it. Cary opened it from time to time, consulted with whatever he kept in there, and she laid awake nights wondering what it was, what arcane secrets or hidden power Cary consulted within it. And now it's here. Ready for her personal inspection.

"Go get it," she says. "Bring it to me now."

"And I need a swizzle." Mimi stands and points at Gordie, sizes him up. "You wanna swizzle? You old enough? You aren't, are you?"

Gordie shakes his head, but Melissa hardly notices, her thoughts are wading through sludge, she knows what's in the briefcase is better left alone, but she's gonna make herself find out. This trip was always gonna be difficult, painful, that was always obvious, but to tear open old scars—only an idiot or a masochist wants that.

The woman gets up and goes into the other room while Gordie raises his eyebrows at Melissa in silent alarm: *Is this okay?* Melissa nods, and he follows Mimi out of the room.

Melissa's alone then, breathing steadily but rapidly, feeling the dreadful complications of everything rising around her, she will never be free of this, it will follow her forever. The fucking red briefcase. She can see it now—that weird color, like blood on chocolate, like old boxcars, like a bad dye job.

They come back in—Mimi has it in her hand and she hefts it onto the pale ottoman in front of where she was sitting. "Here," she says, "take a good goddamn look. Fuck it with your eyeballs, take it, you can have it, whatever's yours."

And there it is. The red briefcase.

Actually, it's really more of a chestnut rose, a reddish-coffee color. It sits there with an air of evil sentience, one of those eldritch horror movie books, its watchful gaze daring Melissa to touch it. It's flat, unremarkable. A slight rip in the bottom corner, scuff marks here and there. Not meant to impress.

Gordie waits warily in the doorway, watching as the woman slips past him and down the hall. "I'll keep an eye on her," he says to Melissa.

You'd better not! a voice chimes in. Melissa hardly hears, the briefcase has every ounce of her attention, she pulls the ottoman closer, looking at what lies upon it, afraid to touch it, afraid it might electrocute her with the power of its purpose. So many hours with that thing in the same bright room, looking at it, contemplating it, wondering what terrors it held. It seemed then to draw the light toward itself and still does, a red-rust black hole, a malignant entity that only eats and never gives.

In one smooth move, like a snake-charmer carefully but assertively handling a cobra, she reaches out, undoes the latch, and flips it open.

It's a standard briefcase interior, pockets for folders and little empty elastic pen holders. There are papers, which she picks up and examines—insurance papers, it looks like, marriage papers, birth announcements, maybe a deed to the house, divorce papers, lives gone wrong. She glances over these with a sense of sadness, it's plain this wretched broken unhappiness is due mostly to her, who knows what transpired after all this, who can speculate about what abuses and affronts and transgressions took place within these walls, but Melissa does know one thing for certain—not many couples can weather the death of their only child.

You can have whatever's yours, Mimi said. Was this, all of this, this mess, *hers*?

And there's little Joshua James's birth certificate. *5.1 pounds*, it says. A standard preemie. And his birth notice, clipped from a newspaper. And his death notice.

Below that is a binder. Or more like a folder, really, a child's folder for school, it has childlike doodles all over it, as if Cary—apparently a terrible artist—sat in court and sketched on it as the facts of his son's accidental death swirled around the room again and again. Melissa opens it, catches a glimpse of several newspaper articles, her own younger serious face in black and white newsprint, and closes it again. With a scraping in her gut, she understands now what's in there, she takes a deep breath and wipes the tears that are just now beginning to dampen her eyes, and opens it again.

The first article is folded in half, and she peels it back to see her youthful self looking back. Not thinner, not exactly, but less experienced and maybe more harried and tormented, if that's possible. Her hair, though—at least that was nice. It's an article from *The Birmingham News*, there's young Melissa again in a courtroom, photographed from across the chamber, wearing her handcuffs and that horrible full sleeve cotton dress her lawyer insisted she wear, like something from an Amish barn dance.

Nurse Accused of Infanticide, the headline says. The article mentions her name, and little Joshua James Newcombe, and the parents Mimi and Cary Newcombe, of Mountain Brook, AL. Back then Melissa made a point to stay away from any newspapers, they would only drive her batty, their idiot forecasts and fallacious speculations, so she had no idea what was written about her other than what her mother told her. Most of it was certainly nasty, but it was better to let it go by unopposed and unattended to—that way, maybe in a couple of years it would wither away, become obsolete, scrub itself from modern awareness. And it has, mostly. Except for the burly guy and his masked buddies and all the blood-colored blood they brought with them.

Gordie, half in and half out of the doorway, his drape of hair shines in the light from the kitchen like a girl in a shampoo commercial. "Still in the bathroom," he says, updating Melissa. "Must be number two."

But she's not paying attention, she's looking for a route—a road stretching out in front of her, a highway, a county two-lane, a fucking deer trail—some way, any way, to help her get through this collection of lies and slanderings. Against her better judgment, she keeps looking through the clips, seeing more and more images of herself. *Renegade Nurse Kills Infant,* says one. *Baby Dies of Accidental Overdose,* says another. *Nurse To Undergo Psychological Evaluation. Investigation at Children's Hospital—Baby Deaths Under Suspicion. Nurse Charged With Murder. Nurse Charged With Manslaughter. American Nurses Association Criticize Charges of Lethal Nurse. Former Nurse May Plead Insanity. Nurse Rejects Insanity Plea. Reckless Nurse Cleared of Charges. Homicide Nurse Fired From Job.*

It's like a series of vicious and self-loathing diary entries. How many people read about this, how many news programs used her as their sordid bait to draw eyeballs? That time in her life has taken on a corroded quality, her memory hazy and indistinct, she's done her absolute dead-level best to consciously block it out, it's the only way to live with herself, time has moved on and closed the door and done what it could to make sure these things will never come up ever again. But yet, plainly here they are.

Down the hallway the toilet flushes, and then comes the sound of the door opening and Mimi stepping out. "A drinkie-wink, sweetie-girl?" she calls from the hallway. "I'll make you one if you promise not to do anything weird."

Gordie raises his eyebrows at Melissa, but she's too far in the past. "Make her one," he says.

"*All righty, lovelies,*" Mimi singsongs boozily from the kitchen. "I'm havin' a fuckin' stiff-ass Goose, no tonic. And if you wanna murder that tiny-pricked bastard, I'll help you strangle him myself." There's the opening of a fridge, the clink of ice cubes. "*Fuck* Cary."

Fuckfuckfuck! another voice calls.

Melissa keeps going. More details of the investigation, quotes from her old boss, Dr. Elliot McEllis. *Who the hell with the last name McEllis,* the hospital staff would joke all the time, *would name their poor child Elliot?* But it happened, and there he is, bald head and heavy black mustache, sweet man but looking like an old-time matinee villain, giving quotes to the two Birmingham newspapers, plus *The New York Times, The Denver Post, The San Francisco Examiner, The Chicago*

Tribune, and *The Chattanooga Times Free-Press*. Melissa has no idea the story got so big. She thumbs through the rest as the articles go back in time in reverse order, catching only fragments of headlines—*Rogue Nurse, Lethal Accident, Murdered Child.* In many of them, little Joshua James's picture is there, a wrinkled little preemie drooling at her in smudged black and white. One article toward the end though catches her eye: *Nurse and Murdered Infant Father Suspected of Failed Affair.*

You fucked him, girl! a hoarse old man's voice yells from behind her, from the back of the room.

She stops on this one, she scans it, her eyes hardly daring to move from line to line. The article's dated Aug. 4, 2004, there's the usual picture of her in her scrubs—her Catarina smock, shapeless pants and sensible shoes, she's actually pretty sexy in this one, in a nurse-next-door kinda way. And there's a picture of Cary—Cary Newcombe, slightly greying even then, sharp in a suit. It's kinda coming back to her now, he fancied himself an accountant playboy. This picture must have been a publicity photo from his...his what, his firm? She thinks for a moment, her memory like an open hole in the ground, unearthing itself one shovelful at a time. Yes. He worked at a firm, *Newcombe Martin Hoyle*, it was called. Right, reverse alphabetical order, Melissa's brain itches but can't quite bring it into focus.

Investigators are looking into tips that deadly nurse Melissa Sweet and slain infant father Cary Newcombe had an affair a year and a half prior to the infant's death. For now, speculation that the alleged murder is retribution for a failed relationship is the primary motive. Investigators are following every lead.

Her chest constricts with a new weight. Affair? What affair? *A year and a half previous,* it said. She and Cary? What the fuck? This episode is ancient history, put out of her mind, purposefully so—it's too distressing to keep fresh and relive every single fucking agonizing day, there are so many things—*many many things, girl, you have no idea*—that have passed into the foggy mists of yesteryear, that's the way it should be. Except this was only five or so years ago now. So many details lost, yes, but not a fucking *affair,* no way. She could hardly remember what that guy—*Cary, for God's sake, his name's Cary, he told me his name was hell during elementary school*—what his face looked like without seeing his photo. There's no way she had a fucking affair with that guy, it's like someone discovered a crawlspace inside her no one knew was there, like a tumor but opposite, instead of a mass there's an abscess, a void, a null. *Cary Cary carycarycary.* They were a thing? She and Cary-fucking-Newcombe? *Really?*

Bits of memory bobble to the surface, like debris from an underwater wreck—his jokes that were always too vague to be funny, his comic-book chin, his upper lip, so thin as to not really even be there. *Cary Nuke'em.* She reads the paragraph again: *Investigators are looking into tips that deadly nurse Melissa Sweet and slain infant father Cary Newcombe had an affair a year and a half prior to the infant's death. For now, speculation that the alleged murder is retribution for a failed relationship is the primary motive.*

Mimi comes into the room with a wooden bamboo tiki-tray, and two sweating glasses on it. Limes have been neatly quartered and placed along the rim, and there's a little bowl of salted nuts and little tented napkins. "Here," she says. She puts the tray down next to the briefcase and takes a seat on the couch.

"*Shit,*" Gordie says suddenly, lunging from the doorway, "*watch it—*"

Melissa, still faraway, glances up to see Mimi sitting there across from her now, glaring at her, her face fiercely set, her eyes little black holes—yellowjacket nests in the ground. Instead of a vodka tumbler in her hand there's a stubby little black pistol. Before Melissa can react, Mimi pulls the trigger and the thing goes *POP! POP!* and Melissa feels the whizzing of hornets in the air, there's a sudden pain in her ear, like a bee sting, and then a puff of leather as one of the bullets whistles through the chair behind her.

Without thinking she raises her own gun—she forgot it was next to her on the chair, but evidently her hand didn't—and pulls the trigger. The sound is weirdly different from Mimi's gun, but all she can see is the woman's bee-nest eyes, a little hole appears in the wall behind her but Melissa must've pulled the trigger again because the woman's blouse blooms black, a funeral pansy pinned to her breast. Mimi's little gun fires again twice—*POP! POP!*—but these shots go wide, and the woman crumples sideways over on the couch.

"What the *fuck*!" Gordie cries, and wrestles the gun away from Mimi. She's writhing now, hunched over like someone's kicked her hard in the gut. Melissa checks herself—she's okay. Except—*my ear*—her ear stings. She raises her hand and feels a wad of flesh hanging off, without thinking she pulls at it and feels it come away, like a big hangnail. Her hand is wet and a single bright red rivulet of blood runs into her palm.

Gordie's standing over Mimi now, the little snub-nosed pistol in his hand. "What the *fuck*!" he says again. "Where did this fuckin' thing come from?"

Melissa stands shakily and goes over as Mimi slides slowly off the couch onto her knees, and twists and squirms on the carpet, which smears red and pink all around her. "*Fuckin'...*" she says, trying to sound fierce but not quite making it. "Fuckin' crazy-ass *bitch.*"

"You gotta aim for the body, you dumbass!" Gordie's gibbering voice echoes in the room as he hops from foot to foot. "Aim for the head and you miss!"

Melissa's ear hurts. It's like a headache but worse—sharper, burning and stinging. "Sorry," she says, pressing her hand to her ear. "It's not my fault, Mimi. I did my best."

Mimi's face is a grimace of pain and hatred as she looks up. "*Fuck you, you fuckin' whore. You slut. You fuckin' babyki—*"

That's when Melissa shoots her again. In the little hollow between her right eye and her nose—the sinus. Mimi's face jerks and her eyes go suddenly wide, as if she can't believe what's happening, how terribly awful things have become.

victor

1

The silence is weird—it's a stupendous, padded, *loud* sort of quiet. The grandfather clock in the corner ticks nervously to itself. Mimi's body motionless, as though she's sleeping with her eyes open, a gush of blood has seeped from the hole and runneled down the frown line along her mouth.

"What the actual *fuck*," Gordie says, through clenched teeth. "It was under the goddamn *napkins*."

Nap-ikin! Nap-ikin! a voice says in a terrible Japanese accent.

A chill skitters down Melissa's back. She steps over Mimi and goes into the kitchen. The fridge is a deluxe model, the kind that she's only ever seen on a showroom floor, a glass full of ice sweating near the sink, on the far end of the counter a drawer's half-open and in it Melissa can see a screwdriver and some scattered nails and batteries, a flashlight, a hammer, and a cloth tape measure. Junk drawer. This must have been where the gun was kept. Maybe Mimi remembered it at the last minute, or maybe it was planned all along, Melissa's too confused, too numb now to speculate.

"Okay, this is okay," she hears herself whispering, or maybe it's in her head. She goes back into the living room to see Gordie still standing over Mimi's body. The pink stain on the carpet has grown larger.

"Do you think she maybe has, you know, files?" Gordie says without looking up, his face frozen and fixed, seeming to study the woman, or maybe look through her. "Some kind of little black book? Numbers and names and contacts?"

It's not a bad idea. Melissa's brain isn't working right now, she would never have thought of that, how awful this would have been bearing it all alone, at this point conversation in itself is a big help, a huge distraction. But there's another shadow over her now, something new to her, at least—a fresh darkness, something bigger and bleaker than even she expected. *An affair? A fucking affair, with Cary?* It's in the papers, and though they get things wrong sometimes, drastically sometimes, it's too plainly stated to seem like idle speculation.

You fucked him, Mimi said, *and now you can't even get his name right?*

"Hello?" Gordie looks up. "Melissa? You still with us?"

Melissa nods vaguely, she's on the brink of tears, needing to put this latest shitstorm out of her mind. "Yeah, sorry, address book." She has no idea where it could be. Mimi's purse? The junk drawer? The briefcase? Maybe Gordie knows, he seems to know everything else, pieces of her are starting to crumble off, and like a little old lady she needs his help, she tries not to think of the spooky implications of this. "Why are we looking for an address book?"

"For the dude, Melissa." Gordie's voice, like he's talking to a child. "For whatshisname. Cary."

"Oh. Right."

"Okay, let's start in the kitchen," he says, and she nods and follows him in there, for some odd reason it feels better, there is sanity in kitchens—food, stovetop, fridge, technology, chemistry, it's science, science is good, you can trust science. Gordie's going through cabinets and drawers, pulling them out and emptying them one by one on the floor, as silverware and pottery and tools clang and clatter.

"Shouldn't we be wearing gloves or something?" Melissa asks. Her brain is better, but other stray thoughts come and go like fireflies in a night sky, fleeting, gone before she can process them.

Gordie stops emptying the drawers and gives her a dubious look, *It's a little late for that, don't you think*? it says. She's seen that look before, in the worst moments of arguments, the nadirs of breakups and even in the disbelieving faces of the frat pledges surrounding Michael Morbid and Kevin Schiemann. Gordie goes back to searching, now in the cabinets under the sink. "You're making me nervous, maybe you can check the bathrooms or something?" he says over his shoulder. "Or the bedrooms?"

"Right. Yes. Sorry." She moves around the island in the kitchen, pulling herself along with her hands like a child just learning to walk, down the corridor that leads into the back of the house. The hall is wide, with framed photos on each side, and though she tries not to look at them, there are brief glimpses of a happy family, a threesome—mom, dad, little baby. Her stomach clenches, nausea rolling and whirling, and she almost pukes but manages to keep going, down a small set of stairs. A bathroom on one side, with a small bedroom opposite, and another bedroom at the end of the hall.

Melissa pokes her head into the bathroom, a dark windowless chamber, outfitted in red-rust red—*of course it is*—then looks into the bedroom opposite. Cramped, with a desk and a crisply made bunkbed, prints of dogs and baseball players on the wall. A BB gun leaning in a far corner. This was to be the baby's room, this is where little Joshua James was supposed to be, he would have been three and a half years old now. Her stomach grabs again, from the pain of this moment and also from broken possibility, from what might have been. Better to keep going, down to the first-floor bedroom.

In there, a huge bed sprawls against the wall, among the biggest beds Melissa has ever seen. So big she could lay sideways across it and not touch both edges at once. At the near end of the room is a chest of drawers, some of them hanging half open, with clothes and nylons strewn about, and a big bathroom and a walk-in closet next to that.

From the kitchen comes a huge, brassy racket—the kid still at work.

"Hey, Gordie," she calls through the doorway, unsure of her own intent, but her voice sounds strong and optimistic all on its own, "there's a lotta stuff back here!"

"Good, that's good," comes the reply, several rooms away. "After this I'm gonna check the garage." He sounds focused, mentally far away, which is all for the best because she sure as hell isn't. She goes to the chest of drawers and forages inside it, there's the underwear and pantyhose and socks and tights and, not surprisingly, far in the back corner of the bottom drawer, a large plastic vibrator in faux woodgrain. It has a little slip-switch, and Melissa takes it out and thumbs it on. A loud, insistent electric buzz fills the room.

Do it! a voice says. Melissa powers it down. Jeez, how could anyone get off with that? Even the rich are hard up.

She moves to both end tables on either side of the bed, nothing but reading glasses, a couple of romance novels, several ChapSticks and bobby pins and some sort of pills. *Zolpidem.* Ambien. Melissa's starting to think she and Mimi have more in common than she realized. Absentmindedly she swipes her forehead and is surprised to find a sheen of sweat on her brow, it isn't even close to hot in here. She mops her face with her shirt sleeve, the ceiling is low and textured, like stucco, subtle colors swirl here and there, cream and vanilla and coffee. She crouches and looks under the bed—a lone sock, a fly swatter, a dusty empty water glass—and that's it. Must be the first bed in history with nothing interesting under it.

The bathroom's mostly empty too—makeup and hairbrushes and lotion and a medicine cabinet full of pill bottles, Melissa's too tired to worry about it, let the poor dead woman have her privacy.

Only the walk-in closet now. Melissa goes in and turns on the light. Perhaps a hundred dresses and tops of all colors hang in there, with shoes and shoe boxes and hats and sweaters on the shelves above. An entire life, privileged and posh and put away. Top of the line. And boxes—so many boxes that the idea of going through each of them brings back that surge of despair, it hits her again and staggers her like a heavy surf, she leans on the doorjamb and closes her eyes, the cascading dread and hate and fear, the stippled vortex of violence that has all but submerged her now. And then the newspaper. That article. *An affair,* they said, she and Cary, how could they think that, let alone print it?

"What are you doing back there?" Gordie's voice, gruff and determined, from the front.

"I'm not doing anything!" she calls, but the clothes all around muffle the sound and she wonders if her voice is loud enough. "Just looking."

"Well, hey, c'mere. I think I got something."

2

Melissa returns to the kitchen to see the woman's purse open on the counter. Gordie's dumped it all out and spread it around—cosmetics, hair bands tangled with strands of black hair, aspirin, a crumpled pack of cigarettes, earrings, and a battered little grey notebook that looks exactly like where somebody would keep their numbers and addresses. But Gordie isn't looking at that. In his other hand he's holding a piece of paper, with a torn-open envelope.

"This is it," Gordie says, glaring at Melissa with fierce, nostril-flaring determination. He has a funny way of looking at you when he does something he considers good and worthy, like a proud little boy bringing you a dead frog. "Here we are."

Melissa takes the paper from him. After her horrible experience with the briefcase, she's afraid to read it, but makes herself do it anyway. It's a letter from Mimi's ex-husband all right, from Cary, written in a strangely chilly and formal tone. Most of it's about lawyers and settlements and percentages—ah, so they *do* hate each other. But the last paragraph is the one that pulls the air into her lungs, she seems to regain a bit of herself in the seeing of it, in its own way it's nice how hatred brings her back to herself.

One more thing, the letter says. *She's up in North Carolina. A little town out near the far western tip living with her mom. Started working as a fucking nurse again. Can you believe it? Guess they'll hire any stupid cunt up there.*

North Carolina, she reads it again and a thought rings in her brain—*Cary Cary,* she thinks, *he did it, he's the one.* But this is followed by a more frightening thought—*That's Cary's handwriting, I know that longhand*—and another clang of darkness rings inside her, the handwriting is disconcertingly familiar.

Melissa shuts her eyes and leans against the counter, stars shooting in the blackness behind her gaze, geometric patterns of phosphenes. It's not fear but the same old misery, the one that took up residence in her gut and eats at her from the inside.

"We got him," she hears Gordie say, and when she opens her eyes, he's there, flush-cheeked, that wicked smile on his face. He holds up the envelope. Melissa sees it's addressed to Mimi, presumably here at this house, but the return address says *Cary Newcombe, 111 Oak Trace, Vestavia, AL 35991*, plain black and white in his hurried, almost unfinished script.

Gordie shakes the hair out of his eyes and begins a clumsy dance shuffle. But rather than what she expected—a kind of Viking-rock chant to celebrate his *Skuggämän* revenge fantasies against the world finally coming due—instead it's a graceless pop-and-lock step, right there in the kitchen. "*Whoomp*, there it is," he says, breakdancing terribly, "*Whoomp*, there it is..."

3

They take the backroads back to the motel, staying always on the outskirts, away from people, but still there are lights and convenience stores and gas stations, you can't get away from those anymore. They cruise into a no-man's land—topless joints on the dark end of a commercial strip, discount furniture, auto detailing, small engine repair, *Melissa's Country*—she's begun to think of places like this as her own, her territory, her most proper domain and herself its proper Queen, No-Man's land, indeed. Dinner is Chinese takeout from a boxy little place along the way, Gordie gets Hunan pork while Melissa goes with the vegetable lo mein, and at the drive-thru the little age-spotted woman, her peach-fuzz lips pressed thin, gives Melissa a long, stern survey, her eyes roaming across her wild blonde hair, her bruised neck, her sweaty face luminous in the neon-lime glow. Melissa allows herself to be inspected, digested, there's no point or no way to hide it now. No point in much of anything lately.

They return to the room and sit in silence on their unmade beds. Gordie eating and smacking in the soft murmur of the interstate, but Melissa can't eat, that parasitic dread is getting stronger and stronger, a dead smell coming from somewhere she can't locate. It isn't Cary's letter—plainly he, and maybe Mimi too, were, are, behind the sudden attack, that's obvious now, his casual words fill her with rage and a desperate need to get back at him, to strike out and hurt him.

Jack deserves revenge, and so does her mother, and also Noah—poor crazy Noah. No, that's not what eats at her. And it's not the burnt umber briefcase, that rust-red totem of everything Melissa fears and hates, those newspaper clippings claiming she and Cary had an affair, though she can't remember even remotely anything like that. She does of course remember Cary's face, stolid and sad and even handsome in his grief. But only from far away, never close up. There's no recollection of his body—no collarbones, no breath, no eyebrows.

No, the thing that keeps returning is the fact that she knew his handwriting. She still knows it. From where, she can't say, from what occasion she can't recall—back to that sun-blind part of things that trauma has burned from her brain, back to the blank spots on the map, *Here Be Dragons*. All of which dovetails depressingly with the alphabet soup of prognoses the papers tossed her way—*Mentally unstable*, they said. *Unreliable. Obsessive. Bipolar. Schizophrenic. Schizoaffective.*

She can't eat. She sets the carton of lo mein on the table between the two beds, and Gordie looks over at it with ravenous teenage eyes. "Are you gonna eat that?" he asks, his mouth full. Melissa shakes her head.

Incoherent. Demented. Paranoid. Psychotic. It makes her want to cackle wildly, to heave things across the room. It's so easy to bandy these terms about, so effortless to label and assign devastating medical diagnoses to anyone and everyone without a second thought, they don't know her, they never knew her. Besides, if the sickness was that bad, her lawyers could have claimed insanity, it would have been way too easy. But in her (admittedly flawed) recollection, that convenient little back door out of her self-created mess got rejected pretty early on. Her lawyers were young and green and in over their heads, but they got her off, somehow they fuckin' got her off.

One thing's certain though, she needs help, and has needed it for a long time. There were antidepressants and anti-anxieties after the trial, but those prescriptions are long lapsed, and anyway she also needs some relaxation time, time to think, time to convalesce and get her energy back.

Convalesce? You only had three years, Mel. You need more than that? What're you, fuckin' geriatric?

The rubber room then. Is that what she needs? Goddamn *shock treatment*? A straitjacket, a lobotomy? Whatever you wanted to call it, the ugliness of those years is coming back to her now, she tried to leave it behind but now she sees it follows her wherever she goes. *The past isn't even past.* There are tales of soldiers, Viet Nam vets, who mentally buried traumatic events, episodes their minds wouldn't or couldn't let them relive—they blocked it. When she thinks about those newspaper articles, they seem to reference a shadow person named Melissa

Sweet—*Sweet Melissa*—whom she doesn't even know. A stranger. The memories from that time are like photos albums of your friend's friends—you recognize the faces and the places, but you weren't there to enjoy it firsthand. The memories that do stick are more sensory and tactile—the cologne a policeman wore, the rasp of the hospital staff's smocks, the moaning ambience of the psych ward, the old paint peeling from the chicken-wired windows. The relief of her mother and Noah coming to visit, waiting for her, sitting with worried faces in plastic chairs in drab lobbies. But not much else.

The streetlight, pale, almost blue, seeps in through the closed curtains. The sound of Gordie eating, chewing, masticating, his plastic fork scraping the food carton, it's grating but comforting.

Then a cold, wretched thought grips her—*He's here, right, Gordie's here, but how can you know for sure?* How can you know anything? Years of bad memory have been resettled, disappeared from her mind, there's so much she's taken for granted that turned out to be wrong. So much she counted upon which was proved demonstrably, undeniably false.

Melissa, baby, you're tired. This stress is really getting to you. Let's get some sleep.

She squints her eyes until the light in the room stretches, splinters into fragments. The baby comes to mind again, the little preemie, little Joshua James. The cold overhead light of the empty room. The IV. *Hep-lock, not Heparin, you fuckin' idiot.* How could anyone know? It was an accident, purely an accident, and an easy one too, it really was.

They're right. I'm sick. Delusional. Deranged.

Another surge of queasiness. She opens her eyes and looks at Gordie. He's done with his takeout and is starting in on Melissa's now. He's wearing the same t-shirt from three nights ago, *Skuggämän,* it says in bloody, rusty red, and there's a man, a Viking by the looks of things, fighting off a hungry pack of polar bears in the snow. *Skuggämän.* What kind of name is that? She's never seen him wash his clothes or his hands. He's showered, but come to think of it, never sneezed, never pissed or shat. He's hardly slept. Mostly he sits quiet and stays out of the way and watches TV and gives her advice. He seems to have a weird, wily genius for what to do next. She thought it was because he's a teenager, a boy, a dude, one of those nerdy guys who's good at tactical, mechanical things like Risk and D&D and fixing cars. But—

—Maybe it's something else, Mel, dear. Something... else.

"Hey," she says quietly, her eyes closed now, trying to keep her voice from quivering, "can I ask you something?" From the sound of things, Gordie seems to pause, maybe glancing at her with his mouth full. "I need to know something."

"Yeah? This shit is terrible, how am I supposed to eat this?" She opens her eyes to see Gordie toss the half-full carton across the room, where it hits the wall and makes an oily splat, and rebounds into a trash can. Perfect shot. A perfect dude-shot.

She laces her fingers across her chest like a corpse, and takes a deep breath. "Are you really here, Gordie? Are you…real?"

"What?" He seems amused at the question. "Am I really here? Jesus. What do you think?"

What do you think, Mel? Huh? Huh? What do YOU think, Mel?

"I…I don't know what I think." The patterns on the wallpaper are throbbing now. The voices are with her again, in fact they're always with her, sometimes it's easier to drown them out and it's hard to understand what they're saying anyway, some are ubiquitous background noises like passing trucks or barking dogs, and some are just inarticulate howls of rage and frustration.

"Let me put it another way," Gordie says, belching and stretching out on the bed atop his bedcovers. "Have I been with you this whole time? Is that what you're asking?"

"Yes. Sure, I think so."

He laughs. "Would it matter? If I was or if I wasn't? Would that change anything?"

"I…think it would, yes. For me it would."

"Or am I in here, you mean?" Gordie taps his temple. Melissa nods again, less sure of herself, the curtains behind him are rippling in the slight breeze. Or are they? What breeze? There is no breeze. "Honestly," he says, "if I was or wasn't, there's nothing about it either way that would make a rat's shit of difference. My life was over when you brought those two assholes over to my house, lady. However it's gonna end, it'll be the same. Then or tonight or tomorrow, it doesn't matter."

"What do you mean? It matters to me." She waits for Gordie to say something, but he doesn't. The tears are starting up now, splintering the lamplight even more. "I'm sorry, Gordie, I really am. If I could do it over, I would. I should have let them just…fucking kill me."

"But hey—instead they killed us both." The lamplight glints in Gordie's eyes and makes them unreadable. "Your life's over. Mine's just beginning."

The phrase echoes in her head: *Mine's just beginning.* Is he speaking metaphorically or literally? *Mine's just beginning.* Is that "mine *is* just beginning" or "mine *was* just beginning"? Either way, it's a tragedy, it's a tough question to ask—*Are you really here?* It sounds so stupid. *Are you really alive, or are you a ghost? Are you here with me in the room, or am I alone right now, talking to myself and having massive paranoid delusions?*

The last several days click through her brain like a slide show. She drove the car, every single mile. She's been the one to fill it up at the gas stations. She's been the one to buy all the food. If you really think about it, Gordie hasn't done anything, she seems to remember him interacting with people, with Mimi, but not really, not consequentially, it's as if he isn't there, as if he could be retroactively deleted from every situation, from this moment and from the ones that came before, and nothing at all would change. As if he's just a figment of Melissa's imagination, her sick, delusional, psychotic imagination. She rolls over to the wall and closes her eyes.

4

Sometime later in the night she ascends from the deep, comes awake. Something's wrong, outside the window, in the parking lot, several car doors have quietly shut in short succession. Shadows flit out on the sidewalk, but—her mind fully conscious now—the motel has been mostly empty since they checked in, the two of them are among the only ones inhabiting this flea-shit inn, and now it sounds like several people are arriving all at once. Arriving right outside her door.

Gordie's bed is empty. As if it's never been slept in at all. She glances at the trashcan in the corner, looking for the oily stain. It's there, for sure, a big brown splat, along with the lo mein, looking like a squirming knot of fishing worms.

Another shadow flits, another car door shutting softly in the distance.

There's a lot of them out there.

Clad only in her t-shirt and underwear—no matter the season, she always sleeps hot—Melissa rolls off the bed and crouches in the darkness and skitters low and slow, creeping around the corner and into the bathroom. She waits there in the shadows, one veiny hand on the sill—*looking more like an old lady every day, honey*—and peeks out into the main room. Shadows crossing the curtain. Lights come and go, others flutter and die, a quickening, a storm-cloud feeling of descending doom. She can practically see them out there, with their dark eyes staring, their hands ready with guns and the guns ready too, their deep black infinite hollows eager to spit fire.

On the other wall is a window with frosted glass. It may not be too late. Praying no one's there yet, she wrenches it open. In the front now, the men are at the door, she can hear them, and the window in back is wide but thin, not made for human egress but Melissa's scrawny and at least it's not the louvered kind with metal rods everywhere, so she stands on the toilet seat and pushes her upper body outside just as the front door caves in.

The men come pounding inside, yelling and screaming her name, but in the cinderblock rear of the building she drops to the ground and rolls like she did when she was little, and sits upright. In a blink she takes it all in—an old forgotten strip of weeds behind the motel, a place no one ever comes, and several feet away the ground tumbles down into green-black darkness—kudzu and ivy and a weedy ravine of trash and broken glass. There might be a thin ribbon of wet at the bottom, hard to tell from here. Across the ravine another parking lot stretches out toward a dead abandoned shopping center. It could be a haunted house, if ghosts went shopping.

Before she can stop herself, she pushes headfirst down into the void, dewy weeds slapping her face, scrabbling over pieces of cinderblock and shattered ten-gallon buckets, and then she hits the kudzu slope and her shoulder twists hard and she tumbles again, trying to catch herself with her hands but missing. She slides onto her aching arm and face and skids down several more feet over rocks that tumble with her, and finally comes to rest on her back in a cold cold muck.

For a moment there's nothing—the signal of the world around her recedes and advances like a camera unable to find its focus. The pain in her shoulder snaps her back, it's fierce and immediate but she's felt worse, she lays motionless in the mud and the weeds as the damp crawls up her shirt and soaks into her hair. The thick foliage has closed again over her, voices chattering above now, hard to hear what they're saying, nor can she see them, only the dark rims of the ravine and the cold lonely stars above the night—the world seen from the inside of a grave. A flashlight rakes across the opposite bank and picks out the trash and the cinderblocks and a discarded tire, Melissa lays as low as possible, shivering now, and holds her breath in case it fogs up into the air. For a moment she's in some bad WW2 movie, maybe a trench-coated gestapo thug on a motorcycle is searching for her, to torture her perhaps, or reveal himself secretly to be working for the resistance. The flashlight crawls across the bank again, and the voices, men's voices, with their bloodhound determination, who can say if it's Moreau or the cops and it doesn't really matter now, but the circle of light crawls across the bank and down into the creek and she forces herself to lay still as it slides across her body, its spidery touch skittering across her skin, but her shirt is dark and muddy and soaked with water and the light skates right across and doesn't stop.

The voices grow dimmer as the men leave, mercifully they go somewhere else, maybe around to the front of the building, or maybe it's a trick to get her to expose herself, Noah would do that when they were younger and healthy, use every tool he had to convince her the playtime—the teasing, the taunting which could often get brutal, more violent than their mother or any adults really ever knew—he would convince her that it was over, he would let the relief flood in, just to launch back into it at the last moment worse than ever, it was a cruel trick and surely these men know it too.

But they really are gone. Melissa springs up, scrambles up the shadowy opposite bank and over the cinderblocks and into the parking lot of the derelict shopping center. She lurches across the open space, over ghostly parking spaces, and takes shelter finally against one of the brick pillars of the awning, her skin exposed in the night and freezing now. A rusted marquee, a sidewalk, big black windows that glare inside into nothing, into the dusty void beyond the world. A sense of helplessness presses into her, cuts into her flesh—she's wet and alone, no money, no coat, no car. Not even clothes or shoes or pants. A glimpse of herself in the store's plate glass shows what a strange, slimy creature she's become—a long-legged corpse in her panties and t-shirt and skinny and wet and cold. Sweet Melissa, like some night-crawling thing suddenly exposed.

When she peeks out from behind the pillar, there's just the parking lot, slanting slightly away and downhill, the low motel across the way, but the moonlit forms and oblique shapes of the world around her—the red and blue pulsings, garish and bright, from in front of the motel, skittering off shiny surfaces and complicating the dark, something's off—corners oddly refuse to meet up, planes don't correspond, the shimmering night sky like a proscenium arch. And beyond it the lonely highway seeming somehow closer now, while the bricks of the pillar in front of her are sharp in detail but strangely distant and out of reach. The horizontal lines of the world twist and warp, the leaning trees, the bulbous night clouds buckle the straight lines like gravity.

She sits on the bench there, huddling to herself, not sure what to do. Then she gets up and limps around the far side of the building, toward the forgotten feral curtain of black and green that edges behind the store, shuffling along in the shadows, around the corner and threading through the dumpsters in the loading bay and off to the far side. Now she's behind Hornbill Hardware—the silence here is blanket-heavy, and there's a sour, grassy smell of refuse and wet sawdust.

When she peeks out at the parking lot, the perspective has changed, it's far enough down to see partially in front of the motel. A posse of police cars has gathered there, stationed at odd, impatient angles, anonymous uniformed men coming and going like dwarves and goblins in a subterranean mine. Faint bursts of fiendish babbling, police radios echoing off the vast spaces between the buildings, the flashing colored lights turn the night into a wicked carnival, the soft breath of the city beyond humming to itself, a watercolor glow smeared across the sky, a dreaming city at rest.

Not far away now is the truck stop, shuttered and dark. Half a dozen 18-wheelers huddle outside it, their cabs closed, motors humming quietly, parking lights radiant in the early morning mist. Melissa scuttles along, sticking close to the walls and the brick pillars, and then with a huff of gathering desperation, she leaves the shelter of the shopping center, like swimming out over a great oceanic abyss, across the open depths of the parking lot. No one seems to notice as she shuffles along, in their looking they're too busy to see her, and she creeps over to the hulking shapes of the parked trucks that purr to themselves in their sleep, long rectangular beasts of the night with metal sides cold and hard and indifferent. She slips into a long corridor between two of them and feels swallowed, as if she'll never come out, but then she does, the flashing police lights diminished now, and the night air hits her again, cold and wet, and if she doesn't get warm soon things will turn bad. She moves along the trucks, all of them peaceful and still, it must be three or four in the morning.

But then—a faint noise. Music. Coming from somewhere. She follows the sound, toward the end of the line of trucks, until it's clearer. It's coming from a large, high semi—*Peterbilt*, the grill says, Melissa remembers Billy Dickie talking excitedly about those rigs—its pale hide almost orange in the sodium arc lights. It sits high on night-black wheels, and the cab is dark, but music, beautiful music, drifts out from a slightly opened window.

Melissa looks down at herself—bare wet gooseflesh legs shivering in the dark, her muddy-bloody t-shirt like a short dress. Back toward the motel, the flashing red and blue menagerie of lights, the infernal hobgoblin workings of the cops back and forth, and she knows she doesn't have a choice—she gathers her courage, throws herself into fate's mercy, and knocks on the door.

At first there's nothing, she wonders if the music's only in her head. She pounds again, louder now and more desperate, her heart pounding too, and this time there's the unmistakable sense of shifting weight inside, of someone moving around. In a moment, the window rolls down, and Melissa says a wordless prayer to herself, more a silent moan than a coherent plea, that everything will be okay.

The face that looks out at her is dark and thin, with a scrim of salt and pepper beard. A black man. She blinks up at him, her mind teeters with what to say and how to say it, like a soldier in a minefield she's immobilized, *paralysis by analysis*, standing frozen in the midst of a tinderbox. His eyes crawling up and down her body, her bare legs, her stained t-shirt.

"I don't want it," he says, and rolls the window back up.

"Wait! Wait!" She finds her words now and her urge to move again, and pounds on the door with the flat of her palm.

"I don't want it," the distant voice comes from inside. "Get the hell away!"

Melissa skitters back. She's both repelled and compelled in this moment of grave danger, in a sane situation she would gladly do what he asks, but that circumstance—that *type* of circumstance—passed a long time ago. Instinctively she steps up onto the running board and reaches into the crack of the window with her fingers—that's all that will fit—and waggles them at the man inside. "Please! Please, mister! I need your help!"

There's a palpable hush now, it's dense, as though the cab weren't hollow at all but solid. Melissa waits, listening, on the far side of the truck the red and blue lights of the cops flicker and flash against the flat planes of the motel and the empty buildings and on the dew-wet pavement.

Then, from inside the cab, "What do you want?"

Her own horrific reflection in the window stares back at her, and she says, "I—I'm cold and wet. I need warm."

"I gotta wife, lady. I don't do lizards."

That causes Melissa's mouth to snap shut. *Lizards?* What? Her throat is dry, her body wracked now by shivers and she bobs up and down. She *really really* needs to get warm soon. "I'm freezing out here, mister! I need some help!"

The dark face appears in the window again and appraises her through tired eyes. "You know what time it is?" The music inside is still quite loud—frantic jazz, a chatter of saxophones and *click-clack* drums, some freewheeling subterranean Chicago cats from decades ago.

"I'm sorry. It's just—" She doesn't know what to say, how to appease him, how to get him to let her into the warmth, it occurs to her to claim some kind of assault, or some other terrible misfortune, but the look in his eyes is old, wary, sad in a way and perhaps visibly kind, but wise to trickery. "I just need some clothes," she says. "Nothing else, I promise. Then I'll go."

There's a pause in the morning, a stillness in the air, the world has stopped, nothing happens, no one breathes, not even the flashing red and blue lights seem to take a breath.

Then, "*Goddammit,*" the man says with an air of helplessness, and the oxygen rushes back into the world. "Go around," and she does, she hops down and circles the cab in the front and goes to the passenger side, where a hundred yards away the cops still work. With a huge brown hand, the rough hand of a sailor or a soldier, a workingman's hand, he reaches over and unlocks the door.

Melissa opens it and heaves herself up. The cab's bigger than it looks, it reeks of sweat and food and feet and something else, some kind of sweet smoke she can't place. It's dark inside, and she can only get glimpses of the man in the driver's seat—midnight skin, stout arms, sagging of cheek and jowl and chin. But his eyes, deep-set gems in a Bronze Age idol, are gentle.

"Let me see what I got back here," he says over the music, it's louder now, the old stuff, fierce horns blazing and piano pounding and wild. "Got my own little stash back here, but not any lady clothes."

Melissa settles on the passenger seat with one leg under her, hugging herself, suddenly shy and sheepish, trying not to shiver and hoping the blood on her shirt isn't too obvious, or at least mixes okay with the mud. The man digs under a pile of clothes in the far back corner of his sleeping cab, it's a mess back there—empty potato chip bags, soft drink cups, fast-food wrappers kicked into the corners.

"Goddamn, I'm sorry, lady. I ain't got nothing." Melissa hears herself let out a breath—a deflation of despair and unceasing stress, as if the world is conspiring against her. Of course it is, it always has. The man sees this, and his eyes soften. He says, "Did you get yourself into trouble? Or outta trouble?"

Melissa supposes she did—both—but not the kind the man's thinking of. She nods vaguely. *Now comes when he puts me out,* she thinks.

Instead, the man asks, "What's your name?" Melissa considers lying, but that time is past now. In a thin voice she tells him, and the man answers, "Call me Victor. This here's my rig." He nods at something taped to the dashboard, a polaroid photo. Melissa sees a middle-aged black woman, sweet-faced and heavy, her hair in a greying halo around her head. "Gwendolie. Twenty-one years, me and that one. Waitin' for me at home. Like I said, I don't do no lot lizards."

Lot lizards. Ah. With a snap of understanding, Melissa knows now what lizards refer to, who they are, what they do—and a plan clicks into place. She has to convince him that someone, some asshole trucker, got pissed and put her out, but she must construct it so it seems inevitable, airtight, it's almost better to stay quiet in her performance, her shivering and teeth chattering speak for themselves.

Victor pulls a towel from the mess in back and throws it onto her. "You welcome to get warm back there." He pats the bedroll behind him, a heavy coverlet, like a sleeping bag. "Where'd you come from? You piss somebody off? You ain't runnin' from them cops, is you?" He nods at the funhouse spin of red and blue lights, he stares at her, a lopsided assessment, but there's a light in his eyes. He's joking.

She laughs. It sounds weirdly convincing, not too loud, like it's actually funny, of course she didn't, *haha.* "If they'd actually goddamn *do* anything, I'd go ask for help," she says. "What's going on over there?" Trying to sound innocent, free of *those* kinds of worries.

"Who the fuck knows, always something going on in that dump. Every time I come here, something going on over there."

Melissa doesn't answer. She crawls in back and settles herself under the covers. It's tight, it really is like a sleeping bag. The warmth wraps her all at once. Victor reaches over and flips off the jazz and the sudden quiet is loud again, louder than the music. Victor doesn't seem to notice. "You look tired," he's saying. "I'm gonna let you crash for a while, but I gotta get going near daylight. Try not to get mud on my shit, okay?" Melissa shivers again before the world closes in, irises itself down to black.

5

Voices. Voices wake her up. With her eyes closed and her breathing thick and slow, she finds herself curled into herself, hands tucked under her chin. The words *woman, blonde*, and *deadly* flutter around the little sleeping chamber, so close she could reach out and snatch them from the air. Some man talking, a Southern accent, deep and slow and smug in its certitude.

"Yessuh," Victor replies in that tired acquiescent way everyone's heard a million times before, and which makes Melissa's heart sink every time she hears it again. "I sure will." Then the *whik-whik-whik* of the window rolling up.

She raises her head, opens her eyes. Victor in the passenger's seat, slipping on an old red knitted hat. It isn't cold in here—matter of fact, it's quite stuffy now, the skin between her chin and neck is clammy and her shirt's damp with more than mud or blood. The hat might be the kind of thing he wears when he goes somewhere or maybe when he leaves the cab, she knew a fellow like that, another boy she dated—Craig was his name, Craig something or other, he worked at a movie theater and though he had the most beautiful dark head of hair he wore the same nasty sky-blue beanie every chance he got, even in sweltering heat.

Victor catches her eyes in the rearview mirror. "Coffee," he says. "What else you want? You hungry? Donuts?"

Melissa doesn't answer. Her words keep just out of reach, back down inside herself, as if talking were some great cough of regurgitation to dislodge them. When she gets a glance at herself in the mirror—blonde scribble of hair around her head, eye bags, skin splotchy and flushed—she looks like a more-than-slightly ill fifteen-year-old. Or maybe a fifty-year-old. As if her body and soul were being reclaimed and reprocessed, growing older and younger at the same time, acid hunger eating at her belly, she only had a bite or two of the lo mein from last night before she tossed it away—wait, was that her, or Gordie? *Gordie, where's Gordie?*—but she nods and falls back into the bedroll. He knows about her now, but yet he said nothing to the cops.

Victor shuts the door and the blast of morning air chases itself around a bit before succumbing to the smell of feet. It feels good to be alone again, even for a moment. The ceiling of the sleeper compartment is faux leather, rust-red—*of fucking course it is*—and chipped and needing repair, and there's a little shelf with paperbacks, Chester Himes, Dashiell Hammett, Malcolm X. A few well-thumbed girly books. A crumple of candy wrappers down near her feet, and work boots and old socks—that's where the smell is coming from. She runs her fingers through the tangles in her hair, knowing she doesn't smell too good herself. She'd been lucky to find this guy—beyond lucky. He could have easily been some pervert or serial killer.

No no, sweetheart, the pervert serial killer, that would be you. Even in these tight quarters, the lines still aren't meeting up, it's like wearing someone else's glasses, something's wrong, some essential scaffolding inside of her has collapsed, but she doesn't know how to fix it. And then there's Gordie. Without him she'll be lost, how can she do it without Gordie?

Lunatic. Deranged. Psychotic.

She wipes her nose with the back of her hand and smears it on the bedspread. Sorry, Victor.

But if Gordie isn't here, hasn't been here, then where is he? Where is everybody?

And then, just like that, a darkness comes on, passes over her like the shadow of a great bird, as if she's disconnected from herself, her body not a part of her at all, as alien as all the rest. *And maybe poor Seth was innocent, you ever think of that? Maybe it was Dr. Larry or Wilston, maybe Seth and Teddy had nothing to do with it, maybe you marked them for nothing.*

Okay. Gordie. She traces it back, looking for the seams, the weak link, and finally there it is—how did she know to come to Alabama? Gordie was the one who saw the license plates, right? That clammy doom comes again—asylum visions and patchwork portraits, mosaics of herself made up of mosaics of herself, too many different versions of Melissa, all of them ailing in different ways. She stretches out in the tight cab, she needs a ball of thread to find her way back out of the labyrinth again. *Jack, Moreau, Gordie.* Mimi's husband Cary, who more and more now, even through the nuthouse reasoning, she's sure started the whole fucking thing. His address is tattooed onto her brain. She repeats it to herself again, just for good measure.

A rush and a clatter makes her flinch, and then the passenger door opens and a blast of cool, fresh air pours in. Victor's back. Melissa pushes herself up to a sitting position.

"Gotcha a chicken biscuit," he says, handing it over. It's warm and heavy and smells like life itself. "Coffee and donuts too. Blueberry." He climbs into the passenger seat and gives her the coffee, it's tall and hot, and seems to warm her too from the inside. She wonders where he got them—no doubt the truck stop is open now. It's pale outside, and toward the motel, the cars are still there, but the cops are mostly gone, once in a while a lone figure strolls into view to sit in the black and white, or go back to the room. A tow truck has backed up to Gordie's GTO and started loading it onto the flatbed. That insatiable darkness gnaws at her again—she's stuck now. Stranded. No clothes, no car, no way to get around.

"Look," Victor says, catching her eyes in the mirror. "They told me about you, Melissa Sweet." The eyes blink, heavy with knowledge, seeing her in her true form for the first time. "I wish you woulda just come clean to me, 'stead of having to hear it from them."

Melissa coughs, swallows deliberately, with effort.

"Now, I don't know what kinda bullcrap you got yourself involved with, and I don't wanna know. I ain't gonna judge you on that. I knowed some women who done some things and most of them was put to it by bad men or bad situations. Or both. But after you eat, I want you gone, all right?"

There's a moment of quiet, a pause in the air, and Melissa can only nod, at the food and at the ultimatum both. The lure of breakfast takes over, Melissa's stomach is a hole, she fills her cheeks and burns her lips on the coffee, while Victor seems to eat without a care and scans some small community paper he picked up somewhere. The sun's up now. The chill is already going away.

"Ah, horse dookie," he says with a snap. "Almost forgot—got you some clothes. They may not fit, but at least they's girls' clothes." He reaches into the floorboard and tosses a rolled-up paper bag he brought with him into the back. Melissa digs them out and holds them up—a floral skirt, some lint-pilled purple wool tights, or maybe leggings, a yolk-yellow sweater and a berry-red—*of course, what else?*—football jersey that's way too big but looks nicely worn-in. In fact, the numbers have practically peeled away. The back has only a partial name: *McG ady.* And *Roll Tide.* Someone's cast-offs.

"Where'd you get these?"

"Truck stop's got showers in the back and they's a lost and found in there. I dug around in it lookin' for things that might fit."

Melissa pulls the leggings over her knobby, skinned-up knees, which look the same as they did when she was twelve years old, and surprisingly, even though they're a size or two too big, she enjoys the feel of them on her body, they hide and enshroud her. She wrestles her muddy-bloody t-shirt over her head and slips into the jersey. Too big for her, she was right—*You need to eat more,* a voice tells her—but it's still good to have it. Despite the few hours' rest, she still feels depleted, probably in shock, she's worried she might get sick from the wet and cold and terrible upset of the night, the constant body-seizing stress of her life.

"Were there any shoes?" she asks. Victor shakes his head and goes back to his paper.

Outside, across the sea of pavement, the cops are mostly gone. The car's gone too. *My God,* she thinks, *what is happening?* This new weird stress, the uneasy notion that her thoughts won't line up, the absence of connection—she lays back down, the feet smell is strong again and mingled with the funk of food and grease, making her want to gag.

"Now don't get too comfy back there, missy," Victor announces, looking into the mirror. "Me and you's done. I gotta get on the road, I'm makin' Memphis 'fore four o'clock."

Melissa squeezes her eyes shut. In the hush of early morning, static bursts of police radio talk again, little aural explosions of sound skipping across the flat expanse, it's probably as much in her head as it is outside in the damp air. "Could you drop me off somewhere?" she asks.

There's another pause. "I gotta get goin', lady." The tone in his voice is still kind, but skeptical.

"Look. Victor, please. You've been so good to me. I don't need money, I got money." This isn't true. Her purse is back at the hotel. Surely it's in the cops' property room back at the station now. "But I gotta get somewhere. I got nobody else, Victor."

"Well let's call you a cab."

Melissa's eyes are still shut, as if by not seeing anything it might set it all right again.

"Look. You caught up in that business over by the motel. They lookin' for you. I don't want no trouble. I keep it nice and clean, my books are spotless."

She's not sure what to say. What *can* she say? There's too much to say, tidal waves of things to say, but there's no opportunity to really be heard.

Victor turns sideways in the passenger seat, it's a struggle for a man of his age, his brown eyes are weirdly suddenly sad. "Look, I ain't holdin' it against you. My daughter…" He takes a moment to gather himself, turns back around. Wipes the corners of his mouth with a thumb and forefinger. "My little girl was kilt. Domestic abuse, boyfriend, the whole thing. So I get it, believe me, I get it. Seen it on you the moment you came up, it's why I let you in, I seen you needed help."

"Oh shit, Victor, that's...that *sucks.*" And it does. Millennia of women wronged by men, too vast to contemplate, her eyes still closed, it feels better that way, to drift and drift and drift...*Just go back to sleep,* she hears herself tell herself.

"Yeah." Victor clears his throat. "What happened over there? I mean, I know what the cop told me. But what cops say happened and what really happened is usually two different things." Melissa doesn't answer, too afraid to speak, her thoughts cascading again, too hard to single out just one before it's gone. "Boyfriend?" Victor squints at her reflection in the mirror, dark eyes looking into her core. She nods. "He dead?"

She shrugs, one shoulder, *I dunno.*

"Well, maybe he still alive then. That's a start. Killin' ain't no good for nobody. Ain't nobody learn nothin' that way." Victor collects the garbage in the passenger seat floorboard, stuffing it into the fast-food bag.

"Please, Victor? I don't have anybody else."

Victor's eyes won't meet hers in the mirror. A half-minute or so passes, traffic's picking up outside, she can feel the vibrations of his thoughts working, gears turning in his mind. Finally he looks into the mirror again. "This place you wantin' me to take you. Ain't too far away?"

"It might be on the way," she says. "It's..."—she needs a good lie, something that sounds workable—"my dad's place. He's...he's expecting me."

"Well. I'm headed west, is it west?"

Melissa doesn't know, it's probably south, she can only shrug again, she remembers a sad stray dog she came across once, too scared and confused to go anywhere on his own, frozen in his place of abandonment. He could only stand and shiver.

But the options in Victor's eyes flit this way and that, and then finally he says, "Goddammit," and exhales loudly through his nose, it's his version of a sigh. "But we gotta get going, I can't have no foolin' around, if I'm late I'll be in the doghouse." Despite his complaining, Victor's voice is clear. Simple and straight—no crinkles, no contradictions.

"I can tell you where," she says, sitting up. "I'm ready. Ready Freddie."

Victor opens the passenger side door and steps stiffly down—his body displaying his age, he walks like an old man—and goes around the front of the truck. He's a big guy, with a big guy's front-loaded belly, and the nurse in Melissa sees that if he isn't careful he'll be having hypertension in the not too far future, if he doesn't already, if not a stroke.

"Thank you, Victor," she says from the sleeper as he comes back around and heaves himself up into the driver's seat. "Can I give you some money?"

"I don't want your money," he says. "You just take care of yourself. All right?"

"I will," she says in a small voice. Then, "Can I ask you a question? A...a crazy question?"

The big man buckles himself in. "I guess you about to."

"Are you really here?"

Victor pauses. "What?"

"Are you really here?"

He laughs, a strange sound in this gloomy bog of her life, this terrible cheerless world which surrounds her, and he starts the truck with a roar and a hiss. "Well, despite what my wife would tell you, I guess I am." He laughs again. "Sometimes I wish I warn't, but I guess I am."

6

She climbs in front to the passenger seat and tells him Cary's address—it's south, as she suspected, not west—but he knows the general area, so they drive, the truck groaning and shifting and shuddering with the change of gears, through empty outlying streets and into the city proper. It's still early. The town is the same as before—old trees and hills, root-rutted sidewalks, wide empty streets. Further along, little hydrangea plants wilt on both sides, as if some city council member found funding enough to plant them but not care for them.

A torrent of emotions tries to push their way into Melissa's brain, but she shoves against them and keeps them out. The truck, pulling a fully-loaded semi-trailer, wheezes up the grades, but Victor knows what he's doing—his dark face is relaxed. Soon they're on a smaller highway pointing south, over mountains and into kudzu canyons, the malls and hospitals looming on the sides of the roads as on the way to Mimi's house. As they pass Melissa glances over there, as though she can see through the curtain of trees and telescope into the living room, she wonders if Mimi's still there, still spread out on her pink-stained carpet.

After fifteen minutes or so, Victor veers the truck off the highway and into a commercial area—a wide, tilted boulevard of fast food and banks and hotels. He pulls the rig into a neighborhood, past manicured lawns and two-story ranchers, trucks like this aren't common back here, the roads are too thin and winding. Victor's face is stony and he says very little as he steers, hands carefully placed like an old man at ten and two, and Melissa gets the feeling that he knows he's doing something he shouldn't.

"Why are you helping me?" Melissa says, hugging her knees. The purple tights are itchy, and their too-large size makes her feel like some kind of wacky children's book heroine, Pippy Longstocking or Holly Hobbie or Raggedy Ann, one of those adorably disheveled girls, she thinks back to the days when she would read those books and expect the world really to be like it was pictured in the pages, full of whimsy and adventures and afternoon tea. And then the hard, head-on crash of knowing that it wasn't, and it would never be. Those books were lies, they led her astray, as a kid, worries flooded into her life almost immediately—parents, school, friends, boys, weight, sex, health, the mental health of her family—and it seemed to her the authors of those books failed to prepare their readers for the antagonism of the real, hard world.

"Aw," Victor says. He rolls down his window and spits. "You 'mind me of somebody, is all," he says.

Fuck it all to hell! a voice yells from somewhere.

"Your daughter?"

"Nope."

"Who?"

"Oh, this lady." Victor wipes his mouth with the cuff of his sleeve. "Gave me my first job ever, washing dishes in this soup kitchen she was runnin'. She was kinda my teacher, you know, my mentor. Livvie was her name, God, I loved her. Sorta pretty for an older lady. Like my mother even after my real mother died. And after I grew up and moved away we mostly lost touch, only talked to each other every several years."

Victor straightens up in his seat, the seat belt cutting into his girth, his shirt beige and tight and stained from yesterday's sweat, and the big pizza tray of the wheel spins as his hands work it. "One day out of nowhere I get a letter from her. Say she was looking at being homeless. I was like, *whoa.* Kinda sudden, you know. So I wrote her back, sent her a check for hunnert and fifty bucks. We kept a little more close in touch then, and I sent her money when I could. Then a letter came one day, saying she wasn't looking at being homeless now, she really actually was."

"Oh, wow. What happened? Did you take her in?"

"Couldn't. Me and Gwendolie was in a rough spot then and it woulda tipped us over the edge. Can't say I blamed her. So I couldn't send Livvie money 'cept secretly. So that's what I did, but a hundred dollars here and there don't help much no way. Had to watch one of my favorite ladies, my angel, my mama when I didn't have a mama, get homeless. She'd send photos, sometimes of her day, her world, herself, and her looks would change with every one. Said she was in a shelter, but they didn't allow nobody in until 9 at night, she had to be gone all day, and that sun, you know, that weather, it does things to you. Skin hard as leather. Lips thinned out. Hair went all dishy gray—wrinkles, eyes got deader and deader. And then one day the letters just stopped."

The wind whistles through the crack in the window. Melissa stares at her knees, so far away and disjointed, like some kid's bad perspective drawing.

"Never heard nothing else from her." Victor's voice is hushed and timid now, turned inward. "Beautiful lady, treated like that." His face still stony but his eyes are glassy, glassier even than when he was talking about his daughter. "Poor people, people on the bottom, they ain't got no help, no chance at all. We all's just climbin' to the top as best we can."

He clears his throat, adjusts himself in the chair, and says, "All right, I think we gettin' closer. But this rig ain't gonna squeeze into these tight-ass little roads."

The truck moves slowly up the lane, sliding past putting green lawns and older modest homes tucked back among the long shadows of the trees. Melissa looks out at the houses—the porches, the tasteful shutters, the carefully chosen cranberry for the front doors—and sees their address numbers are sometimes visible, but they aren't making much sense anymore. Why was she coming here again? Why would she put herself in such danger again?

"What's the address?" Victor says. Melissa tells him. "All right, it's just a bit more up here. I think it's through there." He points beyond a row of houses rimmed by pine trees, to another street, just beyond. To Melissa they look like something from a children's drawing, all skewed angles and leaning walls. *There was a crooked man, and he walked a crooked mile*, she thinks stupidly, and tries to put it out of her mind, but can't. *He found a crooked sixpence upon a crooked stile. He bought a crooked cat, which caught a crooked mouse, and they all lived together in a little crooked house.*

The rig hisses and shudders to a stop in the middle of the empty road. "This is far as I go, lady. I get too far back in here, I'll have to back it out, and me—I got to hightail it to Memphis." He turns to Melissa, and she tucks a greasy lock of hair behind her ear to meet his gaze. "You gonna be okay? I done lost one friend, don't wanna lose another."

He was quite handsome at one time in his life, but now he's thick with age, sunken eyes and a sad face. Happens to everybody, if they get to live that long. She leans over and kisses him on the cheek, then wipes away her own dampness there.

"I'll be fine. I promise"

Her hand finds the door handle on its own, and it opens easier than she thought it would. She slides down the impossibly long distance to the ground until her foot finds the pavement. Her purple tights are itchy, and she's already wanting to take them off, to rip free of them with relief, like a cheap bra after a long workday. “You go on,” she says, “I’m meeting somebody here in a bit.”

“Your dad?”

“That’s right. Dad.”

Victor squints, gives her another look. “You need money? Don’t mess with me.”

“Nope. And thank you for everything. You’re a sweetheart.” She shuts the door with a confident slam, which she hopes convinces him she’ll be okay, and she grins at him through the window. But then she has a thought and raps the glass with a knuckle. He leans over and rolls it down.

“What was your daughter’s name?”

His eyes brighten, his face opens just a bit, the first time she’s seen this. “Tamara. Tammi Rae.”

Victor nods and guns the rig, and it slowly pulls away, belching smoke and most likely waking up the neighborhood. Melissa watches it get smaller and smaller, and then disappear around the corner.

Well. She turns and considers the neighborhood again. All the houses look cold, closed up, the blinds drawn. If there are people in there, they’re still asleep. She wishes she could sleep, but if she laid her head down now, she’d sleep for a thousand years. In her purple tights with no shoes and her blood-colored football jersey, she starts making her way up one of the driveways, through the backyard and into a bony stand of autumn trees that leads to the other backyard and the other house, the one where Cary lives.

joshua james

1

The grass is an impossible shade of green as she shuffles around the side of the house, the weeds a little ill-mannered for this neighborhood, wet with dew and dampening her tights-feet. She crosses the front yard, leaving footprints, to check the mailbox—*111 Oak Trace,* it says. This is the one. She turns and takes it all in. The house is a meek rancher—*Divorcery is rather shite for the finances, huh, Cary, old boy?* a voice says from just across the road, brutish and slurring—but it lists dreadfully to the right, leaning like a tumble-down old barn in the Appalachians. Above her, the sky feels close, the clouds grey and low, the sun's gone away after a brief hello. There's a drifty quality to her movements now, she understands she's disengaging from herself, hands loose on the wheel of herself, as if neither her brain nor her body will quite follow her orders, she thinks maybe checking the front door is the next step, where's Gordie to tell her what to do?

She mounts the porch—little umber flowers and a pair of weathered, unraveling wicker chairs—and tries the knob. Locked. Of course it is. But there's a view into the side foyer window, white curtains obscuring most of the liminal space beyond, she goes down and around, off the porch and wading through bushes to another window, she cups her hands against the glass to see this one lacking any curtains at all—just a simple front bedroom, a mattress and an unmade bed, bare and bleak with a silent air of neglect. A high tinnitus whine starts up from somewhere, a floating whistling that veers in and out of the trees and above the empty street. Melissa knows enough by now to understand it comes from her and not from some neighborhood metal shop somewhere.

She drifts to the garage and bends down and tugs the handle. It won't budge. *So,* she thinks with a weird stab of pride, *Gordie isn't right every goddamn time.* Around the far side of the house, a mossy brick retaining wall forms a shady corridor leading into the back. She scuffs along trying to look like she belongs there despite her clothes. The corridor, wet and damp—footprints comically visible in the dewy grass, a cartoon villain's clues—leads around to the backyard, and the wooden deck she passed on her way in. It's a family kind of deck, low and sprawling and half-rotten from damp, where kids play and parents sip cocktails on Saturdays. A sadness yanks at her, a leftover from the world she wanted. The back door's a solid pane of dirty glass, old fingerprints and dog nose-smears, but the frame is strong. Also locked. Off to the side, though, a little weather-chewed back door opens into the garage, her hand reaches forward—out of perspective, she's watching it onscreen like in a movie now, some old lady's hand, thin and haggish—and tries the knob. This one's unlatched, Gordie's right, it's always the garage, and she pulls it open and quiet as a shadow she slips inside.

At first it seems she's seeing things again. There's no car in here, but the perspectives still are not meeting up—the garage door weirdly far away and tilted off its axis, like a movie-screen seen from off to the side—and the sheetrock walls are dramatically, almost violently, chipped and gashed, vicious holes and hacks ripped into the plaster, as if someone has taken the claw end of a hammer and gouged it away. It looks like a torture chamber. Surely not—even with a chaotic and jumbled brain such as hers, this is improbable. But someone in here has had a series of very bad days.

The door leading into the house, though—it's blessedly, gloriously open. She creeps inside.

It's another utility room—in this one, a washer and dryer stuffed side by side in a hallway that leads to a kitchen. The kitchen is itself a kind of hallway—not a chef's kitchen but a galley, the kitchen of someone in a hurry, where soup is microwaved, sandwiches are compiled, frozen dinners are thawed. Jack would hate this kitchen. Piles of empty cans of beer in a trash bag in the corner, crusted plates and pots in the sink that might have been clean a week ago. Melissa listens for any movement, any snoring or sleeping breath huffing in empty space, a sense of nearness or air disturbed, and finds none. No one home, not even at this ungodly hour.

The kitchen spills into a larger family room, with a raised ceiling and a stone fireplace, the house might have been nice if someone wanted it to be, but now the only furniture is a solitary couch which looks rescued from a yard sale, facing the empty fireplace, and just like her house, the floor slants, she sees it right away. A hallway beckons off to the back of the house and also that bedroom she saw earlier, just off this room, as bereft as it was from outside the window.

Melissa takes stock of this empty place, this vacant house, this unfamiliar roof above, the air around her tight like a second skin, and also feeling as if she's gotten weirdly good at this by now, this creeping around in other peoples' lives and peering into their private thoughts and intimacies. She might have missed her true calling.

Beyond the hallway, a large rectangular living room opens up, where a recliner lounges in front of a TV. Empty beer bottles and plastic Solo cups next to the chair, this place reeks of *single dude*. A strange, domestic impulse comes upon her to turn on the TV and sit in the chair and lose herself in the morning shows—news now, then *Don Ho* and the soaps, and later *Gilligan's Island* and *I Dream of Genie*. But nah, the news sucks and she always hated the soaps. And Cary's furniture looks greasy and unwashed.

Cary. When his name comes up, strange little memories rise up to nip and pluck at her, like tiny little fish from below. His boxy chin, that sexy thinning hairline, the soft lobes of his ears. Hard to tell if these memories are real or just imagined sense-impressions, momentary synaptic tantrums firing into being and fading even quicker, thoughts put into her head by that insidious newspaper, because when she tries to remember more of him she can't.

Before long she's back in the kitchen—the morning light's cheerier here, ready for a young mom and a kid and a plateful of sticky breakfast. The refrigerator's mostly bare: ketchup, mustard, mayo, soy sauce, pickles, eggs, hamburger buns. Half a six of imported beer. Deli-sliced meat rigor mortising in a half-open Ziploc bag. Collapsing oranges just now beginning to explore their fuzzy afterlife.

She gets a glass from the cabinet and fills it with water and takes her time drinking it. Gotta stay hydrated. An urge comes over her from deep within, it's been yesterday since she's used the bathroom, it's pushing at her—hey, at least *that's* still working the way it should—and she puts the glass back and goes to Cary's bathroom and lowers herself to the seat to take a pee and a poop. In this empty house, she has an urge to write a poem about this moment, the lonely little profundities, the murmuring wisdom of the voices in her head. It's a terrible idea, no time for that kind of thing now, but hey, here we are.

2

While the world flails on,
And fights like ghosts in your head,
A quieter song comes to the fore.
The sound of snowmelt and

Sunrise, the scrape of scabs
Healing and bones knitting together.
But for the broken and the haunted,
For the fractured and the fallen,
There are... there will be... there are—

Ah, fuck it. Sucks anyway. She wipes and flushes and goes back into the main room. The foyer windows look out at the neighborhood—no one in sight. It's like being a child, the days when she was young and skipping school, hiding ashamed behind the chairs and looking out from the window at the stolen yard, the embezzled sunshine, the guilty reproach of all that unearned free time. Here the shadows are vague but still long, the edges of things bright despite the lowering sky, despite the aching inside of her. The pain is so great it's unnamable—heavy and thick, encasing her like an atmosphere, it's too late, that's why the poem sucked, she'll never get out from under it.

Feeling depleted from everything, the constant stress and the lack of sleep and food, she goes to the front bedroom, the one with the bare mattress and no furniture, she sits on the bed, and then lies down. Despite the room's lack of cheer, the mattress is good and firm, Cary may not have much talent in the way of interior decoration, but he knows a good box spring. She rests her head on the bare pillow, thinking strange thoughts, smelling strange aromas, wondering how all this happened to her—

—and a flash arrives, a face, two eyes, someone lying in bed, staring up at the ceiling just as she's doing now. It's her dad's mom, Gran-Gran. Melissa, no more than four or five, pushing open the guest-room door, the one far down the hallway, to see someone, to see Gran-Gran in bed. But the old lady is different tonight—bloody, splattered, mapped with gore like a cartography of rust-red roadways, from her hands and arms to her body, all the way up to her face. Her bloody face, those bloody eyes, staring upwards as if from a mask. Young Melissa standing there who can say how long, maybe a noise, maybe a peep, and there's a scuffle from behind her and the room is filled with adults and someone pushes her back, hustling her away, outside and eventually down to the neighbor's house at the bottom of the hill as red and blue carnival lights flashed in her driveway. That had been the last time she ever saw Gran-Gran, aside from the nightmare visions of her scuttling down the hill on all fours, hands curled into claws, bloody and grinning at her through the window.

The sickness, the disease, the *linger-long something wrong,* it's in their family, it's ancestral. The worm in their brains and there's nothing they can do about it. Gran-Gran had it too. Her father's mother. And her father. And Noah. And her. A blood inheritance—a curse.

3

Sometime later—could be minutes, or hours—a sharp bomb-blast of nerves causes Melissa to sit up. Was that a not-so-distant rumble of thunder? She's been sleeping, her head full of fog. After a moment, the rumble comes again, on the other side of the house. It's not thunder, it's the garage door closing. Which means the first noise was the garage door opening.

Somebody's home.

This bare bedroom, just off the main room, is completely exposed. There's nowhere to go, she could skitter into the closet like a roach caught in sudden light, or dash into the other parts of the house—with the split plan, each section its own little dead-end trap, no egress except locked windows. Or sprint out the front door, run away and never ever come back.

No, she's too tired, too lethargic, too drowsy, she wants only to slip back into sleep, dip into dreamland and slumber blissfully away. If Cary finds her, if it ends that way, so be it, all things have to end somehow, part of her wants to slip off her clothes and receive him on this bed, legs spread, her womanity displayed in all its soft and boundless welcoming.

The car door closes with a dull thump. But now there's another slam of a car door, unexpected, this one out front. Melissa rolls off the bed, surprisingly sure on her feet for one so weary, she goes to the window and peeks outside. A car at the curb, parked near the sidewalk. The light's different now—it's flatter, it's afternoon, early evening, a light rain draining the world of color. She slept most of the day.

But then her heart kicks hard against the wall of her chest. Coming around the car, like a circus grizzly on two legs, is the big guy, Moreau. He's got wraparound sunglasses and a sand-colored camouflage jacket that's weirdly improbably too big even for him—it's like he's wearing the jacket of a giant—and he slouches up the wet weedy sidewalk out of sight of the window, up to the front porch.

Melissa turns slowly, in the shock of things her body threatening to become unmoored again—and now there's rustling in the kitchen. She peeks around the half-closed door to see Cary, his hair a tad grayer and higher on his forehead now, a tad thicker through the belly, standing at the kitchen sink. Wearing a crumpled suit. Drinking a glass of water. It's the same glass she used.

A pinprick of sadness jabs her, a needle-stab of regret and yearning and a wretched, unnamable desire. Now that she sees him, she can feel the soft pads of his long fingers, the two-tiered slope of his nose. It's more in the sense-memory of her body than in her brain, his long hairless feet, the part in his hair and his shrewd brown eyes. There's a new weakness in her knees, another jumble in the stomach, those days so caustic and painful to her now, still she could disappear into them and never make it back.

The front doorbell rings, and Cary goes out of sight to open it. From the sound of things, he lets the big man in. The door slams, shaking the house. "Damn, dude," she hears Cary say. That voice. "Chill."

"Sorry," the big man mumbles, and with his words a strong ghost-hand seems to reach out and crush Melissa around the throat. Cold shivers as that voice comes back to her again—deep, chesty, full of its own misery but lashing out in mirth and malevolence instead. Pain made manifest.

Weighty footsteps as they head back toward the kitchen. Cary returns to the sink while Moreau sits at the table, the chair creaks under his weight. From Melissa's vantage point behind the crack of the door, the table looks improbably small and genteel in front of him, like a kid's playset. Water runs, hands are washed, another glass of water downed. "Got any beer?" Moreau asks, and Cary shakes his head. *But you do, Care*, Melissa thinks, remembering all at once her pet name for him. *It's in the fridge.*

"There'll be beer at the party. I don't want you drinking, anyway. I need you straight for this."

"Straight for all the hot chicks? The black and white chicks"

"Yeah, it's stupid. We have to do crap like this every year." He stares out at the backyard, for a moment letting his thoughts roam around.

"Why black and white? Spy versus spy kinda shit?"

"The fucking firm. Part of their whole PR thing." Cary regards the man with reluctance. Melissa can tell he doesn't like Moreau, doesn't respect him, he never could hide his contempt. "It's supposed to be a nod to whatsisname, that writer guy, Capote or whatever. He's from Alabama, and he used to throw these fancy black and white parties, these elegant occasions up in New York. So we have a theme every year, and this year we're doing a Truman Capote black and white ball."

"Fancy. You're not expecting her to show up though?"

Cary goes to the table and sits down. He rubs his face, his fingers are the fingers of a surgeon, a pianist. They were the sexiest part of him, Melissa remembers now, she was always a sucker for nice hands. "Kinda hard to do that at the biggest party in the city, you know?" Moreau opens his mouth, but Cary cuts him off. "But no. I need you there. I can't be worried and still be, you know, workin' the crowd. You sure we don't need the other guy, whatsisname?"

"Garza's scared of her, that pussy. Haven't heard from him, far as I know he's back home, fuckin' *chinola*."

Behind the door, Melissa takes a quiet, shuddering breath. Her hands are shaking, she can make her presence known, end this whole thing right now—step out, reveal herself, and allow events to take their terrible course. It would be the end of all this horror. In the empty bedroom there's nothing even remotely resembling a weapon, only a mattress and a pillow. When she checked, the closet was empty.

On top of it all, she's still exhausted. Fear is hard on the body. With a kind of acceptance ringing in her head like dull bells, she goes back to the bed. She wonders if she should find a hiding place, but now the energy has dissipated, she crawls across the cool of it, so nice, it feels better to lay here. And the men are right there, not thirty feet away. Just a door between them and her and not even closed all the way, this whole thing could end right now if they would just push it open and look inside.

The sound of someone getting up and rambling around the house—drawers opening, toilets flushing, teeth being brushed—and she waits for the inevitable shock, the *Holy shit! What the fuck!* But no one comes through the door. Somewhere a phone rings, a dreadful sound, empty and hollow, full of demand, and footsteps back to the kitchen.

"Hey," Cary says into the phone. "You get any sleep?" There's a hush as the whole house seems to lean in and listen, even Moreau. "More than I thought," Cary says. "You got your mask?"

Mask, Melissa thinks dreamily from the bare plateau of the bed, *mask, a mask, a ma-ask*. Of course, there's a mask. It's a black and white ball, of course it is. She remembers Capote—that short, mewling man, the toast of all the talk shows and the pompous literary set. Cigarettes and bowties and that wide, froggy frown. Apparently he knew how to throw a party. The flesh of her face feels like a mask now.

"We're basically ready," Cary says in the other room. "What time should we pick you up?" Moreau's thick huffing breath fills the silence. The air in her own lungs rustles in and out but it doesn't seem like her hearing and her thoughts and her body are connected anymore. "You want to come here? Or we can meet you somewhere. Yeah, no, that's great. I get to drink tonight."

Cary's relief is familiar, of course it is, Melissa has new flashes of him now—his hairy knees, his gentle knuckles, his neck, strangely narrow for a man. "Bird-neck," she would tease him, and his temple, which wasn't nearly as gray just a few years ago, losing a child will do that. "Are we getting dinner?" Cary says into the phone.

Kissing his temple, kissing dry lips... Melissa drifting, balled up now on the bare mattress, wafting in and out.

"Okay. See you there." She turns over, the mattress fabric massive in her vision as her face lays cool against it. All he has to do is come through the door, *Please come, please, Cary, open the door, it'll all be over, you can kill me and I can get warm, I can sleep and this will all be over. Please.*

But he never does.

4

By full evening—Melissa guesses it must be around 7 PM, but the whirligig entropy in her head has got her inner clock all screwy—the men gather their things and go out on the porch. Through the window, she sees Cary dressed now in a black tux, spiffy and new looking. Moreau still sports his weirdly oversized jacket, as though he has no other clothes, this is his true skin. The light rain has backed off to a steady drizzle—*What's the fookin difference!* a voice yells from the far side of the house—and after a hurried check in the mailbox, they squeeze into Moreau's little car.

But Melissa's ready now too and she springs into action, flinging open the bedroom door and dashing into Cary's other bedroom to frantically search the jumble of his bedside table. Then the bathroom, and then—*oh shit, yeah, the kitchen*—and she races back to see on the counter what she's looking for. Car keys.

Of course, there's a peach pit ape, and of course it's howling.

As Moreau and Cary out front take off, she dashes out to the garage and climbs inside Cary's little car and shoves the keys into the ignition, praying praying praying, *please please please.* It comes to life immediately. On the overhead visor there's a garage door opener, and she presses the button and it opens slowly, slowly, interminably slowly, taking goddamn forever. She throws the car into reverse, jerks down the driveway and into the road, and takes off after the other car, buzzing as if every need in her, her sense of right and wrong and her very existence, were located atop those four moving wheels ahead of her.

In the drizzle, a ghostly mist rises up from the streets, and her hand finds the windshield wipers and turns them on, and they sweep out a languid *shwock shwock shwock.* A picture of Moreau's car is firm in her mind—a grey-blue sedan kinda thing, characterless and unremarkable, purposefully so, almost an antique and weirdly, perfectly unfitting for the walking talking grizzly of a man driving it. At the four-way stop, she searches and sees nothing—empty streets in every direction, houses colored in compliant shades, wet old trees, buzzed grass with the lawnmower lines still visible. Melissa wipes snot from her nose and tries to think—*Where would they go?* Toward town, of course. She takes a right.

Four frantic minutes later, in which the refracted jumble of visual geometry makes her lean more on instinct than on her own eyes—and the drizzle's not helping at all—she sees them stopped at a traffic light. *Over here! Over here!* a woman's voice calls triumphantly from somewhere outside as she pulls up, two cars behind. It would be so nice to have Gordie here to share in this moment. There's a church at the intersection, a strange five-way junction which threatens to addle her brain, but when the light turns green, Cary and Moreau keep going straight, right toward downtown, her car tails them now, several cars back, their brake lights radiant in the mist, her peripheral vision blurring and blocky like a poorly rendered video game—she dares not move her head now, her eyes lurch this way and that in her sockets—but her hands seem to know what to do. More neighborhoods, the constant gray smear of trees overhead, damp children staring from yards, their eyes strangely old and wise to her deceptions.

After a couple of miles, passing self-storage units and Jewish Community Centers and the black, hulking shapes of apartment complexes, Cary and Moreau's car veers into a parking lot. It's a steakhouse on the margins of a commercial district, *Mario's*, the sign says, and below that, *The More You Have The More You Want*. Their car glides to a stop around the side, and despite the rain they take their time getting out, slowly stretching, as if they've been on an all-day drive. Melissa watches from near the entrance as they mosey across the cracked pavement, talking, hands in motion, Cary in his tux, Moreau in his damp, desert storm camouflage.

When they're inside, she circles the building, and pulls in behind the dumpsters and the frying oil receptacle, which smells of last week's french fries. The need to urinate is strong in her now, a burning and pushing at her bladder, but there's no time to step away, and anyway, who hasn't peed on the side of the road hunched down beside the car with the door open? But right now she's boxed in on all sides by condos and restaurants and pet clinics, she doesn't know what day it is anymore, but she knows there's nowhere private right now to piss. The windshield is a dreamy, floating shimmer of rain, the refracting evening traffic and the dark trees across the road writhing in the breeze, they're like little kids trying to get her attention. A dazed feeling comes to her, that occasional unmooring, the fire in her bladder and another spread of time, it might have been ten minutes, might have been an hour.

But when the grey shapes of Cary and Moreau come back out, her body snaps by itself into perfect bloodhound vigilance, she could spot them anywhere. And now there's a woman with them, running around and ahead with an umbrella and heels—young, attractive, helpless. She's wearing a white gown with a black wrap draped over her shoulders, looking like a model from the 1950s. What do they call those things? *Shrugs.* Nobody wears them anymore, it's like an artifact from a forgotten civilization, alien from Melissa's own antiseptic reality of pressboard and collection agencies and Kmart jeans, from her life where the future's pinched down to mean maybe the next two weeks. But this woman, poised and elegant as a picture in a book. She looks cold.

The three of them take off in Moreau's Honda, circus performers in a clown car, and Melissa tails them through the commercial area—fast food and banks and pharmacies and paint stores—and eventually out the other side. Here the world is green and silver and gloriously natural again, and beyond the trees there are hills, and beyond them are bigger hills, and she follows the car, sometimes becoming nearly unmoored and forgetting why she's after them, sometimes forgetting who exactly is inside the car—then with a start and a sudden blink she'll come back and adjust herself in the seat and rededicate herself to the matter at hand.

Their car heads eastward, eastward, wet in the gathering darkness, just a Tetris pattern of glowing brake lights, and then a hard left, and Melissa hangs back at a safe distance as together the two cars climb a long, steep inclining road that weaves higher and higher now through the increasing canopy. Blackbirds scatter from the road, and she follows around and around, up and up, the little car shifting gears internally through eons of green, beyond horses in the rain, and even the smell now is different, cooler and loamy and primitive.

Eventually the road flattens off to a treelined bluff that overlooks the entire city. Red Mountain, so named because of the bloody red rust of the iron ore found here, the "Pittsburgh of the South," through the trees the night panorama is a glittering carpet of color and diamond lights that bleeds out into a far plain, spreading into the north and the rainy vastness beyond.

Moreau's car turns into a long, manicured drive, with landscape lighting. On the corner, backlit and crowned by the misting rain, stands a filthy man in furs, maybe homeless but definitely hirsute and savage, with a long staff and holding it up like a Bronze Age sentry watching them as they pass. Melissa and the man meet gazes, and as her car passes his nod of acknowledgment sends of thrill of dark wonder or terror down her spine, in the rearview mirror he raises his other fist in the air, and then he's gone.

The chattering all around her is worse now, next to her and from the backseat and even from outside, a mostly low clamor of voices, with an occasional shriek or whistle or child's moan rising above the din. She tries to tune it all out as best she can.

The lane widens and Moreau's car approaches a parking lot, and beyond that—an angular building with the words *The Aerie* written above it in a slash of lively red neon, which seems to ignite the soft rain around it. It huddles on the edge of the cliff, overlooking downtown Birmingham, in the distance rain drifts in ribbons of fog across the high-rises. Their car glides up to the front, where several valets lounge under the awning and out of the damp, but the big man waves them away. Melissa hangs back, and watches as Cary and the woman inelegantly pry themselves out—no other way to get out of that tiny car—and hustle inside. *Pussies*, a voice says from the back seat—Melissa actually turns to see if anyone's back there, of course not, that was obvious—but sometimes it's good just to make sure.

Moreau pulls away in the car, and she watches him drift down among the lanes, looking for a place to park. He finds one midway from the entrance, and he climbs out and meanders through the other parked cars toward the lodge, wearing a hat now, a fancy fedora kinda-thing—*homburg, it's called a homburg,* Melissa vaguely remembers some gangster wearing one of those—to protect him from the drizzle. But instead of going inside, he makes for an empty area off to the edge of the awning, and finds himself a nice little nook behind a yellow concrete bollard in a far corner of the entranceway. From her car, Melissa watches as several of the valets approach him, then shrink back in apparent fear or intimidation as he surely promises many terrible things in return. They retreat to the front doors and leave him alone, where he lights a cigarette and settles himself into the shadows to scan the other cars and people coming up.

Her brain is threatening to unmoor again—it's like a stripped nut turning and turning on its screw, never catching until at last it does—and she gently presses the gas. Instead of approaching the front door, she pulls to the side of the building, to the employee parking area. Her bladder is burning again now, pushing hard at her belly. She finds a parking spot against the building and takes half a moment to back into it—she learned that from Gordie, much better for a quick, painless egress, should she need one. For an eternity then, she sits idling behind the wheel, it might have been seconds, or minutes—the weight of things pins her to the seat, the dull rain splatting, a muffled rainstorm in her head now and a desperate reluctance about what she must do, and yet an unstoppable drive to do it.

Before she can become unmoored again, she turns the car off, climbs stiffly out, and in her purple tights and Roll Tide jersey she limps shoeless across the glittering wet asphalt. Everything careens from one state to another, from one emotion to another, there's a frightful numbness here in this damp dark cliffside place. But there is one thing for which to be grateful. Before she left Cary's house, she took the time to dig into his utility drawer and find the very most needed thing of all—an old, wooden-handled, sweat-stained clawhammer. That part at least is certain.

5

Melissa comes around the corner of the building and stops there. In the flickering floodlights, various cars cough up their passengers, many of them wearing their masks already, or let the valets take their keys and drive them away. Beyond, the dark hunched shape of Moreau still watches from the far corner, more a shadow in the rain than anything, he seems to scrutinize everyone coming and going with sharp eyes. And as her thoughts threaten to strip the nut again, she considers what to do next—she could go back around the building, all the way around to the other side, then sneak up behind him and hammer a brand-new hole in his head. Yeah, maybe that's the best way—swing for his crown, knock his brains in, even through the hat the crunch would feel splendid and good, like the crack of an eggshell. She can feel herself physically warming to this idea, a hot blush in her cheeks, a quickening of the pulse, her lips flushed and swollen, a surging sensation of violent almost sexual desire.

Just then, headlights swing around, another car approaching, more guests to drop off, and put her in bright relief. She freezes. Her purple tights, her wet oversized jersey, number 17—for a moment she's as brightly lit as a mannequin in a window display. Moreau's head gives a slight twist before the car's lights veer off and lose her, the dim oval of his face turned her way, tiny in the distance like a shelled peanut—but when it passes and her eyes readjust to the darkness, he's no longer there, no longer at his perch.

Shit. She retreats to Cary's car, opens the door, gets back in. Did he see her? Soaked now, her hair hanging in strips, she starts it while slumped in the driver's seat, watching for a flicker of movement, anywhere, in any direction, a sound or slip of footfall or breath. Moreau's a butcher, and if luck isn't with her he'll drag her off into the trees and wring her neck like a chicken. The advantage of surprise is long gone, the best thing now would be to get the hell outta here and never ever come back, to run and flee and try to forget about all of this. But she's come too far—the murders, the meds, the blood tracked across several states. And Jack. No, the urgency of her need is a physical thing now, a mass with heft and shape, a tumor of violence behind her eyes, it has a sentience, a personality of its own.

The windshield is dark with rain. The car idles softly, its humming quiet and nearly inaudible. But then, bringing with it a cruel dread, the unmooring steals over her again, creeping across her like a cloud eclipsing the sun. It happens in stress, she's learned—her mind emptying out, an unnerving but undeniably pleasant blankness crawling across her brain and body. Briefly she wonders if it's better this way—Moreau will come across her, silent and still as a statue, and as unaware, and slit her throat then and there without even a fight. Or maybe he'll pass right by her without noticing.

That's when the shadow appears. It steals from around the front of the building, as knobby and hunched as a troll from a fairy tale. His dark profile leers out, head wild with hair even with the hat and the wet, grim against the parked cars and the low trees and the mist. *Skuggämän*, it all makes sense, coming finally to make his claim.

Melissa watches as the shape proceeds—slowly, inching across the dark parking lot. With her right hand she nudges the car into drive, *Relax, girlie,* a voice tells her, *best just to breathe, it'll all be over, just give in to it, let it take you, a gentle tide pulling you guiding you lulling you out to sea...*

The shadowman comes on, creeping across the pavement on his strange, clawed feet, nose like a beak, slipping between the darkness and the rain, aware of everything, *slowly, slowly, slowly the tide pulling you out...*and just as the creature steps in front of her, she slams the gas and the car roars forward and the shadowman pivots and fires his pistol, and there's a gruesome crunch as the car spikes into the one across from it, Melissa's thrown forward into the steering wheel, snapping her collarbone and cracking her nose, the horn barks loudly and blood spurts...

...and then there's nothing. The silence of aftermath, the soft sigh of consequence.

6

The two empty sleeper chairs, their footrests kicked mysteriously back, as though past parents' worry were still here, ghosts still lingering in fretful witness. The port to the IV already in his arm, no flush or gloves needed this time, just pure perfect contact, her hand finds the cannula and she steadies it and tightens the barrel of the syringe. He's ready for the push. Her eyes flicker to the name on the baby's wrist—Joshua James—just to make sure, and it is, he even—

7

A clicking. Regular and cheerful. Breaths. Ragged breaths, and uneven. The blinker ticks to itself in mindless jolly timekeeping.

She waggles her fingers—her body can move and breathe and feel the tide of pain that's flooding in and taking over her body like the unmooring itself. Blood, warm and thick as cream, seeps from her nose, and there's a dull ache in her chest that feels like someone kicked it, but it was only the steering wheel. For the thousandth time she thinks *JackJackJack, I need you…* But Jack's not here. Nobody's here, not even Gordie. She's all on her own.

Painfully, she opens the door, and like food tilted from a plate, she spills from the car. For a long time her body hunkers there with her legs puddled beneath her, feeling the various agonies that announce themselves all over again, the throbbings, the achings, the bleedings, the wet and the sticky and the cold-burning all at once. With a force of will she makes herself stand, one piece at a time, until she's mostly upright. Her right collarbone shouts in pain, and her head wants to tilt to one side all by itself to keep the pain at bay, the body knows what to do. And there's a sharp stabbing ache in her left shoulder, she pulls the neck of the jersey away to expose a wound in the grey light, a round hole, like a carpenter bee has bored a home inside her body. *Skuggämän* got her.

But then her eyes creep forward, beyond the car door, over the wet hood, toward the front of the car where he grins at her. *Skuggämän* is there, and his grin is filled with blood.

He's pinned between the front of Cary's car and the opposite car, propped up by it or hoisted by it, she isn't sure which, but he grins and leans over the hood, his two thick arms propping himself up, like a mechanic inspecting the engine. He laughs weakly. Wetly. The rain on his face and the skyline at his back make it hard to see him, but it's him all right, Moreau in all his bushy, sandy glory.

"Fuckin' good one," he says in his Southern accent, he laughs again and it's the sound of soggy nightmares. The homburg hat—it looks like something from the old country, from *The Godfather*—rests on the hood, as if placed there.

Feeling like an old arthritic woman, Melissa bends and peeks below the cars to see a pair of denimed jeans, mannequin's legs, lying detached on the ground underneath—motorcycle boots and frayed cuffs and faded at the knees. This causes her no consternation at all—it merely *is*, as she *is*, and Jack *was* and Seth and Teddy *were*. She straightens up, her joints creaking and popping, she wipes blood from her face and rubs her hands on her purple tights. Doesn't say a word.

Moreau's gun is gone, knocked or dropped somewhere, under a car or flung in the bushes or maybe a thousand other places.

"*Fuckin' crazy bitch,*" Moreau says now, the humor leaving him. "No wonder Cary wanted you gone. Fuckin' babykiller and psycho-girlfriend all rolled into one." He spits onto the hood, and in the dim light the sputum mixes with black rain. The man's voice surprises her all over again, how weirdly reasonable it sounds coming from that ogre, that ignoble savage who murdered her mother and brother and fiancé.

She waits for him to speak again, and when he doesn't, the silence becomes unbearable. "It was a mistake," she explains for the thousandth time, her voice tired, almost a whisper. "Only an accident."

Moreau tries a laugh, but it comes out more of a gurgle. "Yeah?" He lowers himself on the hood, lets himself rest now on his elbows. His head hangs low, a line of bloody drool strings from his lip, it swings and catches the light as he moves, bobbing back and forth. "You kill his kid when you can't have what you want. Fuckin' rad. You got balls, girl."

Movement back toward the edge of the building catches her eye. Two people stand there now, silhouetted against the misty radiance of light from around the other side, as though their curiosity cast a glow. The collision and the shot were quite loud, quite violent—at least Melissa thought they were—but now it all seemed to have happened a thousand years ago. Acoustics are weird in a place like this, and the comings and goings are busy on the other side of the building. It might have been less apparent than it seemed.

When she turns back, Moreau's lying on the hood now, head turned as if listening to the motor. His wet-twig hair, eyes calm and watching the tangle of trees that borders the parking lot. Beyond him, the lights of the city gleam and throb. She reaches out, takes the homburg and puts it on her head. It's too big, but it shields her from the rain. Moreau doesn't say anything. The indifferent city glimmers beyond him, his breathing slows and slows, and then she's alone.

8

You kill his kid when you can't have what you want. What does that mean? When you can't have what you want? She only wanted to be left to herself, to live her life in peace, if that was at all possible with her sad inheritance of foul blood. Plainly it's a lie, another of Cary's falsehoods meant to make her the villain of his story rather than the other way around. She'll ask him when she sees him.

She limps toward the staring people and they make a space for her to pass, a man and a woman, astonished at her exploits and her grotesqueries...or maybe it's the deathlight in her eyes and the blood seeping from her nose, hard to tell at this point. In their elegant black and white, their hands carry masks—*Oh yeah, right, it's a masked ball*—dripping in the rain. She holds her hand out, and without any hesitation the man passes Melissa his own. It's simple and black, the kind she's seen on superheroes and bank robbers in the comics, the little charming old-fashioned thing that frames the eyes, like Robin. She takes off her hat, situates the mask, and replaces the hat. That's better. Somehow she's ready now in a way she wasn't before.

At the corner, she peeks around—cars lining up, waiting for valets, the young men taking keys and hopping into cars and heading off, the hammer's tucked safely in her waistband, the metal just one more point of cold against her skin. She waits until all the valets are gone for a second and it's just a line of cars ready to be served, and then she steps out, limping calmly and surely down the sidewalk like she belongs there. Certainly the occupants of the cars puzzle over her and the burdens of their attentions are heavy, but she holds her head high and strolls as confidently as her broken body will allow, she's a dancer or performer, part of the show, she tips her homburg to a rakish angle as suited security boys burst out from the club's front door and scurry past her, and with her good hand she catches the door before it closes and goes inside.

It's loud in here, the chatter and the music, but she has the presence of mind to stop before anything else and examine the door. There's a lock, a solid brass deadbolt thing above the handle, and her hand casually, experimentally, reaches out and flips it, it's practically brand new and rotates without hesitation and clicks into place. It's a good solid door and they're outside now and she's in.

It's cold in here too, the AC is running despite the rain, the long, elegant foyer is decked out in a kind of—*What did Jack call it? Mid-Century Modern?* One of his favorite styles, he would go on and on about it, telling her of Mies and Brazil and Scandinavia, and how it all came to America, everything so clean and with a hint of space-age glamour. And there's a chessboard floor and butterfly displays on the wall and bright bomb-bursts of flowers on the table. Melissa squints, surfaces reflect, everything shines and everything's alive, details prism, lines throb and oscillate, and a low noise rises in and out now like the buzzing of crickets. The smell of food—lobster and crab, fried onions and green peppers, salad dressing, tangy and sweet—clenches her stomach as she steadies herself against the wall. Her bladder now really is burning, but she makes herself to go through the vestibule and into the main room.

Smartly dressed people cluster here and there and look Melissa over, watch her as she passes. At least she thinks they're people, because unnervingly now everyone wears their masks. Many of them are not simple at all but strange and distorted—bird masks and grimace masks and jeweled glittering things that deform the faces. Everyone wears black and white—black tuxes, white dresses, it's a voluptuous scene, this masquerade, they leer at her through ill-fitting eye holes, but in her private charade, *I'm part of the show*, no one reaches out to stop her. She wipes blood from her nose and tries to hold her head high, to keep her back straight, to *belong*, she tells herself to be proud, she fought for her right to be here, *killed* for it, goddammit, what the hell did they do to get here? She pulls up her droopy tights, adjusts her jersey, straightens her hat, and keeps going.

The main dining area is wide and circular, and features a lowered, recessed floor, a dancing area, *boogie time*, with big plate glass windows and doors that open onto the grand balcony outside, which itself overhangs and overlooks the Christmas-tree lights of the city. Above the burble of voices there's music, a live jazz combo sparkling out a cover of something or other, *Moondance,* maybe—*It's a wonderful night for a,* and after a few soft shoe moves, she always had it and she still does, she drifts off around the periphery toward the far side of the big room, holding onto the inside railing for support. The floor is slick and wet, her teeth starting to chatter, looking this way and that for Cary, but it's impossible to pick him out from the others. Everyone's the same, black or white, and the lights outside fling themselves up at her, the lodge listing to starboard now, as if the entire place could wobble and crash down onto the city below. The masks, the blocky cubist faces turned her way, watch her with dead eyes. *A dancer, I'm a dancer,* she chants in her head. *A healer, a dancer, it's a wonderful night for a...* Bathrooms in the distance, vast and far away, a men's and a women's, and the burning in her crotch again, but there's no time for that, Cary will leave or at least become unavailable, he'll evacuate the premises, *evacuate*, and she presses her own burning bladder back down, thinking of all the people in all those stalls evacuating themselves, clearing their bladders and their bowels and shuffling back to the party with their asses unclean.

She ventures a word out loud, or at least she thinks she does. "Cary?" There's no answer, but even more dark, dead eyes turn her way. "*Cary?*" Louder now—"*CARREEEY!!*"—but the white noise in the room is too loud, and the dark holes in the masks, the drinks sweating in their hands, the glasses shiny and reflective. Waiters halt now and stare, chairs are slid back as the masks stand and strain to get a better look. Above her a myriad of floating lights, little white lights embedded there, they seem to be sending a secret message, maybe Morse code or one of those spy encryptions. The unmooring is threatening to take over again, a numbness in her feet and fingers, a chatter of cold in her teeth, but she forces herself to keep shuffling. "*Cary?*"

She's most of the way across the room when, over the music and the conversation, a voice near the windows says, "*Oh my fucking God.*"

The sound hits Melissa, it's electric, that voice, Cary's familiar obnoxious petulant whine. White shirt and bow tie, like on the porch of his house, standing near a table, he's also wearing a mask now, a black mask, round and soft, Spanish somehow, more Zorro than Batman, but it's Cary. Hair slicked back from the wet. The slant of his posture, his bad knee, which he injured in high school.

"Melissa." He takes off his mask to look at her better, or maybe for her to better look at him. "What the *fuck*…?" He glances around, probably hoping to see Moreau. But the big guy's not here, he's still out in the parking lot, *haha*.

Her purple tights-feet slosh. She takes off her own mask and drops it, she should have cleaned herself up, should have stopped in the ladies' room for at least a comb-through of her hair, even with the hat. But it's too late, at this point the attention of everyone on this side of the club is all hers. It's shameful, her crimson and purple in a sea of monochrome, can't even get that right.

That's when—*thump!*—something falls to the carpet. Behind her, a knife on the carpet. A steak knife, small and clean, but far away, as if down in a hole. It must have fallen from a table as she brushed by it. Slowly she bends to pick it up, bending at the knees, *gotta be careful, don't ruin your back*, and stares at it as if it's an artifact from another civilization. Maybe it is.

"Ma'am, do you need help?" a voice says, and someone comes to her, comes *at* her from behind, small and rotund, maybe to help or maybe not, but she slashes the business end of the knife around at the black holes in the mask and knocks it askew. The woman, it's a woman, shouts, "*FUCK*!" in a flabby voice, and retreats holding her bloody face with two cherubic hands.

The crowd of people gawking at her fight to clear her path, they back away. Nearby, a woman says, "*Arnold? Where's Arnold?*" And now the band across the room tumbles to a jazzy, inelegant halt, the people watching her form a kind of gauntlet, their masks moaning and leering and grimacing—and at the end of the line, the interior of the angle, the drain through which she must flow, there is Cary.

"Hi, *Care*," she says, trying to sound happy to see him. The nickname appeared on her tongue unbidden, by itself—old buried selves resurfacing, coming to light again, always more to learn. Everyone in the room staring at her now with inscrutable black and white cubist eyes.

"*What the fuck?*" Cary says again, almost choking it out. "What are you doing here? Where's—where's my guy?"

"I wanted to ask you a couple of questions, if you don't mind." Using the handrail, she goes down the shallow carpeted steps toward him, she imagines herself a movie star, a swank starlet, so elegant, this place.

Cary's looking at Melissa's groin with distaste, and she sees a dark strain spreading across the crotch of her tights. She's pissed herself—she finally did it. Behind her, wet footprints not entirely from water trace down along the stairs. Murmurs from the crowd around her. Her gaze rediscovers the knife in her hand. With a new determination, she points it at Cary.

"Tell them, Cary, tell them what happened."

There's movement behind her—"*Ma'am, here, let's—*" and a man steps in, a manager maybe, hands raised to seize the knife, but she spins and swings at him. She's quicker than even she remembered—her reflexes are savage and tight and her riposte barely misses skewering the man. He ducks away, retreats, melds back into the crowd. "*Security*!" she hears him yell. "*Hey, security!*"

"What do you require to go the fuck away?" Cary's voice is calm but his eyes dart back and forth, a caged animal. "This woman is *sick*," he says to the people in the room. "She's…*unwell.*"

"My family, Cary." Like a lover, cooing into someone's ear. "They're dead now thanks to you. The men you hired. Even my fiancé. He's dead now and he was everything to me."

A wail rises from the crowd, high and keen, like an auctioneer. The woman Cary was with, the woman with the shrug, glances from him to Melissa, her face anxious, unready for this, Melissa wishes she were better prepared too but how do you get ready for something like this? "Tell us all, Cary," she says. "Tell us how you pulled it off."

"*What?*" His voice, short and thin and clipped, that old peevish frustration, but then he sees the people turning to him, their faces expectant, ready for his explanation, his volley.

Melissa drifts to a halt. Her body's a dead weight, her knees tremor, it's all she can do to keep from collapsing, the knife almost drops to the floor, this whole terrible matter almost falls apart right here. "Tell them the truth. Or I will."

A sneering smile from Cary. Something inside him still smolders, that old sense of pride or vanity, that dry arrogance which made him so easy to annoy. "Tell them the truth? *Really*? You don't remember, do you?" And then, as an afterthought, "*You sick bitch.*"

"Come on, now," a man's voice in the crowd says, maybe over by the bandstand. "Let's stop all th—"

"Let her talk!" a sharp voice calls out.

Ha. Too many faces, too many eyes, all of them staring at her with their unreadable scrutiny, the people shift and shuffle with that wisdom given only to crowds, that collective genius which hungers to witness something real, it doesn't matter if it's a car wreck or a bloated body at the bottom of a well, carnal appetites must be fed. Cary turns to them now, the room of them, the malformed faces leering at him too. A woman holds a flip phone pointed his way, and instinctively he straightens his tie.

"Yeah, let her talk, *Care*," another voice says, and Melissa sees its Cary's date, the woman with the shrug. "What have you got to hide?"

Cary's eyes dart here and there, he wipes his lips as he seems to contemplate getting into it. "Look, this woman—" he says, pointing at Melissa, and then stops. "Okay. All right. This woman is nuttier than a fuckin' candy bar. We had a thing, a very brief thing. A long time ago. A month at the most. Until I realized how sick she really was."

Melissa approaches, slowly, step after step. The knife, lowered now, wavers at her side.

"Told me she was pregnant with my kid." Cary retreats, and coughs, dislodging phlegm like horrible memories, and he stretches across a table for a glass of water, not his own, and drinks from it. "I had no idea what to believe. Of course, I wanted her to get rid of it, it was the best option, I would've taken care of the whole thing. But she *refused*. Said she wanted that baby. And I could see in her eyes that something was wrong in there. Next thing I know," Cary says, "that goddamn baby was born *dead*."

A soft gasp from the crowd. Eyes blink, more feet shuffling.

Miscarriage, the word appears in Melissa's head, not for the first time, but for the first time in a long while. *Stillborn*. Her punctured shoulder aches but she resists the urge to wilt, willing him to shut up but unable to utter a word.

Cary wipes a hand through his wet hair, takes in a deep breath, feeling his way again through the memories. "She stopped answering my calls. Started parking outside my house. Watching me through the windows. Fucking *stalking me*. And I called the cops on her. Had her arrested, but like a putz, after that, after everything, I didn't press charges. I felt sorry for her."

Melissa can feel the crowd is repulsed by her presence, her damp, her filth, her sickness, she can taste it in the air, but they want to *see* now, the ravening crowd must feed. "But tell them the truth," she says weakly. "Tell them about who you hired."

Cary retreats until he bumps against the plate glass door to the outside. But his eyes are full of bright fire now. "So, I'm a putz, right? An idiot. And she had a miscarriage. A motherfuckin' *stillborn. And she goes back to work!* I have no idea how they let someone sick as her do it, but they do. A year later, when my wife Mimi and I have a little boy, a little preemie boy, who should be on the fucking maternity ward? *Her.*"

All this chatter, all these words come at Melissa like wasps, her face feels swarmed and stung, her skin hurts. The masks all stare back, some still perplexing, some of them dark accusing bloody inhuman eyes that want to impale her if only they can get close enough, she's running out of time.

Cary chokes now, swallowing sudden emotion, wasted already from unearthing nasty business that's not really that long ago. "And she killed that little boy. Our little boy. Joshua James, my firstborn—my *real* firstborn. Killed by this sick *fuck*."

"Here's what happened," Melissa says, raising a finger to the crowd, not wasting a breath, not listening, not sure if anyone can hear and not caring either. "That baby, Joshua James—he died, but it was an *accident*. You hear? An *accident*."

Her head pounds, but more like a fever than a headache. *Miscarriage* is still bright in her thoughts, hard to see anything else now. So much not to think about, so many buried moments.

A murmur rises within the crowd, the witnesses, several voices, *Enough,* and *Stop them*, and *Somebody help her!* And in the plate glass window next to Cary, a night vision appears, a reflection creeps closer—a goblin, inhuman, small, hunched, hatted. It's the shadow from inside her house come to make his claim. *Shadowman. Skuggämän.* A knife in hand. Except when she moves, the reflection moves. It's her, the reflection is her, she's the shadow.

People close around her again, ready to crowd her, hands ready to snatch her away, there are more of them than her. But her point is made now and the knife drops to the carpet. She doesn't need it anymore.

"Tell them," she says with open hands, *see, unarmed, no harm no foul,* turning to Cary again, "How you hired people to kill my family." Despite her pain, the righteousness of *Skuggämän* soaks her, fills her up, and she turns back to Cary. "Baby? *Care*?" she whispers now, sweetly, sarcastically, and moves toward him.

He backs away, pushing the glass door open with his ass as he retreats, and he totters out onto the patio. Instantly the night comes inside, bringing a cool evening damp with it, and the first promise of winter. She holds the door open with her foot, and the broad gleaming view of the city is there behind him, painted like a theater backdrop or a green screen. A wet breeze blows out here—honeysuckle and kudzu and iron rain. Chairs and tables crowd the space, damp empty fireplaces, with a wet metal railing on the far side that seems to drop off into nowhere. The rain has lessened but not stopped.

"Will you tell us the truth, Cary?" she asks, for herself and all the people behind her, knowing he will not. "For all of us?"

"You sick *fuck*. We had a fling. That's all it was, a summer fling. We fucked in the park near the tennis courts. *Drunk*. That was all it was, but you wanted to keep the fucking baby, like a lunatic you wanted to keep it. And when it died, you couldn't—"

"Please," another voice says behind her, and she turns to see a young woman, a waitress by her uniform, approaching slowly and carefully, hands raised in surrender. "Please. Let me help." Gently. Humanely. *I'm on your side*, the hands say.

But Melissa steps out into the wind and lets the door swing closed behind her. Now all the people are on the other side, watching through the plate glass. She takes a fire poker from nearby, jams it just so between the handles to secure them both. Good as locked, now it's just she and Cary.

Thick drops of rain fall from the trees and the wind. "You got me pregnant," she tells him, quieter now, her voice bruised from unwanted memory, "and then she—she died. And *you were glad! You were glad!*" She pulls the hammer from under her jersey.

Someone rattles the door but it only opens an inch or so. A clear tableau behind her now of black and white faces, masks watching them through the glass, with the reflected lights of the city superimposed onto them. They're like gods, gaping old gods, rising above the skyline.

"I didn't know what to do, you fucking idiot!" Cary yells, his tone still whiny, still shrill. He can't seem to take his eyes from the hammer. He may even recognize it as his own. "I was a kid! You were a kid! We were fucking kids! What is this, some kind of weird repressed-memory thing?"

From the dark abyss below comes the high faint whine of sirens. They're coming up the drive. She advances again, slicing the air now with the claw end of the hammer.

"You hired people," she growls, feeling feral, in better command of her body again, no unmooring anywhere right now at all. "You had people come in and kill my family."

"*You killed my fucking baby, you sick FUCK!*" Cary's shrieks, like a woman. "I didn't want anybody dead! It wasn't my fault!"

Melissa swings the hammer at him, hard, and he tries to grab it, but they both miss. He skitters back to the edge of the steel handrail.

"*Stop it*," he says, his voice newly calm, sober now, impressed with her tenacity and seeming to understand there's nowhere else to go. "I'm sorry. I didn't mean it. Melissa, stop."

Melissa swings again and connects this time, with his collarbone, and there's a satisfying crunch.

"*Aaaagh!*" Cary cries out, and reaches for the hammer again, but fails.

"*Tell me what you did,*" Melissa says, almost a whisper. "*When my baby died, you were happy about it.*" She swings the hammer again, wildly now, and it connects with Cary's chin and rips it open, big pads of flesh peeling off like chunks of soap, and he reels back, half over the railing. The great black-green abyss yawns below him—far down, a canopy of night trees, bunched like broccoli, with the lights of the city shimmering gold and red and silver beyond.

The gaping faces in the window are grouped now like zombies from a cheap horror movie. Her friends in oblivion—they're here, it's a show, she's putting on a show just for them.

The hammer's yanked then, and Cary's leaning over the railing with his hands out, trying to pry it from her grasp. But she has a better grip—the white-knuckling started when she pulled it from her waistband—and she wrenches it away, and with a scowl swings at him again and connects with his neck.

There's a *TCHOCK!* like cutting cabbage, and the claws sink into and get caught in the little cords and sinews inside him. Cary's eyes go suddenly faraway and his body shudders, and in a kind of slow motion he doesn't catch himself now but instead topples over the railing, the tendons in his neck striate and pull and for a moment are the only things holding him up and keeping him from the fall. And then with a spurt of black blood they rend and split, and his body cartwheels lazily down into the darkness below.

The crowd on the other side of the window utters a collective *Ah!* Then there's a terrible, airy silence.

9

He even looks like Cary, like a little old man version of him. Thumb on the plunger, she licks her lips, dry and chapped as always. She thinks of Cary, the crinkles of his eyes, the little double chin that's cute now but maybe not so much when he's forty. Then the darkness comes, a storm outside the window, and her own child, preeclampsia they told her, it's what they wrote on the certificate. But Melissa knows it's different than that, she never had a name, she was unwanted, unneeded, a hindrance—her life ensnared in the tangles of power before it had even begun. She was rejected by Cary, by her father, she died of a broken heart, and Melissa's heart died along with her, and she presses the plunger, she watches the liquid, clear and watery and clean without a single bubble, slip down the cannula and into the little boy's body.

10

There's a great crash then as a glass window shatters—a man down the other side of the balcony, metal chair in his hands. Melissa drops the hammer onto the deck, and turns to the vastness beneath her, the black, cloudy, shimmering plain stretching like diamonds out into the darkness beyond, into the rivers and mountains and the nameless places in between. She steps up onto a chair and puts one foot on the railing, and wonders if right now would be a pretty good time to finally spread her wings.

a note from the author

SHADOWDAYS had a weird gestation. Before it was a novel, it was a screenplay, which had been optioned several times, and then, despite everyone's best efforts, languished for years in development. Some really talented and fun people were willing to play in my sandbox, and were set to produce and star and shoot the thing, and I got terrific notes from some of the best professionals in the business. But the movie was not to be.

And that's okay. Because I like the novel best of all.

The project was suggested by my own genetic experience. Sadly, some of the folks on my mother's side fell victim to a particularly vicious strain of paranoid schizophrenia. It ravaged my aunt's mental health, ruining her life from a young age, and eventually crept into my brother's and my mother's lives, taking over the latter halves of theirs. For all I know, I have some of it too—we're all on a spectrum, of course. So, this book is personal—not just a dark, pulpy tale, but an expurgation of sorts, a coming to terms with our family situation, even as I say goodbye to them.

I did research on paranoid schizophrenia—what it is, where it comes from, how it targets the brain—so that all the elements were honest, or at least used in knowledgeable ways. For years I read books and articles, I studied YouTube videos and haunted forums and chatrooms and Reddit threads. I made lists and notes and watched films. Sometimes I worried that my dark, pulpy story wasn't representing the mental health community with grace, that it wasn't necessarily uplifting, that it wasn't helping anyone and that I was making a less-than-stellar impression for my friends who are suffering.

But in the end, I'm a storyteller, not an essayist or topical writer, and a pulpy one at that. I tell stories about people, and people aren't messages (though they are messy), and the best stories don't preach or have morals. So I allowed myself to tell my story the way I wanted to tell it. When my people wanted to do bad things, I agreed to let them. I'm okay with it. I honored my family in my own way. It's a sweet-hearted story, in its own way.

If you or someone you love is having trouble, help is available. In my own personal journey, I've found therapy to be a lifeline, a tool to be used in good times and bad. Also, medications like antidepressants have come a long way. Don't hesitate to find a good local professional who understands you and your particular situation. They can steer you in a more specific direction.

Thank you for reading. Here's to stories, here's to messy people, and here's to good mental health—for you, for me, for all of us.

#

~

#

Special thanks to Shane Meador, for the many beer-and-Mexican-food sessions talking about the story, and to Jaime Byrd, Adam Cohen, and the good folks at Blind Lyle Films for their input as well. Thanks to Carrie Preston, Robert Longstreet, Chris Bauer, and the wonderful people at Daisy Three Productions. Thanks also to Jennifer Trudrung for being my first reader, to John Palisano for his editing expertise, and Scarlett R. Algee, Sean Leonard, and all the JournalStone folks for believing in this story. And special thanks to Robert Kolker, and his definitive account of mental illness in families, *Hidden Valley Road*, which served as an invaluable resource for this book.

about the author

Polly Schattel is a writer and filmmaker. She lives in Asheville, NC with her wife and two dogs and two cats.